Andrews

A Wing and a Prayer

headline

First published in Great Britain in 2002 by
HEADLINE PUBLISHING GROUP

First published in this paperback edition in 2016 by
HEADLINE PUBLISHING GROUP

1

Cataloguing in Publication Data is available from the British Library

ISBN 978 1 4722 3775 0

Typeset in Janson by Avon DataSet Ltd, Bidford-on-Avon, Warwickshire

Printed and bound by CPI Group (UK) Ltd, Croydon, CR0 4YY

HEADLINE PUBLISHING GROUP
An Hachette UK Company
Carmelite House
50 Victoria Embankment
London EC4Y 0DZ

www.headline.co.uk
www.hachette.co.uk

For Theresa Scully, Mary Deverey, Kay Looby, Gret Bracken, Brigie Delaney, Carmel Healion, Concepta Guinan, Bridie O'Brien, Ann McCourt, Molly Minnock, Bernadette Hickey, Katherine MacDonald, Colette Grennan, Kathleen O'Brien, Marie Looby and all the other members of the St Carthage's Women's Group. Thank you for your friendship and the great *craic* we have on Monday mornings.

Lyn Andrews
January, 2002

Prologue

———❦———

Liverpool 1917

'IS IT A BOY or a girl?' Mary Callaghan asked. Even though she was exhausted there was a note of apprehension in her voice.

'It's a girl, luv, a fine 'ealthy girl, just like yer Daisy.' Ma Mulligan, the local midwife, beamed as she handed the infant, wrapped in a clean towel, over to her mother.

Mary bit her lip as she cradled her new daughter close to her. 'Oh, God luv her! Jack's not going to be very pleased.'

'What's not ter be pleased about? She's perfect, 'e should be grateful.' The woman was scandalised. So many of the babies she delivered were stillborn, sickly or deformed.

'I know. I'm happy, but ... you know ... after the last time ...'

'That should make 'im even more grateful and don't let yer mind dwell on that, Mary, girl.' She began to collect together the accoutrements of her trade from the room where she'd delivered the child, one of the two Mary and Jack Callaghan rented in Portland Street, off Scotland Road.

The house was like so many others in the festering slums of Liverpool: old, damp, teeming with vermin and bugs, half falling down because it was so dangerously in need of repairs. Repairs that would never be done. There were fourteen people crammed into the two-up two-down house with one shared earth closet in the yard and no piped water.

Mary bit her lip again as her glance went round the room. They had little enough. The heavy chenille curtains that covered the window were borrowed and would have to go back now that their purpose – privacy for a few hours – was over. The bed, a small chest and a rag rug were the only things in the room and it had taken hard work and self-denial to save the money for them. There wasn't much more in the kitchen: a few bits of furniture; the bare essentials for cooking and storing. She tried hard to keep everything clean, as did most people. She took turns with the other women in the house to scrub the cracked and broken steps at the front door and to keep the yard and privy as hygienic as their circumstances would allow. Many women gave up the struggle, or their health simply broke down. The slums claimed those most at risk: the old, the sick and babies. Mary held her child tightly.

The midwife noted the gesture and knew what was in the young mother's mind. 'Yer should rest now, luv. I'll inform meladdo in there that 'e's got another daughter and by God I'll swing fer 'im iffen 'e starts on at me! Nice way ter be goin' on, I must say, and with a war on!'

Mary managed to smile at the older woman. 'I'd even forgotten about that these last hours.'

'Yer 'ad a right ter, girl. An' isn't Jack the lucky one not ter be gettin' slaughtered like the lads over in Flanders? It's shockin', that's what it is.'

'He doesn't think he's fortunate. And I do worry about him just the same.'

'Sailin' on them new-fangled "convoys" is a picnic, even in the stokehold. 'E's in a "Reserved Occupation". Fine fer 'im, I say. God knows 'ow 'e wangled it.' Contempt was written all over her face. She had no great opinion of Jack Callaghan.

'You'd better send him in,' Mary urged. She was so tired that she wanted to get this over and done with.

Ma Mulligan smiled grimly. She liked young Mary. She was a fine-looking girl, with clear blue eyes and soft, light brown hair worn in the cottage-loaf style, and she'd help anyone in any way she could.

'What will yer call 'er?'

'Ellen – Nell for short. It was Mam's name, God rest her.'

'Aye, God rest 'er indeed, she was a good woman. But she was wore out with 'avin' ter cope with all this!'

Mary looked down at her baby, wondering who she would look like. Herself or Jack? Two-year-old Daisy was like her in looks but not in temperament.

'I'll send 'im in,' the midwife said firmly.

Mary stroked the soft, downy little head, still apprehensive although profoundly thankful.

The door opened and she looked up at her husband of three years. He was a handsome lad, she thought. His skin was olive, his eyes and hair so dark that he could pass for an

Italian or Spaniard. His clothes were not new but they were well cared for and he took pride in his appearance. 'Black Jack' Callaghan, people called him. Oh, yes, he was handsome, but lately she'd begun to realise he had other less attractive qualities. He spent his money freely and on things she considered wasteful: drink, cigarettes and gambling. They were luxuries the poverty-stricken inhabitants of Liverpool could ill afford.

'A man's got to have his few pleasures, Mary,' had been his reply when at the end of his last trip he'd been short of more than half his earnings. He'd gone on to point out to her what a pit of hell the stokehold he worked in was. She knew that. She didn't mind his few pints and packets of Woodbines, but what had happened to the rest of it? To her consternation he'd laughed and when she'd pressed him he'd become angry and had told her not to meddle in his affairs. She had enough to manage on – hadn't she?

As he looked down at her now, she held out the precious bundle. 'Isn't she beautiful, Jack?' she asked.

He kept his hands in his pockets, his dark brows drawn together in a frown.

'She told me you managed to have a healthy girl. You could do that all right! Another bloody girl! But my son – all that I ever wanted – was born dead! Don't expect me to be happy or proud in any way!' He turned from her and walked out, slamming the door behind him.

Mary felt tears prick her eyes. She'd never forgive him for those words. How cruel he was. Deeply hurt, she held the baby to her breast. Well, she loved her and she had enough love for both of them. 'I love you, Nell Callaghan. You're very precious to me and I'll see you do well in life if I have to work my fingers to the bone. You'll have a better life than your mam has.'

The tiny fingers closed around her own with a strong tenacious grip and Mary smiled.

'You're a strong little lass. We'll get through, "on a wing and a prayer", as my mam used to say. You see if we don't, Nell.'

Chapter One

Liverpool 1938

'OH, GOD, NELL! WHAT am I going to do?' Daisy
Callaghan's pink-and-white-complexioned face crumpled with anguish and fear. Her pale blue eyes were full of
tears and she twisted a strand of curly hair around a plump
finger that her sister could see was trembling. She was a pretty
girl. She herself thought she was a bit too bonny and plump
especially when not in a state of abject misery and despair.

'Oh, Daisy! Are you sure? Are you absolutely certain?'
Nell Callaghan's dark eyes were full of anxiety and sympathy
as she reached out and took her sister's hand and squeezed
it tightly.

They were so different in looks that people who didn't
know they were sisters were surprised when they realised.
Daisy was like her mother, small and plump with Mary's light
brown hair and blue eyes – although now there were strands

of grey in Mary's hair and she had lost some weight. Nell was like her father. She was tall and slim with chocolate-brown eyes and hair so dark it looked blue-black in certain lights.

Daisy dashed away a tear with the back of her hand and sniffed. 'I'm not wrong. I *couldn't* be wrong about something like . . . this. Oh, Nell, I wish I was dead!'

Nell was deeply concerned. 'No, you don't! Don't even think like that! Oh, Daisy, how could you let him . . . ?' She couldn't finish. She didn't want to hurt her sister. Daisy was in a terrible state and an equally terrible predicament. The very worst thing that could happen to a young unmarried girl was to get pregnant. And that was the condition that Daisy had told her she was in. But Nell's shock soon gave way to deep sympathy. Poor Daisy. How easily and totally in love she'd fallen with handsome Sam O'Grady, with his blond hair and deep blue eyes that were always alight with some form of devilment. And he could entice the birds off the trees with the Irish blarney he'd inherited from his parents. No, poor Daisy had stood no chance against the full battery of his charms.

'You're going to have to tell Mam,' Nell said gently.

'Oh, Nell, how can I? Sam doesn't even know yet.' Daisy was trembling now and on the brink of hysteria.

Nell squeezed her hand again. '*We'll* tell her. You know I won't leave you to face it on your own.'

'Will you, Nell? I . . . couldn't bear . . .'

'Hush now. Wipe your face and tidy your hair and we'll go down and face the music together.'

Daisy did as Nell suggested and Nell sat on the bed and watched her. What exactly were they going to say? How could she utter the words that would shock, hurt and humiliate the mother she loved so much? There had been a special bond between her and her mother for as long as she could remember. She caught a glimpse of herself in the mirror on the wall of the bedroom the sisters shared. She was two years younger than Daisy but she often thought she looked and acted as though she were the elder. She also knew in her heart that no man would ever take advantage of her, no matter how much she might love him. She sighed. Chance would be a fine thing. There wasn't a lad she knew in the entire neighbourhood that she'd consider walking out with, let alone marry.

Daisy looked a bit calmer now and, getting to her feet, Nell gave her sister a hug. 'Everything will turn out fine, you see if it doesn't.'

As they went downstairs Nell hoped she'd sounded more confident than she felt. She was dreading this as much as Daisy was, but for different reasons.

Mary was sitting in the old armchair by the kitchen range. She looked so tired, Nell thought, but her day started at four o'clock in the morning. She got up, raked out the range and put on the kettle and a pan of porridge for their breakfast. She made sure things were tidy and the room warm, then she walked to the fruit market, pushing her empty barrow in the dark, down the silent cobbled streets. Nell knew it was hard in winter for her mother to leave the comparative warmth of the house but Mary protested that she had to work and was grateful for both the barrow and her 'pitch' at the corner of Great Homer Street and Scotland Road. Nell wished her da was different and gave the family more of his wages, but like Mam she had had to come to terms with the fact that he would never change his easy come easy go attitude to life. Nell glanced across the room to the single bed, crammed into the alcove, where their benefactress slept fitfully. For forty-five years Annie Garvey had pushed the barrow from which she earned her living around the streets of Liverpool until she was too old and worn and ill to carry on. The poor old soul, who hadn't a relative in the world, had been destined for the Workhouse until Mam had taken her in. Annie had been so grateful that she'd bequeathed the means of her livelihood to Mary in return for a comfortable home in which to live out the rest of her days. Oh, Da complained about the old woman but after a few heated arguments Mam ignored his demands.

Things had become a little easier when first Daisy and then Nell herself found work. It was in an animal feed factory and the work was dull and dirty and paid a pittance, but they seldom complained.

She pulled her mind back to the situation that faced them.

'Mam, we want to talk to you,' she announced quietly.

Mary sat up in the chair and smiled. In their different ways they were both very attractive girls and she was proud of them. Oh, Daisy was a bit of a handful at times, but what young girl wasn't? She smiled again. Well, not all of them. Nell had never been any trouble but then Nell had been special since the day she had been born and Jack had rejected her.

'A deputation, no less! Come on then, tell me. What's the matter now?'

Nell glanced over at the old lady.

'It's all right, Nell, she's had her medicine. She's asleep.'

Nell looked down at her feet and plucked at the waistband of her skirt. 'Mam . . . well . . . we—'

'Oh, for the love of God, Nell, spit it out!' Mary interrupted, suddenly feeling apprehensive. There was no sparkle in Nell's eyes, just . . . fear?

'Mam, it's . . . me,' Daisy stammered.

Nell pulled herself together. 'What she wants to say, Mam, is that she's . . . she's . . . in the family way.' There, she'd said it, but she couldn't meet her mother's eyes.

Mary drew in her breath sharply and slumped back into the chair. 'Oh, dear God! Daisy, tell me it's not true! For the love of heaven, tell me it's not true!'

'It's true, Mam. I wish it wasn't but it is and I . . .' Daisy couldn't go on. There was a lump in her throat and her heart was thumping and she felt sick.

'It's Sam O'Grady, Mam,' Nell said flatly.

'It would be! Oh, Daisy, how could you? How could you let him do this? He's disgraced you. He's a fly-by-night glib-talking wastrel! The whole family are the same!' Mary dropped her head in her hands. She should have seen this coming. Daisy was too naive. She'd been walking around in a daze since that feckless Irish charmer had walked her home from work. He was all Daisy talked about. She should have watched Daisy more closely, given her stern talks about letting him take advantage of her. It was no use now. It was far too late, she'd only be slamming the stable door, the horse had long bolted. And it wasn't just Daisy who would be publicly humiliated when this got out, it would be all of them, and she'd worked so hard all her life to bring up a respectable, God-fearing family – and she'd had no help at all from Jack.

Even now he was down in the Golden Fleece in Burlington Street drinking, wasting what money he had left from his pay-off on his last trip.

Daisy had sunk down on the battered sofa and dissolved into tears. Nell, glad it was at least out in the open, was torn between comforting her sister or her mother.

'Mam, we . . . she's so sorry and it takes two and you know what he's like!'

Mary got to her feet. 'Oh, I know what he's like all right! I wish to God I didn't! Get your shawl.'

Daisy dabbed her eyes and looked up at her mother in confusion. 'What for? Where are we—'

'We're going to sort this out here and now before a word of it gets out.'

'But, Mam . . . can't we wait?' Daisy begged.

'No!' Mary was firm.

'Mam, let's wait until Da gets back at least?' Nell begged, thinking it wasn't fair to leave everything to her mam. She had enough on her plate as it was with old Annie, Da and their young hooligan of a brother, Teddy, to see to.

'If we wait for him we'll wait until past midnight and do you think he'll be in any state to be of any help?' Mary demanded.

Nell knew she was right. 'I'll go for him, Mam. I'll go down to the Golden Fleece and bring him home.' She didn't relish the thought one bit but she wasn't going to let Mam shoulder the burden of their disgrace alone.

Mary sighed deeply and sat down again. 'You're a good girl, Nell. It'll be better if I have him with me for a bit of support.'

Nell took her heavy black shawl from the hook behind the door.

'Daisy, pull yourself together, girl, and put the kettle on. I could do with a cup of tea,' her mother instructed wearily. 'It's going to be a long night.'

As Daisy reached for the heavy black kettle she felt a bit better. At least Mam knew, that was half the battle, and she was so thankful that Nell was going to bring her da home reasonably sober. Her sister might even find the courage to tell him before they reached home. It *was* going to be a long night but she felt better than she had for days.

Nell drew her shawl tightly around her. It wasn't raining yet, but it was threatening to and it was cold and windy as she walked up the narrow street, trying to form the words of the excuse she would use to tear her father away from his cronies. Just as she turned the corner into Limekiln Lane there was a scattering of feet and suppressed childish laughter followed by the clattering of an empty tin can and the frightened yelping of a puppy.

'See 'im run! Look at 'im go!' one cried.

Nell recognised the voice and, lunging out, caught the jacket collar of the voice's owner and yanked him into the circle of light thrown out by the gas streetlamp.

'Teddy Callaghan! You flaming little hooligan! Get home now before I box your ears until your nose bleeds! Hasn't Mam got enough to worry about without you running the streets with those other horrors and getting up to no good? I'll swing for you yet!'

'Ah, Nell, gerroff!' her eleven-year-old brother cried,

trying to wriggle free of her grasp. 'We was only havin' a bit of fun, like!'

'Just what were you doing? I thought I heard a puppy.'

'You did. It was only a bit of fun, I told you!'

She shook him again and clipped him across his left ear. 'Go and find the poor animal and bring it here. I'll wait and don't you dare to run off. If you do and I catch you, I'll run you straight down to Rose Hill nick and let the scuffers sort you out!'

He turned pale before disappearing. A few minutes later he returned, clutching the scruffiest, most underfed mongrel puppy she had ever seen.

'So, this is what you call a bit of fun? You . . . you cruel little sod! Tormenting a poor, weak, terrified little creature. Take that can off his tail at once and then you can take the poor thing back to where it belongs!'

'It doesn't belong to no one, honest, Nell. We found it lying in the gutter.'

The puppy looked up at Nell with sad brown eyes.

'Well, it belongs to someone now.'

'Who?' he demanded.

'Me! Take it home and give it a few scraps and a bit of milk and then get yourself to bed or I'll tell Mam what you were doing and then you'll be for it!'

He looked up at her, his eyes full of outrage, dirt streaking his face and a ring of jam around his mouth.

'Do I have to?'

'Yes, and wash your face! God help me, what did I ever do to deserve a brother like you?'

She gave him a shove and turned away. He could learn

how to treat poor defenceless creatures properly. The puppy wasn't exactly something her mam would welcome right now and she hadn't meant to adopt it but it had looked so pitiful her heart had melted. Maybe it would distract Mary and Daisy a little until she got back with Da. And, with the thought of the task before her weighing her down once more, she set off for the Golden Fleece.

Chapter Two

THERE WERE FAR TOO many pubs and alehouses in the neighbourhood, Nell thought as she walked along. And far too many men who frequented them, whether they could afford to or not. Someone had once told her that there were over seventy and she could well believe it. Da had only been home three days and it was another four before he sailed again. By that time he'd be flat broke. Well, he wasn't getting any of her hard-earned wages this time. Mam was going to need every penny to provide some kind of a wedding for Daisy. She didn't think to question the outcome of tonight's events. Sam O'Grady would have to marry Daisy, it was as simple as that.

Despite the weather the door of the Golden Fleece was wide open and there were loud drunken roars of laughter coming from inside the smoke-filled room. She took a deep breath to give her courage. The smell of cigarette smoke and sour ale filled her nostrils. God, it was awful, but at least it was easy to pick out her da from the throng, she thought as she elbowed her way through. He was the tallest man there, and the best dressed. His appearance was another thing his wages went on: good, if second-hand, stylish clothes bought in New York when his ship docked there.

''Ere, girl!' a large, red-faced, bleary-eyed man yelled at her. 'This is the fellers' bar, the snug's around the back!'

'I know that and it's a pity you haven't got the sense to stay away from both!' she retorted angrily, in no mood to explain her presence to drunks.

'Youse better watch yer mouth, girl!'

'Oh, go to hell!' She had almost reached the corner where Black Jack Callaghan was propping up the bar with his mates from the stokehold. Suddenly she was caught by the arm and whirled around. Instinctively she lashed out, catching the man a swipe across the face.

He uttered a roar like a wounded bull but she deftly moved out of his reach. She was past caring about herself anyway.

'Da! Da, for God's sake, let's get out of here!' she cried, tugging at his sleeve.

'Nell, what the hell are you doing here? Can't you see I'm enjoying myself with the lads?' His tone was genial and he smiled expansively at the group of half-drunk friends he'd been carousing with for the last three hours.

'The lads!' Nell muttered, casting her eyes to the smoke-stained ceiling. 'Da, we *have* to go home! It's very important! It's very urgent!' she shouted above the din.

'What the hell is so important that I have to leave the lads in the lurch?' His good humour had disappeared. He was annoyed that she was making a show of him in front of half the neighbourhood.

'Da, it's Mam and our Daisy! Please, Da, you have to come,' she begged.

He looked a little concerned.

'Better go an' see what's up, Jack. Then cum back, there's plenty left in the kitty yet. Gerroff with yer.'

Nell shot the man a grateful look, then took her father's arm again and propelled him towards the door.

It was a relief to be outside again. No one could call the air 'fresh' around here but it was better than being half choked in there, she thought.

'Now, just what the hell's the matter? It's not right that a man's kids come to the boozer and plague the life out of him, make a show of him in front of his mates.'

She fell into step beside him, her shawl pulled close to her face. 'Mam needs you.' She was trying to summon up the courage to tell him about Daisy.

'What for? She's never needed me before. She gets on with things, your mam does.'

'Well, she . . . we all need you now.'

'Is it young Teddy?'

'No. For once it has nothing to do with that little hooligan.'

'He'll end his days on the gallows, will that lad! She spoils him.'

It was on the tip of Nell's tongue to reply that if he was home more often Teddy's behaviour might not be so bad. 'It's . . . it's . . . our Daisy.'

'What's wrong with her? Is she sick? Is her having some

kind of pain or other the reason why I've been dragged away from my night's enjoyment?'

'It's not just a pain. She . . . well, you know she's been courting Sam O'Grady from Eldon Street, she—'

'Your mam never told me she was courting,' Jack interrupted.

'She did, Da, you just didn't listen. You were too interested in the horse that would solve your money worries for life.' Except that it was still running months later, she thought. He'd lost a week's pay on that nag.

'Is he one of that tribe of Irish down there?'

'Yes, but you can't hold that against him. Grandad Callaghan was Irish. But . . .'

'But what? Out with it, girl, and we can get it sorted and I can go back to the lads.'

She felt as though she could scream. Did he care nothing at all for them, his family? 'She's in trouble. He's put her in . . . in the family way,' she blurted out, her annoyance banishing her trepidation.

He stopped and grabbed her arm. 'She's what?'

'You heard me, Da. Now can we go home?'

A red flush of anger tinged Jack's cheeks. 'By God, I'll kill the little tart! I suppose she's been flaunting herself around the neighbourhood, the little whore! By God, I'll take my belt to her!'

'Da! It's not *all* her fault! He's no good, you know he isn't.'

'It's her own fault that she was carrying on like some common trollop from Lime Street! What the bloody hell was your mam doing while all this was going on?'

Nell was stung. 'It's not Mam's fault either! You know how

hard she works. She's out in all weathers with the barrow to make ends meet.'

'Oh, I'm to blame now, am I?'

'No! No one ever said anything like that, Da!'

'But you think it.'

Oh, this was terrible, she thought. He was working himself up into a temper and that was the last thing Mam needed.

'Da, you know that's not true! We all know that the sea is in your blood. It's your life, it always has been. Mam . . . we . . . all understand that if you were to get a shore job you'd be miserable and we don't want that. We all *understand*, Da, it's just that at a time like this, Mam needs your help and support. She wants to go and see Sam O'Grady tonight and I said I'd come down for you. You didn't want her to come, did you? I put it as best I could, so as not to embarrass you.'

Mollified, Jack nodded his head and they walked the rest of the way in silence.

'Oh, Jack, thank God you're here!' Mary cried, getting to her feet as they walked through the door. At the table Daisy's hand began to shake so much that she slopped the tea from her cup.

'Aye, well, it's important,' Jack said sourly.

'Where's Teddy?' Nell asked.

'In bed and with the warning that if he dares to come down he'll get the hiding of his life. He brought a scruffy little dog home and said it's yours. It's in the scullery.'

'It is mine. But never mind that now, Mam. I . . . I told Da on the way home, didn't I?' She turned and looked at her father.

'She did indeed and by God, Mary, what the hell were you thinking of, letting her go carrying on with the likes of him?'

The light of battle came into Mary's tired eyes. 'Now you listen to me, Jack Callaghan, I've done the best for *all* of you, *all* my married life! We share the responsibility. She's your daughter!'

'It's no use getting into a slanging match as to whose fault it is,' Nell interrupted. 'It's happened and we have to sort it out!'

Jack turned on Daisy, who was crying quietly. 'Will you shut up that bloody noise and tell us what the hell you were doing letting him take advantage of you?' he roared.

In the corner old Annie stirred in her sleep.

'Oh, Da! I love him! I really love him and he said . . . he promised . . .' Daisy sobbed.

'Oh, I can imagine what he bloody promised! As for all that rubbish about "love", it's "lust" he meant and you fell for it like the bloody stupid little tart you are!'

Mary was indignant. 'She's not a tart, Jack, and don't call her one!'

'She's as bad as one.'

'Oh, Da! I'm not . . . bad,' Daisy wailed.

Nell went and put her arms around her weeping sister. 'Da, it's no use calling her names now and you know how thin these walls are—'

'Nell's right, Jack,' Mary interrupted. 'It's bad enough without having her next door with her ear glued to the wall knowing all our business and passing it on.'

Slowly he nodded. He was furious. Furious with Daisy for

21

being such a fool. Furious with Mary for allowing this to happen and furious that his good name would be dragged through the muck of the gutters. They were all to blame. Humiliating him in the eyes of the neighbourhood. Amiable, easy-going, smartly dressed man of the world Black Jack Callaghan would be pointed at, sniggered about and ridiculed for having a stupid daughter as free with her favours as Daisy.

'I'll get my coat,' Mary said firmly.

'You stop snivelling and get your shawl,' Jack commanded Daisy.

Daisy looked fearfully from her mother to her sister. 'Can . . . can Nell come too, Da, please?'

'What the hell for? Do you want everyone in bloody Eldon Street to see the entire Callaghan family marching down there at this time of night?'

'I don't mind, Da,' Nell offered.

'Well, I do. You can stay here in case meladdo in bed decides to come down and have the place up.'

Knowing further argument was useless, Mary nodded her agreement. Pushing his daughter before him and followed by his wife, Jack left the room.

Nell sat down and covered her face with her hands. Oh, God, what a night! She had wanted to go and give her mam and Daisy some support but she'd done enough arguing with her da. She got up and felt the teapot. It was cold. Well, she'd make a cup of tea and then decide if it was worth waiting up until they returned.

It was only when she went into the tiny scullery that she remembered the dog. It was lying in a corner on an old bit of sacking.

'Oh, I'd forgotten all about you.' She knelt down and stroked it gently. It was all skin and bone and probably alive with fleas. 'You're a real little scruffbag, aren't you? Still, I can't throw you out. But it's a fine time to come into this house and this family, with holy murder going on.'

It snuffled, trying to raise its head, and she picked it up, regardless of its filthy state. It nestled against her and she sighed. 'I should call you "Trouble" but you've already had enough to put up with without having a name like that. Seeing as you're such a scruffbag, it had better be "Scruffy". Well, I'll make the tea and you can come into the kitchen with me and we'll wait for them to come home.'

She was dozing in front of the fire, the puppy asleep on her lap, when a movement from the bed disturbed her. She got up, still holding the animal, and went over to the alcove.

'Annie, what's wrong?'

The old woman looked at her curiously. 'You're a good girl, Nell. Your mam needs you, especially now.'

Nell was surprised. 'You mean you heard . . . everything?'

'I'm not *that* deaf, girl. Daisy's a little fool. She's not the first and she won't be the last to trust a man's promises. But you take care, Nell, don't you make the same mistake.'

'I don't think I'll ever love someone enough to do anything like . . . that.'

'Oh, you never know what the future brings, girl. I saw all kinds of things when I tramped the streets of this city. You take care.'

Nell smiled down at her. She wasn't as feeble as people thought she was. 'I will, Annie. I'll probably end up an old maid.'

'Not you, girl. There's someone out there for you.'

'You'll be telling me next that you can see into the future. I remember when I was younger you read the tea-leaves. There was always a crowd of women here on a Monday night peering into empty teacups.'

'Don't mock an old woman in her dotage.'

'I wasn't. Can I get you anything? A cup of fresh tea? I'll make one, then you can read my fortune from my cup.'

The old woman grinned, revealing a few yellowed stumps of teeth. 'No, no tea, thanks, but get under the bed and fetch out my box.'

Nell put the puppy down on the hearth and reached under the bed for the old, battered tin box that contained Annie's few belongings.

'Here you are, shall I unlock it?'

Annie nodded, taking off the key she wore on a long chain around her neck and handing it to Nell.

The lock was a bit stiff but finally Nell opened it.

'That little tin. Take it out, girl.'

Nell did as she was bid, retrieving a small tin that had once held Gold Flake tobacco.

'I want you to have that, Nell. I want you to keep it but don't open it until I've gone to my eternal rest. Promise me?'

Nell was bemused but she felt she should humour the old woman. 'Of course I'll promise, but you've years yet.'

'I wouldn't be too sure of that, girl. I'm tired now, all that shouting and crying has got me down. But just you remember, be good to your mam, Nell. She's a fine woman who deserves better than the one she got out of life's bran tub.'

Nell tucked the blankets around the frail little form and glanced down at the box. She wasn't going to spend the rest of the night wondering just what it contained. She knew it wasn't money – it didn't rattle and besides poor old Annie had none of that, not even a penny to bless herself with. She'd take it upstairs later.

She was dozing again when Teddy crept into the room, looking very sheepish.

'What in the name of God are you up to now?' Nell hissed, glancing across at Annie.

'What's wrong with me da and our Daisy?' he whispered.

'There'll be plenty wrong with you if Da comes back and finds you down here.'

'I've never heard Da so mad, Nell. Why was he shouting and bawling at Daisy and Mam? Where have they all gone?'

He looked so pale and tearful that Nell relented. 'Sit down on the hearth or you'll freeze. Don't disturb Scruffy though.'

'*Is* he yours? Is that what you're calling him?'

'It's "yes" to both questions but *you* can learn to look after him. You can have some responsibilities for a change.'

He was contrite. 'I'm sorry now that I tormented him. Where've they gone, Nell?'

She sighed. She'd have to tell him something. 'To Eldon Street, to see Sam O'Grady.'

'What for?'

'Because . . . because he and Daisy will be getting married.'

'Really? Why was Da yelling at her then?'

'Because he doesn't like Sam O'Grady and neither does Mam. In fact, I don't like him much myself.'

'Then why is Daisy marrying him?'

'Because she loves him, little fool that she is. Now you'd better get back to bed or you'll get a hiding – and don't be asking any more questions about Daisy.'

The lad nodded and got up. It was a perfectly reasonable thing to get married, but why they'd all gone to Eldon Street at this time of night he couldn't fathom. He shrugged. Who could ever understand grown-ups? You only had to look at Nell keeping that scruffy little dog to know they were half mad. Still, he was glad she was keeping him. He'd never had a pet before. Mam had always told him it was hard enough to feed them all without feeding a dog as well. At least something good had come out of this topsy-turvy night.

Chapter Three

———◆———

DAISY HAD STOPPED CRYING, for which Mary was grateful. At least they could now present a dignified front.

The only lights visible in Eldon Street were those of the gas lamps, which cast small circles of feeble yellow light, further diluted by the misty drizzle now falling.

'What number is it?' Jack asked in a hoarse whisper.

'Nine,' Mary answered grimly. 'But for God's sake don't have the street up by hammering on the door.'

'What kind of fool do you take me for?' he replied sharply, before trying the front door and finding it unlocked. That wasn't unusual; the O'Gradys, like everyone else in the street, didn't need to lock the door. They had nothing worth stealing.

'Do they have the whole house?'

'Of course they do, there's about fourteen of them,' Mary snapped.

'God, it stinks!' Jack said scathingly.

'Well, she's not much of a one with the housework, from what I've heard. They must be like sardines in a tin and just as smelly and oily. Go on, knock. I don't want to be here all night.'

Jack rapped smartly on the door of what had once been a parlour. There was no sound from within so he hammered on it again.

Mary closed her eyes as the noise echoed through the silent house.

Daisy drew closer to her mother, upset and frightened. But at least, she told herself, the bad part would soon be over and then she could look at the future in a far different light. She loved Sam and he loved her. In the next few minutes the nightmare she had endured for days would be a thing of the past.

At last there were sounds from within and the door was opened a crack.

'Who is it out there an' at this time of night?' a woman's heavily brogued voice demanded quarrelsomely.

'Jack Callaghan and I want to speak to that lad of yours.'

'An' which lad would that be? Sure, I've eight of them.'

'Sam, and I want to see him now. I've my wife and daughter with me and we don't intend standing out here all night.'

The door opened and a stout woman with grey, greasy hair that framed a pasty face stood in the aperture.

'Jesus, Mary an' Joseph! What is it ye want with my Sam at this hour? And now haven't ye woken himself and he with the sick stomach on him.'

Looking past her they all saw another figure materialise from the gloom.

'Maggie, what for have ye the door open? It's so cold it would perish the crows.'

'Ah, Patrick, would ye get back in there. This feller wants ter see Sam.'

'What for?'

Mary was fast losing patience. 'I've no intention of standing here and discussing the matter. We're coming in and we're going to see your precious bloody son.'

'Come in then, ye can sit on the bed and say what ye've come for.'

'Thank you, but we'll stand,' Mary said cuttingly.

Maggie O'Grady pulled an old shawl around her and disappeared while Mary tried to see what else was in the room, apart from the bed. The whole place obviously needed a good scrubbing out.

'I'd offer ye a cup of tea or even a drop of the good stuff, iffen we had either,' Pat O'Grady said affably.

'Thank you, but we haven't come on a social visit.' Mary's tone was still icy.

Rubbing his eyes and running a hand through his thick curly blond hair, Sam was ushered in by his mother. His drowsiness left him as he saw Daisy and her parents in the room. He felt panic rise up inside him. Oh, God! There could only be one reason why they were here. The eejit of a girl must be pregnant!

'Right, you! I want to know what you're going to do about the condition you've put our Daisy in?' Jack demanded.

Maggie crossed herself and let out a wail.

'That's not going to help anyone!' Mary snapped at her.

'By all the holy saints, what have ye done to the girl?' Maggie demanded of her son.

'What . . . what's she told you?' Sam demanded cautiously. Oh, she'd been willing enough, eager even, and she'd been good. He'd enjoyed himself. She'd been easy to handle except for that moonstruck look that was always in her eyes and her constant demands for declarations of undying love. Which of course he'd sworn.

'She's told us that she's in the family way and you're the father and now I'm telling you that you're going to marry her.' Jack's authority was impressive.

Sam felt trapped. No! Oh, no! He didn't want to be tied for life to Daisy Callaghan with all her simpering stupidity. 'How . . . how does she know it's mine? How do I know she's even after telling the truth?' he blustered.

His mother let out another wail and crossed herself and his father just stood glaring at him.

Daisy was distraught. 'Oh, Sam! How can you say such things? You know I've never let any other lad . . . I love you. You know there's never been anyone else.' She dissolved into tears.

'I understand what you're implying and I'll beat the living daylights out of you if you say it again!' Jack yelled, oblivious to the fact that now he would have everyone in the house up and probably next door as well.

Maggie let out a screech. 'Sam O'Grady, you've the heart across me! Haven't I warned ye time and again where all yez womanising would take ye? Aren't ye the biggest eejit in this city. But ye'll marry the girl. Them's decent folk.'

Mary noted that Sam's father seemed to have no intention of taking part in this conversation.

'Ma, I'm not marrying her! I . . . I don't even love her! I won't be tied for life to the likes of her!' Sam shouted, his voice quavering with fear.

Uttering a roar that seemed to shake the room, Jack caught the lad by the shoulder and slammed him against the wall, banging his head hard against it.

'If I have to break every bone in your miserable bloody body, I will! If I have to drag you by the scruff of your neck up the aisle, I will! By God, you'll not humiliate us all! You'll marry her!'

Sam winced and turned pale. Jack Callaghan was a big man and one used to fighting. All the members of the 'black gangs' fought amongst themselves and anyone else stupid enough to antagonise them. Jack meant what he said. Sam'd be half killed. There was no way out of it. He'd get no help from his da, who was afraid of his own shadow, nor his mam either.

'All right! All right, I'll marry her.'

The vice-like grip slackened and he breathed again.

'I'm glad you've seen reason, but if you try to scarper or go back on it, you'd best reserve your plot in Ford Cemetery!' Jack looked at the lad with contempt. He'd come across his type before. Full of fancy chat but with no guts.

'Sure, there'll be no need for that! I'll see he keeps his word,' Maggie said fearfully. The lad was an eejit to have taken advantage of the daughter of a man like Jack Callaghan.

'Right then, I'll be round to see you about the . . . arrangements tomorrow,' Mary said firmly, suddenly remembering the time. Outwardly she was calm but inside she was fuming.

'I'll be waiting on ye, Mrs Callaghan. And I'll see to it that this fine bucko here goes to see Father Mannion,' Maggie replied, glaring at her son.

Once they were back in the street, Daisy started to cry.

'Oh, Mam! Mam! How could he say those terrible things? How could he?'

'If you'd behaved yourself he'd have had nothing to accuse you of,' Jack snapped at her. 'And you ... we ... wouldn't be in this mess.'

'But I believed him, Da! He swore he loved me, he was always saying that. I wouldn't ... couldn't have done ... anything if I hadn't believed him!'

She stopped and grabbed her mother's sleeve. 'Mam, I ... I ... can't marry him! Not after what he's just said! He doesn't love me! You heard him. I was just ... easy.'

Jack glared at her. 'You've made your bed and now you'll bloody lie in it.'

'Marry in haste, repent at leisure.' Mary thought how apt the old saying was. Despite her anger, she felt sorry for Daisy. The girl did love Sam. She'd believed all the lies he'd told her and now to be rejected like that was heart-breaking for her. Still, there was nothing could be done about it now. Daisy had to make the best of her marriage. Just as she'd learnt to do all those years ago.

'Well, Mam?' Nell asked, getting up stiffly and rubbing her eyes as they all entered the kitchen.

'He'll marry her. Your mam is going round tomorrow to

sort it all out. Now, can we all get some sleep? A fine shore leave this is going to be.'

'Go on up, Jack. It won't be so bad, you've another four days left yet,' Mary said flatly.

'And won't I be glad when they're over!' he retorted angrily as he went upstairs.

Nell could tell by the look on her mother and sister's faces that it had not gone smoothly.

'I'll make us all a cup of hot tea, then, Mam, you go up, you look worn out. You're not going out with the barrow tomorrow, are you?'

'I'll have to, Nell, to pay for a wedding. Daisy, luv, you go on up and try and get some sleep. It's not been an easy day for you either.'

Nell looked at her mother quizzically. She appeared to have forgotten her anger with Daisy.

'Mam, what went on?' she asked, placing a mug of tea in her mother's work-worn hands.

'Oh, it was terrible, Nell. I feel so sorry now for my poor girl. He refused to marry her, said how did he know it was his? How did he know she wasn't lying?'

'Oh, no! He said all that in front of her?'

Mary nodded. 'She just . . . sort of crumpled. At least she didn't break down until we got outside.'

'Oh, poor, poor Daisy!'

'Your da threatened to break every bone in his body and he finally agreed, but it's going to be so hard on her. Your da has his faults, but at least he loved me, still does in his own peculiar way.'

Nell reached out and took her mother's hand. 'Mam,

there's nothing else she can do, is there?'

'Nothing. I hope to God that the child will give her all the love she'll need, so that she can see some point to her life. Oh, Nell, why did this have to happen?'

'I don't know, Mam. I really don't, but I'll do everything I can to help you both.'

'I know that, luv, and we'll get through it somehow.'

Daisy had cried all night and by morning was worn out and red-eyed. Nell had listened to the muffled sobs and her heart went out to her sister. Now, as she got ready for work, Daisy again broke down.

'Nell, I don't want to go to that house there ever again! They were . . . awful, the house stank, it was terrible and I can't face them!'

'Then don't go. Mam won't make you. I'll go with her, if she wants me to. But we've got to go to work, we can't afford to lose a day's pay and you know there's plenty of girls waiting to step into our jobs.'

Daisy was appalled. How could she go to work? 'But what will I say! I look awful! People will notice and ask!'

'Say you've got a head cold. You look as though you have. You've got to pull yourself together, Daisy, so people won't suspect. Won't *know* what he said.'

Daisy dashed away the tears with the back of her hand. 'You're right, Nell. I'll try but it will be so . . . hard.'

'I know that, but I'll help you. We'll get through it.' Nell spoke with a confidence she didn't feel.

Somehow they *did* get through the day but they were exhausted when they got home. When they walked in the door they found Mary with her Sunday coat and hat on. Of their father there was no sign.

'Oh, Mam! I can't face it! I'm too tired and sick,' Daisy wailed.

Nell laid a hand on her mother's arm. 'Mam, I'll come with you. She doesn't feel up to it, she *has* had a hard day.'

Mary looked at her elder daughter with some impatience. She was tired out too. She'd had little or no sleep and had had to go out with the barrow. The weather had been foul and customers few. It had been a long day.

'All right. You stay here and see to your da – whenever he decides to come home – and our Teddy. Make sure he doesn't get up to any mischief and for God's sake tell him to give that blasted dog a good scrub with carbolic. I can't understand you at all, Nell.'

Nell shrugged apologetically. 'I don't know why I said we'd have him, Mam, but I've told Teddy he's got to look after it. It just might make him more responsible. I'll wash my face and hands and tidy my hair. It won't take a minute.'

As they turned into Eldon Street Mary sighed heavily. 'Well, I wonder how many of them will be in to hear that their fly-by-night brother is going to get married. There appears to be a tribe of them, and you should have seen the state of her and him! Oh, Nell, I've worked so hard for all of you and now I have to see our Daisy reduced to marrying into this.' She reached out and pushed open the dirty, pitted door from which the paint had long since peeled off.

As she followed her mother Nell caught her breath at the odours that assailed her nostrils. Mary knocked loudly on the kitchen door.

'Ah, it's yourself, Mary. Come on in. I've the tea wet an' waiting on ye,' Maggie said cheerfully.

Mary pursed her lips. She had no wish to be on first-name terms with this slattern. The kitchen appeared to be crowded with kids of all ages.

'Is there nowhere else we can go, Mrs O'Grady? Somewhere more . . . private?'

'Sure, 'tis only the family that's here.'

'And they have a right to sit in their own kitchen, Mrs O'Grady,' Nell said tactfully, 'but perhaps you might like time to . . . talk to Mam, woman to woman, mother to mother so to speak?' She too had no desire to discuss the reluctant bridegroom in front of this crowd.

'Ah, well now, ye might be right. Theresa, boil up that kettle again. We'll have a fresh pot – bring it down to us in the room below.'

Mary cast a grateful glance at her daughter and followed the woman back down the dark, dank lobby.

'We'll have to sit on the bed.'

'That will be no hardship, Mrs O'Grady,' Nell said pleasantly, averting her eyes from the piles of rags and old papers that seemed to serve as bedclothes.

'Right, did you send him to see the priest?' Mary asked.

'I did so. His Reverence wants to see the pair of them as soon as possible. He was scandalised, as well he might be, and me not missing Mass on a Sunday for years! "Maggie, how did you let this come about?" he says. "Father, aren't I on me knees prayin' to Our Lady and all the Blessed Saints to turn that lad away from his wild ways—"'

'Yes, that's all well and good,' Mary interrupted, 'but I'd

like to get this wedding over and done with as quickly as possible before Jack – Mr Callaghan – goes back to sea. I'll rig her out and provide a bit of a "do" afterwards.'

'Aren't ye the kind an' generous woman. Myself, I'll be hard put to turn that tribe out decently.'

'You're surely not intending to bring them all?'

'And why not? Haven't they the right to be there to see their own brother wed?'

'I think what Mam means is that we'd like it to be a very quiet wedding with not a lot of fuss, under the circumstances,' Nell intervened.

Mary seized upon it. 'Nell's right. That's just what I mean. Now, where will they live?'

'Sure to God I couldn't fit another bairn in this house. There's sixteen of us already.'

'I have no room either,' Mary stated firmly.

Maggie looked at her intently. 'Isn't himself away at sea most of the time, and there's only the four of ye?'

Mary sighed but she had made up her mind that the pair were not going to live with her. Sam O'Grady had a job. He was a porter at the fish market. He could afford to put a roof over their heads. 'And I intend to keep it just the four of us. Surely you understand that. It's hard enough to keep a decent roof over our heads, clothes on our backs and food in our bellies. They'll have to look for a room. Can't Father Mannion at Our Lady's help?'

'I'll ask him,' the woman said grudgingly.

Mary got up. 'Right then, I'll see that they go and see his Reverence and get a date, then I can start to . . . organise.'

Chapter Four

———◆———

WHEN THEY GOT BACK Jack was in, sober and reading a copy of the *Echo* someone had left on the tram. Daisy was staring into the fire, holding a cleaner but decidedly damp puppy, wrapped in a bit of old blanket, on her knee.

'Well?' Jack asked, putting down the paper. He hadn't been giving much attention to the events that were taking place in Germany where an Austrian house-painter called Adolf Hitler had rapidly risen to power.

'The pair of them are to go to see Father Mannion as soon as possible. I said I'd rig her out and pay for a bit of a do but they'll have to find themselves some sort of a room to rent. I'm not having them and she can't fit another single soul into that house.'

'Was . . . was he . . . there?' Daisy asked.

'No, thank God. I told her to ask Father Mannion if he can help with lodgings. I want it all over and done with before you sail, Jack.'

'Before I sail! You've got no chance, you know how long it takes the church to get it all organised.'

'We'll do it,' she replied firmly.

'Oh, this is turning out to be a really great leave!' he snapped sarcastically.

Mary lost her temper. 'All you ever think about is yourself, Jack Callaghan! Well, wouldn't you sooner come home on your next leave and have it all settled and done with? There'll be gossip, but it'll be a nine-day wonder and you won't be here to have to put up with it! I will!'

'Don't you go taking it out on me, Mary.'

'Mam, Da, please? Hasn't there been enough fighting?' Nell pleaded.

Jack picked up his newspaper again.

'I'll finish up early tomorrow, Daisy,' Mary went on coldly, 'and you'll have to get off an hour early too, then we'll all go to see Father Mannion. You can go to town on Saturday for an outfit and I'll see Peggy Draper about some ham and tongue and a few cakes. Now get to bed both of you and, Daisy, put that animal down. He'll be warm enough on the hearth.'

The next afternoon Daisy managed to get off an hour early, pleading sickness, and because she did look awful, the foreman agreed. When she got home Mary was waiting.

'Get changed and be quick. I sent our Teddy down to her in Eldon Street to tell her to get him to the Parish House by five.'

'Mam, do I have to go?'

'Of course you do! You managed to get out of going to see

her last night.' Daisy knew there was no hope of a reprieve this time.

Sam O'Grady was already there when they reached the Parish House, with a tidier, cleaner Maggie. She looked grim and so did Sam.

'Right then, let's get the formalities over and then I'll have a word with you two – alone!' the parish priest said ominously.

'Father, I . . . we'd like to get it organised as soon as possible. Jack has only two days left before he sails again.'

'But, Mary, I don't think it can be arranged that quickly.'

The priest had known Mary Callaghan for years, for she had gone to him for advice in the early days of her marriage, when she had begun to realise how irresponsible her new husband was.

'Please, Father! You know . . . what Jack's like?' Mary pleaded, ignoring the interested gaze of Daisy's future mother-in-law.

'I know, Mary. You've a heavy cross to bear.'

'Life would be much . . . easier, Father.'

'Well now, if they are not going to have a full Nuptial Mass I could do it on Sunday, in the afternoon, before Benediction. Of course it all depends on the Registrar, but I'm sure if I explain . . .'

'Oh, that would be a big relief to me, Father. Jack doesn't sail until eleven o'clock in the evening, something to do with the tides. I'll make sure she's here, dressed in something decent. Did you – were you able to help with lodgings?'

'I was indeed. The Flannagans in Silvester Street have a

room they will let. They can go and see it after I've finished with them,' he ended firmly.

Mary nudged Daisy in the ribs.

'Thank you. Thank you so much, Father,' Daisy managed to get out, although there was a catch in her voice. This wasn't how she'd envisaged the future at all. Before she'd found out about the baby, she used to dream of the wedding dress she would have, the flowers, the music, and then a home of their own, no matter how humble. Now there was only to be a quick service, no long white dress and a small room in another slum house.

Mary was on her feet, her hand stretched out to the priest. Following her lead, Maggie too stood up and thanked him. Like Mary she would be glad to get out and go home.

Daisy never wanted to go through the following hour ever again. Her cheeks had burned with shame at the dressing down both she and Sam received from the priest. He made her sound like a fallen woman and Sam an irresponsible, sinful seducer – which he was, she thought bitterly.

When the interview was over they went, in total silence, to see the front downstairs room that was to be their first home. It was hideous. It came furnished but there wasn't much in the way of actual furniture. What there was was old and dilapidated and she shuddered when she saw the blankets on the stained and lumpy flock mattress. She had been on the verge of tears all evening. She wished he would just say *something* to her but he didn't and he left her to walk home alone while he went to drown his sorrows in the Royal George. She had nothing, *nothing* to look forward to and that night she cried herself to sleep, railing at Nell's comforting words. 'You aren't going to marry a man who won't even speak to you!' she sobbed and buried her head in the pillow.

The following day Mary was distracted trying to get things organised, keep up with the housework and go out with the barrow. Saturday was one of her busiest days and she had her regulars to think of. It was cold and damp but she hardly noticed it as business was brisk and her mind elsewhere.

'Mrs Callaghan, you don't seem to be your usual cheerful self today. Is there anything wrong?' Alfred McManus asked solicitously.

Mary managed a smile. He was a pleasant enough man. A bachelor in his forties, she judged. He had a good job too. Some kind of a foreman down on the docks, he'd once told her. He'd been buying his fruit and vegetables from her on Saturday mornings for the past five years. 'I'm sorry I'm a bit down in the mouth today, Mr McManus, problems at home.'

'Nothing serious?' He knew her husband went away to sea and that she had two grown-up daughters and a son of eleven, who he gathered was a bit of a tearaway. With his father away so often it wasn't any wonder. She'd told him all about old Annie Garvey and his admiration for the kind-hearted, hard-working, respectable woman had grown.

'My daughter Daisy is getting married tomorrow. It's all a bit of a rush. We . . . we wanted to get it over before Jack sails.'

'I see.' He inspected the carrots she held out. Surely she

would have been able to plan around his trips. And it wasn't a usual day for weddings, unless of course . . .

He nodded. 'The carrots'll be fine, Mrs Callaghan, thank you.'

'Anything else?'

'A couple of those oranges. I like a bit of fruit now and then.'

Mary selected two, held them out for approval and then slipped them into the hemp bag he always used.

'Well, I hope it all goes well. I'm sorry I've no less, Mrs Callaghan,' he said apologetically, holding out a white five-pound note.

'Oh, I don't think I can change it.' She searched through the small leather bag attached to the top of her apron, bringing out a handful of coins. 'No, sorry, I can't. Are you sure you haven't anything less?'

He searched his pockets while a small queue formed behind him. 'You go ahead and serve someone else while I root around,' he urged.

She turned to the woman who was behind him and for the next five minutes her attention was diverted from him. She did hear someone shout his name but took no notice. At last when there were no more people to serve she looked around. He'd gone. Well, that was a bit odd, she thought. He'd never done anything like that before and he owed her almost five shillings. Five shillings that would have paid for the boiled ham from Peggy Draper and meant five shillings less on the slate. She hated owing money but there were times when she had no choice.

The afternoon was drawing in, the winter dusk falling and

she was preparing to finish up. What bits that were left over she could use herself. She was cold, hungry and tired and could murder a cup of tea.

'Have you finished, Mam?'

Mary turned at the sound of Nell's voice.

'I have, luv, and it hasn't been a bad day. What did you get?'

Nell held up the Blacklers' bags. 'A nice wool dress for me and a lovely costume for Daisy.'

'Did it run to hats and stockings?'

'It did. Come on, we'll give you a hand and when we get home we can have a fashion parade.'

Mary smiled tiredly at her daughters. She had had word from Father Mannion that the Registrar had agreed and the service would take place at three o'clock tomorrow.

'Will you go over to Lizzie Cassidy and see what flowers she's got left? Tell her I'll take them all and pay her next Saturday.'

Daisy stood silent and dejected while Nell went across to the woman who sold flowers, returning with some chrysanthemums, a few carnations and some dark green foliage. 'She said take them for free. I'll get a bit of ribbon and make up a couple of posies.'

'Let's get off then. I've the barrow to drop off at Henry Street stables, your da and our Teddy's shirts to iron and a couple of jellies to make yet. Your da's promised to get a bottle of port, sherry or Madeira wine and some ale. He couldn't run to whiskey.'

'I think they're lucky to get anything decent to drink at all,' Nell said.

'I just hope to God she doesn't trail all those kids around here!' Mary sighed as she manoeuvred her heavy barrow over the cobbles.

'She won't, Mam, and anyway it will all be over in half the time a wedding usually goes on for.'

Daisy sniffed as she trailed behind her mother and sister. How could they be so matter-of-fact about it? Her heart was broken, her life ruined and all they could worry about were the O'Gradys.

''Ere, Mary, luv, I believe congratulations are in order,' Edna Stanley from two doors down shouted as they turned into Portland Street.

'They are, Edna. Only found out myself a couple of days ago. It seems the pair of them were planning to elope and we couldn't have that,' Mary shouted back. It was the excuse they'd agreed on to try to save face.

'God, that one doesn't miss a thing!' Nell hissed.

'Well, once I'd seen Peggy Draper I knew it wouldn't take long for the entire street to get to know about it.'

'I didn't know they were that serious!' Edna called back, oblivious to the blushing Daisy.

'Neither did we, Edna. Well, I can't stop, I've a million and one things to do.'

'Well, good luck to the pair of them. I hear they're going to Silvester Street to live.'

'She doesn't give up easily, does she!' Nell said heatedly.

'You might like to come in for a glass of sherry, Edna, tomorrow afternoon,' Mary called. 'Bring your Tom with you.'

'Ta, luv. I'll do that.'

'Well, what could I do?' Mary said in response to Nell's startled expression, as Edna finally went back inside.

'Where's your da?' Mary asked of young Teddy who was lying on the floor, playing with the puppy.

'Dunno, Mam.'

'Oh, isn't that just great! Well, let's get started on the tea.'

'Mam, sit down for a few minutes. I'll make a cup of tea; you look perished. Daisy, why don't you go and get changed into your new stuff. Show Mam how nice it looks.'

Daisy shrugged and left the room.

'Oh, Nell, I'm worried about her, I really am.'

'So am I. She's not a bit happy at all and you can't blame her. I had a job even to get her to look at things. Mam, I feel so sorry for her. She hasn't even mentioned where they're going to live, apart from saying it's a tip!'

'I pray to God that once they're wed and in their own place, he might come around to trying to make the best of it.'

'That's all we can hope for, Mam,' Nell replied sadly.

She had made the tea and had seen to Annie who was having one of her bad days – she was crippled with arthritis and when it was cold and damp her joints swelled so she could barely move – before Daisy finally appeared in her finery.

'Oh, Daisy, luv, you look lovely!' Mary cried, meaning every word. The pale green two-piece costume was fashionable and looked smart. Underneath was a cream rayon blouse with a Peter Pan collar embroidered around the edges. She wore a cream, wide-brimmed hat trimmed with a green ribbon bow.

'With her good shoes and my best handbag she'll look great, Mam. We'll *all* look great.'

'That won't be hard to do compared to what *that* lot will turn up in. I just hope they won't make a show of us, not with every woman in the street either out on their doorsteps or peering from behind their curtains.'

'Can Scruffy have a bow around his neck for the wedding, like?' Teddy asked.

'Oh, aren't you a case, Teddy!' Nell laughed, trying to lighten the mood. 'Don't you think Scruffy has had enough what with having tins tied to his tail?'

'He looks great now, Nell! I gave him another good wash and he's eaten everything I put down for him.'

Mary raised her eyes to the ceiling. 'We're causing enough of a spectacle as it is without making it worse by dressing up a flaming mongrel!'

That night Nell was the last one to go to bed. She'd helped Annie to get settled for the night.

'You'll feel better with that hot brick in the bed,' she soothed.

'Some days it's so bad that I wish the good Lord would take me. It's pure agony.'

'All those years of being out in all weathers.'

'I know, Nell. I just hope your mam – God bless her – doesn't end up the same way.'

'I'm going to make sure she doesn't. I don't know how – yet – but I *will*.'

'The last thing she needs is all this fuss and palaver over Daisy.'

Nell sighed. 'I know. I feel so sorry for Daisy.'

'Well, at least he's marrying her.' There was a note of bitterness in the old woman's voice.

'But what kind of a marriage will it be? It's . . . it's a life sentence.' Then: 'Will you be all right next door?' she asked to change the subject.

'I'll be fine, better than having to sit here with all the noise and carry on. A few hours' peace and quiet in Florrie Ford's kitchen will be a treat.'

'Yes, I suppose it will. No one's looking forward to tomorrow.'

'Except your da. He knows he'll be well out of it all by ten o'clock,' Annie finished scathingly.

After another sleepless night Mary got up to a fine, bright winter morning. She thanked God it wasn't raining or they would all have been soaked and shivering walking to church. She had had an argument with Jack who wanted to meet his mates for a swift half in the Golden Fleece before the wedding. Reluctantly he had agreed to forgo it, thankful that his ship sailed that night and he would be well away from all of them for two weeks.

Nell had spent most of the morning helping Mary tidy up the house, lay out the food and drink, make the posies and a couple of buttonholes, and keep Teddy and the dog out of everyone's way.

'If you dare to poke a single finger into those bowls of jelly I'll kill you!' she warned, finding him staring at the two bowls that had been left out on the window ledge all night so the jelly would set.

'How else can you tell when they're ready?' he demanded indignantly.

'You just shake the bowl gently. Get inside and get washed and put on your good clothes or there'll be no jelly or cake or anything for you.'

'Ah, Nell, do I have to just yet? I hate that collar, it's tight and all scratchy! All me mates will be skitting me.'

'And all your mates' mams will be wishing they could turn their lads out in a decent shirt! Get in with you now!'

As the afternoon approached Mary had become more flustered and irritable. It didn't help that Jack had gone to the pub after Mass and hadn't come back until half past one.

'Oh, Nell, will this day ever end?' she asked as they laid out the plates of sandwiches and cakes, cups, saucers and glasses.

'It will, Mam, don't worry! The table looks well, our Teddy is still clean and tidy, Da *did* bring home the drink, we'll all look smart and Daisy will be fine.'

'She doesn't look it. She's hardly said a word since she got up and when I went up last time she wasn't even making an attempt to get ready.'

'She's plenty of time yet and I'll sort her out.'

'Oh, who the hell is that?' Mary exclaimed as the door-knocker rattled loudly.

'Mam, you stay there. I'll see who it is.' Nell wondered who it could be. No one ever used the knocker, the neighbours pushed open the door and yelled down the lobby to announce their arrival.

Opening the door, Nell looked up at the well-dressed man who stood on the doorstep. 'Oh, sorry, are you . . . Daisy?'

'No. No, I'm Nell. Can I help you?'

'I hope so. I buy my provisions from your mother every Saturday and yesterday I didn't have change . . . and . . .'

'Nell, who is it? Don't be keeping them on the doorstep, it's cold out there.' Mary's voice came down the lobby.

'You'd better come in, Mr—?'

'McManus. Alfred McManus.'

She smiled at him. 'Follow me.'

'Oh, I couldn't intrude!'

'I'll get no peace if you don't. Come in.'

Reluctantly he followed her.

'Oh, good Lord! Mr McManus!' Mary cried.

'I'm sorry to bother you. I forgot about the wedding, but . . .'

Mary patted her hair into place. He was the last person she had thought it would be. 'You're not bothering us at all. Please do sit down.' She was so thankful the place was tidy.

'No. No, really. I just wanted to pay you. I got distracted by a chap I haven't seen for years – well, not since we left school actually, and it wasn't until much later that I realised I hadn't paid you. I went back but you'd gone. One of the other women gave me your address. So, please take this with my apologies, then I'll be on my way.'

'That's very kind and considerate of you. Please do stay – and maybe have a drink?'

He began to protest but when Jack appeared and all was explained, he insisted the man have a drink.

'There's not many fellers in this city who would be so honest or thoughtful. What'll you have?'

'Well, a small port, if you have any.'

'We do indeed,' Jack said expansively, thinking that 'a small port' wasn't what your average working feller drank. Not when there was ale and rum on offer, courtesy of the landlord of the Golden Fleece, seeing as he was one of his best customers.

'Well, where is the bride? I'd like to drink her health – and her husband's of course.'

'Upstairs,' Jack nodded. 'You know what women are like, mate.'

'No, not really.'

'Aren't you married, er . . .'

'Alfred, and I'm a bachelor.'

'Aren't you the lucky one!' Jack said, knocking back his second tot of rum in one gulp.

Mary glared at him. 'Daisy will be down soon. Would you . . . would you care to stay? It's only going to be a short ceremony and there's plenty of food and drink for afterwards.'

'Can't have you going off to . . . ?'

'Priory Road,' Alfred supplied.

'To an empty house in Priory Road when there's a good do in the offing. Have another one!' Jack was feeling far more cheerful, ignoring the looks his wife cast at him.

'That's very kind of you, er, Jack.'

'Some of the neighbours will be popping in later. If you feel as though things are a bit . . . awkward, we'd understand.' Mary had picked her words carefully. He was a cut above them. He had a good job and a house in a decent area of Liverpool. His clothes were high quality and he had a silver

51

pocket watch on a chain in his waistcoat. She refused to even think about the O'Gradys.

'Mrs Callaghan, I'll be only too delighted to accept.'

'It's Mary. This is Nell, my younger daughter and the young lad with the scruffy little dog is our Teddy.'

Alfred stood up and shook hands with them – even Teddy. 'I'm very pleased to meet you all,' he said sincerely.

Nell smiled at him. He was very stiff and formal, but maybe a few drinks would liven him up. And he had had the decency to come down here on a Sunday to pay Mam what he owed.

He smiled back. The place, although small, cramped and sparsely furnished, was spotless. Jack was very convivial, Mary welcoming and young Nell was a real beauty, although she obviously didn't realise it. He wondered was the bride as good-looking?

'Nell, luv,' Mary whispered, 'go and get our Daisy down here. We'll have to be leaving in a minute and your da's had enough to drink already. Father Mannion will have a fit if he smells his breath!'

Nell did as she was bid and returned with a nicely turned-out but very tearful Daisy.

'Oh, luv, you look beautiful!' Mary enthused.

'You do indeed, Daisy!' Jack added, the circumstances of this wedding temporarily forgotten.

'Might I add my congratulations and praise?'

Daisy smiled politely at the stranger but she couldn't have cared less.

'Right then, we'd better get off. Teddy, you walk where I can see you. Nell, perhaps you'd walk with . . . Alfred.' She found it hard to call him by his Christian name. It seemed so odd.

'Of course I will, Mam.' Nell smiled.

'Might I be so bold as to offer you my arm, Miss Callaghan?' Alfred ventured.

She looked at him with amusement from beneath her long dark lashes. He was so prim and proper, it would certainly give the neighbours something to talk about.

The little procession made its way on foot to Our Lady's in Eldon Street with the bride and her father not far behind. As was the custom the women and girls of the neighbourhood stood on their steps to call blessings and discuss the outfits.

'Who's that feller with Nell Callaghan?' Edna Stanley asked her neighbour in a loud whisper.

Nell grinned to herself, pleased to be distracting attention from Daisy's hasty marriage.

'God bless the both of yez!' Florrie Ford cried as Daisy passed.

Edna crossed herself.

'What's up with yer, Edna?' Florrie hissed.

'Did no one tell 'er it was unlucky ter wear green?'

'Oh, shurrup with yer auld wives' tales!' Florrie said impatiently, but Edna shook her head ominously as they passed by.

For Daisy the whole afternoon went in a blur. She'd heard herself, so calmly and quietly, reply to Father Mannion's questions as she promised to love, honour and obey Sam O'Grady until death would part them. She managed to smile as she was congratulated by her family and his – all sixteen of them for, to Mary's chagrin, Maggie had brought every one.

Packed as they all were into Mary's small house there was nowhere she could go to seek refuge. All she wanted to do was hide. To get away from all these people, even Nell, but there was no way out and at the end of it all there was the walk to Silvester Street to start her married life with a man who didn't love her and never would.

For Daisy Callaghan her wedding day was the unhappiest day of her life.

Chapter Five

———◆———

ALFRED MCMANUS BECAME A regular visitor. He had enjoyed himself at Daisy's wedding and after a few drinks had become less buttoned-up. Mary, feeling sorry for him, had asked him to come for his dinner the following Sunday and his visits continued through spring and into early summer.

Jack, on his visits home, still found him a bit too strait-laced, but he was always willing to pay his round on the few occasions when Jack managed to persuade him to join 'the lads' in the Golden Fleece.

After feeling a little embarrassed at first, Mary found his advice very helpful.

'You know, Mary, you could save yourself time and effort if you bought two days' supplies at once. In this cold weather they will keep fresh, as long as you keep the frost off them. I don't say do it through the summer months, but it's light and much warmer then anyway. Every other day you could spend a couple of hours at home, take things easier. You work very hard.'

'That's a great idea, Alfred. I should have thought of it myself. These cold, dark mornings I'd give anything for an extra hour in bed,' she'd replied, touched that he was so considerate. He'd been just as helpful with her worries over Daisy and Sam.

'Oh, sometimes I despair, Alfred, I really do. I had hoped things would get better, but they haven't,' she'd said after a recent visit to Silvester Street.

'When she has the child it might help, particularly if it's a boy. What man wouldn't be pleased and proud to have a son and heir?'

'Well, Jack certainly was when I finally had our Teddy. I lost a boy, the year after I had our Daisy.' She'd remembered the day Nell had been born and Jack's treatment of his younger daughter. She would never forget that day or his words.

'I'm sorry, I didn't know that. It must have been hard for you both. But young Teddy isn't a bad lad, he just needs a firm hand. Give him plenty of chores to do, that will help you and give him less time to hang around street corners and get up to no good.'

'You're right again and I could do with some help. Nell's very good but I feel she should be going out and enjoying herself more, she's twenty-one now and I want her to meet a decent lad.'

'Nell's far more . . . sensible, Mary. She'll take her time . . .'

'Unlike our poor Daisy.' They were back to the old problem.

'Don't worry too much, Mary, I'm sure things will be much better in a few months, especially, as I say, if the child's a boy.' He paused, then added wistfully, 'I know I'd be delighted to have a son.'

Mary looked at him enquiringly. 'Did you never consider marrying, Alfred? You're a fine man.'

'Once or twice, but I had to see to my old da. Mam died when I was young and Da had an accident on the docks and was crippled. That's how I got my job – as a sort of compensation. I looked after him until he died. Sometimes I feel like a pea rattling around in that empty house. But I'm afraid I'm too old for things ever to be any different now.'

'Oh, don't say that, you'd be a good catch for a lot of young women.'

'I suppose I would, if you put it like that. I could offer a good home, a regular wage, no need to go out to work, I'm temperate in my habits—'

'I wish Jack was,' Mary interrupted. 'Life could have been much easier, but you know Jack.'

'You'll not change him now, Mary.'

'Don't I know that well enough.'

'But I suppose you would be glad to see Nell make a good marriage?'

'I would indeed. She'd make a lovely wife and mother.'

He leaned forward in the chair, clasping his hands, wondering if now was the right time to voice the thoughts he'd been having for a good few months.

'Mary, do you think . . . Well, what I mean is . . . would you be happy about me asking Nell to walk out with me? I know I'm a lot older and she's a very attractive girl, but I could offer her so much and I would like to have a son or daughter or both.'

Mary was a little taken aback. She hadn't known he was interested in Nell. Oh, he was always polite and seemed to get on well with her younger daughter, but she *was* much younger than him.

She thought carefully about her reply. She didn't want to insult or upset him. 'I really don't know, Alfred. I'll ask her, it's all I can do.'

'I'd be grateful if you would, Mary.'

'Let me think about it for a week, Alfred. I'll tell you next Sunday, if that's all right.'

'That will be fine. I've been wanting to mention it for some time. Will you ask Jack his opinion?'

'No. Jack's never really had much time for Nell, not since the day she was born.' She smiled wryly. 'He wanted a son, you see.'

'Well, I'll leave it in your hands.'

'Thanks. I *will* give it a lot of thought.'

She did think about it a great deal and the more she thought, the more reasonable it sounded. He could offer Nell a very good life. One that would be secure, without worry, without slaving as she, Mary, had had to do all these years. Not exactly a life of leisure by some people's standards, but a damned sight easier than her own. He was over twenty years older than Nell, but he didn't drink heavily, he didn't smoke, he didn't gamble and he certainly wasn't a womaniser. She'd always sworn that Nell would have a better life than her own and Nell could do far worse than Alfred McManus. Well, she'd put it to Nell and see what she said.

'Alfred asked me something last Sunday,' she said after tea was over, the dishes washed and dried and Teddy and Scruffy safely dispatched to play on a piece of waste land down Athol Street.

'What?' Nell wasn't giving her mam her full attention, she was leafing through a magazine she'd been given. It was very tatty, she being its sixth or seventh owner, but it did give the latest styles for summer.

'Put down that magazine and listen to me. It's serious.'

'What then? Is it something to do with Daisy?'

'No, it's not, for a change. It's something to do with you and your future.'

'What future?' Nell hadn't given that much thought.

'Alfred asked me to ask you if you'd consider going out with him, seriously.'

Nell was startled. 'Mam!'

'Wait now before you start to get on your high horse. I know he's a lot older but he has a good job, a whole house to himself, he's no vices and you'd never have to go out to work again – there's not many girls or women from around here who can look forward to that! I just want you to consider it carefully. I know you're only twenty-one and I was very surprised myself when he asked. I was saying I wished you'd go out and enjoy yourself more.'

'Mam, you can't be serious? Alfred? Alfred McManus!'

'Nell, I said I'd ask you and now I have. Just bear in mind all he can offer *and* he's an educated man. I don't want to see you end up like our Daisy.'

'I've more sense than her, but Mam . . .'

'That's all I'm going to say about it, Nell.' Mary busied

herself folding up the pinafore she'd been wearing.

Nell was bemused. 'When does he want an answer?'

'I said I'd give him my verdict on Sunday. Mine, not yours – yet. Will you promise to just think about it?'

'I'll think about it, Mam, but . . .'

'Right, that's enough for me. Now I'm off to my bed, I've had a headache all day. I think it's the heat. It's very hot and sticky for June.'

When she'd gone Nell got up and went to sit on the front doorstep to wait for Teddy and the dog to come home. What on earth was Mam thinking of? Alfred was an old man with very strait-laced views and practically no sense of humour. It would be nice to live in a house in Priory Road and never have to worry about money ever again or have to go to work, but . . . Alfred? She'd been out with a couple of local boys, nothing serious, but she'd found them a bit juvenile. She knew she was attractive, many people had told her so, but that hadn't had any bearing on her decision not to consider a local lad seriously. She also knew that many of them called her 'stuck up' and 'snobby'. But she couldn't help how she felt . . .

Her attention was diverted by the sight of Daisy walking slowly up the street. She was very big now and pregnancy hadn't suited her. She looked bloated, her face puffed up, her hair straggling, the smock she wore over a skirt creased and grubby, her shoes broken down and she wore no stockings. Nell sighed. She looked nothing like the young girl who'd been married just five months ago.

'What's the matter?' she asked as she helped Daisy inside, noting how hot and clammy her sister felt. 'It's stifling in here, because of the range. Do you want to sit in the yard? Our Teddy has cleaned it up a bit.'

'God, no! The privies stink in this weather. It would turn your stomach.' She paused. 'I've left him.'

Nell's eyes widened. 'You've *left* him?'

'Where's Mam?'

'Gone up to bed for an early night.'

Daisy clutched her sister's arm. 'Will you call her, Nell? I can't take another day of it! I hate him! I bloody hate him!' She began to sob uncontrollably.

'Oh, Daisy, sit down and tell me what this is all about.'

'No! I want Mam!'

Nell sighed. 'All right, I'll get her. Stop crying, please.'

Daisy eased herself into the armchair and waited until Nell reappeared with Mary, who looked pale and tired.

'Daisy, what is it now, luv?'

Daisy started to cry again. 'I *hate* him, Mam! I can't stand it any more. He hardly speaks to me. Now he's gone off again with his mates, into town for a few bevvies and a bit of a laugh, because he never gets that at home, I'm too bloody miserable! That's what he said! Oh, what does he expect? But he . . . he's . . . meeting some girl or other, I know he is! He's suddenly started to get dressed up to go out and he won't tell me why, or why he's spending more money than we can afford. Look at me, Mam! I've no stockings and hardly a shoe to my foot! I've nothing for the baby, nothing at all! I can't afford anything! I can't stand it any more, Mam! I want to come home. Please, Mam? Don't send me back, Mam? I'm begging you.'

Mary shook her head sadly. 'Oh, Daisy, luv, what can I

say? You took your vows, before God. For better or for worse. You're not the only woman who has to suffer.' She thought briefly of all the years of hard work and deprivation that she'd suffered. 'There's no going back on your promises, Daisy.'

'What about his promises?' Daisy cried bitterly.

'Daisy, your da made the same promises and he hasn't stuck to them, but I've *had* to! Look at the likes of Bessie Weaver from further down. He belts hell out of her every Saturday night and has she left him? No. She can't. There are hundreds of women and girls trapped in miserable marriages. Where would we all go, Daisy? No one will take us and our kids in, clothe and feed us. Oh, luv, I'm so sorry for you, but you can't stay. Your da and Father Mannion would go mad. Have you talked to his mam?'

'No! What help do you think I'd get from her? She couldn't care less about any of them and his da is just as useless!' Daisy was distraught and her shoulders shook with her sobs.

'Will I go to the Dispensary and get something to calm her?' Nell asked. Daisy was in a terrible state.

Mary was upset and worried but she *had* to send Daisy back. 'Would you, Nell? I'll put the kettle on. You just sit there and rest, Daisy. You shouldn't be getting into a state like this, it's not good for the baby.'

'Oh, to hell with the baby! I don't want it!' Daisy cried.

'May God forgive you, Daisy O'Grady! That's a terrible, wicked thing to say! So many babies die around here and you don't know what it's like to lose a child!'

Daisy was instantly contrite, remembering the brother who had been stillborn. 'Oh, Mam, I'm sorry!'

'And so you should be! You'll love it when it's born and you've not long to wait now.'

Daisy's sobs diminished as Mary busied herself with the kettle and teapot.

Teddy arrived and was sent to wash his face and hands and get himself to bed without asking any questions.

'They gave me some of this stuff,' Nell said, finally arriving back. She handed over a small bottle to her mother while she regained her breath. She'd run there and back and she was hot, tired and sticky.

'This will do. Measure out half a teaspoon and give it to her, Nell, while I pour the tea.'

Nell did as she was told, then stroked the damp strands of hair that clung to her sister's forehead. What must life be like for poor Daisy? She was so young, with so many years ahead of her.

Mary gave her a knowing look over the top of Daisy's head.

'When she's calmed down, I'll walk back with her,' Mary said quietly. She wouldn't have stood by and watched her daughter be mistreated, if Sam had been a wife-beater, no matter what Jack said. But he wasn't and so she could do nothing about Daisy's predicament. To condone her walking out on her marriage was against everything she believed in.

'Let me take her back, Mam, you need an early night. I don't mind.'

'You're a good girl, Nell.'

Daisy lost her temper. It wasn't fair! Mam didn't want her but Nell could do no wrong. 'That's all you ever say!' she screamed. 'Oh, *she's* the good one! *She's* perfect. It's all you ever go on about, Mam, flaming Nell! Nell! Bloody Miss Prim and Proper!'

'Daisy!' Nell was shocked and hurt.

Mary's whole body went rigid with rage. 'That's enough of that, Daisy! I won't have it! You brought all this on your own head! Yes, I wish you did have the sense Nell has, then I wouldn't be out of my mind with worry. I'll take you back myself. Now sit there and be quiet, I'll not have you saying such things about your sister who only ever thinks of us and not herself!'

When Mary had taken a silent and mutinous Daisy home, Nell went upstairs. Daisy must be so unhappy to have gone for her like that. She'd never, ever said anything like that before. She thought about her own position. Was Mam right? Was the future Alfred offered – free from worry, debt, work and an unfaithful husband – to be considered desirable even if that husband was much older and more strait-laced? She certainly wasn't in love with him, but maybe in time she could learn to love him? And just look where love had got Daisy.

Chapter Six

AFTER SHE RETURNED TO the dismal and depressing room in Silvester Street, exhausted and utterly miserable, Daisy fell into a grief-sodden sleep. Of Sam there was no sign. She was certain he was out with some girl, while she . . . Oh, why, why hadn't Mam let her stay? Surely she could understand. Adultery was a sin, but how could she prove it? And even if she did, there was still no way out of the life she loathed.

She was awakened by a searing pain coursing through her. 'Oh, God! This must be the start of it!' she thought in panic, trying to get off the bed. She had to get some help. She couldn't stay here in this room alone, she'd die, she just knew she would.

She dragged herself to the door and then the lobby. The humid night air wafted in through the ever open front door and she felt dizzy. She was sweating with fear and pain.

'Mrs Flannagan! Mrs Flannagan, help me! Please help me!'

she cried as she hammered on her landlady's door.

It was at length opened by one of the younger Flannagans.

'Please, get your mam, quickly! Quickly!' she begged as another pain tore through her.

Kate Flannagan appeared in the doorway and Daisy grabbed her arm. 'It's started, I know it has!'

'God Almighty, Daisy! Get back to bed, luv. Where's your feller?'

'Out. Out and I don't know where!'

'Bloody typical! Fellers! Neither use nor ornament! 'Ere, lean on me, luv. Is there anyone else?'

'Mam! I want my mam! Please get her. Please?' Daisy was terrified, she had never known that there was pain like this. No one had really told her what to expect. They'd just said it was damned hard work. She must be dying! She *must*!

'Get inter that bed, I'll send our 'Arry fer yer mam. An' what about the midwife, shall I send fer 'er as well?'

Her neighbour was taking it so calmly. 'Yes, yes please. Oh, don't leave me, I can't bear it!' she cried as Kate Flannagan turned towards the door, after helping her on to the bed.

Kate bawled down the lobby for Violet, her eldest daughter, and Harry, the most sensible of her many sons. They appeared and were given the instructions, then Kate turned back to Daisy.

'Oh, I'm dying, I know I am!' Daisy cried as another contraction distorted her features.

'No, yer're not, luv! It's yer first an' it can be a bit frightenin', like, but it'll be all over soon. When yer've 'ad eight like meself, yer won't pay it any attention. It's like fallin' off a log!'

Daisy didn't believe her and prayed Mam would come soon.

Mrs Hannigan, the midwife, arrived first and was very matter-of-fact about Daisy's condition.

'I'll time the pains. You just tell me when one's started and when it's over.'

'Oh, Mother of God, I'm going to die! It's going to kill me!' Daisy wailed.

'No, it's flaming well not! Pull yourself together, Daisy! It's a bit painful for a few hours and then it's all over. You're a healthy young girl, you're certainly not dying.'

She was interrupted by a knock on the door and went to open it.

'Oh, so you've finally put in an appearance!' she said cuttingly to Sam who was holding on to the doorpost to keep himself upright. 'And I see you started the celebrations early!'

'Who the hell are you?' he demanded.

Daisy let out a piercing scream.

'Jesus! What's up with her?'

'She's started and you can't come in here!'

'I pay the bloody rent on this kip!' he blustered.

'I don't care if you own the whole bloody street, you can't come in. Go and ask Kate can you wait in her kitchen.'

Sam made to push her aside and caught sight of Daisy writhing with agony on the bed.

'Christ! I've changed my mind. I don't want to go near *her*!'

'Well, that's nice I must say! She didn't get into that state all by herself! I hope Kate chucks you out in the street to wait!' Mrs Hannigan replied coldly.

It was Nell who came downstairs to open the door in response to the distant thunder of the hammering that had aroused the whole house. She'd thrown an old shawl over her nightdress.

'What's the matter?' she demanded of the untidy, bespectacled lad.

'Me mam sent me down 'ere ter tell Mrs Callaghan ter gerrup ter our 'ouse smart, like. Yer sister's 'avin' the baby.'

'Oh, God! I'll go and get her. You stay there.'

The boy pulled a face as she disappeared. Waiting here hadn't been mentioned by his mam but he supposed he'd better do as he was told, or he was bound to get a box around the ears.

Mary dragged her clothes on, helped by Nell.

'I'll come with you, Mam.'

'No, Nell, you stay here, luv. It's no place for a young single girl. She'll be fine, she's probably more frightened than anything else.'

'I told the lad to wait, is there anything I can get to give her?'

'No, luv, but thanks all the same. Don't stay up, babies won't be hurried and you've work in the morning.'

'So have you, Mary.'

'Well, that's of no consequence now. Go back to bed or that flaming dog will have our Teddy up and the whole street barking like that at the commotion.'

Nell went back upstairs, wondering how Daisy was. It was all a mystery to her and would be until she had a child of her own, but she knew poor Daisy must be going through agony. She prayed that when she'd finally had the baby, Sam would alter his ways.

When she reached Silvester Street, Mary was breathless with hurrying and worry, but Kate Flannagan reassured her that Daisy was fine as she ushered her into the room.

'I've got 'im in me kitchen. I'm tryin' ter sober 'im up, like!' she added.

'Oh, God! That's all we need!' Mary exclaimed irritably.

'Well, at least 'e's cum 'ome!'

Mary nodded. Jack had been away when Daisy and Teddy had been born. She prayed that Sam wouldn't reject the baby the way Jack had done with Nell. It would kill Daisy, after all she'd gone through.

It was dawn, still warm and humid, when Mary finally took her grandson in her arms.

Daisy was exhausted, her nightdress and hair clinging to her with sweat, but so very thankful it was all over. She'd never experienced such pain before, and it was hard work, yet it had been worth it. She smiled up at her mother. 'Oh, I never want to go through that again, but he's . . . he's beautiful.'

''E is an' don't they all say the same thing, Mary?' Kate Flannagan said.

'They do, Kate! But we all forget the pain soon enough. Have you a name for him, Daisy?'

'Joseph John Patrick.'

'That's a mouthful.'

'John after Da, Patrick after Mr O'Grady, and Joseph because I like it.'

'I suppose we'd better get the father in 'ere, 'angover or no 'angover,' Kate said laconically.

'I'll get him,' Mary said firmly, handing Daisy back her son.

He looked as if he had a bad hangover, Mary thought after Violet Flannagan had opened the kitchen door. He'd been asleep in an old chair and was pale and dishevelled.

'You've a fine healthy son, if you'd care to go in and see him.'

Sam stood up with a groan. 'Oh, God, my head,' he muttered.

Mary ignored the complaint. 'And try and look delighted about it because if you don't and you upset Daisy, I swear I'll swing for you!' She was having no repeat performance of the day Nell had been born.

He pulled himself up tall and straightened his clothes. 'I *am* delighted. I wanted a son.'

'Don't most fellers get what they want, and I'm not just talkin' about babies!' Kate muttered to Mary as they watched Sam walk unsteadily through the door. Then, with a sigh, they began to tidy up.

Nell was up and dressed when Mary returned home. She hadn't had much sleep worrying about her sister and thinking about Alfred.

'Is it all over? Is she all right? Is the baby all right?'

'It's yes to all those questions, Nell. You've got a nephew.'

'Oh, Mam!' she cried with delight.

'Joseph John Patrick O'Grady. He'll get Joe for short.'

'Who is he like?'

'His da, I'd say, but they change.'

'I'll boil the kettle, Mam. A cup of tea and then you get some rest. It's too late to go out with the barrow now.'

Mary sank down on the sofa. 'Thanks, luv, and I think I

will have a day off, but not to laze about. This place could do with a good turning out and I've been meaning to change poor Annie's bed and get the blankets washed. They'll dry quickly in this weather.'

'Ah, Mam, can't you leave all that?'

'No. I'd never forgive myself if I wasted a whole day!'

'Can I go and see them after work?'

Mary smiled. 'I'm sure she'll be dying for you to call. Now get off with you. I'll sit here for a bit before I start.'

The day couldn't go quickly enough for Nell, but at last she walked down Silvester Street with a spring in her step.

She knocked on the door then opened it. Daisy looked very tired, she thought.

'Oh, Daisy, let me see him! I've been dying to come all day.'

Daisy proudly handed him over.

'Isn't he beautiful! Is Sam pleased?'

'Yes, he is. Needless to say he's down the pub with the rest of *that* lot. God knows what time or what state he'll come home in, but I don't care!'

Nell stroked the soft little cheek. 'I do envy you!'

Daisy was surprised. 'Do you really? I mean . . . this room . . . those awful O'Gradys . . .'

'You'll get out of here soon and you don't have to have his family in on top of you all the time. Oh, look at his tiny little fingers! He's perfect!'

Daisy smiled. 'I want you to be his godmother.'

Nell's eyes were shining. 'I'd love to be. Will it be soon?'

'When Da comes home. It's only a week away.'

'He'll be so proud of you, Daisy. And of little Joseph too.'

'Perhaps he'll have forgiven me for the . . . disgrace.'

'He's done that already, Mam said so. I'm sure things will look up now, Daisy, I'm positive.'

On her way home Nell was lost in thought. She had never imagined she would feel so deeply about a baby. It amazed her. Her thoughts turned to Alfred McManus. There was no one else in the neighbourhood that she was remotely interested in, she was twenty-one, and he could offer her so much. But what would it be like being married to him? She couldn't bear the thought of never being able to have a baby of her own. And if she were to have a child she certainly didn't want to try to bring it up in circumstances like her sister's. She wanted a decent house, not a slum, enough money and above all security. He was the only one who could offer all that.

'So, how is she?' Mary asked as Nell arrived home.

'She's great and so is Joseph. Oh, Mam, he's gorgeous. She wants me to be his godmother.'

'I should hope she does, you're her sister.'

'She's waiting until Da comes home for the christening. The O'Gradys are all down the pub.'

'I suppose Sam's got a right to celebrate.' Mary sighed. Before Nell could reply Teddy burst into the kitchen followed by a now much fatter and larger Scruffy, who was his constant companion and whom he was trying to train, without much success. His mother had threatened that if she found one more little puddle, he was out on his ear.

'Mam! Mam! Tommy Ford said I'm an uncle! How can I be an uncle when I'm only a kid?'

Mary smiled and Nell laughed.

'Of course you're an uncle, it doesn't matter about your age. You could be a baby yourself. Daisy's your sister. "Uncle Teddy".'

'I don't want to be an uncle!'

'You've got no choice. Now get yourself and that animal out of the kitchen that I've just scrubbed. I'll call you in when your tea's ready.

'Will you make up Annie's bed, Nell? I took the blankets down to the washhouse then put them over the line. They should be dry by now. Then could you go and get her from Florrie's?'

Nell did as she was asked. After she'd made up the bed she went for the old woman.

'Are you tired?' she asked as Annie gripped her arm and walked slowly up the street.

'Not too bad, Nell. Florrie's good but it's so crowded in there with all those kids.'

'I know. Your bed's all ready and it's nice and fresh and Mam will have the tea on soon. I went to see Daisy and the baby.'

'Did you? And . . . ?'

'He's beautiful.'

'Oh, they are, luv, when they're that age.'

'Did you never want any, Annie?'

'No, luv. You know I've no one in the world. But babies can give great happiness.'

Nell nodded her head in agreement, thinking that poor Annie's voice held a note of regret.

After the meal was over she touched her mother's arm. 'Mam, can I talk to you?' she said quietly.

'What about, luv?'

'About Alfred.'

Mary looked a little apprehensive. 'Come into the scullery then.'

Nell leaned against the sink in the tiny, dark room. 'I've been thinking, Mam, and . . . and I'll go out with him, but nothing serious . . . yet.'

'Does this have anything to do with Daisy and Joseph?'

Nell nodded. 'It made me realise that if I never had any children of my own I'd be devastated.'

'You could do a lot worse than Alfred, Nell.'

'I know, Mam. I've only got to look at that room that Daisy's living in. I don't want to end up like that.'

'Well, if you're sure, I'll tell him when he comes on Sunday. It would be a weight off my mind to see you settled.'

Chapter Seven

———◆———

ALFRED WAS DELIGHTED WHEN Mary informed him of Nell's decision.

'I wasn't at all confident, Mary. I'm so much older than her.'

'She knows that. It doesn't matter.'

'I'd like to take her somewhere special; I've been giving it a lot of thought. A young girl must like to dance but I'm afraid I'm hopeless. I thought about taking her to the Hippodrome – you don't get the riffraff in there. And maybe something to eat afterwards?'

'Oh, I think she'd love that. What time will I tell her and what day?'

'Saturday. I'll call for her at seven o'clock, if that's convenient.'

He was so polite and considerate. Nell did like to dance but Mary was certain that what Alfred had planned would please her just as much, if not more. If this was the way he was going to treat Nell, then she had no qualms at all. She'd sworn that Nell would have a better life than she had had and now it looked as though she would have. Nell would never end up like poor Daisy.

'Mam, what will I wear?' Nell asked after Mary had imparted the good news. 'People like us don't go out for meals in restaurants, I've nothing suitable at all.'

'Can you get off work an hour early one day and go into town? I heard that Blacklers have some nice rayon dresses at very reasonable prices and it's so warm that you won't need a coat or jacket.' Mary wanted Nell to look her best and not show any of them up.

'I'll try.'

'I want you to get a hat. Respectable women always wear a hat and gloves.'

'Oh, Mam, I think gloves are taking it a bit too far!' Nell laughed, but was pleased none the less at the idea of the hat.

After she'd helped Mary to tidy up she went around to see Daisy.

'Can I hold him, please?' she begged. Joe was so precious.

Daisy smiled and handed the baby over, glad of a respite. She was supposed to stay in bed for another week but how could she? She thought. There was no one to see to household chores and she got no help from Sam or his family. Her mam came when she could and Mrs O'Grady had been a couple of times, but her mother-in-law had only wanted to chat, not do anything constructive.

'While I'm here, is there anything you want me to do, Daisy?' Nell offered, having taken in the state of the room. It was untidy and not very clean. Clothes, baby things, newspapers were strewn around the place. The dishes were dirty, there were soiled nappies in a bucket of cold water and Daisy looked tired, untidy and somehow older-looking. She had put on weight and still wore the cotton smock she'd worn while carrying Joseph. It was grubby and creased.

Daisy had noted the expression on her sister's face. 'I can't do everything, I get no help!'

'Here, take him. I'll do the dishes, rinse out the nappies and do a quick tidy up. Have you eaten?'

'I had a bit of tripe and onion earlier on. It's no use trying to cook a meal for him, he eats at his mam's,' Daisy said bitterly, taking her son in her arms. She watched Nell as she darted around the room gathering up clothes, nappies and newspapers and dumping them on the table to sort out. Oh, how she wished she'd never met Sam O'Grady!

'I've got a bit of news for you,' Nell said, thinking it would take Daisy's mind off things.

'What?' Daisy asked without much interest.

'I'm going to the Hippodrome on Saturday and then for a meal out. Imagine – a meal out!'

She'd captured Daisy's attention. 'Who with? Who can afford things like that?'

'Alfred McManus. Oh, I know he's years older than me, Daisy, but—'

'God, Nell, he's an old man! He's nearly as old as Da!'

'He's not *that* old!'

'Why are you going out with *him*? What's wrong with the fellers around here?'

'Nothing, except that . . . well . . . I don't fancy any of them.'

'You can't be serious, Nell. Do you fancy him?'

'Oh, I don't know, Daisy, and that's the truth. He can give me a good life and well . . . you've got Joseph and I'm not getting any younger . . .'

'Oh, for God's sake, Nell, you're only twenty-one! I'm twenty-three and bloody look at me! I look thirty-three!'

Nell began to fold some clean nappies. 'That's part of it, Daisy . . . I . . . I don't want to be . . . like you.' Nell immediately regretted her tactlessness.

'Oh, I see! You'll marry him for what you can get. A good steady job, a nice house, never having to go out to work again. There's a name for girls like you. You're a gold-digger!' Daisy cried vindictively.

It wasn't fair! It wasn't bloody fair! Oh, Nell would get what she wanted, she always did. Mam's little favourite!

'Daisy! That's not true and it's . . . cruel!' Nell was shocked at her sister's bitter outburst.

'It *is* fair!' Daisy said vehemently. 'Oh, go back home to Mam!'

'Daisy, I didn't come here to upset you, really I didn't.'

'You came to gloat! Poor Daisy. Stupid Daisy. Go home, Nell!'

Hurt and bewildered, Nell walked back to Portland Street. Even the comic sight of Teddy taking a very reluctant Scruffy for a walk on a piece of old rope failed to amuse her.

'What's the matter?' Mary asked as she walked in, looking up from her darning.

Nell sat down and told her.

'What terrible things to say! But, poor Daisy, she hasn't much of a life and never will have, now. I'll go round to see her later on and have a word with her. I don't like you falling out. You're not a gold-digger, and I won't stand for talk like that.'

'Oh, Mam, you'll only make things worse.'

'I won't! I'm not having you two at each other's throats.'

Nell sighed heavily. It was no use arguing, but she still felt shocked at how much Daisy envied her.

After Nell had gone Daisy broke down and wept. Nell would have everything she didn't have or could ever hope of having. She looked around her, wrinkling her nose. The room stank. The window was warped and wouldn't open to let some air in. The place needed a good clean but she had neither the time nor energy nor inclination. She knew she looked a mess but why bother? No one noticed. No one cared.

Joseph was crying and she pulled herself together. He probably needed changing. More bloody washing! He demanded attention morning, noon and night and she was so tired. She was always tired.

She was trying to get him back to sleep when Sam opened the door.

'Oh, so you've finally decided to come home!' she snapped. She could tell he'd been drinking.

'Oh, for Christ's sake, don't bloody start the minute I set foot in the door!'

'I've got good reason to "start" as you call it! I'm stuck here in this bloody . . . midden while you and that tribe are off down the pub!'

'I always go to me mam's for Sunday dinner, and I like a drink after it!' he said sullenly.

Daisy turned on him. 'Oh, isn't that nice! A happy family get-together! And what about me?'

His expression changed. 'What about you, Daisy? Look at the cut of you! What feller would want to be seen out with you? You're a bloody mess. You stink, your hair is like rats' tails, you're fat and blowsy, why the hell should I care anything about you? You trapped me into marrying you because you knew I wouldn't willingly spend my life with the likes of you! A feller wants a girl who's good-looking and good for a bit of a laugh, not a screeching, fat, dirty tart!'

Daisy screamed and caught the nearest thing to hand, a half-cold mug of tea, and hurled it at him. 'Get out! Get out of here! I hate you! I hate you! I hope you get bloody run over by a tram!'

The door slammed, making the dirty dishes on the table clatter and the baby cry fretfully. Daisy sank down on a chair. She *did* hate him! She hadn't known how much until now. Oh, God, he must hate her too, she thought miserably. She was fat, smelly, blowsy and utterly charmless. She had nothing to look forward to while Nell had everything. In that moment, torn apart by jealousy and despair, she began to hate her sister.

Nell didn't go around to see Daisy, Mary had forbidden it. She had been shocked when she'd gone to see her elder daughter. Somehow Daisy seemed to have changed. She was bitter, sullen, resentful.

'Daisy, it was dreadful of you to upset Nell and I *don't* favour her!'

'Yes, you do, Mam, you always have. Anyway, if you've

come round to nag me, then I don't want to listen to you. It's bad enough me having to put up with *him*.'

Mary could see all the aching misery and despair in Daisy and her heart went out to her.

'I didn't, but I will nag you about pulling yourself together. You *do* look a mess, and this place *is* a tip.'

'What do you expect, Mam?' Daisy demanded.

'Daisy, your da and I lived in a tiny place when we were first married and I had you and Nell but I never gave up. I kept my self-respect. I worked hard, you know that. It wasn't until after Teddy was born that we got the whole house to ourselves. Your da will be home soon and he'll be horrified at all this. I'll come down every afternoon when I've finished and help you clean up. Get yourself sorted out and here, get something decent to wear for the christening.' Mary handed over three pound notes.

'Don't have the O'Gradys looking down on us. Don't sink to their level, Daisy. Now, is there anything in this place to eat?'

As she took the money Daisy still felt upset and resentful, but the offer of help with the housework and a new outfit cheered her up a little. At least there was a glimmer of hope on her bleak horizon.

When Jack arrived home Mary informed him that he had a fine grandson, but that there was great animosity between their daughters. He'd shaken his head, called Daisy a fool and Nell a bit of a heartless madam, Teddy a tearaway, the dog flea-bitten and had then gone down to the Golden Fleece to cheer himself up.

Mary sighed and picked up his seabag full of dirty washing. He never changed. He never allowed anything to upset him and always left her to do the worrying. At least, he had given her some money towards the christening, something she hadn't expected him to do. She'd put her foot down about a do afterwards, though. It was strictly family and surely to God there were enough of the O'Gradys without providing food and drink for the neighbours as well.

Jack had promised to be back from the pub to see Alfred when he arrived to take Nell out that evening. He hadn't arrived, however, when Nell came downstairs in her new outfit. Mary smiled affectionately at her.

'How do I look, Mam?'

'You look great, luv. Give us a twirl.'

Nell did so. She'd taken more care with her appearance than usual. She'd suffered a night of agony due to a head full of pipe cleaners to make her dark hair curl. The pale blue rayon dress with its white Peter Pan collar and short puff sleeves looked smart and crisp. It was set off with a narrow white belt, pintucking on the bodice and a row of small white buttons down the front. Her hat was small: she didn't think the wide-brimmed straws suited her and they looked very middle class. She had even managed to buy a pair of white gloves – cheap ones, at the market – and wished she had white shoes with peep toes, but her good tan court shoes would have to do.

'I'm nervous, Mam.'

'Well, don't be. You look very respectable and he'll be delighted with you. Why wouldn't he? It's not every day a man of his age walks out with a lovely young girl like you.'

'Oh, Mam, stop it!' Nell laughed.

To her surprise Mary suddenly jumped up and hammered on the kitchen window.

'Teddy Callaghan, get down off that wall! Get down this minute and come in here! God Almighty, that lad will be the death of me!'

'Mam, he's not bad, he's just mischievous.'

'I'll mischief him, he has me heartbroken.'

A hot, dishevelled Teddy, followed by an equally hot and scruffy dog, came into the kitchen.

'Mam, I wasn't doing nothing!'

'How often have I told you about jumping the jigger walls? You'll fall one day and break something and then what'll we do?'

'Me da said he played jumping the jigger walls when he was my age.' Teddy was outraged that he was being punished for just doing what Da had done when he'd been a kid. Of course that was hundreds of years ago, but things like that didn't change.

'Give that animal a drink of water and then go down to the bottom of the road and see if there's any sign of your da.'

Thinking he had got off lightly, Teddy did as he was told. Mam would be so preoccupied with Da and Nell and that Alfred feller that no one would notice him on the walls. His mother's lecture hadn't bothered him at all and he certainly wasn't going to abide by her rules.

Alfred and Jack arrived together.

'I met him coming up the street. God Almighty, that Fred Higgins from number twenty can't half talk. I wouldn't mind, but it's all bloody rubbish. I told him straight. There'll be another bloody war before long if someone doesn't do something about that bloody Hitler feller and I remember the last one!'

'Oh, Jack, don't be going on like that,' Mary chided.

'Well, it's true, Mary. You can't shut your eyes to it, or bury your head in the sand like a bloody ostrich, isn't that right, Alfred?'

Alfred nodded slowly. He too remembered the last war, although he did his best to shut it out of his mind. The nightmare conditions of the trenches in France and Belgium still disturbed his sleep.

'Oh, Da, can't we forget all about it?' Nell said impatiently.

'You look very . . . nice, Nell,' Alfred said hesitantly. She did. She looked very smart. Smart enough for the Stork Hotel in Williamson Square where he had reserved a table. He was doing things in style. He knew he had much to offer her, but he was very conscious that she was still so young. Thank goodness she wasn't in the least like her fast and foolish sister. 'Are you ready?'

'Yes, Alfred, thank you.' She suddenly felt very shy. She tried to pull herself together as he held open the door for her.

They got a tram to West Derby Road and when they reached the theatre he bought her a quarter of Everton mints, a quarter of lemon drops and a programme.

'Oh, you shouldn't be spending so much money on me, Alfred!' she said as she settled herself in the red plush of the best seats in the house. 'These must have cost a fortune.'

'I'm not a mean man, Nell. I'm careful, as your mam knows, you've got to have a bit put by for a rainy day.'

'Oh, I wasn't criticising you!'

'I know that, so let's sit back and enjoy the show.'

She smiled at him and he smiled back and she thought how much younger he looked when he did so. He must have been quite handsome when he was a young man.

She relaxed and watched the show, which they both enjoyed, but when they emerged into the warm dusk she felt a little apprehensive about the table booked in the hotel. She'd never been anywhere as posh as the Stork. On the tram journey to Williamson Square she hardly uttered a word.

She was even more overawed when he ushered her into the hotel foyer. Everything was painted in shades of pale green and cream. There were gold-framed pictures on the walls, easy chairs of tan leather, small ornate tables and the carpet was dark green with a pattern of sprays of cream roses all over it.

'It's . . . it's very . . . nice . . .' she stammered, feeling even more nervous.

'It is. I wanted to take you somewhere really classy. Follow me, I'll ask that feller where the restaurant is.'

She followed him, not daring to look around, and they were led into a dining room every bit as stylish as the bar lounge. The waiter held her chair out and she sat down gingerly. It looked very fragile.

She took off her gloves and thanked the waiter who had passed her a menu. Oh, God! she thought. What should she choose? She didn't feel very hungry and wished she hadn't eaten the sweets.

She looked over the top of the menu at Alfred.

He smiled at her. 'I think we'll both have the soup and

then the plaice,' he said confidently, as though he had been in and out of here all his life.

Nell was thankful and smiled at him. She would have to get used to things like this if she was to seriously consider marrying him.

It had been a very pleasant, if a little nerve-wracking evening, she thought as they walked back home from the tram stop.

'It's been such a treat, Alfred, thank you,' she said shyly as they reached the door.

'I'm really glad you enjoyed it, Nell, I'd hoped you would. Well, would you consider . . . er . . . letting me take you out again?'

She picked at an imaginary thread on the cuff of her glove. 'I . . . well . . . yes, please, and we'll see you tomorrow for the christening?'

'You will indeed. I hope . . . I mean . . . your mother has made me seem, er . . . part of the family.'

'She has and I would like to go out again, maybe next week?'

'Next Saturday? We could go somewhere different if you want to?'

'Oh, the Hippodrome was just great, but you don't need to take me for a supper. Fish and chips from the chippy will do.'

He was glad that she'd accepted and that she didn't always want to be taken for expensive suppers, but he couldn't see himself eating fish and chips from a newspaper in the street.

'Well, then, that's settled. I'll see you tomorrow, Nell. Goodnight.'

'Goodnight, Alfred, and thank you again.'

Mary was waiting for her, still darning socks, when she got in. The dog was lying at her feet asleep.

'So, luv, how did it go?' Mary asked.

'Great, Mam. Where's Da?'

'No prizes for guessing that one! Down the pub with the lads! I've told him that hangover or no hangover he's coming to Mass with me in the morning. His Reverence will be scandalised if the baby's grandfather can't even get himself to Mass and he's not showing us up in front of that lot! Now, tell me everything.'

Nell took off her hat and gloves and put the kettle on the range. She could have a good chat with Mam before Da came back and disrupted their peace.

Daisy had taken her mother's words to heart and had smartened herself up. Leaving Joseph with Kate Flannagan, she'd gone into town and bought herself a new dress and hat in C & A in Church Street. It was what Mam would call 'cheap and cheerful' and no doubt Nell would have something more expensive and stylish, but at least it was new and she felt a bit better by the time they all arrived. She hadn't spoken a word to Sam since he'd slammed out. She didn't care where he'd been or who with, she just hated him with a burning ferocity.

'You look well, Daisy,' Mary commented as Daisy held her son out for his grandfather's inspection.

'He's a fine big lad, Daisy! Just don't let him grow up like this hooligan here,' Jack said, smiling with pride.

Teddy was stung. 'I'm not a hooligan, Da!'

'That's a matter of opinion!' his father retorted. He'd just had to give the lad a talking to about his general behaviour, something Mary had insisted upon but which Jack really felt was unnecessary. Boys would be boys.

Teddy looked mutinous. He hated having to wear a starched Eton collar and the suit Mam had bought him for best. It had knickerbockers and a belted jacket and he felt a real sissy in it. His mates all skitted him – out of earshot of their mams of course. Still, at the prospect of jelly with hundreds and thousands on it and custard as well as cup cakes and butterfly cakes and lemonade he cheered up.

'Are that lot going straight to church?' Mary asked, glancing around. She was glad to see Daisy had tidied up.

'Yes, and so is he.'

'What's up with him?' Jack asked.

'Oh, he's just being awkward,' Daisy replied, glancing at her mother.

'You know what he's like, Jack.'

'I wish I didn't,' Jack replied drily.

It wasn't until the ceremony was over and they had all returned to Portland Street that Daisy had time to look at her sister. Nell looked different, more grown up and much, much smarter than herself. She noticed how solicitous Alfred McManus was towards her. Treating her like a bloody queen. Oh, yes, she was certain Nell would marry him and in her heart of hearts she knew that in the same position herself, she'd jump at the chance of all he could offer. She dragged her gaze away as her mother-in-law, in a very garishly coloured dress and equally awful hat, borrowed from two of her better-off neighbours, approached with a glass of sherry.

'There ye are, Daisy. Now be getting that down ye, a drop

of the good stuff will do ye good. Ye should get out more. Make our flamin' Sam take ye out!'

'Thanks, but I don't want to go anywhere with him!' she replied cuttingly.

Nell had gone into the lobby to see Alfred out.

'I hope it wasn't all a bit too noisy for you.'

'No, although I must admit that Daisy's in-laws are very . . . boisterous.'

'They're flaming rowdy and will get worse as time goes on. They won't go home until the drink runs out. It was nice of you to describe them as merely "boisterous"!'

'So, will I call for you at the same time as yesterday?'

'Yes, that would be great.'

'Then goodbye until Saturday, Nell.' He bent and kissed her lightly on the cheek, then, feeling embarrassed, drew away and hastily left the house.

Nell felt a little embarrassed too, then she shook herself. She'd better get used to the embraces and kisses.

As he walked up the street to the tram stop Alfred was deep in thought. He was sure she liked him, she wouldn't have said she'd see him again if she didn't, but he mustn't rush her. When he asked her to marry him, and give him the thing he most wanted – a son – she had to be sure. He told himself to be patient. Only time would tell.

Chapter Eight

AS THE SUMMER DIED and autumn passed in misty mornings and evenings, interspersed with howling gales which heralded the approach of winter, Nell got used to Alfred McManus's ways. Each Saturday night they went out, usually to the music hall or the cinema, and on Sundays he came for his lunch and, if the weather was fitting, they went for a walk or a tram ride or a sail on the ferry. Occasionally they had a supper out but he always bought fish and chips on Saturday nights, enough for all of them. Mary would send Teddy up to Kellys' with a big bowl and Alfred insisted they eat them at the table. Nell was almost certain now that when he asked, she'd agree to marry him. She'd thought about it all often. Especially after he'd taken her to see the house in Priory Road.

'Mam, it's so big! Well, it seems like it compared to this house.'

'Of course, it's not in a slum, is it? That's a decent,

respectable neighbourhood. What was it like?' Mary had been full of curiosity.

'It's very clean and tidy. The rooms are a bit . . . well, dark. The paintwork is all brown. In fact, everything is brown.'

'That's soon remedied.'

'There's wallpaper in every room, except the kitchen. Mam, it's got a proper kitchen with a gas ring for the kettle and a gas stove. No more having to swelter in summer because we have to keep the range on. It's got shelves all lined with oilcloth and red quarry tiles on the floor. All the other rooms have lino and it's all shiny, you can actually see the pattern,' she'd enthused. Mary had looked down at the well-scrubbed but faded lino that covered her kitchen floor. 'There's a pantry, with shelves and a marble slab. Oh, Mam, you should see the parlour! There's a rug in front of the fire, a really good gateleg table and chairs, a sideboard and a glass cabinet! Imagine, Mam! A glass cabinet and it's full of stuff! It must be worth a fortune.'

'It probably is. It must all have belonged to his mam or even his granny.'

'There's three bedrooms, all with good furniture and quilts. The privy is still in the yard, but there's one for each house.'

'Is there any kind of a bathroom?'

'A small one. But all tiled and the bath is huge!'

'Holy God, if I had all that I'd think I'd died and gone to heaven! Imagine a bathroom! Running water, hot water! What wouldn't I and all the women in this neighbourhood give for things like that! Oh, life would be so much easier,' Mary had sighed.

Nell had nodded her agreement. That house was a dream come true. She'd never seen anything like it.

Soon it would be Christmas, she thought as she walked down the street, her head bent against the biting wind. It was a 'lazy wind', Mam said. It went straight through you, instead of going around you. She smiled to herself. She was almost certain that Alfred was going to propose before Christmas and that her Christmas present would be an engagement ring.

She arrived home to find Mary setting the table and her da reading the *Echo*, his face serious. Teddy was sprawled on the rag rug in front of the range feeding Scruffy with the bits of gristle and bone that he'd managed to beg from the butcher. He'd been trying hard not to get into trouble, hoping that this year Santa would bring him the box of lead soldiers he coveted, but he was aware of a recent lapse from the good behaviour, provoked by being called a 'cissy' by his mates. His mam would be likely to hear of it eventually.

'Oh, it's cold enough for two pairs of bootlaces out there!' Nell remarked, laughing, as she unwound the handknitted scarf from around her neck.

'Don't I know it, luv. I was perished standing there all day. By the time it came to finishing up I could hardly feel my hands.'

'Mam, you should wear those gloves with half the fingers cut out. It would help. Here, give me those, I'll finish laying the table.'

'Well, there's a good pan of scouse, that'll warm us all up. Jack, what's up with you? You look dead serious.'

'I am, Mary. Things are getting out of control over in Germany. That feller is too bloody big for his boots and I don't trust him even if Chamberlain does!'

Mary looked worried. 'Oh, please God it won't come to a war.'

'Well, if he carries on like this, that's how it's bound to end up.'

Mary crossed herself before returning to the big black iron pot that held the stew, while Nell cut thick slices from the loaf. Scouse wasn't the same without bread to dip in.

'Our Daisy was round earlier on,' Jack said casually.

'You never told me. What did she want? Is the baby all right? Is she all right?' Mary demanded.

'She looked frozen, but Joe was happy enough. I think she came looking for money.'

'Did you give her any? That feller keeps her short.'

'I gave her a few shillings, I couldn't spare any more. Billy Mac down the pub is making remarks about how much is on the slate. I'll have to pay up or I'll never hear the end of it. I don't come home on leave to listen to him whingeing and moaning about the price of a few bevvies.'

Mary raised her eyes to the ceiling. He didn't change. Always thinking of himself.

'Teddy, will you shift yourself from under everyone's feet?' Nell instructed her brother.

'And take that dog and those bones out in the scullery while we have our tea. You know I can't stand him begging from the table,' Mary added, thinking she'd go and see Daisy later on. The poor girl had hardly anything in her pocket. Sam O'Grady was as bad as Jack with regard to his pay and responsibilities, and she'd heard rumours about him and Frances Walshe from Hepworth Street.

They were all deep in their own thoughts when the sound of the doorknocker made them look up. 'Who can that be? Don't let them in and go ruining our meal,' Jack said, irritably.

Mary returned with a soberly clad, solemn-faced Mr Broadhurst.

'God Almighty! What the hell have you come for?' Jack cried upon seeing the local undertaker.

'I'm sorry to disturb your meal, but it's a serious matter concerning your son.'

'What the hell have you been up to, you little horror?' Mary demanded.

'I was with a very recently bereaved family, Mr and Mrs Dodd, when we were interrupted.' He paused, as was his way.

'Right, meladdo, what have you done?' Jack demanded.

Teddy looked from his father to the undertaker.

'It was only a bit of fun, Da! Just a bit of a joke, like! It was all Tommy Ford's fault, he said . . . he dared me . . .'

Jack got up and caught the lad by the back of his jumper. 'Never mind Tommy Ford, what did you do?'

Teddy dissolved in tears.

'A group of boys, including that one there, burst into the parlour and shouted, "Have yer any empty boxes?" and roared with laughter. My clients were very upset.'

Jack cuffed his son around the ear, but was fighting down his amusement.

'Well, that's the end of your Christmas presents, meladdo!

You apologise this minute! You're a disgrace to us all!' Mary fumed.

A very sheepish, white-faced Teddy apologised profusely, in tears at the thought of waking up on Christmas Day to no presents at all.

Mary saw the undertaker out, banishing Teddy to his bedroom.

'I tell you, Jack, that lad will end up in Walton Jail!' she fulminated when she returned to the kitchen, glancing anxiously at a shocked-looking Annie in the corner.

'Oh, for God's sake, Mary, where's your sense of humour?' Jack could hardly keep his face straight and Nell was grinning.

'You've got to see the funny side of it, Mam! "Any empty boxes"!' Nell laughed.

Mary smiled. 'Oh, I know, but he has to learn how to behave. And it's not right to upset the bereaved,' she added soberly.

'Where are you going tomorrow night, Nell?' she asked later as they were clearing the table and Jack was engrossed in his newspaper.

'I don't know, Mam. Usually Alfred is full of plans. You know how methodical and punctual he is. But when I asked he just said, "Wait and see." It's something special.'

'Do you think he's finally going to pop the question?'

'I don't really know for certain, Mam, but I think he might.'

'You know how happy it would make me, Nell. When I see what our poor Daisy has to put up with I worry myself sick.'

'I know, Mam,' Nell answered quietly. She had tried so

hard to heal the rift but Daisy had grown more and more cold and bitter towards her. Still, it was worth putting up with all that just to see Joseph who was such a placid, happy baby.

'Well, it's about time he made his mind up. The pair of you aren't getting any younger,' Jack remarked from behind his newspaper.

'Oh, Jack! She's only a slip of a girl!' Mary protested.

Nell laughed. 'He thinks I'll be an old maid. A "spinster of this parish", don't you, Da?'

'Ah, give over with the jokes. I'm off down the pub.'

'When is he ever anything else, unless it's down a back jigger playing pitch and toss,' Mary whispered to Nell.

When Alfred arrived on Saturday evening Nell knew that tonight was the night. She could tell by his face and she smiled at him.

'Well, where is it you're off to?' Mary asked.

'I thought a nice, quiet drink in the Stork,' he replied meaningfully.

Mary hid a smile. 'You're very fond of that place, aren't you?'

'It's very nice, Mam. Select,' Nell added, securing her hat with a long and dangerous-looking hatpin against the force-nine gale that was blowing outside.

'Well, I'll see you later,' Mary said, smiling as Alfred ushered Nell out.

Nell kept up a flow of harmless chatter until they were seated in a corner of the lounge bar of the hotel, then, picking up her drink, she looked enquiringly across at him. 'This feels special somehow,' she said.

'I hope it will be, Nell.' He looked flushed as he drew a small leather-covered box from his pocket. 'I went into town and bought you this. I hope . . . I sincerely hope, Nell, that you'll like it and that you'll consent to be Mrs Alfred McManus. I know I'm a great deal older than you and . . . mm . . . er . . .'

She leaned across the table and placed a hand on his arm. She couldn't let him struggle on. 'Alfred, I'll be delighted to marry you. I'm very . . . fond of you. You're a good, kind, generous, thoughtful man. The lads around our neighbour-hood are hopeless. There's not a one I'd take seriously. They all act like kids, even Da acts like a kid at times. I've always felt that I was more . . . mature than most girls of my age, so I'd very much like to marry you.'

He was so relieved. He'd been practising his speech and the answers to all the arguments she might use but she had put him out of his misery immediately. She was indeed someone he'd be proud to have as his wife and the mother of his children.

'Thank you, Nell. You won't be sorry. I hope you like this.'

She smiled and opened the box. It was from a very good jewellers, T. Brown at the bottom of Lord Street. Inside was a beautiful ring, a red garnet surrounded by diamonds. She didn't know anyone who even had an engagement ring.

'Put it on, Alfred,' she instructed a little shyly.

He slipped it on her finger and she held out her hand to admire it.

'When . . . er . . . when do you think . . . ?' he pressed.

'Let's say early in the New Year.'

'Why not New Year's Day?'

'Oh, I think Mam would like a bit of time to save up.'

'She doesn't need to save up, Nell. I'll contribute as much as I can.'

'Let's leave it until the end of January, just the same.'

'Very well.' He raised his glass. 'Here's a toast to the future Mr and Mrs McManus.'

Nell's smile was one of genuine affection. She couldn't honestly say she was madly in love with him, but she *was* fond of him and it would make Mam so happy and relieved.

When they got back Jack had just come in and Mary had relented and allowed Teddy down for his supper.

'Mam, Da, Alfred and I . . . we're engaged.' She held out her hand and Mary gasped. No one she knew had ever had an engagement ring; they were lucky if they got a wedding ring and usually, that yo-yoed between the owner's finger and the pawnbroker's.

'Oh, Nell, luv, I'm so happy for you both!' she cried, hugging Nell tightly. This is what she'd prayed for.

'Congratulations, Alfred!' Jack pumped his flushed future son-in-law by the hand.

'Are you going to marry him, honestly?' Teddy demanded. Alfred McManus was such an old man and Teddy thought he was far too serious.

'I am, Teddy, and you be careful or I might have you as a pageboy,' Nell laughed.

'Ah, you wouldn't do that, Nell, would you?' The lad was horrified.

'Of course I won't!'

Teddy was very relieved.

'Have you decided on a date yet?'

'Mary, for God's sake, the man's only just got engaged! Time enough in the future to be thinking like that,' Jack cried.

'Well, actually, we were thinking about the end of January,' Nell informed them.

'I wanted to make it New Year's Day, but Nell dissuaded me.'

'What's the matter with New Year's Day?' Jack demanded.

'Nothing, Da. I just wanted a bit more time to get things organised.'

'What's to organise? Our Daisy was married in a right rush.'

'Jack, it's up to them,' Mary said firmly.

'Aye, all right then. Fancy last orders down the Fleece?' Jack asked. Well, now there was something to celebrate!

Alfred looked from Jack to Nell, not really wanting to go but not wanting to offend anyone either. He wasn't comfortable in the company of Jack or his mates.

'Oh, go on! I don't mind. It is a celebration. Mam and I have got plenty to talk about.'

Jack needed no further encouragement. 'Right, I'll just get my cap and muffler.'

'And you, meladdo, you can take yourself off to bed, but leave that dog down here!' Mary instructed her son.

Teddy was even more relieved to get out, thinking they might well change their minds on the pageboy idea. He'd sooner die than wear one of those terrible soppy-looking outfits.

'Is it *really* what you want, luv?' Mary asked, putting the kettle on.

Nell was admiring her ring. 'It is, Mam. He's a good man and I'm very fond of him.'

A shadow crossed Mary's face. Was affection going to be enough? Still, it quite often mellowed into love and her mam had often quoted the saying: 'When poverty comes in the door, love flies out of the window.' There was plenty of evidence of the truth of that all around her. No, Nell would have a good life.

'So, will you have the works? White frock, flowers, music?'

'Nothing too grand, Mam. Alfred said you don't have to worry about saving up, he'll contribute and I know he will.'

'That's very good of him, but I'd like to pay for something.'

'I know, Mam, and so does Alfred. We can talk about that later. I'd like a Nuptial Mass, with flowers and candles and music. I don't want a very expensive wedding dress, it's a bit of a waste of money.'

'Nell, you only get married once, God willing.'

'I know, but I'll wait and see. Will you come with me to choose it?'

'Try and keep me away!'

'What about Daisy? I want her to be my matron of honour, but . . .'

Mary looked a little grim. 'Leave Daisy to me, luv.' It wouldn't be easy to persuade Daisy, she thought regretfully. It would only add to Daisy's resentment and jealousy, but she'd have a damned good try.

'You'll be moving straight in with him then?'

'I can't see us having a honeymoon, so I will. There's not much to take really. Just my clothes and a few bits and pieces. Who will we invite?'

'I think we'd better start and make a list.'

'I don't want anything too big.'

'I know, but you know what they're like around here, they'll all expect to be asked to the do and don't forget we'll probably be lumbered with our Daisy's in-laws.'

'Oh, God, Mam! Not all of them! Alfred will be mortified!'

'And so will I. Let's make it very clear that the invitation only applies to Sam's mam and da. We don't want to be providing drink to that tribe.'

'Will we all fit in here, Mam?'

'We have done in the past and Alfred's got no family, has he?'

'He has a cousin or someone who lives in Wales, but he hasn't seen him for years so he might not come.'

'I might take Teddy to the forty-shilling tailor, see if I can get him something decent, but cheap.'

'Can't Da bring him something?'

'I wouldn't trust him. He'd come home with something totally unsuitable.'

'What will you wear, Mam?'

'I don't know.'

'You always said that if you came into money you'd buy a fur coat.'

'Oh, that was just me being daft! We can't afford fur coats, not even second-hand ones!'

'Well, what about something with a fur collar and cuffs? It's a winter wedding so it wouldn't look out of place. Mam, I'll buy it. You've always worked so hard and you've never had anything really nice or a bit of luxury.'

'Oh, give over, Nell! What would I look like?'

'Very smart, Mam! You deserve it!'

'I never even had a coat until a while back. I always used to wear a shawl, still do on the barrow.'

'I know and that's why I want to treat you. Da never has, he's too selfish, so please, please let me buy it for you? I've money saved up and I'll get the rest from Alfred. Please, Mam?'

Mary felt a rush of tenderness and gratitude. Nell was the best daughter anyone could wish for.

'All right, Nell, thanks! Oh, would you just think. Me, Mary Callaghan, with a coat trimmed with real fur!'

'And a hat. Don't forget about a hat, Mam!' Nell laughed, getting up to make the tea.

They'd just started to make a list of names, when: 'What's up with your da? He knows the door's open, what on earth is he knocking for?' Mary cried, annoyed at being interrupted.

Nell was on her feet. 'Maybe Alfred's having a bit of trouble with him. He's probably been "celebrating" a bit too much. I'll go.'

'I'd better come with you. If he's paralytic it will take all of us to get him to bed!'

A lad about Teddy's age was standing on the step, shivering.

'What the hell do you want? Who are you?' Mary demanded.

'Me name's Vinny Flannagan. Me mam sent me. Yer've ter cum right away.'

'Is it Daisy? Joseph?' Mary cried.

'No, missus, it's 'er feller. Sam. Sam O'Grady. Some feller called an' told 'er 'e'd 'ad an accident, like.'

'What kind of accident?' Nell demanded.

''E got run over by a bus. E's in the 'ospital.'

'Oh, Mother of God!' Mary cried.

'Which hospital?' Nell demanded, fear rising within her.

'The Royal. Will yer cum now?'

'Yes! Go on, get back and tell Daisy I'm on my way.'

'She's gone ter the 'ospital.'

'Where's the baby?' Nell demanded.

'Me mam's mindin' 'im.'

'Get off with you, tell your mam I'm going to the hospital and that Nell will look after Joe! Shift yourself!'

'Mam, get a cab! I'll get my coat and go round there!'

'What about your da and Alfred?'

'I'll leave them a note. You should be able to get a cab from Scotland Road. Never mind the expense. Oh, poor, poor Daisy!'

Chapter Nine

———◆———

MARY HAD A LITTLE difficulty with the ward sister, a
sour-faced, aggressive woman in a blue dress with
heavily starched cuffs, apron and cap.

'His wife is with him, we don't allow other relatives. Who
are you and I'll tell them you called,' she barked. Then her
mouth snapped shut like a steel trap.

Mary was annoyed with her officious attitude. She had no
intention of being bullied by a puffed-up spinster of a woman.

'I'm his mother-in-law and my poor daughter will be out
of her mind. She has a young baby, she needs comforting, she
needs someone to reassure her. I am going to see her even if I
have to call a doctor out here!'

Grudgingly the woman indicated a bed down the other
end of the half-lit, white-tiled ward, and Mary walked on.

Daisy was sitting in a chair, just staring at her husband's
unconscious form. He had his arm in a sling and a bandage
around his head. He didn't look too good at all.

'Daisy, how is he?' Mary asked quietly, placing a hand on Daisy's shoulder.

Daisy's eyes were full of tears. 'Oh, Mam! It . . . it's dreadful!'

'What happened, luv?'

'He was drunk. He stepped out into the road and under a bus.'

'How bad is he?'

'He's got a broken arm, a cut on his head but . . . but . . . oh, Mam!' Daisy broke down.

Mary gathered her in her arms. 'Daisy, luv, what is it?'

'Mam, they had to amputate his legs, they were so badly damaged . . . just a mangled mess of bone and flesh. He'll be a cripple, Mam, he'll never walk again and I'll have to do everything for him. How can I manage with no wages coming in?'

'Oh, Mary Mother of God! The poor lad.'

Daisy drew away from her mother. 'Poor lad! *Poor lad!*' Her voice rose until it was almost a scream. 'What about *poor* me? He'll never work again, what am I supposed to do, Mam? We'll all end up in the Workhouse!'

'Daisy, hush, you'll have Sister down on us in a flash and like a ton of bricks. I've already had a run-in with her. She'd be only too happy to throw us out,' Mary admonished, although deeply shocked herself.

With a great effort, Daisy became calmer. 'Mam, what am I going to do?'

'Don't say things like "ending up in the Workhouse". You know I would never let that happen. You'll have to go back to work, luv, but don't let's talk about that now. Come home with me, we can't do anything to help him just sitting here. Nell's gone to mind Joseph so don't worry about him.'

Daisy reluctantly agreed and Mary led her down the ward.

'If anyone else comes, it'll be his mother and I don't advise you to try and stop her seeing him,' she said to the sister, who glared at her.

Nell had taken Joseph home to Portland Street and when Mary and Daisy arrived she looked anxiously at them.

'Well, what's the bloody fool done now?' Jack asked. Nell had insisted he stay up and wait with her.

'Jack, it's serious. Nell, luv, put the kettle on.'

'How serious?' he demanded.

'He'll never walk or work again. He's broken his arm and has a cut on his head. They'll heal, but they had to . . . cut off both his legs they were so bad.'

'What the hell will they do?' he gaped, glancing at the ashen-faced Daisy.

Mary tried to stay calm. 'First of all we're going to have a cup of tea. Then Daisy and little Joe are going to stay here, she needs a decent night's sleep. It's been a terrible shock for her. We'll sort something out in the morning. Nell, they'll have to squeeze in with you.'

'They can have my bed, I'll sleep down here on the sofa. Annie won't mind.'

Mary shot her a grateful look. 'That's true, she's sleeping so much lately. She hardly knows night from day and she's getting very confused about other things.'

'She's nothing but a bloody parasite,' Jack muttered.

'Jack, I'm not going into all that now.'

'Fine bloody Christmas this is going to be and it all started out so well. I suppose it will put the mockers on Nell's wedding.'

Shocked and upset though she was, Daisy raised her head. 'Nell's wedding?'

'Alfred proposed to Nell earlier and she accepted. The wedding was planned for the end of January, but now . . .'

'Oh, so I'm going to be blamed for ruining things, I suppose?' Daisy cried.

'Daisy, don't be stupid!'

'I'm not being stupid! It doesn't matter that I'll have to slave all my life to keep Joseph and that useless, drunken, cheating sod! It doesn't matter that we'll all have to live in that poky horrible room for ever. Oh, don't let Nell get upset! Don't let anything spoil *her* day!'

'Daisy, just stop that! It's *not* true! You know I'll do anything, anything to help you, you're my sister!' Nell cried.

'It *is* true! You all blame me! When it's me who's suffered, having to put up with him and now . . . oh, I wish I was dead! I wished he'd get run over and now he has but I wish he was dead!'

Mary slapped her hard. 'Beg God to forgive you for saying that, Daisy! I never thought I'd see the day when one of mine would wish someone dead! It's a sin!'

Daisy was crying noisily.

'Mam, don't hit her again. She didn't mean it. She's terribly upset!' Nell begged.

'In the name of God Almighty! Will the three of you stop screaming at each other like fishwives! I won't stand for it!' Jack thundered and they all fell silent, Mary shocked and furious, Nell biting her lip, upset and hurt, and Daisy sobbing more quietly, impotent anger, jealousy and despair making her shake.

Mary tried to calm herself. 'Your da's right. We're all getting hysterical and it will upset the baby.'

'To say nothing of me!' Jack grumbled.

'Let's deal with the sleeping arrangements. Nell, there're some spare blankets in the cupboard in our room. Bring them down here and we'll air them in front of the range. Daisy, take Joseph up and get him settled, then the pair of you come back here while we get this sorted out. God, what a night!'

'Mary, do we have to sort it out now?' Jack demanded irritably. He was tired and hated rows.

'Yes, we do! I won't have those two at each other's throats. It upsets me terribly.'

'Families always fight.'

'Not every family and not like this. Oh, Daisy has changed so much.'

'Well, what did you expect, the way she carried on? She should never have got mixed up with that lot.'

'There's no need to rake all that up again, Jack. It's in the past, it's the future that worries me now.'

She made another pot of tea and sat at the kitchen table until, to her father's annoyance, Nell had arranged the blankets around the fire.

'They're blocking out the heat!' he complained.

'Well, it's not as though it's freezing in here and they won't be there all night!' Mary snapped tiredly.

'Is he settled then?' Jack asked of Daisy. She nodded.

'Right, all of you, sit down here with me,' Mary demanded.

Both girls reluctantly did so but Jack made no move. Typical, Mary thought angrily. He was making it quite clear that he wanted no real part in this discussion.

'Daisy, you've had a terrible shock, we all have, but we have to get things sorted out. First, I want an end to all this jealousy and rowing with Nell. You chose to marry Sam, just as Nell has chosen to marry Alfred.'

'No, I didn't, Mam! I *had* to get married!'

'Well, that was your own fault for carrying on like a bloody floozie!'

Mary glared at her husband. 'Jack, that's not helping anyone.'

'Daisy, I'm really sorry about . . . everything. You have to believe me.' Nell reached to take her sister's hand but Daisy pulled away.

'Oh, leave them, Mary! If Madam there doesn't want to make up with her sister then it's her lookout!'

'That's all very well, Jack, but you don't have to bear it every day.'

Nell tried again. 'Daisy, let me help you?'

'I don't want your help! I don't want anything from *you*!'

Mary passed a hand over her aching forehead. Daisy clearly wasn't going to relent. She'd have to think about that later, for now all she could do was at least try to sort out the practicalities.

'You'll have to get a job, Daisy. I'll help as much as I can and so will your da.'

Jack was outraged. 'Don't rope me in, it's her own fault.'

Mary was fast losing all patience. 'How can it be her fault that he walked in front of a bus?'

'He was drunk! If she'd been any kind of a wife he wouldn't have got drunk!'

'Oh, so I suppose I'm not much of a wife then either? The state you come home in from the Golden Fleece?' Mary shot back.

'If that's the way you're going to carry on, I'm going to bed!' Jack retorted, getting to his feet.

He had only been looking for an excuse, Mary thought. As usual, leave everything to Mary.

'I want both of you to think about things. About the way you treat each other. We used to be a close family, now we're tearing it all apart.' She stared miserably into the fire. 'Oh, tonight started out so well, I'm sorry, Nell.'

Daisy jumped to her feet. 'That's right, Mam, apologise to *her* again! I'm going to bed!'

Mary felt defeated and depressed. Obviously Daisy wasn't going to be reconciled. It was useless to ask her to be matron of honour now, she might even refuse to go to the wedding.

Sam O'Grady's condition improved a little, so his mother said when she called to inform Daisy of her husband's progress. Daisy had refused to go to see him.

'I've tried, Mrs O'Grady, I really have. I can't do a thing with her these days,' Mary had apologised as she'd shown the woman out.

'Ah, God, what's to do with them these days, Mary? We never carried on like this, an' sure, isn't it 'is own fault for gettin' fallin' down drunk, the eejit!' Mrs O'Grady had replied.

'Well, she'll have to do her duty by him when he comes home. In sickness and in health,' Mary said firmly. She would take Daisy back to her home even if she had to drag her there. Who else would look after Sam? Certainly not his mother if she judged the woman's earlier attitude and comments correctly. Still, he wouldn't be out of hospital for a while yet and therefore that problem could be postponed.

'I asked Alfred to wait, but he wouldn't,' Nell said to Mary as they sat at the table with papers scattered around them. The church had been booked, the Registrar contacted, Father Mannion would see to the music and the candles, and Mary would provide the flowers even though they were expensive at this time of year. Nell was going for her dress on Saturday afternoon and Mary was going with her. They were making a list of the guests and of what food and drink they would have to provide.

'You can't blame him, Nell. Just because Sam O'Grady was fool enough to walk under a bus, it's no reason for postponing the wedding.'

'I wish Daisy would change her mind about not coming.'

'She won't,' Mary said in a clipped voice. 'At least she'll be here for the wedding breakfast. She's not going to escape altogether. People will talk, ask why she didn't go to the church, but that can't be helped.'

'We'll have to make an excuse.'

'I'll think of something. Is young Nancy quite happy at being a bridesmaid?'

'She was delighted when I asked her,' Nell replied. Nancy, although a good deal younger than herself, was her closest friend at work and had agreed to be her bridesmaid after Nell told her that Daisy wasn't really up to it with all the upset over Sam.

'Well, I'm glad you've chosen long sleeves and taffeta otherwise she'd catch her death of cold. I just hope your da can get me those tinned peaches and pears, there's not a one to be had. I'm certain people are starting to hoard food.'

'Oh, Mam, do you really think so?'

'I do and I'm not going to be left behind. I've told your da to bring stuff home each trip and he said was I thinking of starting a black-market business.'

Nell smiled. 'And are you?'

'Don't ask daft questions. You know I would never do anything like that. How can you take advantage of people's misery? No, it will be for our own use only. Now, are you certain about this outfit for me?'

'Of course I am, Mam. I want you to look like the Queen.'

'It's *your* day, Nell, not mine.'

Nell reached across and squeezed her hand. 'Mam, if you hadn't had the barrow I would never have met him.'

Mary looked across at the tiny form of the sleeping Annie Garvey and smiled.

'I'd never even have had the barrow if it wasn't for her, God love her, and I don't think she'll be with us for much longer,' she finished sadly.

Chapter Ten

—•—

THE MORNING OF NELL'S wedding day dawned clear and cold and Mary sighed with relief. It could have been foggy, raining or blowing a gale. There had been a heavy frost last night and now everything was covered in a sparkling white mantle. Even the yard didn't look too bad. The only thing they'd have to watch out for was slipping on the icy cobbles. Uttering a sigh, she turned away from the window. There wasn't time to spend admiring the lacy patterns the frost had made on the glass. She had too much to do and so many things to think about.

She raked out the range and rekindled the fire with the remaining hot ashes and wooden 'chips' as firewood was called. At least there was no need to worry about the jellies. It was freezing in the scullery, so they'd be more than set. She'd get the sandwiches and rolls done, then cover them with a damp cloth to keep them fresh. She wanted to get as much done before anyone came down. This morning Nell was having a lie-in.

As she worked, Mary lost herself in the memories of herself and Nell trying on dresses and coats in Blacklers, assisted by two very pleasant sales women.

'I think this will suit you very nicely,' one had said, holding out a brown coat with a deep cream-coloured fur collar that cost nearly six pounds ten shillings.

'Oh, it's gorgeous, Mam!' Nell had exclaimed.

The coat was now hanging on the back of the bedroom door, covered with brown paper. Nell had insisted she get a fur hat to match and she'd bought a nice chocolate-brown wool dress to go underneath. She had her good brown shoes and she'd thrown caution to the winds and bought a brown handbag and beige leather gloves. For the first time in her life she would feel elegant. Nell would look beautiful and she didn't want to let her down.

'I can always pawn them if I need to!' she'd laughed on their way out with the bags and parcels.

She smiled to herself. Jack always looked smart and for once Teddy would too. She knew he hated the suit she'd bought him but she didn't care. Today the Callaghan family were going to be very stylishly turned out and the neighbours would be agog. Her expression clouded; the light in her eyes died. All except poor Daisy. She'd felt heartless, but she'd finally ordered her back home, to get their room ready for Sam's return. She'd given her daughter some money then and last week given her more, telling her to get some kind of a costume and blouse. She'd urged Jack to dig into his pocket for money for accessories for the wedding. Daisy, she knew, had used all the money for other, more important things, like food and clothes for Joseph, and she had no real interest in smartening herself up.

'Mam, what are you doing leaving me in bed while there's so much to do?'

Mary turned to see her daughter in her nightdress in the doorway. 'Nell! It's your wedding day, you're entitled to have a lie-in.'

'Don't be daft. Here, let me finish those. Is there any more meat paste?'

Mary put two jars of Shippam's Beef and Ham Paste on the table and put the kettle on.

'Just think, Nell, from now on you'll never have to mess about with dirty, temperamental ranges. Think how clean everything will stay with no ash or soot.'

'I'll still have the coal fires, Mam.'

'I know, but they're not half as bad.'

'What time are the flowers arriving?'

'Lizzie Cassidy said she'd be here at eight o'clock sharp.'

'At least they won't wilt in the yard.'

'No, but they might get frostbitten. In fact, I think it's still freezing so we'd better cover them with a bit of old sacking. Now, just let me check your da and our Teddy's good shirts before I go and wake them.'

'Is there anything else I can do?'

'No. Just go and see to yourself.'

Nell put down the knife and caught her mother's hand. 'Oh, Mam, I'm nervous. Am I doing the right thing?'

'Nell, everyone is a bag of nerves on their wedding day and wonders if they're doing the right thing. Go on up with you.' She didn't add that there were a lot of women – herself included – who knew they'd definitely done the wrong thing where their choice of husbands was concerned.

As the morning progressed things became more chaotic. Mary was demented trying to keep her son clean and tidy and away from the cakes and lemonade and constantly interrupted by Jack regarding the whereabouts of shirts, socks, handkerchiefs and shoe polish.

The flowers had arrived and Teddy was put in charge of them. He had tied a bow of white ribbon around Scruffy's neck, which he hated and which he was frantically – and with much barking and whining – trying to scratch off.

Annie Garvey watched everything from her bed in the corner and occasionally smiled, before drifting into sleep again. The previous night Nell had been unable to get to sleep and had gone down to make herself a hot drink. She'd moved quietly, not wanting to disturb Annie, but the old woman had been awake.

'Are you happy, Nell?' she'd asked.

'As happy as I'll ever be,' Nell had replied, sitting on the edge of the bed.

'What's that supposed to mean, girl?'

'Of course I'm happy. Mam's happy, so is Da . . .'

'Don't you get wed to please your mam. It won't work.'

'I'm not, Annie.'

'I know there's someone out there for you and it's not Alfred McManus. Take care with him, Nell. He's not all he seems to be.'

'Oh, Annie, is this more of your fortune-telling?'

'Maybe it is and maybe it isn't. Do you still have the tin box I gave you?'

'Of course, and I haven't opened it.'

'Maybe you should.'

'No. I promised I wouldn't until you . . . oh, let's not go on about it any more! I'm going to try and get some sleep. Is there anything I can get you?'

'No, girl. I'm tired, I'll go to sleep now.'

As Nell had climbed the stairs she'd thought her mam was right. Annie was getting very strange.

Nancy, Nell's friend from work, arrived at the same time as Daisy and in a moment the kitchen was crowded.

'Nancy, luv, will you go up to our Nell, it's getting like Lime Street Station in here,' Mary said, feeling flustered.

Daisy looked resentfully at the girl who disappeared into the lobby. Mary, seeing her elder daughter's sour expression sighed. Daisy hadn't made much of an effort. The navy-blue two-piece costume wasn't too bad, nor was the cheap white blouse, but Daisy's shoes were broken down, she wore no stockings and her legs were blue with cold. She had a battered old handbag and a borrowed hat but she hadn't washed her hair or put a bit of lipstick on. Mary felt so sorry for her.

'It's a damned good thing she's not coming to the church, the state of her!' Jack said in a loud whisper while Mary fastened his collar stud.

'Honestly, Jack! What a thing to say, you know she's got no money!'

'Don't let's start on that road, Mary.'

'Well, keep remarks like that to yourself or you'll ruin everybody's day!' she hissed back. 'I'm going up to see how Nell and Nancy are getting on. For God's sake don't let our Teddy get dirty and keep him away from the food!'

'I'll be a damned sight happier when we get this over and done with,' Jack muttered. What was it with women and weddings, turning the whole thing into a three-ringed circus?

'So you can start on the booze?' Mary asked, but she was laughing as she ran up the stairs.

'Oh, Nell!' she exclaimed as she opened the bedroom door.

'Isn't the dress beautiful, Mrs Callaghan!' Nancy enthused.

'You saw it in the shop, Mam.'

'Oh, I know, luv, but with the veil and everything it looks just gorgeous! No, don't come near me until I've taken this dirty old pinny off!' she admonished as Nell stretched out her arms. There were tears in Mary's eyes as she gazed at her daughter. The dress was pure gleaming white satin in a very plain bias cut. It had long tight sleeves and a high neck edged with satin ribbon. It had a sweeping train, the hem of which was bound with satin ribbon, and where it joined the bodice there was a huge bow. The wreath of mock orange blossom and the short veil suited Nell, making her hair look even darker than it was. She looked like a princess, Mary thought. Oh, at that moment she was so happy. Everything she had ever wanted for Nell was bound up in this day.

'What about Nancy?' Nell asked.

'She looks great too. That dark-red shot taffeta suits you, Nancy, you being so fair.'

'Mam, will you get yourself ready!' Nell urged.

'Oh, it won't take me long, Nell. Not like your da, it takes him hours, God knows why. Now, don't go sitting down, you'll get that bow and train all creased. And don't let it trail in all the dust and dirt of the street. Nancy, you carry it.'

'It's part of my duties, Mrs C. I asked Mam about everything. I've never been a bridesmaid before.'

'Mam, will you just go!' Nell laughed.

After a very short time, it was Nell's turn to exclaim with pleasure when Mary re-entered the room.

'Oh, Mam! It doesn't look like you! You look . . . great! Like a proper lady.'

'Oh, she's right, Mrs C. You wouldn't be out of place in the Adelphi!' Nancy added.

Mary blushed and patted her hat with a gloved hand. 'I might look the part but as soon as I opened my mouth everyone would know I'm a barrow woman.'

'There's nothing wrong with that, Mam. You've worked hard all your life and you shouldn't be ashamed of the way you earn your living or of your accent either. Now come and give me a hug before you go down.'

When Nell and Nancy came into the kitchen, Daisy wasn't sorry she wasn't going to the church like everyone else. Her eyes filled with tears of self-pity. Nell had everything, even the big wedding that she'd always imagined she'd have. She couldn't keep the memories of her own wedding day from crowding back into her mind. The brief ceremony. No music or flowers. A sullen, bitter bridegroom and she had looked so dull and plain. Nell looked so beautiful, the dress set off her slim figure and dark hair and eyes perfectly. Daisy'd always been 'pleasantly plump', as Mam put it. Now she realised that she was fat, as her husband had called her. Why couldn't she have been the one who took after Da? Even Nancy, whom she'd always thought to be a bit on the plain side, looked far better than she'd ever done.

'By God, don't you look like a queen!' Jack cried in stunned admiration as he took the hand of the daughter he'd never really forgiven for not being a boy.

'Thanks, Da. Do I really look . . . nice?' Nell was overcome. For the first time in her life her father admired her.

'Nice isn't the word for it, Nell. You look beautiful; you've done us all proud. He's a good feller, a bit strait-laced, but all right.'

'I know, Da. What do you think of Mam?'

'She looks great. She's a good-looking woman when she's dressed up. Real fur, no less!'

'You should take her somewhere nice tomorrow to show her off. The Stork or somewhere.'

'Nell, fellers like me don't go to no hotels or restaurants. I'd feel a fool and so would your mam.'

'Just the once, Da? It would really make her happy,' Nell begged. 'It's my wedding day and you can't refuse me!'

Jack relented. Mary did look attractive and smart. 'I'll think about it. Now, we'd better get a move on or Alfred will think you've stood him up!'

Daisy sat in the silent house. Her da had never even said a word to her and she'd always been his favourite. She might not have been there, he'd ignored her so totally. Now he was promising to take Mam out somewhere posh and he'd never ever done that before – but Nell had persuaded him. Well, she wasn't staying here to be ignored when they came back or looked on with pity by the family and friends who would all compare her to her sister. She was going home and she was taking Joseph with her and she was never going to come here again.

When the wedding party returned, only Mary realised that Daisy wasn't there.

'I'll sort her out tomorrow,' she whispered to Jack who had failed to realise that his elder daughter was missing.

The little house was bursting at the seams as one by one all the neighbours 'popped in'. They spilled out into the back yard and on to the front steps even though it was bitterly cold again. But there was plenty of rum and whiskey to keep them warm.

For Nell the whole day had passed in a dream-like haze. It didn't feel as though it was all happening to her, that now she was Mrs Alfred McManus. Alfred had been delighted with her, stunned into silence for a few seconds, then openly admiring and proud. Now, with the train of her dress looped over her arm, she was dancing with her father in the tiny front room.

'Are you happy, Nell?' Jack asked.

'I am, Da! No one could ask for more.'

'You've fallen on your feet there. You'll be a lady of leisure now!'

'I want to go on working, Da, but Alfred won't let me.'

'You must be mad, girl! Getting up at first light in the middle of winter and slaving away in that bloody factory is not what I'd choose to do, not when I could have a lie-in. I wish I didn't have to strain and sweat in a bloody stokehold and with the bloody ship pitching and rolling and making the job twice as hard and dangerous. You just think yourself damned lucky he doesn't want you to work. And I can understand him. What would people say? They'd say he couldn't support a wife and in his position it would be humiliating.'

'I know all that, Da, but what am I going to do all day?'

'Keep house, shop, cook, do his washing and ironing, isn't all that enough to keep you busy?'

'I suppose it is.'

'And it's a decent house, not a bloody kip in a bloody slum. Your mam works her fingers to the bone, always has done, to keep this place halfway decent.'

'She works too hard, Da, and she's not getting any younger.'

'Neither am I!' he retorted, knowing she was having a dig at him.

'Jack, I think it's time my wife and I went home,' Alfred interrupted, taking Nell's arm.

'It is.' Jack relinquished his daughter to her husband. 'This lot won't go home until morning, if they go home at all.'

'We'll have to say goodbye to everyone, Alfred,' Nell reminded him.

'Let's make a start then. I've sent young Tommy Ford to go and find us a cab. I don't know what your brother has been drinking but he looked very pale when I saw him. And, Nell, you can't go on the tram dressed like that.'

Nell laughed. 'Wouldn't that cause some comments? I'd be mortified. And so will Mam be if our Teddy's drunk!'

'Mary, we're leaving now, but I want to thank you for all the trouble and expense you've gone to to make this day so special,' Alfred said seriously to his mother-in-law.

'Mam, it's been great, thank you! Thank you so much!' Nell added.

Mary hugged her but felt a dart of apprehension. How would Nell cope with the physical side of marriage? She hoped Alfred would treat her with patience and sensitivity.

As they settled themselves in the cab the same thought occurred to Nell. Oh, she knew all about the consummation of a marriage but she was very nervous. Would it hurt? How long would it go on for? Would she enjoy it? They were questions she would soon find the answer to.

As if he had read her thought, Alfred patted her hand. 'Don't worry, Nell, things will be fine and who knows we might get lucky and I'll be a father in nine months' time.'

She smiled at him. 'Yes, we might. I'd love a baby, Alfred, I really would.'

Chapter Eleven

———◆———

NELL GAVE A FINAL polish to the last glass and sat back on her heels to admire her handiwork. Once a fortnight she took out the entire contents of the glass cabinet and washed and polished every piece. The first time she had done it she had been so careful, afraid in case she broke something. It was all so beautiful and delicate. Alfred had informed her that the glasses and dishes were very fragile and had great sentimental value, having been collected over the years by first his grandmother and then his mother. Now she wasn't too afraid to handle them. She'd got used to them. The way she'd got used to everything. But she just couldn't think of everything as belonging to her. This was Alfred's home and she was his wife but she felt that she was only a custodian. She was just looking after things for him until the next generation came along.

'Nell, are you there, luv?'

Nell got to her feet. 'I'm in here, Mam!'

Mary pushed open the door. 'Oh, it's lovely and cool in here. I'm completely worn out.'

'You look it, Mam.'

'It's so hot and dusty out there. It's got to be the hottest August ever. Thank God it's nearly September and it should get a bit cooler.'

'You sit there and I'll make us a cup of tea. I've just finished these.'

'I'll come into the kitchen. I never feel at ease in here.'

Nell smiled. 'I used to feel like that, but I don't any more. You get used to it. You get used to a lot of things. You just sit there and rest.'

Mary leaned back in the chair gratefully. It was so cool and sort of restful, but then it should be restful, there was never any commotion of any sort in this house, unlike her own. She'd spoken the truth when she'd said she was worn out. The intense heat seemed to have sapped her strength and her back was aching. It ached a lot these days. She must be getting old and all that lifting and bending didn't help.

Nell came in with a tray. 'Here we are, Mam.'

'I'm being treated like a lady, on a tray no less.'

'Well, you are a lady to me, Mam.'

'I've never owned two cups that matched, never mind a proper tea set. You're right, I could get used to this, Nell. It's a little palace of a house compared to mine. You've got so much. Decent rugs on the floors, good curtains on every window, a runner up the hall and even carpet on the stairs. You know I scrub my stairs every week. I scrub the whole house. I sometimes wish I had a Ewbank carpet sweeper, but seeing as I've got no carpets it would be useless. You've sheets on the bed and pillowcases and that lovely eiderdown and bedspread and then there's all your thick, soft towels. I could go on and on.'

'It's very nice to have all that, Mam, but it's not . . . everything.'

Mary looked at her closely. 'Nell, is something the matter?'

'Nothing.'

'There is. I'm your mam and I can tell by just looking at you. Is it Alfred?'

'Not really, well . . . It's me, I suppose. I just can't . . . I don't know if I like being married, Mam.'

Mary looked at her quizzically. 'What do you mean by that, Nell?'

'It's . . . it's all such a . . . disappointment.'

'A disappointment? You've got all this and you're "disappointed"? Poor Daisy would kill for the life you have. You don't even have to go out to work. Does he keep you short?'

'He is careful but we don't want for anything. I wish he would let me work, Mam, I really do. The time drags and I feel so . . . useless. With just the two of us the place doesn't get dirty and he's very tidy.' Obsessively tidy, she thought.

Before he went to bed each night he folded his newspaper and added it to the pile in the scullery. He wound the clocks, checked the doors to make sure they were locked. Placed his boots by the scullery door and if she hadn't plumped up the sofa cushions he did them. She wouldn't have minded a bit of mess now and then. At least the place would look lived in. The days passed so slowly, especially the afternoons, and she got terribly bored, but she couldn't tell her mam that for how many women did she know who had so much time on their hands? Not one.

'Well, if you've got so much time to spare, you could give me a hand.'

'You know I'd love to but . . . but Alfred says I've plenty to do to keep things "ship-shape".' It was one of his expressions and she was rapidly learning to hate it.

'You have indeed.'

'Oh, Mam! I do spend all Monday washing and ironing. I shop every other day, I bake three times a week and he always has a good meal ready on the table, but I could still work at something, part-time.'

'Now just stop complaining, Nell. You know he has a position to keep up. Even if you don't care what the neighbours say, he does! Don't let me hear you complaining again.'

Nell nodded. Mam would never understand. She'd had to work all her life.

'And, madam, when you have children you'll have your hands full then.'

'That's another thing, Mam. I do want children, but . . . but I don't like . . .'

'So that's the reason behind all this discontent and disappointment. There's no baby on the way. Is it his fault?'

'No. No, he's always . . . It's me. I just . . . I'm just not happy with . . . that side of it.' She looked down, embarrassed.

'Nell, you'll get used to it. Does he . . . hurt you?'

'No!'

'If you want a baby so much then you'll *have* to get used to it. "With my body, I thee worship." It's all part of being married. I just wish Daisy had been as reluctant as you appear to be.'

'How is she, Mam? And Joseph? I miss seeing him so much.'

'He's fine. He's getting very noisy and boisterous.'

'It's being with Mrs Flannagan and her kids all day.'

'I know, but what else can she do? She has to work now and you know what that flaming factory's like. I wish I could help with Joseph during the days, but I can't. Your da won't cough up the extra money I would need to cover the cost of staying at home and minding him. He says she knew what she was doing and she shouldn't expect him to go short just because the fool she married walked in front of a bus.'

'Oh, how I wish he . . . but, he'll never change, Mam. We both know that.'

'Of course. That's why you should be very grateful for Alfred's thriftiness. You'll never have to work on the barrow the way I have.'

'Sometimes I wish I could, Mam,' Nell said quietly. Then she smiled, seeing Mary's expression harden. 'I was only joking, Mam.'

'It breaks my heart to see the state of Daisy living in that awful room with no hope of ever leaving it. Oh, if only she hadn't been so stupid!'

'I know, Mam. I feel so sorry for her, but you know what she's like, you know what she thinks of me.'

'I do and it upsets me.'

'I tried.'

'I know. Oh, don't let's go into all that again.' She finished her tea. 'I must go, I've still got work to do and if our Teddy has left that flaming dog in the house again I'll kill him!'

Nell looked amused. 'What did Scruffy do?'

'Only knocked the food press over and ate the rest of the bit of meat I was saving to make a pie. I told meladdo that when we were all out that flaming animal stays in the yard!'

Nell hid a smile. 'Oh, Mam, I'm sorry I lumbered you with him!'

'And well you may be. I'd best be off. You count your blessings, my girl!'

'I will, Mam.'

When she'd gone Nell washed the cups and rinsed out the teapot. Mam would never understand. She loathed the physical side of marriage. The first time she had expected so much, it had hurt terribly, and Alfred had seemed not to care that things hadn't been at all how she'd imagined them. She never spoke of her feelings but submitted with gritted teeth and clenched hands. She was sure it wasn't supposed to be like this. Daisy must have found it very different, but then Daisy had been in love with Sam. She wasn't in love with Alfred, she knew it. Affection just wasn't the same thing. Still, as Mam had said, if she wanted children then that was the price she'd have to pay. And Alfred desperately wanted a son. Sometimes she thought he was getting obsessive about that too, in addition to all his other odd ways that she had never known about until she'd married him. He was constantly economising. He insisted on not having the electric light on during the long summer evenings. He advised her to save all the bits of soap which he then softened and shaped into tablet form. The Sunday joint of meat had to go further than a single meal.

Cold with potatoes on Monday. Minced with cheap bits from the butcher on Tuesday. Scouse on Wednesday. But as she'd come from a home where meat of any kind had been scarce, she didn't complain. How could she?

She'd changed her dress, re-done her hair and had a steak and kidney pie in the oven when Alfred came home.

'It won't be long. I've set the table and I got you a jug of beer from the Dog and Duck. It's on the slab in the larder. I thought you would be thirsty.'

'I am. That's very thoughtful of you, Nell, but a bit extravagant.'

'It's only once and it's very hot. Thank God I've the gas cooker. I know it's stifling in the kitchen now, with the jets and the oven being on. I had to change, I was so hot, but we don't have to keep it on.' She busied herself with the pie and the pan of potatoes while he poured himself a glass of the beer he'd complained about her buying.

'Mam called this afternoon, on her way home,' she informed him as she served the meal. 'She looked exhausted.'

'She must be. This heat is hard to bear. There's not even a bit of a breeze down on the river.'

'I wish Da would give her more money so she needn't carry on with the barrow.'

'Well, he won't and it's no business of ours. It's between them.'

She said nothing until he had finished and she served the sponge pudding and custard.

'She said Joseph's getting to be very boisterous. It's being with the Flannagans all day.'

'Daisy should take more notice of that child. If she's not

careful he'll be running the streets when he's old enough.'

'I know, but what can she do?'

'It's a great pity she hasn't a trade in her fingers. If she'd been a dressmaker or a confectioner she could have worked from home.'

'The likes of us would never have been able to be anything like that, Alfred.'

'Well, at least any children we have will be properly looked after.'

Nell fell silent again. She didn't want to go along that road.

She had cleared away, washed and dried the dishes and put them all back on the dresser and had just sat down to read yesterday's *Echo* – women's magazines were considered a luxury – when Teddy burst in.

'Just how did you get in here?' Alfred demanded of the red-faced and sweating lad.

'I left the door open a bit, hoping to catch a draught,' Nell explained. 'What's the matter?'

'What have I said about leaving the front door open? It's a habit I deplore. It might have been the custom in Portland Street, but it's not here. We could be burgled. We could be murdered,' Alfred said irritably.

Nell ignored him. 'Is it Mam?' she asked fearfully.

'No. Hang on a bit while I get my breath.'

'Then what's the matter? Why have you come tearing in here?'

'It's old Annie, Mam says she's dying and she's asking for you.'

'For me?'

'Yes, for you. You've to come now, Mam said so.'

Nell looked for her husband's approval. He looked annoyed but nodded.

'Wait until I get my hat and bag,' Nell ordered. 'I'll only be a second. Get yourself a drink of water or milk.'

'Is there lemonade?' Teddy asked hopefully.

'No!' snapped Alfred. 'What do you think I am, made of money?' He grunted. Lemonade indeed! Give some people an inch and they'd take a mile!

Both Nell and Teddy were sweating when they reached Portland Street but Nell didn't notice the stifling heat in her mother's kitchen.

'Mam, is she really dying?' she whispered, taking off her hat.

'I'm afraid so. Oh, it had to come, Nell. She's just been getting weaker and weaker. Everyone has been helping out with seeing to her. The neighbours here have been very good as usual.'

Nell noticed her mother looked pale and worn as she sank into the chair by Annie's bedside. 'Why didn't you tell me earlier? I could have come and looked after her. I had the time.'

'I don't think Alfred would have liked it, Nell.'

'But she's . . . she's part of the family!' She was part of the fabric of the house too, she thought. The bed with its blankets and faded patchwork quilt was so familiar that you didn't give it a second glance. Annie's walking stick had been propped up in the corner for years too. As she stooped down to the bed Nell took one of Annie's tiny claw-like hands in her own. The old lady opened her eyes and tried to smile.

'It's Nell, I've come to see you, Annie,' she said.

The old woman looked agitated.

'Mam, I think she's trying to say something.'

'What is it, Annie, luv?' Mary spoke slowly and distinctly.

'The box. My . . . box . . . the little box,' came the hoarse reply.

'Nell, she wants her box. It's under the bed.'

'No, I think she means the little box she gave to me.'

'Which box?'

'Is it the old tobacco tin, Annie?'

Annie nodded.

'She gave me a little box but told me not to open it until she was . . . gone.'

'She's trying to speak, Nell.'

Nell leaned very close to hear the whispered words.

'I will, I promise, Annie,' she replied aloud.

'You will do what?' Mary asked.

'I'll open it. She wants me to open it now. It's at home, I'll send Teddy back for it, with a note for Alfred.'

Mary shook her head. 'I don't think she has that long with us, Nell. Look, she's closed her eyes and her breathing is very laboured. I'll send him for Father Mannion and then for the box.'

Teddy was told to run quickly for the parish priest. He wasn't sorry to go; he didn't relish the prospect of being around a dead person, although he'd seen enough of them. Mam always made him go and pay his respects when one of the neighbours was bereaved.

Father Mannion came quickly and anointed Annie, who hadn't spoken again. One by one the neighbours came to call and Nell made tea. At eight o'clock Daisy arrived with Joseph.

'Mrs Flannagan told me. She heard it from someone in the street. You should have sent for me, Mam.'

'I was going to,' Mary reassured her, 'and it's good of you to come, luv. Here, give him to me.' She reached out for her grandson.

As Nell watched she longed to say she'd see to Joseph – she saw little of him and he'd grown so much – but the expression on her sister's face made her hold back. Daisy looked awful. She was obviously tired. She'd lost weight, so much so that her clothes, which were terribly washed out and creased, hung on her. Her curly hair was snatched back off her face and was held by a piece of elastic. She looked so old, Nell thought with pity in her heart.

'Daisy, sit here,' she offered, getting up.

The reply was sullen. 'I'm fine. I'll stand.'

Florrie Ford nudged Edna Stanley and raised her eyes to the ceiling. 'Yer look all in, girl,' she said, getting to her feet. ''Ere, 'ave my chair, I'm goin' now. Our Maureen's comin' around ternight so I'd best be off.'

Daisy sat down but ignored her sister.

After that all that could be heard in the kitchen was the sound of muttered prayers for the soul of Annie Garvey which half an hour later departed from her body. At last her harsh and lonely life was over.

'She's gone,' Father Mannion said quietly.

'God rest her soul,' Mary sighed, as Nell assisted her to her feet. They had both knelt beside the bed until Annie had breathed her last.

'You've nothing to reproach yourself for, Mary. She'd have

been in a very bad way if you hadn't taken her in all those years ago.'

'What else could I have done, Father?'

'I'm sure you've reserved your place in heaven for your kindness.'

'I hope so, Father, but she was very little trouble. All she wanted was to be part of a family, to live somewhere where people cared for her, and we did. I'll miss her.'

'I'll make all the arrangements.'

Mary sank down on the chair Daisy had vacated.

'I have the Burial Club money for her funeral. She'll not be buried as a pauper even though Jack thinks it's a waste.'

Nell got her coat. 'I'll go for Mrs Hannigan,' she offered, for the midwife also did the laying out.

'No need, luv, I'll send my lad when I get 'ome,' Edna Stanley offered.

The house was much quieter by the time Teddy arrived back. He'd dawdled purposefully both on the journey to Priory Road and from it.

'Here, Nell. Alfred couldn't find it at first,' he said, shoving the box towards her.

'Right, get yourself a drink and then get washed and up to bed,' Mary instructed him.

'What's that?' Daisy asked, curious despite herself.

'It's something Annie gave me a while ago. She made me promise not to open it until she was dead.'

'Why did she give it to you and not Mam?' Daisy demanded suspiciously. Had the old woman left Nell something of value? It would be bloody typical if she had. 'Much gets more,' she thought.

'I don't know. I honestly don't know, Daisy.'

'Well, open it, Nell,' Mary urged.

Nell prised open the lid. 'There's just some pieces of paper . . .'

'Give me that one, it looks like some kind of document,' Mary requested.

'This one just has a name and address on it.' Nell was having difficulty reading the faded scrawl.

'James Burton, looks like forty something Cedar Road in . . . I think it's Aintree.'

Mary looked stunned.

'Mam, what's the matter?' Nell asked.

'This is a birth certificate.'

'For who?' Daisy asked.

'For a David Burton.'

They all looked at each other. This was very odd.

Mary at last fathomed it. 'She must have had a son.'

'Annie? Annie had a baby?' Nell cried.

'And the father was that James Burton?' Daisy added.

'She never said! All this time and she never said a single thing! God luv her! He must have been illegitimate. Oh, poor Annie!'

Nell was shaking her head. Poor Annie indeed. She must have been young when she'd had him. Maybe as young as herself. No one knew if she had lost her parents or been abandoned by them for Annie would never be drawn on that aspect of her life. She'd always denied that she had a family, but had there been brothers and sisters? Had she been disowned? She must have been forced to give David up for adoption.

'But why did she give the box to Nell?' Daisy demanded. 'Did she ever say anything, Nell? Anything at all?'

'No. She did say that she was sure there was someone out there for me and it wasn't Alfred, but I took no notice. She can't have meant it because it was before I was married and she was here after I was married and said nothing more about it.'

'What will we do?' Daisy asked.

Nell shrugged. 'Nothing. What can we do, Daisy? He's probably dead and this David, well, who knows where he is? And it's all so long in the past now, it really doesn't concern us. If she'd wanted us to do something about it she would have let us know sooner. Not after she's dead.'

Daisy picked at her broken nails. So, Annie Garvey had got into the same predicament as herself but obviously there had been no Mr Garvey to demand that this James Burton marry her. Or maybe there had been and he – coming from that address in Aintree, a posh area – had refused to marry poor Annie. Well, it was all water under the bridge now. She had her own miserable life to cope with. Annie's was over, God rest her soul.

Chapter Twelve

＊

'IT'LL SEEM VERY STRANGE in the kitchen now she's gone,'
Mary said sadly when they got back from the cemetery.
It hadn't been an ostentatious funeral, nor had it been a
pauper's one. The women from Portland Street had turned
out in force and Mary was grateful to see the church so full.

'It's bound to seem strange, Mam,' Nell agreed.

'Richie took the bed and I gave Florrie all the bedding. I
didn't fancy keeping it myself.'

'I suppose there will be more room in the kitchen now and
you know how Da always complained about her.'

Mary nodded. Jack had never agreed with her over poor
Annie.

'When will Da be home?' Nell asked.

'With a bit of luck in a few days. He's never sailed on the
Athenia before. He'll be full of praise or complaints, depending
on how he got on. Well, he'll have nothing to complain about
at home now—'

'Except about this bloody war,' Florrie interrupted.

'Do you think it *will* happen?' Nell asked. It was all everyone thought about and discussed.

'Unless there's a miracle and that Hitler decides to behave like a decent human being,' Mary answered grimly.

'Richie said if 'e invades Poland there'll be real trouble an' I believe 'im. God Almighty, I remember the last one. The "war to end all wars" they said it was, an' 'ere we go again!'

'Our Teddy's not a bit happy about being evacuated.'

'Our flamin' Tommy thinks it's all goin' ter be a big joke, a birrof a laugh! God 'elp the poor souls who get that lad, 'e'll 'ave them round the flamin' bend with 'is antics!' Florrie prophesied darkly.

'Will it really be safer for them to be evacuated, Mam?'

'It will if we get bombed, Nell.'

''Oly Mother of God, it doesn't bear thinkin' about!'

'Well, he's all kitted out. All his stuff is ready, wrapped in a brown paper parcel. He's got his gas mask and he'll have to have a label pinned to his coat giving his name and address.'

'Our Tommy says he'll *feel* like a brown paper parcel all done up like that.'

'Alfred's joined the ARP.'

'Aye, Richie keeps goin' on about that. They've both got Reserved Occupations. I said to 'im that it'll be the first 'onest day's work 'e's done in 'is life!'

'I suppose Jack will stay at sea. They'll probably need ships to bring in supplies, like they did last time.'

'In a convoy?' Nell asked.

'Yes,' Mary said and both she and Florrie fell silent, thinking of the menace of the U-boats.

'And there will be rationing?' Nell probed.

'Oh, yes, that won't be long off now. I've a few bits and pieces saved up.'

'Yer know what it said in the newspaper about 'oarding, Mary.'

'I know, Florrie, but I don't intend to make money out of it. We've always shared and well you know it.'

'Well, we'll know what's what on Sunday. Yer feller's gorra wireless, Nell, 'asn't 'e?'

'Yes, he's glued to it when the news is on.'

'Do yer think 'e'd let us cum an' listen on Sunday morning about this "Ultimatum" thing?'

'I don't see why not. Come round after Mass, early Mass,' she added, knowing that Richie Ford liked a pint or two on a Saturday night.

'How did it go, Nell?' Alfred asked when he arrived home, a copy of the *Echo* in his hand.

She put dinner cutlery on the table. 'Not too bad. All of the neighbours went.'

'God rest the poor old soul.'

'Alfred, do you think someone should try and, well, find him? Her son.' Annie's legacy to her had been nagging at the back of her mind ever since she'd opened the box.

'What for? Let sleeping dogs lie, Nell. She had a lifetime to try to contact him and she didn't. What good would it do anyone now?'

Nell sighed. 'You're probably right. Oh, Florrie Ford

asked could she and Richie come round on Sunday morning to listen to the Prime Minister and I said yes.'

He looked irritated.

'Did I do wrong? It is important, isn't it?'

'It's that all right, Nell. It's very, very important. I can't see Hitler backing down.'

'I don't think many people can but everyone's praying he does.'

'We have to be prepared for the worst, Nell.'

'Alfred, can I . . . well, if war does come, I'd like to do something to help. Something useful.' Instead of sitting at home doing nothing, she finished to herself.

'Like what?'

'Nursing perhaps.'

'You've only ever worked in a factory and they'll have plenty of women and girls to nurse.'

'Then in a factory? There'll be munitions work and women did it in the last war.'

'Time enough to be thinking like that when your services are called for. They'll take the single girls and women first.'

'Will Da be safe?'

'Of course, Donaldson Anchor Line are reputable. He's on his way home. The *Athenia* is a fast ship and, besides, even if war is declared on Sunday it will take them a while to get those U-boats out into the shipping lanes. Don't you worry about Jack. Now eat up, the news will be on soon and I want to listen to it.'

On Sunday morning the church was packed and Nell knew that it would be the same in churches all over the country as everyone said desperate prayers for peace. According to Alfred and many of the older men war was inevitable. Some of the younger ones were looking on it as some kind of big adventure, fools that they were, Alfred had said grimly. He and Nell walked home in silence, Nell feeling confused, insecure and a little afraid.

When they got back to the house Alfred fiddled with the knobs of the big awkward-looking wireless while Nell cut some sandwiches. There was half an hour to spare but she'd need that to rearrange the furniture so they would all have a seat and lay the table with the dishes for this far from festive tea party. At ten o'clock they all arrived together: Mary with Teddy, and Richie and Florrie with Tommy, whose eyes lit up at the sight of the food.

'Youse two sit there an' don't say a word!' Florrie ordered the two boys.

'We've had enough out of you two already this morning,' Mary added grimly.

Both boys scowled. Each had a label pinned to his jacket and wore a gas mask in its case slung over his shoulders in preparation for their evacuation later that day. Their brown paper parcels, which contained everything they owned, were waiting at home.

'Why do lads of our age 'ave ter have labels? We *know* our name and address!' Tommy muttered, kicking disconsolately at the kitchen lino.

His mother glared at him. 'I 'eard that, Tommy Ford! Just shurrup or I'll swing fer yer!'

Silence descended and Nell picked nervously at the hem of her pinafore. Alfred turned up the volume and the quiet, tired, sad voice of the Prime Minister filled the room as he uttered the words they had prayed so hard they would never hear again.

The older men shook their heads grimly. Twice in their lifetimes the terrible scourge of war had had to be faced.

Mary wiped away a tear. It was necessary. It *had* to be done, she understood that much, but how they would suffer. She uttered a prayer of thanks thinking of Jack and then was instantly guilty. Maybe Jack and his generation would be safe enough in Reserved Occupations, but what about the young men and boys? Their poor wives and mothers would soon know worry and heartbreak that would scar them for ever.

'What happens now?' Nell asked quietly to break the silence.

'We'll all have a cup of tea. Then we've to see these two to school. The teachers will be there to go with them,' Mary said, trying to sound bright and efficient.

'Do yer think there'll be an air-raid, Alfred?' Richie asked seriously.

Mary and Florrie crossed themselves.

'You never can tell, but I shouldn't think so.'

Richie looked thoughtful. 'Yer never know. That feller might 'ave 'ad the planes ready ter take off the minute 'e 'eard, like.'

Florrie glared at her husband, seeing Nell's frightened expression. 'Mother of God! Trust 'im ter be so flamin' 'appy!'

Alfred tried to bolster all their spirits, his own included. 'I don't think we've anything to be afraid of just yet.' They'd all seen on the Pathé news in the cinemas the indiscriminate bombing of towns and cities in Spain, which had caused the deaths of thousands of civilians.

'Nell, put the kettle on,' Mary said firmly.

'Alfred, do yer want ter go fer a pint? I'm goin' ter the Golden Fleece. We'll 'ear all the plans on the news,' Richie asked.

'Trust you! They're not goin' ter put ale on ration just yet. Mind, there's plenty of women around 'ere who'll be made up when it is! Oh, go on the pair of yez or we'll get no peace. You just be 'ome in time ter see our Tommy off!' Florrie warned.

Alfred didn't particularly want to go all the way to Scotland Road but to refuse would be churlish – especially today – and they might indeed pick up more information. After the pubs closed he'd go for a walk in Stanley Park to think, to try to get things in perspective. He certainly had no desire to hang around street corners with the likes of Richie Ford.

When the time finally came for Mary and Florrie to leave with the boys, Nell hugged her young brother, told him to behave, not get Liverpool a bad name by his trick-acting and gave him half a crown. Tommy Ford looked so pitifully envious that she slipped him a shilling with the admonition not to spend it all at once.

Later, after she'd tidied up the teacups and sandwich plates, Nell sat alone in her kitchen, watching the September afternoon fade into dusk. What would happen now? She desperately wanted to help. There must be something she could do. She couldn't just sit at home all day. Everyone else seemed to be doing something. Maybe Mam could persuade Alfred to let her go to work or even be a fire-watcher? Feeling restless and troubled, she needed to talk to someone now. She wondered how her mother was feeling, having waved goodbye to Teddy. Terror as he was, he was still a little boy, and sending him off into the unknown was deeply upsetting, however much they all made light of it. She had no idea how long Alfred would be out so she left him some ham, cheese and a bit of salad and a note explaining that she couldn't stay on her own and had gone to see Mary.

Everywhere was very quiet, she thought as she sat on the tram. Of course it was Sunday, but it wasn't just that. Everyone seemed to be subdued. Even the conductor on the tram didn't have a single cheerful word, unusual in a Liverpudlian of his profession.

There were no kids out playing in Portland Street. No women sitting or standing on their doorsteps. No men and boys hanging around the corners. The whole city seemed to be holding its breath. Darkness was beginning to fall. Soon the lamps would be lit. She pulled herself up sharply. No, the lamps would not be lit. Not tonight, nor tomorrow night, not until it was all over. The reality hit her hard. The long nights would be pitch dark. How would they all manage?

To her surprise Daisy was sitting in the kitchen with Mary, the baby asleep on the sofa.

'What's the matter?' Nell asked.

'She's had a row with Sam.'

'It was more than just a row, Mam! He was shouting and swearing at me, saying it was my fault he wouldn't be going off to war with his brothers and all the fellers he knows!'

145

'Daisy, luv, I've told you, war is no picnic! Has he ever given a thought to how many of his brothers and mates will die or be wounded? How many other wives will be like you, with crippled husbands?'

'He doesn't think about me at all!' Daisy snapped. Then she turned to Nell, her eyes cold. 'I suppose she'll be sitting at home doing nothing, as usual.'

'No, I won't. That's why I've come. Mam, I want you to try to persuade Alfred to let me work! I'll do anything I can to help!'

'Nell, you know I won't come between a man and his wife. You should both know that.'

Nell sighed. It was no use. Mam took marriage very seriously.

There was a loud rapping on the door and Mary tutted wearily.

'Daisy, go and see who that is, luv. If it's Eddie Molloy tell him to go to hell, I've no lights showing. I swear to God that man takes himself too seriously. ARP warden he might be and he won't be able to get paralytic drunk every Saturday and Sunday night now, but he's a real pain in the neck!'

'I'll put the kettle on, Marn,' Nell said as Daisy did as she was asked. She returned to the kitchen immediately.

'So, was it Eddie Molloy?'

Daisy looked a little pale and shook her head.

'Then who was it?' Mary demanded.

Daisy held out the small brown envelope. 'The telegraph boy said to give it to you.'

Mary looked puzzled but tore open the envelope.

'Oh, Mam! Mam, what's wrong?' Nell cried as Mary let

the envelope fall to the ground, her face drained of all colour.

'Mam? Mam?' Daisy begged.

'Read it, Daisy!' Nell urged.

Daisy read it slowly, shaking her head. When her eyes met those of her sister they were full of stunned disbelief. 'It's . . . it's Da . . .'

Nell snatched the piece of paper from her and scanned the lines. No! No! It *couldn't* be true! It *must* be wrong! It was too soon! Too soon! But it was from the Admiralty; it was official. The *Athenia* had been sunk by a U-boat and there were no survivors. So it had begun. The U-Boats had already been out there, just waiting . . . waiting until it was official and then they'd gone looking for the nearest ship!

Nell threw her arms around her mother. 'Oh, Mam!'

Daisy too was in tears. They'd never see him again. Oh, he'd had his faults but he was still their da and they'd loved him.

Mary was stunned. All she could think of was her Jack. Jack off down the pub with 'the lads'. Jack all dressed up for Mass on Sunday when he was home. Jack the lad, good-time Jack, 'Black Jack' Callaghan. He'd never come home again. He would have stood no chance down in the stokehold. But at least it would have been quick. Better than floundering around in the cold water, dying slowly.

Nell pulled herself together. 'I'll go and get Florrie,' she said, grabbing her coat. Oh, God, what a terrible day it had been. Teddy on his way to heaven knows where and Da . . .

As the door closed behind Nell, Daisy touched her mother's arm gently. 'I'm staying for tonight, Mam,' she said firmly.

Mary was fighting to gain control over her emotions. 'No. You have to go home, Daisy. Who is going to see to Sam?'

'I don't care!'

'Daisy, you should care.'

She shook her head angrily. 'Why? Da was more important to me.'

'Daisy, do this to please me. I'll be fine. Florrie will be in and I'll have Nell.'

Daisy felt the blood of anger flood her cheeks but she said nothing. Silently she began to gather up Joseph's belongings.

Daisy thought the place looked even worse than when she'd left it. She tucked the baby into the bed that she had once shared with her husband. These days he slept in a narrow stretcher-type bed under the window.

'Oh, so you've decided to come home then. I bet she sent you back,' Sam snarled nastily.

'And I see you've been taking your temper out on the few bits of dishes I had!' she retorted, picking up a piece of broken plate and hurling it into the fireplace.

'Don't you bloody start again, you bitch! You left me here knowing I can't see to myself. I'm cold and hungry and you don't even care!'

Daisy's lip curled with contempt. 'You're worse than Joseph! I'm sick of running round after you! You . . . you disgust me!'

He glared at her, powerless. It was always the same, he thought bitterly. The same accusations and recriminations, the complaints, the screaming rows. God, how he wished he could get up and go, leave her and join the Army as his brothers were going to do.

'You're lucky I came home at all! The bloody Germans have sunk the *Athenia*! I lost my da today. Mam had a telegram from the Admiralty and all you think about is your bloody self!'

He didn't reply. She wouldn't lie about something like that. God, it was so hard to take in. But, when he thought about it, he wished he had gone down with the *Athenia* too. It would have been quick. He wouldn't be sitting here a cripple, dying slowly inside. Eaten up with hatred, self-pity, rage and frustration.

Alfred arrived at the Portland Street house at half past eleven. 'I knew there was something wrong when you didn't come home, Nell,' he said, looking anxiously into her drawn face.

'It's Da. He . . . he's lost. They've sunk the *Athenia*. I'll never see him again. I can't believe it. I just can't believe it!'

He was stunned. 'Nell, Mary . . . what can I say? By God, they were quick off the mark! An unarmed merchant vessel carrying women and children! They'll stoop to anything! Now do you see why we have to fight?'

Mary nodded. 'Yes, but . . . but we never expected . . .' Her voice trailed off.

'Isn't there anyone who can come round and help? Sit with her?' Albert asked his wife.

'Who?' Nell wasn't quite sure what he was getting at.

'Well, Florrie?'

Mary raised her head. 'Poor Florrie is in the same state herself. Nell went for her but . . .'

'Florrie had a brother on the *Athenia*,' Nell said quietly.

He said nothing, but after a few minutes as Mary became calmer he cleared his throat.

'Er, Nell, we should be getting home. It takes longer in the black-out.'

Nell looked up at him, confused. 'Alfred, I'm staying with Mam tonight. I can't leave her alone. She hasn't even got Teddy.'

He nodded slowly. Nell's duty to her mother was irksome, but he hoped he wouldn't have to put up with the inconvenience for long. Mary was a strong woman; she'd be able to cope after tonight.

'Right then, goodnight, Mary, and I'm so sorry,' he said kindly, laying a hand briefly on her shoulder.

'She's going to take it badly, I know she is, she's in a daze,' Nell whispered as Alfred went down the lobby.

'Don't worry too much about her, she'll pull herself together in a day or two.'

Nell didn't speak. Pull herself together! In a day or two! How could he be so insensitive? With a sinking heart, she added his insensitivity to the list of reasons why she wasn't happy in her marriage.

She cried herself to sleep that night but awoke in the early hours with a dull dragging pain in her abdomen. She tossed and turned but the pain kept her awake.

At last she got up slowly and quietly: she didn't want to disturb Mam. The lino felt cold to her bare feet. As she pulled herself upright she felt the warm sticky substance flow from her. She wasn't due her monthlies yet. What was happening to her? She sat down gingerly on the edge of the bed.

'Nell, what's the matter?'

'Oh, Mam, I didn't want to wake you.'

'I was awake, luv.'

'Mam, I'm bleeding and it seems to be getting worse.'

Instantly Mary was out of bed and had lit the lamp.

'Oh, God! Nell, you're in a terrible state. Get back into bed, I'll go and get some towels and newspaper. Is it "that time"?'

'No. Why doesn't it stop, Mam?' she gasped.

'I don't know, luv, but let me fix you up and I'll go for the doctor.'

'You can't go out at this hour, there's no streetlights and anyway you know he won't come.'

Mary thought hard. 'I'll go for Mrs Hannigan. She'll come out and she'll probably know more about it than the doctor anyway.'

Nell was shivering when Mary arrived back with the midwife.

'Mrs Hannigan, what is it?' Nell begged. She was still losing a lot of blood and she was in agony now and terribly frightened.

'Were you expecting, Nell?'

'No! No, I wasn't. At least I don't think so. I didn't miss last month. I keep a note because . . .' She couldn't bear to think that she might have lost a baby, even though it may only have been a mere speck. Not that on top of losing Da.

'Well, girl, it's bed rest. Complete bed rest with your feet propped up so they're higher than your head.'

'Will that stop it?' Mary asked anxiously.

'It should do. It might take a day or so but if it doesn't she'll have to see a doctor or go to the hospital.'

'I'm not going into hospital! What about you, Mam, and Alfred?'

'Let's pray you don't have to go. It's probably the shock of what happened to your da, God rest him!' the midwife soothed.

'But Alfred?' Nell persisted.

'Alfred can just see to himself!' Mary said firmly.

Chapter Thirteen

───◆◆◆───

CHRISTMAS WOULD BE VERY different this year for all of them, Nell thought wistfully as she rolled out the pastry for the mince pies. These would probably be the last she would make. Flour and fat were obtainable but the ingredients for the mincemeat weren't. She was determined that she would make it one of the best Christmases ever. They would all need cheering up, especially Mam. The news of the sinking of the *Athenia* had been greeted with outrage, fury and determination to see justice done even if it took years.

There had been many men from Liverpool aboard and there had been memorial services throughout the city – but no funerals. The bottom of the ocean was their grave.

Father Mannion had said a special Mass and it had been touching to see the church packed to capacity and know that all those people were praying not just for Jack Callaghan, but for the family as well. Mam had seemed to draw strength and comfort from it all but it had made Nell thoroughly miserable and depressed.

She had given the house a complete going over and despite Alfred's protests had bought decorations and a tree. He was not very happy about Mam and Teddy coming here for Christmas dinner but she had been adamant.

'Mam is worn out when she gets home. I know she'll have a break on Christmas Eve, seeing that it's Sunday, but she'll be rushed off her feet on Saturday. She has to work now and she won't feel like cooking Christmas dinner for just herself and Teddy.'

'I suppose you're right,' he'd answered grudgingly.

When the pies were cooked she'd take some to Mam's and she'd make up the fire in the range and set the table. It was the least she could do and there was nothing else to do here at home. Except Alfred's tea but that wouldn't take long.

But at least in the outside world everything had slowly got back to normal, she reflected as she sat on the tram. People were calling it the 'phoney war', for nothing had happened. Of course the blackout was rigidly enforced. Alfred went out religiously at seven o'clock each night, on his fire warden's duties, returning at half past eleven for his cocoa, tired and often irritable. She knew that he secretly thought she had had a miscarriage but she was certain she hadn't, although she really didn't know what had caused the haemorrhage. The bleeding had stopped after she'd spent two days and nights in bed. Time on her own had been the last thing she'd needed. Too many empty hours to brood on her da's death.

As she alighted from the tram she spotted Florrie Ford walking along with her shopping bag.

'Are you just going out?' she asked.

'No, luv, I'm going 'ome. 'Ardly anythin' in the flamin' shops, now that I can afford it. I've never 'ad so much money in me life, what with Richie in steady work on the docks an' our Mavis and Jean and Bella working an' the lads sending 'ome money. Just my flamin' luck that there's 'ardly anythin' ter buy. Mind you, I went ter Sturla's an' got some bits an' pieces fer the 'ouse, an' Richie an' me went ter the second-'and shops and bought some furniture. Come in with me, Nell, an' I'll show yer.'

'I will. I'm going in to see to the fire for Mam before she comes home from being out with the barrow – I brought some mince pies.'

'Do yer know, Nell, I 'aven't 'ad a mince pie in years. Couldn't afford the stuff ter make them or the time an' no decent oven.'

Nell smiled. 'You make the tea and we'll have a couple before I start.'

She looked around Florrie's kitchen, pleasantly surprised. There was indeed a change in the room. Previously there had been bare walls and floor, very little furniture and no home comforts. Now there was a rag rug on the floor, two second-hand grubby winged armchairs and a dresser. And there were now chairs around the table instead of the wooden form, and, on occasion, orange boxes. There were also heavy curtains at the window.

'Oh, doesn't it look great?' she enthused.

'I don't know I'm born, girl. And we've got blankets on the

beds instead of piles of old coats an' rags.'

Nell stripped off her coat, hat, scarf and gloves while Florrie made the tea.

'Have you a plate or something we can put these on?'

Florrie went to the dresser and took down a chipped blue and white delftware plate.

'Is Tommy glad to be home?' Nell asked.

'Sometimes I think he is and sometimes he's not.' Nell handed the plate to Florrie who took a mince pie.

'I know Mam's glad to have Teddy back.'

'I don't know what that woman did with them but that lad's changed beyond all recognition!'

'I know what you mean, Mam says the same thing. They're quieter, more polite and he even gets washed without having to be nagged at.'

'Our Tommy washes 'is 'ands before 'e 'as 'is meal, would yer believe! I used ter 'ave ter drag 'im inter the scullery an' yer should 'ave 'eard the cursing out of 'im.'

'Teddy said it was a big house, with a garden, and he used to go and help on the farm. Imagine him helping anyone, let alone a farmer, but he said it was interesting. I suppose it was better than hanging around street corners.'

'Don't expect it ter last, Nell,' Florrie said darkly. ''Ow's your Daisy?'

'All right, as far as I know. I wish she would speak to me. I could help her but she won't hear of it.'

'Stubborn an' ungrateful is what she is, Nell. Just like yer da was.'

Nell nodded. 'How is your sister-in-law?'

Florrie shook her head. 'She's taken it badly, luv. Cryin' all the time, depressed, can't pull 'erself tergether at all. God luv 'im, he was me brother but life goes on, Nell, it 'as ter.'

'I know,' she answered sadly.

She stayed longer with Florrie than she had intended and by the time she had built up Mary's fire, drawn the curtains, tidied up and set the table she realised she would be late home if she didn't get a move on. By now Teddy and Tommy would be home from school, which had reopened, and in Florrie's kitchen, probably doing a jigsaw puzzle, something neither of them would have contemplated before they were evacuated. She smiled to herself as she hurried towards the tram stop in Limekiln Lane. They had both been evacuated to a village not far from the small Welsh market town of Denbigh, where they'd gone to school. Obviously the kind Welsh ladies who had taken them in were far more strict than either Mam or Florrie, but as Florrie had said it probably wouldn't last. Still, it was a relief for Mam to know that Teddy was not running the streets until she got home.

'Here, Nell Callaghan, I want to talk to ye.'

She turned and found Maggie O'Grady confronting her, hands on her ample hips.

'Mrs O'Grady, how are you?'

'Wouldn't I be a damned sight better if my lad was being cared for properly.'

Nell's attitude changed. 'Daisy does the best she can.'

'Well, 'tis not good enough.'

'Look, I've no wish to get into an argument with you, but Daisy has to work, see to Joseph and Sam and try to keep that bit of a room going.'

'Sure, if she had been a decent wife that lad wouldn't be in the state he's in now,' the woman said belligerently.

'It's not Daisy's fault he got himself into that accident. And if you're so worried about him why don't you go and give her a hand?' Nell snapped. 'I don't hear of you putting yourself out. Now, I've a tram to catch.'

She turned away annoyed. The woman was just a lazy slattern. How dare she criticise Daisy. Oh, damn! she muttered as she saw the dim light from the hooded headlights of a tram pulling away from the stop. Now she'd have God knows how long to wait for the next one and the journey took so much longer in the blackout.

Alfred was home by the time she got back and she could see from his face that he wasn't happy.

'Alfred, I'm sorry I'm late,' she said breathlessly. 'I stayed with Florrie much longer than I intended to. You know how she can talk once she gets going. Then I had to go in and see to Mam's place, then I missed the tram because Mrs O'Grady collared me, complaining about Daisy.' She had taken off her outdoor clothes, whipped a cloth from the drawer and quickly spread it over the table.

Alfred, sitting stonily in his chair, was not to be placated. 'I can't see why you have to go to your mother's house and do her housework. Your place is here. I'm tired when I get home. It's a long day. I want to come in to a good fire and a meal on the table instead of a cold, dark, empty house.'

'I've said I'm sorry. I go to Mam's to help her a bit. Surely you don't mind that?'

He shook out his newspaper irritably. 'Aren't we having them here on Monday?'

'Yes, it's Christmas!' She pulled herself up from her tasks

annoyed. 'Just what is the matter with you, Alfred? You seem to have changed. You used to enjoy going to Mam's for your Sunday dinner before we were married.'

'There wasn't a war on then and you weren't my wife. I expect you to act like a wife now. In all respects.'

'Just what is that supposed to mean?'

'You know very well!'

She had had enough of this. 'You think I was pregnant, don't you?'

'I do, and in running up and down to your mother you lost it.'

'How can you think that? How can you blame Mam? It was the shock of losing Da that caused the . . . bleeding! How can you be so . . . so cold and cruel?'

'Because it was my child!'

'Oh, for God's sake, Alfred! I want children as much as you do, but I don't think I had a miscarriage.'

'But you'll never know for certain.'

She was horrified by his words. 'I don't . . . like what you do to me but I don't complain.'

'Like it or not, you'll put up with it until I have a son. I've given you everything! I took you from a slum and gave you a home that's a palace in comparison. You don't want for anything. You don't even have to go out and slave in some filthy dirty factory all day! If I hadn't taken you in you would have ended up like your sister!'

Nell was shaking with rage and humiliation. 'How dare you! How dare you tell me my home was little more than a shack! You were glad to come and sit in it and have your meal off Mam's table. How dare you criticise Daisy and me!'

'I dare because it's all true!'

'Do you honestly think any other girl would have married you?'

'I'm not talking about other girls, I'm talking about you, my wife.'

'You would never have got married, never even have had a chance of being a father, if it wasn't for me, if it wasn't for Mam. She stupidly thought you were a decent, sensitive man and she urged me to marry you. Now you don't want me to try to help her when she needs it.' She glared at him. 'Is this the true Alfred McManus we're seeing now?'

'I couldn't care less about what you or your mother think of me. This is my house, I took you in, I married beneath myself so I could have a son!' He got up and snatched his coat, muffler and bowler hat. 'I'll get something from the chip shop, then I'm on duty!'

The slamming of the front door made the cups rattle. Nell sat down at the table and dropped her head in her hands. He'd only married her because . . . because he looked on her as some sort of breeding machine! Did he care for her at all? He'd openly sneered at her family and her background. Was the quiet and courteous man they'd taken him for only a front? Had she just seen him in his true colours? She had been fond of him. She had hoped it would be enough – obviously it wasn't. She had married him to please Mam and because, if she were really truthful, she had been afraid of being left an old maid.

With a huge effort she got up and tried to push it all from her mind. There was nothing she could do about it. Any of it. She just had to get on with coping with the choice she'd made.

She had tidied up and had his cocoa waiting, wondering if he would come home at all. Just after eleven-thirty she heard his key in the lock. She took a deep breath, wondering what kind of mood he'd be in.

'Your cocoa's ready,' she said quietly.

'Thank you, I'll take it up with me. I'm tired,' he answered coldly.

'Alfred, please don't let us be quarrelling, not now, not for Christmas.'

He hesitated but finally gave a brief nod. 'I *am* tired.'

'Then take your drink upstairs. I'll be up in a few minutes.'

She had to make an effort for Christmas. After that? Well, she wouldn't think of that now. For once, she had plenty to do to keep her occupied.

She'd put up the decorations and dressed the tree with the cheap baubles and tinsel she'd bought. She'd also made some pretty things out of silver paper, pipe cleaners and odd bits of coloured wool that she'd fashioned into pom-poms. She wondered if this house had ever seen such festive preparations. She put up the holly and the wreath she'd bought was in the back yard. Alfred had said he always took a holly wreath to lay on his parents' grave. It was a time-honoured custom. She'd ordered the goose and had made the pudding and the cake. Mam would provide the vegetables and fruit. Nell had some little gifts for Teddy and a nice soft cardigan and a scarf and gloves set for her mam. For Alfred she had bought a new pipe, not too expensive so she couldn't be accused of being extravagant. She wondered if he would give her anything. Relations between them were still cool.

Mary and Teddy arrived at one o'clock.

'Happy Christmas, luv!' Mary said a little tearfully, hugging her. Then she kissed Alfred on the cheek.

'It's good of you to have us, Alfred.'

'You're family, Mary,' he said gravely.

Nell shot him a concerned look before handing Teddy his presents.

'I said no presents until after dinner,' Mary chided.

'Ah, Mam!' He looked to Nell for support.

'And very right too, Mary,' Alfred said to both Teddy and Nell's disappointment.

'I took some things up to Daisy after Mass,' Mary remarked. 'How is she?'

'Miserable and no wonder – but enough of that.' She pulled herself up short as she caught sight of the look on Alfred's face. 'Let me give you a hand, Nell.'

'No, everything's ready, Mam. Just sit at the table, all of you, I'll serve.'

'I'll wash my hands first,' Teddy said seriously.

Mary shook her head in amazement. 'I'm going to send him back to those people in Wales. Look at him. No going on and on about opening his presents, washing his hands; he even combed his hair and washed his neck before going to church!'

'They sound like sensible, responsible people,' Alfred said ponderously.

Nell looked at him again. He'd managed to imply by his tone that neither she nor Mam were sensible or responsible.

When the meal was over and Teddy had at last been able to open his gifts, Mary helped Nell clear up. Alfred had gone into the front room to read the book that had been Mary's gift.

'That's a very nice piece of jewellery he gave you, Nell,' Mary commented.

Nell fingered the small silver locket. 'It was his mam's.' She wondered was if it was some kind of peace offering.

'It's all been very nice. Very thoughtful.'

Nell looked at her mother gratefully. 'Thanks, I wonder if he appreciates all the work that goes into it.'

Mary shot her daughter a calculating glance. She had noticed a coolness between them.

'Do any of them?' She paused. 'Is there something the matter, Nell?'

Nell shook her head dismissively. 'Oh, we had a bit of an argument the day I was late back. That's all.' How could she explain to Mam that she felt sure he had married her just so he'd be able to have children? And she could never tell Mary that it had been partly to please her that she'd married him.

'I wish Daisy would let me do something to help her,' she fretted, to change the subject. 'Was she really miserable, Mam?'

'She was. The place was untidy, dirty, there was hardly anything to eat and she wasn't very happy that Teddy and I were coming here for dinner.' That was an understatement, Mary thought. Daisy had carried on and on about how Nell had everything. There would be good fires in her house, while she couldn't afford coal. There would be plenty to eat, while they had little. There would be gifts for everyone and she had nothing even to give Joseph.

'Oh, Mam, let me take some of this food up to her? I can't bear to think of her being so unhappy.'

'It would only make matters worse, luv.'

'Well, you take it.'

'She'll know where it came from.'

'Does that matter, Mam?'

'No, I suppose not.' She would force Daisy to accept it. It wouldn't be much, but it would help. Despite all her grumbling Mrs O'Grady had done nothing to help Daisy and Sam out for Christmas.

'It'll be your first wedding anniversary soon, Nell.' Mary wanted to take Nell's mind off her sister's plight.

'It will.'

'Do you think he'll take you out?'

'No, Mam. I don't think he's prepared to spend as much on me as when we were courting.' Her mind went back to those days. Had it really only been just over a year ago when he had taken her out for meals, to the music hall and bought her sweets? She was certain there would be nothing to mark their first year of marriage.

Chapter Fourteen

———

S HE HAD BEEN RIGHT. There was nothing planned, nothing mentioned about their anniversary. She was disappointed but it made her think more deeply about the situation she now found herself in. He had made no advances towards her. He had been polite but the easy way they had of talking had gone. She felt very lonely and unhappy. It was no use trying to talk to her mam. Mary had very definite views on the sanctity of marriage vows. Sometimes she couldn't understand her. She'd put up with all Da's selfishness and irresponsibility but she had never threatened to leave him. She had had to work hard to put meals on the table while he had been very well fed indeed and scarcely contributed a penny towards it. There were times when she'd hardly had a shoe to her feet while he had spent his money on flash clothes. Mam never took a drink as many women did to alleviate the worries of everyday life. Da had spent most of his money on liquor. Mam had resigned herself to all that because of the vows she'd taken

– for richer for poorer, for better for worse. Daisy's life must be hell and yet time after time Mam had sent her back to Sam.

She had shopping to do, she thought tiredly. Things were getting scarce. Rationing was having an effect on everyone's lives. She would have to queue for the things she needed and it would probably take all morning. She didn't relish standing in the freezing cold of a winter's morning, but it had to be done. She wouldn't give Alfred the opportunity to criticise her again. There would be no complaints about how she ran the house.

It was freezing. The wind had an icy edge to it. The sky was a dark grey that held the threat of sleet or snow. She wrapped her scarf around her neck and drew her coat closer. Maybe she'd get the tram and go and get her shopping along Great Homer Street and Scotland Road. It would make a change, she was bound to see people she knew and things would be cheaper.

Everywhere was starting to look more drab. Houses and shops needed a coat of paint but people had neither the time, money, nor inclination to be bothered. Other things were more pressing. The women, their coats and shawls pulled tightly to them and headscarves knotted securely under their chins, all wore worried, preoccupied expressions. There were fewer cars and vans on the streets; the trams had hooded headlights and wire mesh over their windows. She felt depressed as she got off the tram and walked towards the junction of Great Homer Street. The first familiar face in the queue belonged to Minnie Harris who had been at school with her and who now had four young children clinging to her skirt.

'Is this the queue for Pegram's?'

'It is and God knows how long it will be before we get served.'

'You're so lucky, Minnie, with all of these,' she said, bending down to chuck them under their chins.

'Lucky! He only has to glance at me and I'm in the club again! I heard you did well for yourself.'

'That depends on how you look at it. I wish I had kids.'

'You've plenty of time, Nell, don't rush. You'll get no peace when you do have any. Tessa, will you let go of me, I can't move!' she said wearily, edging forward in the queue. 'That's a nice coat, Nell.'

It was a good coat. She'd found it in Blacklers and told Alfred that it was a very good buy. It would last for years. She noticed that the one Minnie wore was almost threadbare and too short in the sleeves. Her wrists were red raw with cold; she had no gloves or hat. Then Nell looked at her lovely children. Oh, she knew her school friend would say she would gladly swap with her, but would she really?

'I'm going up to get my veg from Mam.'

'I was sorry to hear about your da. We all were. It was shocking.'

'Thanks, Minnie.'

'My feller's in the Army. At least now I get a steady wage I can work around. Before we never knew from day to day where the money was coming from.'

'Where is he?'

'Training somewhere down south. He says it's great. It probably is, he doesn't have to look after this lot or stand for hours in the cold for food.'

'Alfred's a foreman on the docks. Reserved Occupation. But he's an ARP warden too.'

'You're lucky. So's your Daisy.'

'Daisy? Lucky? She's worn out looking after him and the baby.'

'At least she's got him with her. Who knows when all this will end and if our Alfie will come through it? I worry myself sick over him.'

Nell thought she must really love Alfie Harris, even though she complained about how hard her life was.

At last she got served with the few ounces of bacon, flour and sugar she was entitled to and after paying and putting the bags in her basket she turned to Minnie.

'I'm off now. See you again, Minnie. It's been great talking to you. Take care.'

'Tarrah, Nell, you take care too.'

She walked briskly up the wide thoroughfare, her feet so cold she could hardly feel them. Poor Mam having to get up so early, trudge up to the market and push the barrow back here.

Mary was stamping her feet and blowing on her fingers.

'I'm perished with the cold, Nell!'

'I don't wonder. I've been standing in the queue in Pegram's for ages. It's bitter.'

'We'll have snow before the day is out, see if we don't.'

'I wouldn't be surprised. Mam, if it does snow please don't go out in it tomorrow.'

'How can I do that? I've a living to earn and it's getting harder. There's not much to be had. Did you want serving or is this a social call?'

'I'll have some of those sprouts and a couple of pounds of potatoes. Have you any carrots?'

'A few.'

'Give me them. I'm making scouse. That'll warm Alfred up.'

'How are things?' Mary asked, weighing out the vegetables and tipping them into the hemp bag Nell carried for that purpose.

'Fine, Mam.' Nell rummaged in her purse and passed the coins over. 'Look, I'll take over while you go and get a cup of tea and something to eat in Maggie Black's cannie.'

'You will not. A well-dressed girl like you ruining her clothes dishing out mucky vegetables!'

'Mam, go on. I mean it!'

Reluctantly Mary went and Nell sighed. Standing here for a few minutes wouldn't harm her. She could go home to a good fire and a hot meal. Mam, she was certain, wouldn't have had any breakfast.

She served a few customers, the last of whom had just turned away when she saw Daisy coming towards her.

'Where's Mam?' she demanded.

'I told her to go to Maggie Black's and get something to warm her up,' Nell replied, taking in the old shawl her sister wore over her skirt and jumper. Joseph was wrapped in its folds, asleep.

'Yes, well, you obviously don't need warming up, not with the good coat on your back and the hat and scarf.'

'Daisy, please don't start! I'd give you the coat off my back if you'd take it!'

'How long will Mam be?'

'Not long. Was there something? Can I help?'

Daisy eyed her evasively. 'No.'

'Look, take the rest of this stuff. I'll pay for it. Please, Daisy, take it?'

Daisy faltered. She'd come to ask Mam for money. She had none and there was no fire and not a scrap to eat.

'Please? For Joseph's sake?'

Daisy nodded. It would help. They could have blind scouse. She had no money for meat.

Nell took the vegetables out of her own bag, then began to strip the remains of Mary's stock from the barrow and empty it into the bag for Daisy. Suddenly she felt weak and dizzy and leaned heavily on the barrow.

'What's up with you?' Daisy asked, a little surprised.

'Nothing. I'll be fine, just give me a minute or two and . . . Oh, God! Oh, no!'

'Nell, for heaven's sake what's wrong?' Daisy was thoroughly alarmed now. She'd never seen Nell look so pale.

'I'm . . . I'm losing blood again!'

'Losing bloody? Again?'

'Daisy, go and find Mam, quickly!'

She clung to the side of the barrow. It was happening again!

Mary came rushing back, a piece of a pasty in her hand.

'Nell, Daisy said it's happening again.'

'It is, Mam. I wasn't even doing anything strenuous. I felt a bit dizzy and then . . . Oh, what am I going to do?'

Mary was afraid. This wasn't normal. 'Daisy will stay with you while I call the ambulance.'

'No! No, I'm not going to hospital, Mam!' she cried.

'Nell, you'll have to! Do you want to bleed to death here on the street?'

'It'll stop, Mam. It will! It did last time. Just get me home and I'll go straight to bed. I promise.'

Mary was firm. 'No. This isn't right, Nell. You've got to get it seen to. Daisy, get that bit of a box, she can sit on it.'

Daisy did as she was told and helped Nell to sit down. She'd heard nothing about the first time this had happened. Her eyes widened as she saw the bright stain on her sister's coat and the trickle of blood that was forming a small pool on the cobbles. She'd never seen anything like this. 'You'd better listen to Mam and get it sorted out, Nell,' she said sullenly.

A small crowd had gathered by the time the ambulance arrived. Mary insisted on going with her and Daisy promised to take the barrow back to Portland Street.

'She's very pale, Mam. Will she be all right?'

'You'd be pale too, Daisy, if it was you. I hope to God they can help her.'

'I'll have to go after I've taken this home. Mam, I came . . . to see if you could lend me a few shillings for coal.'

Mary delved into the pocket of her apron. 'Here, luv, take this. You get yourself something to eat from Maggie. You look half starved.'

'Mam, it's not a miscarriage! I know it's not, it can't be!' Nell cried in the ambulance.

'Hush, luv, don't worry about that,' Mary soothed, squeezing her hand.

She was taken to a small white-tiled room in the Women's

Hospital in Catherine Street. Mary was initially refused entry into the room.

Nell lay rigid on the narrow iron-framed bed, dizzy and weak and tired, scared of what was happening to her and even more afraid of what lay ahead. When the middle-aged doctor appeared she answered all his questions carefully.

He looked over his spectacles at her. 'I think from what you've told me, Mrs McManus, that an operation is warranted.'

'No! No!' Nell cried, terrified.

'Calm yourself, young woman. It isn't going to kill you, but these haemorrhages will if they continue.'

'Will . . . will the bleeding stop then? After the operation?' she asked timidly.

'Yes. You should have no more problems. So we'll have no more hysterics,' he finished brusquely.

She lay back on the pillows. She had no choice. She was still frightened. She'd never been in hospital in her life and the people she'd known who had been admitted seldom came out, except feet first. She tried to fight down her panic. She was young and strong. She would be fine afterwards. How could she defy a man of such importance?

'How much will it cost?' she asked.

He looked at her over his spectacles again. 'If you have the means to pay you will receive a bill, if not then you won't be penalised.'

She didn't know what 'penalised' meant; she assumed it meant that it could be free, but Alfred had 'means' so he would have to pay. It might be worth it if it cleared up whatever was wrong with her.

'Can I see my mam, please?'

'Her mother is in the waiting room, sir,' the sister informed him.

He nodded. 'But it will have to be a very brief visit.'

Mary's heart sank when she saw Nell.

'Oh, Mam! Mam, I've got to have an operation and I'm so scared!'

Mary took her in her arms. 'Hush, luv, don't worry. You'll come through it. If they think it's the right thing to do.'

'He – the doctor – said the bleeding would kill me, but, Mam—'

'He knows best, Nell. He's the authority on it. They'll take good care of you here. Hush now, luv. I'll get word to Alfred and we'll come in later on.'

She stayed and Nell grew calmer until the sister came to tell Mary she had to leave.

'Remember, Nell, they know what's best.'

First she had to submit to an embarrassing and painful internal examination. Then she was changed into a white hospital gown. Her hair was tied back and she was given a sedative. The last thing she remembered was the face of the sister and being asked to confirm her name.

When she came round everything was misty, as though fog filled the room. She could hear voices, far away but coming closer. She struggled to get up but then cried out in agony.

'Lie still, girl, you'll burst open the stitches!' a clipped feminine voice instructed as she was pushed back.

'Lie still!' The voice commanded again.

'What . . . what happened? Why . . . is there so much pain?'

'You've had an operation. You were brought in as an emergency, don't you remember?'

Things began to come back to her. 'Mam! Where's Mam?'

'Your mother has gone home. She will be back later, with your husband. I'm going to give you an injection now and you must rest.'

She drifted in and out of sleep, sometimes remembering where she was and at others confused. It was dark when she finally came to enough to realise what had happened. A small electric light bulb glowed from the ceiling and her mother and Alfred were sitting beside the bed.

'Mam!' she croaked hoarsely.

'I'm here, Nell, and so is Alfred. We've been out of our minds with worry over you.'

'How do you feel now, Nell?' Alfred asked. He'd been very alarmed to see Mary waiting for him at the dock gate and even more alarmed when she'd informed him of the reason.

'It hurts and I'm a bit dizzy.'

'That's the medicine, luv.'

'How long will I be in here?'

'The sister said about two or three weeks. It was quite a serious operation.'

'Can't I go home before then?' she pleaded. Two or three weeks! She'd go crazy.

'No, luv, they know best,' Mary replied.

'Your mam's right. You'll have to do exactly as you're told, Nell,' Alfred added.

She felt so tired and sleepy again. 'But I will be fine now?'

'Of course you will, luv,' Mary soothed. Despite her

encouragement she'd been terrified that Nell might die on the operating table.

'I think we'd better go and let her get some sleep, Mary,' Alfred said, anxious to get out of the place. With their smell of disinfectant mixed with ether, hospitals made him feel sick.

Mary patted her hand. 'He's right. You get a good night's sleep, luv, and we'll be back to see you tomorrow.'

Nell tried to argue but found she had no strength. She slept fitfully. She woke once to find a young doctor bending over her. The next time it was the sister and then a nurse, until the winter daylight filtered into the room through the window high up in the wall. She felt very sore, her throat hurt and her mouth was dry.

'Here, drink this. I bet it's the first cup of tea you've had in a while,' the nurse said kindly, helping her to sit up.

'Oh, that hurt!' she cried.

'It will do for quite a while. Drink up, we'll have to have everything spick and span before Matron's inspection. She's a holy terror, and so is Mr Thornton the surgeon who did your operation! We'll all get it in the neck if there's as much as a crease in the bedclothes!'

She drank the tea and allowed her hands and face to be washed. Her hair was brushed, the sheets changed, the white cotton bedspread smoothed out. It was only then that she realised how big a scar she would have on her abdomen.

'Don't worry, it will fade with time,' the nurse had reassured her.

'I didn't think . . .'

'It's a serious operation, and you're only young but it had to be done.'

'I will be all right now though, won't I? I mean . . .' She bit her lip.

'Of course you will. Now, don't move a muscle before Himself and Matron arrive and don't for God's sake ask for a bedpan or I'll be killed!'

Nell managed a smile.

She was very apprehensive when the little group arrived. She thought wryly that the nurse was right. Matron looked to be a real dragon.

She was asked a few questions but mainly they talked about her as if she wasn't there at all. She wondered if she should ask whether everything had gone well. It was her body after all.

'Sir, may I . . . can I ask . . . ?'

'Yes, Mrs McManus?' The tone was cold and clipped.

She quailed a little before the great man's gaze. 'I will be . . . fine now? I mean . . . I will be able to have . . . babies?'

He looked at her askance. 'Babies! Mrs McManus, you have had a hysterectomy. I had to take the womb away. I'm afraid you will not be able to have children. Now you must rest. Proceed, Matron, please.'

She felt cold. Icy cold. What had he done to her? Taken the womb away! And no babies! She would never be able to have children now! She lay back, staring up at the ceiling, the tears slowly trickling down her cheeks.

Chapter Fifteen

W HEN MARY ARRIVED IN the late afternoon Nell was still lying staring at the ceiling.

'Nell, are you feeling better today?'

Nell couldn't reply.

'Nell, luv, what is it?' Mary was very concerned.

'I . . . I . . . asked him if I would be all right to have . . . babies.'

'And?'

'Oh, Mam! Mam!'

'Nell, for God's sake, what's wrong?'

'He said . . . he said I'd never be able to have babies now. Not after a hysterectomy. They had to take the womb away. Oh, Mam, I wish I was dead!'

Suddenly all the shock and heartbreak she'd suffered burst forth and she was racked with uncontrollable, juddering sobs. All she'd ever wanted was a home of her own, a good husband and children. Now the only thing left was a roof over her head and even that looked precarious. What meaning was there to life any more? Why had no one *told* her? It was too late now. Too late for everything.

Mary was horrified. They should have told her before the operation! Why hadn't they told her? Was it because if she'd known she would have refused treatment and maybe died? She took the distraught girl in her arms. Poor, poor Nell. She had so longed for a child of her own. They were not going to get away with this. She wanted answers.

When Nell was a little calmer Mary stood up. 'I'm going to see someone about this. Will you be all right, luv?'

Nell nodded and lay wearily down.

'Can you tell me why she wasn't told before this hyst . . . hyst . . . operation that she would never be able to have children?' Mary demanded of the sister.

The woman looked rather taken aback. 'It was assumed that she would know. It *is* a hysterectomy she's had.'

'Well, she didn't know and now she's broken-hearted. Can I see the doctor in charge?'

Sister looked horrified. 'No one ever asks to see Mr Thornton. You have to understand that he is a very import-ant man with little time to spare to talk to . . . relatives. He must have had a very good reason to do an emergency hysterectomy. Your daughter must have been in grave danger of dying. Now, I have work to do, even if you do not.'

Mary felt exhausted. What was the use arguing? What else could the man tell her that Sister hadn't? It probably *had* been done to save Nell from dying and it was obvious that she'd never get to speak to the great Mr Thornton. She was worried to death about both her daughters, and she felt far from well herself. She was always so tired these days and the pain in her back was getting worse. Maybe she'd have to see a doctor about it, but then look at what a doctor had done to Nell, one far more senior than a Dispensary doctor at that.

She tried to comfort Nell until the sister appeared and told her she must now leave.

'I'll be back with Alfred. Try and get some sleep, luv.'

Nell looked up at her mother with anguished eyes. 'Alfred! Mam, what about Alfred?'

She had tried to dismiss it from her mind. He'd only married her for one reason. Oh, God, what would he say now?

'I'll tell him if you like,' Mary said.

'Oh, would you? It'd be such a relief.'

'Of course I will. Now rest.'

When Mary got outside the coldness of the wind took her breath away and she stopped and leaned against the wall. What *was* Alfred going to say? Poor Nell was so devastated that she'd had to try to alleviate her burden, by offering to tell him. He had promised to call for her and they would then go to the hospital. She would tell him then.

It was bitterly cold outside but in Mary's kitchen it was warm and quiet. She'd taken Teddy in to see Florrie who had been as shocked and upset over Nell's predicament as Mary was herself.

'They're a law unto themselves, them fellers! Treat yer like dirt, they do. Which of us round 'ere knows what that hys . . . hyst . . . means? Oh, God, the poor little luv, it's a flamin' disgrace.'

'I know, Florrie, but you can't even get to see him, let alone ask him.'

'What'll she do?'

'God knows there's not much she can do. Get on with her life like we all have to, Florrie,' she'd answered.

Alfred arrived fifteen minutes early. He was a stickler for punctuality, she thought.

'I thought you'd be ready, Mary,' he said grumpily. He'd had a bad day. The men had been surly and uncooperative, he'd had a row with one of the other foremen and he'd gone home to a cheerless empty house with no meal on the table and no clean shirts. At least before he'd been married Mrs Grenan, his daily help, left the house clean, tidy and warm, with his meal in the oven and his shirts on hangers in the bedroom.

'It won't take me a minute. Sit down, I've got something to tell you.'

'About Nell?'

She nodded. For hours she'd been wondering what exactly she should say to ease the blow for him – and it would be a blow, she knew that. He'd wanted children as much as Nell had done.

'What about her? Is she all right?'

She took a deep breath. 'No, Alfred, she's not. Oh, she's recovering from the operation. Medically there's no serious problem now.'

'Then what's the matter with her?' He wished she'd just get on with it and they could get the hospital visit over.

'It was a serious operation, she might have died, but . . . but when she asked . . . they said . . .' She paused. Oh, there was no fancy way of dressing it up. 'She can never have children. They had to take . . . everything away.'

The room seemed to grow colder, he thought. It couldn't be true, it couldn't! She was a young, strong, healthy woman, she'd have been a good mother to his children. Now . . . now she would never give him the son he wanted so much. A slow anger began to spread through him. Maybe she'd had this condition before he married her? Before he'd even started to court her? Maybe they'd known and hadn't told him? He glared at Mary. He'd taken a slummy into his home and given her everything and now . . .

He got to his feet. 'You'd better go on your own.'

Taken aback, she stammered, 'Why?'

His voice rose. 'Because I don't want to see her! You knew, didn't you?'

'Alfred, what do you mean? Knew what?' She was still confused.

'That she had this . . . this . . . condition.'

'Holy Mother of God! I never knew anything about this "condition", as you call it! She's heart-broken. How can you be so cruel?'

'Cruel! I'm not the one who's cruel, she is. She knew, she bloody well knew how much I wanted a son! I gave her everything! Well, I'm not going to go on supporting her. She deceived me. She can come back here to live!'

Mary was shocked to the core. 'You . . . You're telling me you only married her for . . . for children? That you care nothing for her? She's your wife! You were glad enough to marry her and make your vows before God! How can you just abandon her?'

He was raging. Everything was falling apart. 'Quite easily. She's made a fool of me. I'll not have her over the doorstep again!'

Mary drew herself up tall, her eyes dark with anger. 'Get out! Get out! I'll take care of her, as I have always done! Take yourself back to that empty mausoleum you call a home! It was my poor Nell who made it a home! Get out, I never want to see your face again, Alfred McManus!'

'That suits me fine!' he snapped.

When he'd gone Mary sat down and stared into the fire. She was shaking with rage. How was she going to tell Nell that her husband no longer wanted her? That she'd have to come back and live here? Oh, how she had misjudged him. How were they to know that beneath that pleasant and polite exterior was a calculating, scheming, selfish man. No wonder Nell hadn't been happy. That's what the poor girl had tried to tell her and she'd just brushed Nell's predicament aside. Told her to stop complaining. Maybe Nell knew. Maybe he'd told her. Either way she could understand why Nell hadn't wanted to tell him herself. Oh, it would serve him right that he would have no children. He wouldn't have been much of a father anyway. But she'd better make an effort to get to the hospital, she thought. Nell would be getting worried. Painfully, Mary struggled to her feet once more.

Nell knew by her mother's expression, and the fact that she was alone, that something was very wrong.

'Where's Alfred?'

'He's not coming,' Mary replied flatly.

'Why?'

Mary took her hand. 'This is going to be hard, Nell, but . . .'

'But he doesn't want me . . . now.'

'Oh, Nell, luv.'

Nell turned her face to the wall. Ever since her mother had left she'd been going over and over things in her mind. Things Alfred had said. Things left unsaid.

'I know that, Mam, and in a way I'm relieved. I was beginning to hate living there. Hate living with him, trying to pretend everything was fine . . . with him, and all the time I hated it, loathed it. I clenched my fists and bit my lip to stop myself telling him to . . . stop. He never loved me, Mam.' She paused, gathering her strength, then went on. 'He told me . . . There was a huge row and he told me he only married me for . . . children. He called me a slummy. Said he'd married beneath himself. That he'd given me everything. Mam, he despised us all. I'm well out of it. That place was never home to me. I felt as though I was just minding things. Nothing belonged to me. It's all for the best, Mam.'

Mary was distraught. So Nell had known. She couldn't even imagine how unhappy the girl must have been. And she was so young. She reached out for her daughter. 'I feel so responsible. I urged you to marry him. I just didn't *know*.'

Nell turned to look at her mother.

'Mam, it was my choice, I married him of my own free will. Nothing was your fault. I'll get better, Mam. But if only . . .'

Mary squeezed her hand. 'Don't think about it, luv. Just concentrate on getting well and coming home. Home to Portland Street. I'm not offering you luxury. You'll miss things. You know it's not as comfortable or well furnished as—'

'That doesn't matter, Mam. It's what you make of it that turns a house into a home and it's always been my home. It's not a show house like *his* – and always will be.'

'We'll manage, luv.'

'We will, Mam.' She closed her eyes. 'I'm tired now.'

'I'll go and let you get some sleep. Oh, Nell, it's been a terrible day for you.'

'It has but . . . I'll survive.'

Mary's heart was heavy as she left the hospital. All she'd ever wanted for Nell and Daisy was a good husband and a decent home. Now each was trapped in an unhappy marriage and all hope for both of them seemed to be gone.

When she reached home she was surprised to find Daisy in the kitchen.

'What's the matter? You've not left him again?'

'No. I wish I could. I hate him, Mam! I really hate him!'

'Now what is it?' Mary said wearily, sitting on the sofa.

'His mam came round, on the bounce. Complaining I do nothing for him! She should talk! What did she ever do for him?'

'Did she just come to visit?'

'You know she hardly sets foot in the place, so I told her if she wasn't satisfied then she could flaming well take him back with her! But oh, no, that was too much to ask for! She might have to do some work for a change.' Her mother-in-law's visit had caused another furious row and she was sick of it all.

'He's your responsibility, Daisy.'

'Oh, for God's sake, Mam, don't start on that again! How's Nell?'

'I was wondering when you would come to see how your sister is. She's had an operation.'

'She lost an awful lot of blood, Mam.'

Mary nodded. 'But she'll never be able to have children and you know how she envied you Joseph. And now he doesn't want her. He only married her to give him children. Oh, he's shown his true colours! When she comes out she'll be coming back here to live.'

Daisy looked incredulous. 'He's throwing her out? I always thought he was a cold fish. A real miserable old sod. Well, that will put her nose out of joint. She'll have to come off her high horse, live like the rest of us. Perhaps I'll get a bit of sympathy now.'

'Is that all you can say?' Mary demanded angrily.

'What do you expect me to say, Mam? She's had everything while I've had nothing but drudgery, poverty and hardship! She's had good clothes when I've just had an old shawl and broken-down shoes in the depths of winter. She hasn't had to stand for hours in a dirty old factory and then go home to a cold room, a mountain of washing and abuse from *him*!'

Mary shook her head. 'Can't you find some pity in your heart for her?'

'No, Mam, I can't. Kids aren't everything – they tie you down and plague the life out of you. And she's well rid of him! I can't get rid of Sam so easily.'

Mary sighed. She felt a hundred years old. 'Daisy, I'm not going down that road with you. I'm tired and my back is crucifying me.'

'Have you been to the Dispensary about it?'

'No. What good would that do? I'd be paying out money

to be told there's nothing wrong, except my age and occupation. It's the damp weather. It'll get better when spring and the warmer weather comes. Give me my purse.'

Daisy passed it to her and Mary took out five shillings.

'Here, get yourself something to eat on the way home and get some coal, I don't suppose there's much of a fire.'

'There never is.'

Mary passed a hand over her forehead. Her head was aching. It had been a terrible day for her too.

Chapter Sixteen

———◆———

'ERE NELL, LUV, GIVE me that shopping bag!'

Nell turned and saw Florrie Ford approaching.

'I'm fine, Florrie, really I am,' she protested.

'Yer know what they told yer at the 'ospital. No 'eavy lifting or carryin' an' that bag must weigh a ton. Give it 'ere.'

Nell smiled and handed it over. It was two months since she'd had the operation that had ruined her life and she was still trying to come to terms with it. She hadn't seen Alfred at all, nor did she have any wish to. Mary had gone and collected her things before she came out of hospital. She'd obviously had another row with Alfred but she wouldn't reveal a word about it.

'Yer'll be a good while yet before yer're really fit an' well,' Florrie chided.

'I sometimes wonder if I'll ever be well again, Florrie.'

'Now, don't yer go thinkin' like that, luv. 'Ave yer 'eard from 'im at all?'

'No, and I don't want to either.'

Florrie shook her head. 'God, I can't get over it. I just can't fathom 'im at all. I said ter yer mam, "Mary, what's up with that feller?" 'E seemed so polite an' kind an' generous.'

'That's exactly how he "seemed". He fooled us all.'

'I told yer mam, that girl's been nursin' a viper to 'er bosom! That's exactly 'ow I put it.'

'And I agree, but now it's all over and I wish I could think of some way of getting out of the whole mess. I'm so tired of it.'

Florrie stared at her, shocked. 'Yer don't mean' – she dropped her voice – 'divorce?'

'Lord, no! It would kill Mam and I don't think I could stand something like that. Anyway, I don't think it's grounds for divorce.'

'It's a terrible thing, that divorce. Yer'd be excommunicated.'

'Let's not talk about it any more, please. How's your Maureen?' Florrie's eldest daughter had landed quite a catch for herself, an only son who lived with his widowed mother in a decent house in Everton. She had always been the quietest of Florrie's kids and Florrie was so proud of her. Everything that Maureen said or did was retold with delight and relish.

'She's great. Of course her feller's away training in the Army now but she says his mam writes to 'im every week. Yer know our Maureen was never a one with the readin' an' writin', so the old girl writes fer both of them.'

'Doesn't she mind that? Your Maureen, I mean. I bet she can't say what she really wants to tell him.'

'Oh, she doesn't mind that at all. All the letters are censored anyway.' Florrie frowned. 'It's a pity our Bella hasn't done so well but iffen she 'angs around with them lot from further down she'll go ter the bad! I'm fed up tellin' Richie ter take 'er in 'and. It's like talkin' ter the flamin' wall! 'E takes all this fire-watchin' an' ARP stuff very seriously; no time fer 'is family, like, but plenty fer war duties. And now 'e's lumbered me with his mam!'

'His mam?' Nell was surprised.

'Aye, old Rosie Ford. She can't manage fer 'erself now. Keeps gettin' dizzy spells. An' she's a right tartar, stubborn as a bloody mule! Why can't one of the others 'ave 'er, I asked 'im. 'Aven't I enough ter do? Aren't we overcrowded even with the lads away?'

'What did he say?'

Florrie looked annoyed. 'Nothing. Flamin' nothin'! 'E can be as stubborn as the old girl when 'e wants ter be.'

'When is she coming?'

'Next week. Well, two women inter one kitchen don't go, that's my motto, and it's my flamin' kitchen so she needn't think she's takin' over!' Florrie finished firmly.

When Nell finally got home she was relieved to see that the fire hadn't gone out. She hadn't intended to be out so long but there were queues for every shop she needed. She raked the ashes vigorously and backed the fire up with coal. The cold March wind rattled the window panes and she looked around and sighed. Mam didn't have much to show for all the years she'd been married. There were the bare essentials. A table and four chairs, none of which matched. The old sofa that sagged. A mesh-fronted food press; a scratched and marked old sideboard. There was a holy picture above the mantelshelf but no other ornaments. She wished Mam would let her work but she'd been adamant that Nell stick closely to the instructions the hospital had given her. Well, as soon as she could she'd get a job. There were plenty of them now with more and more men being called up.

She turned as she heard the back door open.

'Teddy, is that you?'

'Yes,' came the reply from the scullery.

'Don't bring that dog in if he's dirty. I've mopped out in here and I don't want to have to do it again.'

The lad came in followed by the comic-looking dog. She had to smile. He was a real scruffbag but he followed Teddy everywhere.

'Nell, can I tell you something?'

'What have you done?'

'Nothing! It's . . . well it's sort of a secret.'

'Out with it then! I know your kind of "secrets".'

'Me and Tommy are going down to the Main Post Office in Victoria Street on Saturday.'

She was surprised. 'What for?'

'Tommy said he'd heard that they take lads of our age as telegraph boys – you know, delivering the telegrams.'

'Don't you have to wait until you're fourteen?'

He looked evasive. 'Not really.'

'Oh, I see, you're going to lie about your age.'

'It's only sort of . . . stretching the truth a bit. We're fed up with school. We want to *do* something! And I'd get a wage too.'

Nell eyed him suspiciously. She could understand how he felt. 'Well, we could do with the extra money.'

'You won't tell Mam?'

'I won't,' she laughed. 'But don't take that dog with you or you'll not get a foot in the door! Now where are you going?'

'To tell Tommy.'

'Well, don't be all night. Mam will be in soon.'

The back door slammed. She'd have to keep it a secret from Mam until he got back on Saturday. Still, lying about your age to the Post Office was infinitely better than lying to join up. She looked around her. The table was laid, the fire burned cheerfully and she had a pan of soup on the range. She'd used everything she could get her hands on in the soup and she hoped it would last two days. She cut thick slices of bread. That would help to fill them up but there was no butter or margarine or even dripping to spread on it.

'Oh, that's a great fire, Nell. I'm perished,' Mary said as she hurried in, holding her hands out to the flames, still wearing the heavy black knitted shawl she always wore except for Sundays.

'Sit down and have a hot cup of tea, Mam. How was business?'

'Not very brisk. All I could get were potatoes and carrots and a few parsnips. All this "Dig for Victory" is making heavy inroads into my trade. People are digging up back yards to grow vegetables.'

'Then isn't it about time you gave it up? I'll get work and with what I hear you can earn these days, we'll manage.' There was also Teddy's wages, if he was taken on.

'We've had this out a hundred times. You're not well enough to work yet.'

'Oh, Mam! I feel great, I really do!'

'Nell, I'm too tired to argue.'

Nell looked closely at her mother and frowned. Mary had lost weight and it didn't suit her. It made her look older and more drawn.

'Mam, are you all right?'

'Of course I am. I'm tired. I'm not as young as I used to be. And my back's still bad.'

'Will you go to the Dispensary.'

'What's the use? It's just age.'

Nell was exasperated. 'Oh, Mam, I give up with you!'

'Nell, I'm fine. I'll manage, I always have done, so let that be an end to it. No more talk of dispensaries or doctors.'

Nell sighed. There was no use arguing when Mam was in this mood.

On Saturday morning Mary could hardly get out of bed, the pain in her back was so bad.

'You're staying in bed, Mam, and I'm going to send for the doctor!' Nell ordered.

'I'll be all right in a bit. Things have just sort of seized up.'

'No you won't, Mam! I'm going to send Teddy now.'

Nell found Teddy in the kitchen.

'Ah, Nell, I'm going into town, remember? The job?' he protested.

'You can go on your way, it will only take a minute. If I leave her she'll try to get up.'

She had tidied the kitchen, made up the fire and managed to find a cup and saucer that matched, for the doctor would be cold. It would warm him up and, besides, she wanted to speak to him privately.

Duncan McDonald was a big burly man with a shock of red hair who had turned down a lucrative position in favour of working with the poor and needy. He crossed to her bedside and lifted her hand, checking her pulse rate. It was normal, but she didn't look well at all.

'Now, Mrs Callaghan, what have you been doing to yourself?' he asked jovially.

'I'm sorry to drag you out. It's my back, Doctor. I can't get up, the pain's so bad.'

'Have you been doing any heavy lifting?'

'Doctor, you know I'm a barrow woman. I sell fruit and vegetables, when I can get them. I've been lifting and carrying nearly all my life.'

He nodded thoughtfully. 'Right then, let's see what's wrong. Nell, I'd like you to leave us, if you don't mind.'

He knew from experience that women like Mary Callaghan would say nothing about what really ailed them in the presence of their children, no matter how old they were.

Nell was worried but she nodded. She would definitely have a word with him before he went.

She busied herself with the kettle and teapot until she heard him come downstairs.

'I've a fresh pot of tea made, Doctor, and . . . well, I'd like to speak to you about Mam.'

He rubbed his chilled hands together. 'The tea will be welcome, it's a raw morning.'

'What's wrong with her? She's been complaining of her back for months but it's just got worse. She wouldn't go to the

Dispensary to see you. She said it was just her age.'

The doctor nodded. 'It is, partly, but I'd like her to see a specialist.'

'Oh,' Nell said, sitting down suddenly.

'Don't be alarmed, lassie, I don't think it's anything serious and you won't have to pay a penny more. It may turn out to be just arthritis.'

'Is she to stay in bed?'

'Yes. She can get up if she feels like it. I'm leaving some tablets for her and I'll send word as soon as I hear from Rodney Street.' He gulped the hot liquid down. 'Now, I'm away, thank you for the tea.'

Nell held out the two shillings and when he'd gone she sat down again and bit her lip. It didn't sound serious. Maybe it *was* arthritis – that was bad enough. But if so, why send her to see some fancy doctor in Rodney Street?

'Has he gone, Nell?' Florrie enquired, coming in the back way.

'Yes, just. Will you have a cup of tea?'

'Thanks, luv. What's 'e sayin' then?'

'He's sending her to see a specialist in Rodney Street,' Nell replied, handing her neighbour a cup.

'Well, who's goin' ter pay fer that? They charge a fortune.'

'I don't know, but he did say it wouldn't cost us another penny. It might turn out to be arthritis. He's left her some tablets.'

'Holy God! Isn't that bad enough? An' the weather's so flamin' damp, which doesn't help.'

'Leave those two gone to Victoria Street?'

'Oh, aye. Couldn't wait ter gerroff.'

'They did tell you they're going to lie about their ages?'

'They did an' I look at it like this: the pair of them will be fourteen in six months' time an' it's not as if they're going inter a trade. It will help with the money an' I might get some peace if 'e's got somethin' ter occupy him. Now, I'll just go up and see 'er. If there's anythin' at all I can do, Nell, yer just have ter ask.'

'Thanks, Florrie, I will.'

Teddy came in an hour later grinning like a Cheshire cat.

'I can see by your face that they took you on.'

'They did. They'll pay us ten and sixpence a week and give us the uniform and the bike.'

'You'll have to take time off school. They won't let you leave and it won't be easy riding all over the city day in and day out. You'll be out in all weathers too.'

'I know all that, Nell, but I don't mind really.'

'Well, I suppose it'll keep you out of trouble. I'll have to write to the headmaster and give some excuse for your being away so often.'

'You can say Mam needs me, she's sick.'

'I suppose I could. It's not stretching the truth too far but you'd better tell Tommy Ford that he can't use the same excuse otherwise we'll have the School Board round here to know what's going on.'

'Can I go and tell Mam?'

Nell frowned. 'No, I think it had better be me who tells her. She'd just get annoyed with you. I'm taking her dinner up to her, I'll tell her then. You get your good clothes off and take that dog for a bit of a walk or he'll drive us mad all day.'

Mary had tried three times to get out of the bed but each time the pain was so great that she fell back, gritting her teeth to stop herself from crying out. It was just arthritis, she'd told herself firmly. She'd be as right as rain after she'd seen this man in Rodney Street; he knew all about backs. Duncan McDonald was a good man. A man you could trust, and generous too. He'd more or less told her that he would pay any fees. She'd be up and about in no time.

'Here's your dinner, Mam.' Nell put down the bread board that was serving as a tray and helped to ease Mary into a better position.

'Don't worry about me, Nell, I'll be up and about in a few days.'

'He told me he was sending you to Rodney Street.'

'That's what I mean, Nell. When I've been up there and they sort it out I'll be back to work.'

'Mam, you're not going to push that barrow another day and I mean it.'

'And just how will we survive?' Mary demanded.

'I'll work. I'll take over the barrow and Teddy, well, he's got a job with the Post Office.'

'He's not old enough to work yet!'

'But he will be in six months' time. What difference will it make? He feels that he wants to help in some way.'

Mary scowled. 'Things aren't so bad that lads of his age need to find proper work. We haven't had an air-raid yet.'

'I know that, Mam, but if he wants to work then let him. And his money will be a help.'

Mary closed her eyes wearily. The pain was always there and it was sapping her strength. For the first time in her life she felt too tired and weary to pit her will against those of her children.

'Oh, I suppose he'll be all right, Nell.'

'He will and so will you, Mam, if you do as you're told. I'll go out with the barrow.'

'Ask for Harry Mercer at the market. I always deal with him and he'll give you good prices. But you'll just have to take what's on offer.'

'I will, Mam. Now get some rest.'

Chapter Seventeen

———◆◆◆———

MARY RECOVERED SLOWLY. IT had been the middle of April before she had been well enough to go the big house in Rodney Street, the Harley Street of Liverpool. She had been completely in awe of the orthopaedic consultant, but he had been very kind and everyone was very relieved when he pronounced that there was nothing seriously wrong, just something he called 'muscular strain'. She just needed to rest, and not to be lifting or dragging.

'You see, Mam. I told you,' Nell had said as they'd left.

'Yer'll 'ave ter do as yer're told, Mary,' was Florrie's pronouncement.

Over the following weeks Mary and Nell had had many arguments over the barrow but by July Mary had worn Nell down.

'You know as well as I do, luv, that fresh vegetables and fruit are getting very scarce. It's time to give it up, Nell, and get a job. I can manage the housework and the washing and ironing. I wanted better for you, Nell, anyway. I didn't want to see you having to be up at dawn and off to the market.'

'I know, Mam. But I thought that . . . well, the barrow was a sort of bequest Annie left us.'

'It was but it's served its purpose now. She wouldn't mind. In the name of God, what's the matter with that dog now?'

They both looked at the scruffy mongrel who was sitting under the table uttering short yelps.

'I don't know and I've enough on my mind without worrying about the dog. What kind of work will I try for?'

'Anything you can get, luv.'

'Nancy has just started in Munitions. She says the pay is great and it would be helping with the war effort. Even our Teddy's doing something useful.'

'Munitions is dangerous and dirty work, to say nothing of having to trail out of the city to Kirkby or Speke every day.' She glared, irritated, at the whining dog. 'Will you put that flaming animal out in the yard before he drives me completely mad!'

'Travelling wouldn't bother me, Mam. I need to earn a good wage to try and buy some of what we need. It'd be nice to have a few "luxuries".'

'I don't like you dealing with the fellers on the black market. Spivs and cheats with no sense of loyalty except to themselves.'

'Well, we'll need the money. We've just been eking out a living for months now. Let's have a cup of tea and we can think about which is the least distance for me to – oh, Mother of God!'

Nell's words were drowned out by the high-pitched wailing of the air-raid siren, a sound they'd hardly heard before that day.

Nell looked wildly about her. 'Mam, just grab your purse and I'll get what I can together, we'd better get to the shelter as quickly as we can.'

The sudden noise of the guns of the nearby anti-aircraft battery propelled them into action. Suddenly the kitchen door burst open and Florrie and her four youngest kids, followed by Richie's mam, crowded in.

'Oh, Jesus, Mary and Holy St Joseph! Mary, I'm scared witless!' Florrie cried.

'Florrie, for God's sake get out to the shelter!' Mary urged.

'I'm not goin' ter one of them places! I've told 'er not ter be such a bloody fool!' Rosie Ford snapped.

'What would *you* do with the stubborn old get?' Florrie fumed at Mary.

'Right, we've no time now to get to the shelter even if we run, and I can't do that!' Mary stated.

'But, Mam, what'll we do?' Nell asked.

'Under the stairs, everyone, including that whining fool of a dog.'

'The dog's no fool, Mary. They often 'as a sixth sense, I bet he could 'ear the planes before we did,' old Mrs Ford said sagely.

Florrie raised her eyes to the ceiling as they all crowded into the space under the stairs.

It seemed as though they had only just got settled in when the all-clear sounded.

'What the hell are they playing at, scaring folk like that,' Florrie said irritably, as she struggled out of the cramped cupboard.

'It must have been a false alarm or just a light raid, or even a raid on Birkenhead,' Nell answered shakily. The sound of the guns and the wailing of the siren had terrified her.

'Nell, make that pot of tea we were going to have before this flaming nonsense started,' Mary urged as she lowered herself wearily into a kitchen chair, feeling a little shaky herself and wondering if Teddy was all right.

'We'll have to be more organised than this,' Nell said as she poured the tea for all of them.

'Well, you take notice of me, girl, them street shelters isn't safe, we're better off under the stairs.'

Florrie glared at her mother-in-law. 'An' what can we get under the flamin' stairs? Nothin', that's what. 'Ow are we goin' ter 'ave a cuppa under there? Yer can't keep dashin' out into the kitchen.'

The old woman ignored her. 'You take more notice of that dog, Mary. 'E's got better 'earing than any of us.'

Mary thought Flossie was right about her mother-in-law. She *was* a stubborn, self-opinionated old woman. She hoped she wouldn't have to spend too long cooped up in confined spaces with her!

Teddy came home at teatime looking a bit pale.

'Were you all right, Mam, when the siren went?'

'Of course I was. We all went under the stairs.'

'I was out in it, I got to the public shelter in Dale Street just before the all-clear went.'

'Holy Mother of God! If I'd known that I would have been worried to death! Haven't you got any sense, Teddy Callaghan!'

Nell glared at her brother.

'I didn't have time, Mam!' he protested.

'Oh, get your tea before I box your ears, big as you are, for scaring me.'

Nell was washing the dishes when she saw through the tiny scullery window the yard door open and Daisy come up the yard with Joseph.

'How's Mam?' she asked Nell who was just untying her apron.

'Not too bad. Our Teddy upset her.'

'How?'

'By telling her he was out during the air-raid.'

'Daisy, is that you?' Mary called from the kitchen.

'It is, Mam. I came to see how you were and to tell you . . . something.'

Nell took Joseph on to her lap as Daisy sat down.

'So?' Mary demanded.

'So I met Brenda Thomas from around the corner, she's working out at Kirkby in a munitions factory and she gets four pounds a week! A week! And if you work nights it's five pounds! But day work would suit me fine.'

'That's what Nancy told me,' Nell added.

'God, what couldn't I do with money like that? Tomorrow morning I'm going to sign on.'

Mary looked anxious. 'How will you manage? It's miles away!'

'They lay on special buses and trains. I wanted to ask you,

202

Mam, if you'll look after Joseph for me? Mrs Flannagan just lets them all run wild, he's getting terrible and she won't be happy with me doing all the extra hours. If you're well enough, I mean.'

'Of course I will but what about Sam?' Mary looked concerned.

'Oh, don't worry about him, I'm going to sort him out.'

'Daisy, just what do you mean by that?' Nell asked, seeing the anxiety in her mother's eyes.

'Never you mind. It's none of your business,' Daisy snapped.

'Just as long as he's going to be looked after, Daisy. I know you need the money badly, so I'm not going to nag you.'

'Thanks, Mam. It was a bit frightening, wasn't it? The air-raid, I mean.'

'It was, let's hope and pray there won't be any more.'

'Mam, was it like this last time?' Nell asked, trying to keep off the subject of Daisy and Sam.

'No, luv, it wasn't. There were a few rocket-type things on London but it was different – more shocking in some ways, but at least there was no bombing of cities and towns.'

'Mrs Flannagan got some wool and knitting needles. She's going to knit balaclavas and scarves and gloves. She says our lads will need them come winter. I got the surprise of my life. I didn't even know she could knit.'

'Why don't you ask her to teach you, Daisy? Then you could do jumpers for Joseph.'

'Oh, Mam, what time do I have for knitting?'

Mary thought that there might come a time when they would all be forced to spend more time in the air-raid shelters.

Today the raid had been light but she was sure it would be followed by others. The Germans weren't going to give up so easily.

It was dusk, the heavy dusk of summer, when Daisy got back to Silvester Street, but she felt so much better. Brenda Thomas had been quite enthusiastic about work, lightly dismissing the fact that it could be dangerous. They had a great time, she said. It was like one big happy family. There was always something going on. You heard all the gossip and they often went on nights out together. It was hard work but no one minded that, after all they were making the ammunition for the lads to use.

'Why don't yer try, Daisy? The money's good. Four pounds a week,' Brenda had urged. And now she'd organised Joseph with Mam, both for this evening and long-term, there was no reason why she shouldn't give it a go.

As she'd walked home her resolve strengthened. She'd missed out on so much by having to marry Sam O'Grady and then having to be a nursemaid to him. It was time she thought of herself for a change. To hell with him! What right had he to tell her what she could or couldn't do?

Her face was set in hard determined lines as she went into the depressing room that she seemed destined not to be able to escape from.

'Where've you been?' Sam demanded. All his good looks had gone since the accident, and his muscles had wasted. He looked like an old man, she thought.

'To see Mam,' she snapped as she began to gather his clothes together.

'What the hell are you doing with my stuff?'

'I'm packing it,' she said, her lips set in a thin line as she stuffed things into a brown paper carrier bag.

'Packing? What the bloody hell do you mean by that? Is this some kind of a joke?'

Daisy turned on him. All her pent-up frustration and anger burst forth. 'No, it's not a bloody joke! I'm going to work in munitions. I'm going to have pals and go out to dances and parties. I'm going to enjoy myself the way I should have been doing except for you! I've bloody had enough of you! I hate you!'

'Christ! I've cursed the day I ever set eyes on you, you hard-hearted little slut!'

'If I'm a slut then it's your fault! I wasn't brought up to live like a bloody pig. You were and so now you're going back to that bloody pigsty you came from! Your mam can look after you because I've had enough!'

'My mam!'

'Yes, your bloody slattern of a mam. Let her clean you up and wait on you!'

She threw the carrier bag on to his lap, grabbed the two handles of the wheelchair and pushed it towards the door.

'You can say goodbye to living here. I'll do the place up when you're not here to make a mess of it.'

'What if Mam won't have me?' he asked sullenly. Suddenly all his will seemed to have gone.

'She's got no choice! I'm leaving you on her doorstep!'

'You bitch! You bloody little bitch! You ruined my life! Now you're deserting me.' He was almost crying, full of abject self-pity.

'And you ruined my life! You remember that! I don't care what happens to you now!'

She ignored the curious looks she received as she pushed him up the street. It was something she'd never done before but she didn't care what anyone thought. She was going to be well rid of him and then maybe she could catch up on all the fun and enjoyment she'd been missing for so long. She wouldn't have to worry about Joseph any more either. Mam would look after him properly, not like Mrs Flannagan who didn't care what any of the kids got up to and then wanted paying.

She hammered loudly on Mrs O'Grady's kitchen door, having pushed a silently furious Sam into the lobby.

'Daisy, why have ye the need to be knocking like that?' Maggie O'Grady demanded.

Daisy looked at her mother-in-law with contempt. She looked as though she hadn't had a wash for a week. The blouse she wore was stained and creased and she had a cigarette dangling from the corner of her mouth.

'I've brought him home.'

'What?'

'Him! Your beloved son that you're always complaining I don't look after properly. Well, now it's your turn to look after him. I've had enough. If you don't want him you can stick him in the bloody Workhouse!' She snatched up the carrier bag and thrust it at the astonished woman. 'Here, I've brought his things, and don't think you can bring him back because I won't be there! I'm going to work in munitions and the hours are long and so is the journey.' She turned and walked away. She felt such relief! Oh, it was as if that awful part of her life was over. She was still only twenty-five now, she could really look forward to living life!

After Daisy had gone, leaving a smiling Joseph with them, Nell's thoughts turned to work. She would try munitions too. Four pounds a week was far more than she could earn with the barrow. She thought of Annie Garvey. The barrow *had* been a sort of bequest. It had enabled Mam to earn a living and herself too for a short while. But Mam was right, Annie wouldn't have minded. No one could ever have foreseen the dramatic events that had overtaken them. The world had gone mad.

She got out the little box Annie had given her and opened it. The piece of paper was on the top and she turned it over in her hand. Why shouldn't she try and find this James Burton? Oh, he'd be an old man now, for Annie had been seventy-two when she died. But what was there to stop her finding him? He might want to know what happened to Annie. He might even have found his son, who, she worked out, would be about Mam's age.

She resolved to take a trip to Aintree the following morning, en route to the munitions factory in Kirkby, seeing as she wouldn't be going out with the barrow.

'He might not want to know,' Mary warned her after Nell had told her of her intention.

'Mam, I might not be able to find him. He could well be dead. But I think, if it's at all possible, she would have liked him to know. I want to at least try – we'll be eaten up with curiosity otherwise.'

Nell caught a number twenty tram that would take her as

far as Fazakerley terminus, which was one of the city's furthest suburbs, made up of newly built, well-appointed council houses and shops, a cinema, churches, schools and a clinic, all of which were bounded by fields and parks. She'd have to get a bus for the rest of the way. She gazed out of the window as they went down Walton Road. Once past Walton-on-the-Hill it became less built up; they were in the suburbs where the houses weren't all crowded together and falling down. There were fewer pubs too. They passed the prison and the hospital and then, further along, the shops and churches of Walton Vale. As the road divided at the Black Bull pub, she got off and crossed over. The tram driver had very kindly given her directions.

There was a big church on the corner of Cedar Road and the houses were substantial Victorian semi-detached with bay windows and small front gardens. It was very quiet, she thought. There was hardly any traffic. The leaves on the trees that lined the road rustled in the breeze and threw patches of shadow on the sun-dappled pavement.

She peered at the bit of paper again. It looked like it said forty-two but she couldn't be sure. The house, when she found it, looked exactly like all the others. The paintwork was fresh, the cotton lace curtains pristine white, all the brass door fittings shone and the garden was well tended. There were even some rose bushes; she could smell their heady perfume. It was a far cry from the Scotland Road area where Annie had eked a living.

She was apprehensive and knocked timidly and then waited. Eventually the door was opened by a tall, thin woman with a lined forehead that looked as if it was the result of a perpetual frown. A clean, plain white apron was tied over a cotton floral printed dress.

'I'm sorry to bother you, but does a James Burton live here?'

The woman looked suspiciously at her. 'And who wants to know?'

'My name is Ellen – Nell McManus and I found this name and address among the things that an old lady left me.' She held out the piece of paper. 'Does he live here? Are you Mrs Burton?'

'Indeed I am not! I'm the captain's housekeeper. Mrs Burton passed away nearly ten years ago.'

'Captain?' Nell asked, surprised.

'Yes. All of his working life was spent at sea.'

'May I see him?' she pressed.

'You'd better step into the hall while I go and ask him. Can't have you standing on the doorstep like some kind of a brush salesman,' the woman said ungraciously.

Nell looked around the narrow hallway. The woodwork was painted in cream and the walls had wallpaper with a small brown diamond pattern in it. The runner and the stair carpet were in a dark brown and the walls were adorned with paintings of ships and nautical scenes. It was a very middle-class home. Would Captain Burton really want to know about a poor old barrow woman? Maybe she shouldn't have come at all, but she couldn't walk away now.

'Come in, but don't be too long and don't expect tea!' was the terse instruction.

Nell was ushered into a comfortable sitting room. There was a big man waiting there, who certainly didn't look his age.

His hair was grey, as were his eyes, which looked curiously at her. He got to his feet and extended his hand. Nell shook it, feeling a little nervous.

'Sit down, Mrs McManus, please. Mrs Armstrong tells me you found my address?' His voice was a little gruff and there was no trace of a Liverpool accent. She surprised herself by how nervous she felt. Everything in this room, including him, seemed to be shouting that she came from a very different – lowly – background.

'I just wanted to talk to you. The address was in a little box, together with a birth certificate, that an old lady left me.'

He regarded her closely, looking puzzled. 'An old lady?'

'Yes, Annie Garvey. She lived with us until she died.'

He suddenly turned his face away from her. He was a tall man, who stood very erect. Had she upset him, she wondered, or was he deep in thought?

'She didn't always live with us . . .' she ventured timidly.

'So someone found her. I'm glad.'

'You do . . . did know her?' she probed quietly.

The room was very quiet; only the ticking of the clock on the mantelpiece could be heard. Nell didn't want to speak further for she was sure that he was about to tell her something concerning Annie's mysterious past.

'Yes, I knew her. I knew her very well. Little Annie. Garvey. With her big brown eyes and her curling hair; she was always laughing and singing and then her brown eyes would sparkle. She was a very pretty girl and I . . . I thought myself very fortunate.' He turned back and faced Nell.

'Did you . . . were you her young man?' He must have

been handsome all those years ago, but how had he come to meet Annie?

'Yes, you could say I was her "young man".' He sat down and stared at the carpet as though she weren't in the room. Again there was a long silence.

'I don't know anything about her early life,' Nell ventured, 'but Mam took her in when she got too old and sick to push the barrow.'

He looked up. 'The barrow? Annie!'

'Yes. She sold vegetables and fruit from a barrow on the corner of Great Homer Street. She lived in our neighbourhood.'

He shook his head in disbelief. 'God Almighty! She came from a good family. Like my own father, hers was a captain. Far too strict, my mother used to say. He ran that household the way he ran his ship. They lived in Litherland; she had two sisters and a brother. A barrow woman? I can't believe it!'

'Well, that's how she finished up.'

He leaned forward, his hands on his knees. His anguished eyes betrayed his feelings. 'I tried to find her. We had a terrible row after she told me that she was . . . expecting. I'm ashamed to say I didn't treat her very well, but I did want to marry her. I wanted to ask her so I searched everywhere but I never found her and of course I was away at sea a lot of the time and then . . . poor, poor Annie.'

Nell was a little stunned but pulled herself together. 'Your name is on the birth certificate.'

'Did she . . . did we . . . ?'

'She had a son. She called him David.'

He uttered a low groan and she thought that now he really did look old.

'She never told us anything about it. She just gave me the box and said I was to open it after she was dead. I . . . I suppose she had to give the baby up.'

He shook his head sadly. She had been the love of his life and he'd lost her. It seemed now that he had lost his only son too, for his marriage to his late wife, who had been called Marjorie, had proved childless.

'You have no idea at all what happened to . . . David?' he pleaded.

'I'm sorry, I don't.'

'Where is she buried?'

'In Ford Cemetery. I could show you if you want to visit.'

'Thank you, but I would prefer to go alone. Thank you for coming, Mrs McManus. I'm glad you did. I just wish she could have got word to me . . . before she died.'

'We would have done had she wanted us to. She'd got very frail and a little confused.'

He nodded and made an effort to control his emotions.

'Is your husband serving in the armed forces?'

'No. He's too old. He's an ARP warden though. We . . . we don't get on. He is much older than me and we have no . . . children.'

'I'm sorry.'

'What will you do now?' she asked.

'I'll go to visit her grave, it's the least I can do. Maybe after that I'll try and trace . . . my son.'

Nell stood up awkwardly. 'I'm sorry if I've upset you. I

never meant to. I just thought it was maybe what she wanted me to do. Find you, I mean.'

'You've nothing to be sorry for. I'm glad you came. I have . . . memories, and all the time in the world to dwell on them.'

'I can give you my address in case there's anything else I can do.' She held out the birth certificate. 'I think this really belongs to you now.'

He took it and nodded slowly and his eyes held the expression she'd seen earlier although now she was certain there were tears in them.

'Thank you for seeing me.'

'No, Mrs McManus, thank you.'

'Please call me Nell, everyone else does.'

He smiled wryly and took her hand. 'Thank you, Nell.'

The housekeeper hadn't said a word when she'd let her out but Nell barely noticed. She was engrossed in her thoughts all the way to the Munitions factory.

'I got the job in Munitions, Mam,' she informed Mary when she got home. 'They'll take as many girls as they can get, the foreman told me.'

'And what about your visit to Aintree?'

She took a deep breath and told Mary everything. When she finished Mary shook her head.

'What a waste of two lives.'

'Three, Mam, if you count this David.'

'He's probably had a decent life. There's no reason why not, if he was adopted into a loving home.'

'But Annie and Captain Burton could have given him a really good life! Oh, Mam, it's so sad. I hope he does find his son.'

'If it's meant to be, Nell, then he will,' Mary said wisely. Despite all that had happened to her down the years, she still believed that they were all in God's hands, come what may.

Chapter Eighteen

———◆———

'HOW'S YER MAM, NELL?' Vera Watson called across the road as both Nell and Daisy got off the bus in Kirkby.

'Not too bad, Vera, thanks. How's yours?' Nell called back.

'Oh, still moaning and complaining! She'd drive yer mad, I don't know how our Cissy puts up with her.'

Nell pulled her scarf tightly round her neck. It was a raw November morning and a mist hung over the surrounding fields and hedgerows. The leafless branches of the trees looked black against the grey sky.

The girls fell into step as they walked towards the factory gates. They had both been working in munitions for four months – neither had had a problem getting a job. It was tiring though, for it was a long day. They went to work in the cold grey morning and came home in the blackout.

There had been a few air-raids in August which turned heavier in September and October and now many buildings lay in ruins or were badly damaged, including the Custom House, Wallasey Town Hall, the Anglican cathedral and Central Station. They, like so many others, had decided it was too far to the public shelter, especially now everyone was prepared. Richie Ford had made the space under the stairs bigger for them and Mary always kept an empty biscuit tin with tea, condensed milk and a bit of sugar (if they had any) there; she'd managed to buy an old spirit stove on which they boiled the kettle. They had an oil lamp which Mary believed was safer than candles but care still had to be taken with it. And she had a pile of blankets stored too. When the siren started they dragged the sofa across to help stop the broken glass and shrapnel injuring them. All the windows were criss-crossed with tape.

'Daisy, a couple of us are going to the Astoria tonight, do yer want to come with us?' Vera yelled from the opposite pavement.

'That'll be great, thanks, Vera.'

Nell said nothing as they walked into the low building. When she finally got home she was too tired to go out again but Daisy seemed to have boundless energy.

She said goodbye to Daisy as they didn't work in the same section, and entered what was known as the Dirty Room. Here she stripped off down to her slip, took off her shoes and her wedding ring and the clips from her hair and moved into the Clean Room where navy blue cotton overalls, a white turban and flat shoes, rather like plimsolls, were handed out. Then she went to join the three other girls she worked with in Group Eight. Their job was to fill anti-tank mines with the obnoxious-smelling TNT that always needed stirring to stop it clouding. They wore gloves and a mask for protection. They also filled 3.8 shells which then went to the women working in Group One, the most dangerous group, to be fitted with detonators. There were frequent accidents, mainly in Group One.

'God, I'm worn out! I heard that the Maypole on Walton Road had sausages and I had to queue for hours after I got home and then hadn't Wilf Chambers, the bloody manager, put them under the counter for his blue-eyed girls and said, "That's it. There's no more"? Well, I got stuck into him!' Ethel Robson said.

'Did you get any?' Nell asked.

'He had to give me them to shut me up!' she said triumphantly.

It was all they ever talked about these days, Nell thought. Food, the lack of it and how to get more.

'Me mam made an egg-custard tart with that dried egg,' Nancy Harding, Nell's young friend, informed them.

'What was it like, Nancy?' Vera asked.

'Bloody terrible. Me auld feller said you could use it to stick wallpaper up with! She chucked it at him! There was murder!' Nancy laughed.

'Well, I'm starting to get stuff together for Christmas,' Ethel announced.

'Are we going to have a Christmas night out?'

'Course we are, Vera. That lot from Group Seven are going to the Grafton. Why don't we go too?'

'I can't dance very well,' Nancy complained.

'Well, yer've plenty of time to learn, haven't yer?' Vera retorted.

'Will you come with us, Nell? You never seem to go out much. Not like your Daisy.'

'Of course I'll come. You can't be a killjoy at Christmas.'

'Then we'll start saving up. Make it a great night. Can you all afford one and six a week?' Ethel asked.

'I think we can manage that. I'll tell me mam it's two and six, that way I'll have a shilling over. She takes every penny I bloody earn, Nell knows that,' Nancy complained, 'Nell even paid for my bridesmaid's frock.'

'We'd all better get cracking or we'll have the bloody foreman in here complaining,' Vera urged, glancing anxiously over her shoulder.

'Do you think old misery guts will put the wireless on so we can hear *Workers Playtime?*' Nancy wondered.

Vera raised her eyes to the ceiling. 'God, Nance, yer're asking for the moon!'

Nell and Daisy met up as they waited for the bus in the bitter November dusk.

'Are you going out tonight, Daisy?' Nell asked.

'Yes. Any objections?'

Nell shrugged. 'So I take it we'll be keeping Joseph all night?'

'Mam doesn't mind.'

'I know that, and I don't mind either, but he hardly ever sees you.'

'I can't help that, there's a war on, you know,' Daisy snapped.

Nell was never so sick of hearing those words.

Mary had made a pan of scouse. She was stirring it when the girls arrived home.

'I don't know about this cheap meat I got, it's more like gristle and bones.'

'Well, it smells great, Mam,' Nell said, wrinkling her nose appreciatively.

'I got some flour and yeast so there's fresh bread too. The flour's wholewheat, you can't get white flour for love nor money!'

'Or a letter from the Holy Ghost,' Daisy said.

'Isn't our Teddy in yet?' Nell asked, taking the dishes from the dresser.

'No. I never know what time that lad will be in and I'm fed up with ruining good food!'

'Don't worry about him, Mam. I'm going out tonight with the girls, will you keep Joseph?' Daisy asked, poking at the fire. 'You can still manage him, can't you?'

'Of course I can. He's getting to be a bit of a handful but that's only natural, he's two and a half and curious about everything. But he's such a good-natured, happy little soul that you have to forgive him for the bit of mischief he gets up to. Now come and get your tea.'

'Mam, I think we're in for another raid. That dog's whining again,' Daisy said.

Seconds later they all looked at each other as the wail of the siren rose to a crescendo.

'Oh, blast them to hell and back! The tea will be ruined!' Mary cried angrily.

'Daisy, get the things, I'll get Joseph and the dog,' Nell urged.

'I just hope to God Florrie stays in her own house.'

'If Richie's mam has anything to do with it they'll all be

under the stairs by now,' Daisy said firmly.

For three hours they sat and listened to the drone of the enemy planes and the shrill whistling that preceded the explosions. Some were very near and of such a force that the whole house shook and little clouds of plaster dropped around them. They knew from the close proximity of the explosions that very probably all the windows were broken. Every one of them was shaking with fear although Mary tried not to show it. The dog sat with his head in Nell's lap, shivering. Mary soothed the baby while praying fervently that Teddy would be all right.

'Oh, Mam, it's never been as bad as this,' Nell said.

'I know, luv, but we'll come through it. They say you don't hear the one that's got your name on it. At least that's what Florrie believes.'

'I hope Mr Ford will be all right. He'll be out, won't he?'

'Yes. Oh, poor Florrie, she's the worry of him too.'

'Well, I'd back his mam against Hitler any day,' Daisy said scathingly.

In her opinion old Rosie Ford had too much to say about everything.

Nell said nothing but she was thinking of Alfred. He'd be out in this too. Would he be cool and efficient or terrified? Probably the former. Still, she wished him no harm.

They were all very relieved when at last at ten o'clock the all-clear sounded and they emerged from their cramped quarters.

'That's put paid to your night out, Daisy,' Mary sighed. 'Put the kettle on while I get Joseph into bed, he's worn out, poor little lamb.'

'It's a good job he's too young to understand and be afraid. Do you think I should go and see if everyone is OK at Florrie's?' Nell asked.

'Suit yourself but I wouldn't go out there yet.'

'It won't take a minute.'

Nell threw her mam's shawl over her shoulders and went out. She found Florrie and her family in much the same state as themselves.

'Oh, thank God yer're all safe. I thought they'd never pack in and go 'ome. I was petrified!'

'Yer'd be petrified of a car back-firing,' her mother-in-law said scathingly.

'I'll swing fer 'er one of these days!' Florrie hissed. 'All she went on about when we was under the stairs was "This country's gone ter the dogs since the old Queen died!"'

Nell looked puzzled. 'Which queen? Queen Alexandra?'

'No. Victoria! I ask yer! 'Ow long 'as she been dead?'

'Must be nearly forty years.'

'That's what I mean! Can yer credit it!' She paused, then went on: 'I don't know where our Bella is. She was all tarted up, like, half an hour before the siren went. Said she was goin' ter meet 'er mates an' they were goin' ter the pictures. I don't believe a word she says. She 'ad all them beads on what she bought off some feller down the dock road. I told 'er she looked like a flamin' Christmas tree. Gerrout of me sight but be in 'ere by ten o'clock, I told 'er! God, I 'ope she's all right.'

'It'd take more than a couple of bombs ter knock sense inter that one!' old Mrs Ford muttered. 'The carry on of them these days. Didn't I tell yer this country is goin' ter the dogs?'

'God stiffen 'er!' Florrie. growled.

'Have you seen Mr Ford and Tommy?' Nell asked. She had no wish to become embroiled in the bickering between Florrie and her mother-in-law.

'God 'elp me, I don't know where our Tommy is but Richie popped his 'ead in a few minutes ago.' Florrie shook her head. 'He says it's bad this time. There's fires burnin' all over the city. The gas mains an' the water mains are all broke, the tram lines an' the telegraph lines are all down. Bloody incendiaries, 'e called them bombs, and if they're not bad enough there's the flamin' landmines. They don't make no noise so yer don't 'ear them comin'. 'E says they just sort of "float" down on green parachutes! 'Ave yer ever 'eard the like? God 'elp us all!' She lowered her voice. 'An' if she says the country's goin' ter the dogs once more, I'll bloody tell 'er ter shove it and the old queen nonsense where the sun don't shine!'

Nell changed the subject. 'We'll have to get to work in the morning somehow.'

'Oh, you make damned well sure yer go, an' fill up as many bloody mines an' things as yer can! God knows 'ow many innocent folk 'ave been killed this night! Time they got some of their own medicine, them Jerries!'

To Mary's relief Teddy arrived home half an hour later. Pale and drawn, he was covered in soot and dust and grime.

'Oh, Mam, it was terrible. We've never stopped! All the phone lines are down and you have to be careful you don't fall into a hole or get run over by the fire engines. There's piles of bricks and rubble and fires everywhere. And people who've lost their houses just standing around, not knowing what to do. It's shocking, Mam, it really is. I came off my bike twice but I'm not hurt honestly!'

'Well, you get a wash, son, and I'll get you something to eat,' Mary said thankfully. At least all her family was safe – for now.

'Tommy and me saw their Bella running down the street and Tommy said she'll get a hiding when she gets home, air-raid or no air-raid,' Teddy called from the scullery.

Mary shook her head. Bella Ford was riding for a fall in her opinion. She didn't envy Florrie at all.

The raids continued but none were as heavy as those at the end of November. People somehow struggled to get to work. It became a matter of pride. The cleaning ladies trudged through rubble-filled streets to arrive early enough for the office workers to attend to the day's business. Gangs of workmen struggled to keep the gas, water, electric and phone lines working. Men who had been up all night went to their day jobs grim-faced and heavy-eyed. No one got much sleep at all, but as Christmas approached everyone was determined to make the most of it and enjoy themselves. The women of Group Eight were looking toward to their night out.

'Your Daisy's going to the Rotunda with her lot, isn't she?' Vera stated.

'Yes, she's got a new frock.'

'She's not half bad looking when she's dressed up, your Daisy. You wouldn't think she was so old,' Nancy mused.

'Oh, aye, she's a hundred and two!' Ethel scoffed.

'Well, I've got to be in by midnight, my feller said! Bloody cheek telling me what to do, my mam was bad enough before I was married.' Vera was indignant.

'Maybe he thinks you'll turn into a pumpkin.'

'Nance, I'm not flaming Cinderella!'

Nell smiled to herself. It was this light-hearted banter that brightened up the long dark cold days. And things weren't too bad at home. Ever since the day Daisy had abandoned her husband she and Nell had seemed to get along much better than they had once done. Mary didn't approve of what Daisy had done but there wasn't anything she could do about it. Daisy was still only a young woman and she had been denied all the outings a young girl embarked on, though in her opinion Daisy went out far too often. Because Joseph was more or less living with Nell and Mary in Portland Street Daisy too spent more time there than in Silvester Street; in fact, Mary had been on the verge of telling her to give up that room and come home to live. She was sure she'd be with them over Christmas anyway. Nell was looking forward to Christmas. Well, as much as anyone could under the circumstances.

That night Nell's contentment didn't last long, though. There was a row between Daisy and her mother when Daisy came to collect Joseph.

'Daisy, I think it's time you went to see how Sam is,' Mary announced. 'It's nearly Christmas and after all Joseph is his son and Maggie O'Grady has as much right as I do to see him. You've never been near since you threw him out.'

'But I couldn't care less about him.'

'Daisy, whether you like it or not he's still your husband.'

'Why should I go around there? All I'll get is the height of abuse from all of them.'

'Daisy, Mam's right, couldn't you make an effort just for Christmas?' Nell coaxed.

'Trust you to side with Mam!' Daisy snapped. 'You mind your own business, Nell!'

'Don't speak to your sister like that,' Mary admonished.

'Nell doesn't have to go and see *him* just because it's Christmas,' Daisy retorted.

'You know that circumstances are different! Take Joseph, just for an hour?'

'Daisy, just once. Just to please Mam,' Nell urged.

Daisy flung her head back impatiently. 'Oh, all right! I'll get no peace otherwise! I'll go next week.'

Chapter Nineteen

------◆------

NELL'S GROUP HAD FINALLY decided to go to the Grafton Ballroom in West Derby Road just up from the Hippodrome where Alfred had taken her when they'd been courting. How long ago that seemed now, she thought. She hadn't heard a single word from him, nor did she want to. She fought hard to keep all those painful memories at bay.

To her surprise she had had a letter from James Burton in which he told her of his thus far fruitless search for his son. He had put notices in both the *Echo* and the *Daily Post* but there had been no response. He hoped she was well and that the bombing hadn't upset her too much.

'Maybe you should go and see him again, Nell?' her mother suggested. 'It might be some sort of comfort he's looking for. It can't be nice to be living alone, except for a housekeeper, knowing he has family somewhere.'

'Maybe I'll go on Christmas Eve. I know Daisy has plans but I'm not going anywhere special.'

'Take that little enamelled brooch Annie left in her box of bits and pieces, he might like to have it as a keepsake.'

'I'm sure he'll appreciate it, Mam.'

'I'll never be able to understand why she never tried to see her family all those years. It must have been very hard for her in the beginning. She wasn't used to that kind of life, and around here too.'

Nell sighed. 'Oh, it's all water under the bridge now.'

'I know. But I still think it would be nice for you to go and see him. I'd ask him here but, well, it's not what he's used to.' Mary suddenly changed the subject. 'Did you manage to get some of that braid?'

'I did. I'll sew it around the collar and cuffs of my good blouse, and my black skirt isn't too bad.'

'Daisy would do your hair, if you want her to. She's a dab hand with hair.'

'That would be great. She's so stylish now, isn't she?'

'She is. She's lost all that extra weight. Her hair is lovely, it's always shining and she's got a perfect complexion. And she doesn't have that permanent frown any more. But I don't know what will become of her, Nell. What's the good of her setting her stall out like she is? She's not free; she can't possibly enter a serious relationship with anyone else.'

'She'll be fine, Mam. She's just enjoying herself and those girls from work that she knocks around with aren't bad. She's making up for lost time.'

Mary paused and looked thoughtful. 'Are you happy, Nell?'

'I suppose I am, but I'm more or less in the same boat as

Daisy. I'm not free either.'

'Well, I still want you both to have a really great time. The Grafton is quite nice, so I've heard.'

Nell smiled at her. The only place Da had ever taken her was to the Stork Hotel, the day after she'd been married to Alfred. The coat with the fur collar, the gloves and the handbag had long since been pawned and unredeemed, but Mary had hung on to the hat. It kept her warm on the way to Mass, and it was a reminder of her one trip out.

The ladies' cloakroom was full to bursting on that Friday in December Nell's work friends had decided was to be their big night out. Girls and women had found numerous ingenious ways of revamping old clothes, hairstyles and make-up, now that everything was on ration.

'God, what a crush! Yer can't get near the mirror,' Nancy complained.

'And it smells like a tart's bedroom with all that cheap scent!' Ethel remarked, wrinkling her nose.

'Oh, thanks, Ethel,' Vera commented drily. 'I borrowed some of our Sarah's best perfume – Evening in Paris. She'll kill me if she finds out and you say it stinks!'

'Yer don't half look different, Nell, with yer hair done like that.'

Nell smiled at Nancy. 'Thanks, our Daisy did it.' She patted the waves and curls that Daisy had managed to produce with setting lotion, hairpins and curling tongs while Mary had smiled at them both, thinking it was the first time in years they'd been so close.

'It's a shame about your Daisy. Young girl like that tied to a cripple,' Vera pondered, seemingly oblivious to Nell's own situation.

Nell just nodded. Daisy had given a very glossed-over account of why her husband lived with his mother.

'God, would yer listen to the pair of yez! It's Christmas, we're out to enjoy ourselves!'

'All right, Nance, if you've finished dolloping all that face powder on, we'll go and get on the dance floor. How's your dancing?' Ethel asked. The ability or lack of it had been Nancy's worry for the past week.

'Shocking. Me mam wouldn't let me practise in the lobby. She said I'd be ruining the lino scraping up and down like a clumsy crab. She says she's sick of having me chanting "one, two, three, dip and turn" like you told me to do, Ethel.'

'God, she's a right misery at times, isn't she, Nance?' Vera sympathised.

'You can say that again, but I'm stopping until the end tonight. I don't care if she belts me when I get home. I'm going to enjoy myself. You don't know, I might cop off.'

'Well, there were enough fellers in there when I passed and most of them in uniform.'

'And we'll never get any if we stay in here all night! They've made the place look so festive with all those paper chains and balloons and that big glass ball that's all coloured and sparkling!' Nancy yelled, elbowing her way through the crowd of women and sighting a half-empty table. To her delight she was asked up the minute she sat down.

'She's a case, isn't she?' Vera laughed as Nancy and her new friend pushed into the crowd.

'Oh, leave her, she's only young.'

'I was just saying . . . er, Nell, don't look now but there's a feller in an RAF uniform coming over. He looks dead handsome too.'

Nell blushed. Nancy wasn't the only one who hadn't been able to practise her steps and it had been a long time since she had danced.

'Excuse me?'

Nell looked up. Vera was right. He *was* handsome. He was tall and well built. The uniform suited him. He had light brown hair that waved naturally and blue eyes that held in their depths a twinkle of interest and humour. She smiled at him.

'May I have this dance?'

She got to her feet, feeling a little shy.

'You're in the RAF,' she commented and then she could have kicked herself. Of course he's in the Air Force, he's wearing the flaming uniform, you fool! she said to herself.

'You're right.' He smiled and she was so relieved that there was no hint of ridicule or sarcasm in his voice.

'Where are you stationed, or is that secret?'

'It's supposed to be a secret but actually I'm at Woodvale, with Coastal Command.'

'Is that near?'

'Just outside Southport. Usually we go into Southport, but tonight I'm here with one of the lads who comes from Everton.'

'What do you do? I mean what does Coastal Command do?'

'Escort the convoys in to give them protection for the last run home – what's left of them. We escort other ships too, although . . .' His expression had changed. He looked grim.

'Although, what?'

'We couldn't save the *Empress of Britain*. We were too late.'
He sounded very bitter.

She remembered the loss of the Canadian Pacific ship in
October. Big enough and fast enough to sail alone, not as
part of a convoy, she'd been bombed not far from her home
port. Coastal Command had not been quick enough to shoot
down the lone German plane. Then, despite being taken in
tow by two Navy tugs, she'd been torpedoed and had sunk.

'How are you going to get home? It's a long way.'

He smiled at her. 'Oh, we'll cadge a lift off someone.' He
paused. 'Now tell me about yourself.'

'Well, I'm living with my mam and my sister and brother.
I work in munitions in Kirkby and this is our Christmas night
out. I've come with the girls I work with.'

'Munitions can be dangerous work, can't it?'

'It can be. There *are* accidents, mainly in fitting detonators.
They blow up. It's not hard work though, and we all get on
well together.'

'And the lads are all grateful that you work so hard.'

'Are you a pilot or . . . something else?'

He grinned. 'A pilot.'

'Oh, God, I couldn't go up in one of those things, I'd be
terrified!'

'I was at first but I got plenty of practise in the Battle of
Britain. I lost a lot of friends then too.'

Suddenly the war seemed to have moved in on them and
Nell realised she didn't even know his name.

'What's your name?'

'John or Johnnie. My pals call me Johnnie.'

'And I'm Ellen, but everyone calls me Nell.'

The dance had finished and he led her back to her seat at the table where a bored-looking Vera was minding the handbags and the drinks.

'Oh, I say, Nell, he was a bit of all right!' she commented as he walked away.

'He was. He's a pilot, Coastal Command out at somewhere near Southport.'

'Oh, very posh! Does he talk as if he's got a plum in his mouth?'

'No!' She laughed. 'Well, I see Nancy has got herself fixed up.'

'Yeah, a sailor! I wouldn't trust one of them as far as I could throw them!'

'Well, we're not exactly footloose and fancy free, are we?'

'No, I suppose not. I shouldn't go on at her.' Vera thrust her face into Nell's. 'Has me lipstick all come off on that glass? I don't fancy going to the cloakroom and fighting me way to the mirror.'

'No, it's fine.'

'Oh, here he comes again, Nell! It looks as if you've clicked.'

Nell felt flattered. He was very nice and he was . . . well . . . young.

'Would you like a drink, Nell? That is if I can get near the bar and if they have anything decent for a girl to drink?'

'Oh, I'd love a small glass of sherry or port, if it's not too expensive.'

'Right. Can I get your friend a drink too?'

Vera smiled. 'I'll have the same, thanks.'

He nodded and elbowed his way to the bar.

'He's a really nice feller,' Vera said meaningfully, 'asking me if I'd like a drink and all.'

'He seems like it, Vera,' Nell agreed.

Vera looked at her closely. There was a trace of regret in Nell's voice.

He came back with their drinks and Nancy, with a young able seaman in tow, came towards them.

'So, who's your friend, Nancy?' Vera asked.

'This is Harry, he's on a warship.' She paused self-importantly. 'He can't tell me which one.'

Ethel and Vera raised their eyes to the ceiling.

'Would you like to dance again?' Johnnie asked Nell. It felt as if it was getting a little crowded around the table.

'You'll have me worn out,' she laughed when they reached the dance floor but the smile on her lips died and she froze in his arms as the banshee wail of the siren drowned out the music. People around them also stood still, uncertain what to do. As the doleful notes of the siren died away Mrs Wilf Hamer raised her baton and the band played on. Taking their cue from them the dancers resumed as did the chatter of voices, but they couldn't drown out the throbbing drone of the approaching raiders.

'Don't worry Nell, I'm right here,' Johnnie said firmly, feeling her begin to tremble.

She clung to him tightly, for the next few minutes were terrifying. There was a huge juddering crash as the Olympia Theatre next door received a direct hit, and the force of the blast ripped off half the roof of the dance hall.

'Oh, my God!' she cried and buried her face in his shoulder as debris began to rain all around them.

A hail of shrapnel suddenly tore through the remains of the plaster ceiling and he grabbed her hand, dragged her back to the table and pushed her under it.

'Jesus! We're all going to die!' Nancy was almost hysterical.

'For God's sake, Nancy, shut up or we'll all be having hysterics!' Ethel yelled at her.

'I want to go home!' the girl screamed.

Ethel slapped her hard.

'Don't you think we all do? No one's hurt, so just shut up!'

'Where's her sailor friend?' Nell asked.

'God knows!'

'He must have gone to see if there's anything he can do to help, like Johnnie has,' Nell said, her voice still shaking with fear.

'Oh, God, I hope it's not going to go on for hours, my feller will kill me if I'm late!' Vera wailed.

'Jesus, Vera, will you stop saying words like kill, it's tempting bloody fate!'

Except for the occasional scream when there was another very loud explosion, no one said anything more. They were only too aware of the flimsy protection the table could give them from shrapnel or falling masonry.

The men in uniform went about their jobs of tending the injured and clearing the dance floor of glass and debris. Within three-quarters of an hour and with searchlights sweeping the now visible sky through the huge gaping hole that had been the roof, Mrs Hamer emerged from under the piano and gave the signal for the dancing to continue.

'Oh, I couldn't move a single step, my legs are shaking,' Vera remarked, clutching the edge of the table for support.

'Well, just shift yourself. Do you want that lot up there to think we're afraid of them? Bloody Nazis!' Ethel's voice was full of scorn.

As Nell emerged Johnnie appeared and took her arm.

'Are you hurt?'

'No, just a bit wobbly – and dusty. I don't think they clean the floor very often here,' she tried to joke.

'Come on then, back to the dance! We can't let the side down,' he urged.

She smiled. It was comforting to have strong arms around you and a broad shoulder to lean on, but she was still trembling inside.

'What time is it?' she asked him as across the room Vera began gesturing meaningfully at her wrist.

'Five to midnight!' he called.

'I had no idea it was so late.' She looked up at the roof. They were still up there, still dropping their bombs on help-less women and children. Would they never go away? She was terrified for Mam and Teddy and everyone in Portland Street.

'What the hell are they doing?' Johnnie said and she looked over to the bandstand where a group of men were setting up a microphone.

'Hush, they're saying something,' she urged.

The dancers gradually fell silent.

'This is the BBC Home Service,' one of the men announced. 'Tonight we've been broadcasting from all over the city and we're ending with a message to London.' He then indicated that Mr Munro, the manager, speak into the microphone.

'Hello, London. I am speaking from the Grafton Ballroom in Liverpool. A few hours ago the theatre next door got it and we've lost half the roof here but everyone's still enjoying themselves! So if you can keep it up, so can we! If you listen carefully you can hear the planes still overhead.' This brought a huge cheer before they were urged into silence and the microphone crackled.

'We can keep it up all right and we're proud that you, Liverpool, are doing the same. So, stick to it, Merseyside, it's worth it!' the cheerful voice of the commentator in London urged.

This brought a huge cheer and the band struck up 'Rule, Britannia', though there were tears in many people's eyes as they tried to sing along.

Vera had long given up worrying about getting home early. There were far more important fears. The raid had started hours ago and showed no sign of being over and it was now after three o'clock. She was worried for her husband and her entire family, for by now half the city must be in ruins and in flames. But everyone still danced and laughed, trying to ignore the noise of the raiding planes.

'If this goes on, there won't be much of Liverpool left,' Nell said, and Johnnie tightened his grip around her waist.

'Don't forget Scousers are a tough lot, Nell! I shouldn't be here, though.'

'Why? You're on leave, aren't you?'

'Yes, but I should be up there shooting the bastards down!' He paused. 'I'm sorry for my language, Nell.'

'That's all right. I've heard worse and I *do* understand.'

It was five a.m. when the all-clear finally sounded.

'Oh, thank God for that!' Ethel sighed with heartfelt relief.

'I'll get the coats,' Nancy offered. 'That sailor said he'll walk me home.'

'I hope to God she's still got a home. I hope we've *all* still got homes,' Ethel said quietly.

'You're going to be very late, Vera,' Nell said, glancing at her friend.

'Don't I know it, Nell, but surely to God getting caught in that raid is something he can't moan about,' she answered grimly.

They all went out into the cold dawn morning.

'Oh, God Almighty!' Johnnie said quietly, then they all fell silent. The road outside, one of Liverpool's busiest, was a complete shambles. There were fires still raging, all the tram lines were down and sparking as water from the broken mains seeped over them. The road was a sea of shattered glass and rubble and there was a strong smell of gas in the air which meant that the gas pipes too were fractured.

'Nell, I'd walk you home, but I'll have to get back, or see how I can be of help to anyone here.'

'That's fine.' Nell nodded. 'Don't worry about me. I'll be with the girls.'

'Stick together, watch out for bomb craters and keep clear of buildings that look as if they're ready to collapse.'

'Will there be anything left at all?' Ethel said in a shocked voice.

'If they can get those fires out it would help,' Nancy's sailor said grimly. 'I hope to God my ship's still afloat, the docks look as if they've been hit bad.' He and Nancy began to swap addresses and make plans.

Nell shook her head in disbelief. She couldn't take it in. It looked as if the whole city were on fire. Oh, God! Just how many people had been killed, injured and made homeless?

Johnnie took her hand and broke her thoughts. 'I'll have to go, Nell, but I'd like to see you again?'

She looked hopefully up at him. 'I'd like to see you too!'

'I don't even know your surname or where you live?'

'It's McManus and I live in number 26 Portland Street!'

'My name's Johnnie Burton and I'll try and get out to see you as soon as I can.' With that he began to walk quickly away towards the nearest flaming building.

Burton! Burton! she thought dazedly, but then told herself there must be hundreds of people with that name.

'Johnnie! Johnnie, what's your father's name?' she called after him.

He turned. 'David! Why?'

She waved him on. Could it possibly be true? Was it fate or just coincidence?

She tried to think positively as she trudged home but it was impossible. They were all tired but the city was in such a desperate state that it took hours to complete their journey.

They were all stunned into silence by the sights they saw. It was like walking in a nightmare. They had to climb over the rubble of what a few hours ago had been houses and shops. They had to make detours when firemen and wardens and council workers said it was too dangerous to go that way because of fires and half-collapsed buildings. They had to thread their way through miles of telephone and tram wires that lay on the ground, like huge black snakes. In some places men were digging frantically with whatever they could use to try to save people buried under the rubble of their homes and businesses. She nearly dissolved into tears at the sight of an old lady sitting on a pile of bricks, rocking a child in her arms, for everyone could tell that the little girl was dead. There were the bodies of animals too. Cats and dogs, and horses that would no longer pull the milk, bread and coal carts.

She had dreaded turning into Portland Street, for she had passed so many streets in which there were huge gaps where houses had stood a few hours ago. She breathed a deep sigh of relief when she turned the corner. With what energy she had left she ran the rest of the way and half fell into the kitchen.

Mary threw her arms around her, tears of relief pouring down her cheeks.

'Oh, thank God and His Holy Mother! Oh, Nell! Nell! I've been out of my mind worrying about you! There was so much bombing that no one could tell me anything. I went out on the streets with Joseph in my arms, begging for any news until Richie Ford made me come home.'

'I couldn't get home, Mam. It took ages. The Grafton had half the roof torn off but everyone stayed and danced!'

'I was under the stairs for the first couple of hours. The dog started his antics about fifteen minutes before the siren went and I just prayed and prayed.'

'Oh, Mam, I would have been so worried if I'd known you were out in it all.'

'It didn't seem that long, Nell, but I've never seen anything like it. I thought the end of the world had come! I've never seen so many planes. What are they trying to do, kill us all?'

'I don't know, Mam. Maybe they are. Is Daisy home?'

'Yes, she got in about half an hour ago. I told her to get a bit of rest as she's insisting on going to work.'

Nell slumped down on the sofa. 'I'll go as well, Mam. I can't let the others down. Oh, Mam, it was awful. You should see the state of the city.'

'I know, luv, Florrie's sister from the south end and all her kids were bombed out. They're all squashed in with her, you can't move!'

'There's so many houses that were hit that people will have to double up.'

'We were overcrowded before, it will be worse now. But what can you say? You can't leave your nearest and dearest out on the street and at this time of year. Oh, this is a lovely Christmas present, isn't it?' She shook her head, on the brink of tears once more. 'I'll make you a nice cup of tea, but I've got no sugar.'

'That doesn't matter, Mam. Is there anything to eat? I'm starving.'

'Bread and dripping is all I can manage until I go to the shops today.'

'That will be great, Mam.'

Despite the traumas of the night Mary thanked God she'd been blessed with such luck. She still had her home and her girls, her son and her grandson were all safe. Who knew what horrors the day would bring to others? She was so tired and her back was killing her but, she told herself stoutly, if both Nell and Daisy could survive the worst raid yet on Liverpool and still be determined to go to work, she could manage too.

'Here, luv, get this down you,' she said, wearily passing the tea to Nell.

Nell was half asleep in the armchair, the terrifying events of the night slowly fading, when she was suddenly pulled back to alertness by Richie Ford's voice. She sat up and blinked. He looked very worried beneath the mask of dirt and soot and exhaustion. But, she told herself, hadn't this night been the longest ever? 'Is Daisy 'ome?' his voice was asking.

'Yes, I'll go and get her,' Mary said, moving into the lobby.

'Yer got 'ome safe an' sound too then, Nell?'

'I did thanks, but . . . but I've never seen anything like it. I was terrified.'

'I know, girl. I was out all night in it. I thought it would never end. There wasn't time ter dwell on it though. No time ter be afraid, yer just 'ad ter do what yer could fer . . . fer everyone.'

'I saw sights on my way home that I'll never forget if I live to be a hundred,' Nell said, gazing bleakly into the fire.

'I know what yer mean, Nell. This is the worst night I've ever experienced and now . . . poor Daisy.'

She rubbed her eyes. 'Poor Daisy? Why? What's happened?'

'It's Sam an' 'is family.'

'What about them?'

Richie looked down at his dirty boots. He'd offered to fulfil this task, but he didn't relish it. 'Their 'ouse got a direct 'it. There was nothin' left, just a mound of rubble. They were all killed outright.'

'Oh, God!' Nell gasped.

'Oh, God is right, luv, and there's so many of them in the same boat. Ternight I wished I 'ad a bloody big gun ter shoot the bastards down with! But, by God, they'll never get the better of us!'

Mary came into the room followed by a white and dry-eyed Daisy.

'Daisy, it's bad news, girl. Sam and all his family are . . . dead. A direct 'it.'

'Oh, God have mercy on all their souls,' Mary said sincerely. Daisy just nodded. It *was* a shock but the events of the night *were* shocking. She'd seen dreadful sights on her way home too, and she simply felt numb.

'It was a mercy in one way, luv,' Richie said.

'How do you make that out?' Mary asked, her arm around her daughter.

'Well, they didn't suffer, Mary. It was instantaneous, so the fireman told me, and he should know,' Richie explained.

Daisy couldn't cry. All she could think of was that she was now free. Free of him, of all of them. She could be like a single girl again.

Nell got up wearily and put the kettle on. 'Will you have a cup, Mr Ford?' she asked mechanically.

'No, luv, there's still a lorra work ter do out there. I just stopped off to tell yer, like.'

Silence descended on the small kitchen. They were all exhausted and dazed.

'You two are going to be too tired to go to work,' Mary said eventually as Nell handed round the tea.

'Mam, we'll have to go. At least I will. Daisy, I think you've a good enough excuse.'

'No, I'll go in. It wasn't as if I was really . . . fond of them. Any of them, God forgive me.'

'Mam, you look all in, will you be well enough to look after Joseph?' Nell asked with concern.

'Don't be so daft, Nell! Of course I'll be fine!'

'Well, we can help you, Mam, over the break. We'll be having a quiet Christmas,' Nell said. She looked at her sister. 'Won't we, Daisy?'

Daisy nodded, but she wasn't really listening. So many people had been killed and maimed and left homeless that she shouldn't think of Sam and his family's demise with thankfulness. If her mother were to discover how she felt Mary would have ten fits. But she wasn't going to be a hypocrite now. She couldn't pretend she hadn't come to hate her husband and his family.

Nell suddenly remembered Johnnie Burton.

'Mam, I was dancing with a lad from the RAF tonight. He was very nice. He would have walked me home but felt he had to go and help as much as he could.'

Mary sighed, wondering if Alfred McManus had come through the night unscathed. 'So?'

'So, just before he left me I asked him his name.'

'Did you not know it before?'

'Only his Christian name. He's stationed out near Southport, he's a pilot.'

'So, Nell, what is it you're getting at?'

'His name's Johnnie Burton and his father's name is David.'

Mary sat up. 'It's just a coincidence, Nell. There must be hundreds of people with the same name.'

'That's what I thought at first, Mam, but what if . . . what if this David is Annie's son?'

'But wouldn't the people who adopted Annie's son have had his surname changed to theirs?'

'They might not have. Not if they wanted him to know who he was one day. After all, his father's name was on the birth certificate.'

'Oh, I don't know, Nell. If the lad's a pilot he might not want to know that his grandmother, poor Annie, was a barrow woman.'

'Oh, Mam, does any of that matter now? The world has been turned upside down.'

'I'd sleep on it, Nell. Give it more thought before deciding what to do.'

'But, Mam, I could help James Burton find the family he's looking for.'

'Just leave it for now, Nell. Christmas is coming and there's so much to do.'

Reluctantly, Nell nodded her agreement. Mam was right. There would be so much to do; there would be so many funerals. They would all have to attend the O'Grady family's and that wasn't a pleasant prospect.

The news over the next few days confirmed the terrible toll Liverpool and its people had had to pay for being the port through which all the aid from overseas passed. Municipal offices, the central police offices, food warehouses in Dublin Street, Princes Parade and Landing Stage, the Adelphi Hotel, the Dock Board offices: the list of property destroyed was endless. In Bentinck Street, beneath the five railway arches, a direct hit had brought down tons of masonry onto the heads of the crowds who had sheltered there. The Olympia Theatre had disappeared of course and Webbs Chemical factory in Hanover Street had gone up like a firework. Huge fires burned in Hatton Garden, St John's Market and Hockenhall Alley. St George's Hall was hit and the Law Library completely destroyed. The Royal Infirmary, Mill Road Hospital, St Anthony's school: the list went on and on, without mentioning the heavy damage sustained by housing.

Liverpool had paid a heavy price, but despite everything the Port remained operational. Liverpool had not given way.

Chapter Twenty

------◆------

THE CITY'S SUFFERINGS WERE not over. On the nights of December 21 and 22 the Luftwaffe came again in force to wreak havoc and heartbreak on an already reeling city.

Mary, Nell, Daisy, Joseph and the dog spent countless terrifying hours under the stairs, Mary with the added worry that Teddy was out there in the virtually unprotected city. The anti-aircraft batteries could do little against the hundreds of enemy planes that circled the city for hour after hour, their targets illuminated by the flames of already burning buildings. With phone lines down the lads who normally only delivered telegrams became the vital links between the police and fire services, the ambulances and hospitals.

Teddy knew he could never tell Mary how terrified he was, how terrified they *all* were. As they rode their bicycles along blazing streets, with bricks and chunks of stone falling about them all, they concentrated upon avoiding the bomb craters and not becoming entangled in the miles of fire hoses and telephone and tram wires. With faces streaked with dirt and dust and often tears of fright, they battled on for hours, taking urgent messages backwards and forwards across the beleaguered city. They had all heard of the fire engine that had plunged into a bomb crater: the entire crew had been killed. As Teddy cycled as fast as he could he fixed his eyes on the roadway ahead. No, these were things he could never tell his mam because for one thing he couldn't find the words and, more importantly, he would never own up to his terror – not even to himself.

Mary was petrified he'd be hit by shrapnel as, for the third consecutive night, she huddled under the stairs, and wondered if anything would be left standing.

'Mam, he'll be fine,' Nell tried to reassure her, as they emerged from their confined positions under the stairs. 'He's come through the last two raids without a scratch.'

'But will it ever end?' Daisy despaired. 'I'm tired out, we're getting no sleep and every time I hear one of those whistling bombs I start to shake.'

'Just thank God we've survived another night,' Mary said gravely. 'Nell, will you go and see if everyone else is all right whilst I put the kettle on? You know what a state Florrie gets in.'

Mary had made the tea and cut some bread by the time Nell came back.

'I saw Mr Ford, he said number thirty-two has had all the windows and doors blown in and half the roof ripped off by a landmine but Florrie is fine. Having old Mrs Ford and her sister and her kids there seems to help. It helps with the shopping too, they take it in turns to stand in the queue. She was a bit worried about Mrs Ford's sister getting bombed out though.'

'If she has been Florrie hasn't a spare inch of space to take them in.' Mary shook her head. 'Well, let's all get some sleep while we can.'

'Mam, it's pointless us going to bed, we have to leave soon anyway, it'll take so long to get to work. It was bad enough yesterday. You take Joseph up and get some sleep yourself.'

'I can't sleep until Teddy gets in, you know that.'

'Well, try and rest then,' Nell urged.

Two hours later, a grimy-faced, exhausted Teddy came home.

'Was it bad, luv?' Nell asked.

'It was. I'm getting so the sound of the siren makes me feel sick and I'm worn out.'

'What time have you to be back?' Daisy asked.

'In four hours.'

'Then have a bit of a butty, a cup of tea and a quick wash, then try and sleep.'

Teddy nodded. He was so tired that he knew he would go out like a light and he was thankful. When he was awake he could remember too much.

Both Daisy and Nell dozed in the kitchen until they were woken by a loud hammering on the front door.

'Oh, now what? Are the blackout curtains pulled tight?' Daisy asked irritably.

Nell stretched. 'I'm certain they are. I'll go, I don't want to wake Mam or Teddy.'

She was astonished to find James Burton on the doorstep. The captain's grey eyes were full of concern.

'Nell, when the all-clear sounded and I heard what a terrible pounding this neighbourhood had taken again, I had to come to see if you were all right.'

Nell's hand automatically went to her hair. She must look a fright, with her hair all over the place, her face unwashed, her clothes creased and wrinkled.

'Oh, that was very good of you. Come in, I'm afraid we're in a bit of a mess.'

'No, I won't intrude.'

'Oh, please? The least I can do is offer you a cup of tea after you've come so far. Did you have to walk?'

'From Rice Lane.'

'That's miles away! And in the early hours of the morning, in the blackout.' And you're no longer a young man, she thought with concern.

'It wasn't too bad, I've a small pocket torch and I really wasn't worried.'

He followed her down the narrow lobby.

'Daisy, this is Captain James Burton.'

Daisy got to her feet and held out her hand.

'I'm Daisy, Nell's sister.'

He shook her hand and then sat down on the sofa, looking around the small, cramped room. They obviously made the best of things but these houses should have been pulled down years ago. He smiled grimly to himself. Maybe the Luftwaffe were doing them a favour in a roundabout sort of way.

'Annie had her bed just there, she could see and hear everything that was going on,' Daisy informed him politely.

He winced. The Annie he remembered would have hated to have been lying in a bed in someone's kitchen. Ever since

Nell had visited him he'd been tormented by guilt.

'I intended to come and see you on Christmas Eve – I can hardly believe that's tomorrow!' Nell said, handing him the best cup she could find, acutely aware of the difference between her home and his.

'I would have liked that, but I realise how busy you are, and now there're these appalling air-raids. Have you coped with the last three nights?'

'Just about. We were in the Grafton Ballroom the night of the first raid. It was terrifying and I thought how dreadful it all was. I never thought it could happen.'

'No one did, Nell,' he said sadly.

'Daisy's husband and his entire family were killed on the first night also. The funeral is tomorrow.'

'Oh, I'm so sorry. You should have said earlier, I wouldn't have intruded on your grief.'

'Oh, that's all right. Things have to go on and we . . . we were estranged.'

'We'll have to go to work in a few hours,' Nell said. 'It's more important now that we do, the things we make are really needed.'

Nell gazed at him thoughtfully as he sipped his tea.

It was really good of him to walk miles to see if they were safe. He was a very kind man. She cleared her throat.

'I have something to tell you, it might not mean anything but . . .'

'What?' He was eager to hear.

'I met a young pilot at the Grafton. He's stationed out at Woodvale, Coastal Command. His name is Johnnie Burton and just before he left I found out his father's name is David.'

The captain sat up. 'Did he say . . . ? Do you think . . . ?'

'I don't know, honestly. He said he'd get in touch, he wants to see me again – he doesn't know that I'm married – but I didn't tell him about you or Annie.'

'Will you ask him if he is related? If you see him again?'

'Of course. It just might be a coincidence but . . .'

'I've had no luck at all. I've racked my brains for ways to try and find David Burton and now that the city is in such a mess it will be even harder to trace *anyone*. It seems pretty hopeless. His name might not be Burton at all. If that's the case I'll never find him.'

'Oh, don't give up. I swear I'll find out something for you, if he does get in touch.'

'Thank you, Nell. It's very . . . good of you.'

He stood up. He'd meant everything he'd said, she was a kind, considerate girl and he liked her enormously. He held out his hand. 'Thank you again. And if we have another raid you must all come and stay with me. It's a bit safer out where I am.'

'Thank you, but my brother Teddy will have to stay and Mam won't leave him. And I won't leave Mam.'

'I can understand that but if things get really bad, the offer is still there. Goodbye, Daisy. I'm so sorry for your loss.'

'He is very nice even though he's a cut above us,' Daisy said when he'd gone. 'Fancy him offering us a place to stay?'

Nell nodded. 'It is terribly good of him, though I can't quite see it happening, somehow.' She sighed, glancing at her watch. 'We'd better get ready for work. It'll take us hours to get there.'

*

As soon as Nell saw her work mates she quickly told them of Daisy's loss.

'I was sorry to hear about yer feller,' Vera said as they all walked to the factory.

'It was shocking, that's what it was,' Ethel stated.

'Well, at least it was quick,' Daisy said solemnly, feeling a bit guilty.

'A blessing really, for him,' Nell added. 'He didn't have much of a life.'

'I'm dreading the funeral,' Daisy said and she meant it.

'I don't blame yer,' Nancy agreed.

As they trudged through the cold morning Daisy found herself shaking her head in disbelief that she was once again free. Free to do whatever she liked – within reason, and after a bit of an interval.

'Well, are we three still going to town on Christmas Eve?' Nancy asked.

'If there's any flaming town left to go to!' Ethel declared heatedly.

'God, I hope they've packed it in. It's bad enough having to sit and listen to the row but me mam drives us all around the bend. Yer know, we can't play cards or read or knit like everyone else in the shelter. Oh, no, we have to pray! She's turning into a flaming religious maniac. Yer should have heard her when I asked to bring Harry home.'

'I didn't think the big romance was that serious. You hardly know him,' Ethel quizzed.

'He got some time off over the weekend.' Nancy was indignant. She liked Harry Larkin. She really liked him. She might even be in love with him.

'So what did they say?' Vera probed.

'I just asked if I could bring a lonely sailor home.'

'A "lonely sailor"!' Ethel scoffed.

'He is! He's got no one. He was brung up in an Orphanage and joined the Navy as soon as he was old enough, so don't you have a go at him and all. Me da said there ain't no such thing as a lonely sailor, they're well known for having a girl in every port and they're not fussy about what kind of girl either. Me mam said she didn't want no hooligan who'd been dragged up in an orphanage over her doorstep. I ask yer! They wouldn't hear of even meeting him so they could see for themselves that he's a nice lad. He's just had a hard life. Yer've got to be tough to be in the Navy and he's Regular Navy too. He hasn't just joined up.'

'They'll change their minds, Nancy, give them time. Just make sure you're in on time and behave yourself and when they see that you're not being led up the garden path they'll come round,' Nell advised.

'Thanks, Nell. At least *you're* not trying to put him down, like some I could mention.'

'Oh, for God's sake Nance, how can we "put 'im down"? We hardly know him!' Vera was exasperated.

'I was just saying!'

'Do yer really like him?'

'I do.'

'Then do as Nell suggests. Behave yourself,' Ethel advised.

'There is one thing though . . .'

'What now, Nancy?' Vera asked looking pained.

'Well, he's . . . he's not the same religion.'

'What is he then?' Ethel demanded.

'Church of England.'

Vera shook her head.

'Oh, Nance, you're going ter have problems there,' Ethel agreed.

Nell hated to see her young friend in this predicament. 'Nancy, you'll have to give it a lot of thought,' she urged.

'Oh, I wish everyone wouldn't go on and on about flamin' religion! I don't care what church he goes to.'

'Yer Mam will. You take notice of Nell and give it plenty of thought,' Ethel advised.

Nancy changed the subject. 'I heard that Madge Collins from Group Three knows a feller who's getting a pile of nylon stockings.'

'Honestly?' Vera demanded.

'Honest to God! I don't know how much he wants for a pair but I'm willing to go to ten shillings.'

'Ten shillings! For a pair of stockings! You must be mad!' Ethel was outraged.

'Well, I'm sick to death of painting my legs with gravy browning and drawing a seam up the back with a pencil! If yer get caught in the rain, it all washes off and makes a shocking mess and me mam's always moaning that I'm wasting good gravy browning and I don't want to give her any more reasons to yell at me.'

'Give me the nod will you, Nancy? I'll have a pair,' Daisy said before leaving them for her own workroom.

'The Merry Widow!' Ethel, a shrewd judge of character, remarked caustically as Daisy walked away from them.

Nell said nothing. None of them really knew how much

Daisy had hated her husband but she hoped Ethel's remark wouldn't set them thinking.

When the sisters arrived home that evening it was to find Johnnie Burton sitting on the sofa in the kitchen.

Nell was surprised. 'Johnnie, I didn't expect to see you so soon.'

'Then you're not pleased to see me?' He grinned at her.

'Of course I am.'

'I couldn't leave the lad standing on the doorstep in the cold,' Mary said. She had been surprised herself when she'd opened the door.

'I managed to get a few hours off so I came to see how you'd coped with the raids.'

'I've already told him,' Mary interrupted, 'we coped fine.'

'I was sorry to hear about your husband, Mrs O'Grady.'

Daisy nodded and smiled. Mary looked at Nell pointedly.

'I haven't enough time to take you anywhere in town but perhaps we could go for a drink locally?'

'That'll be great. Will you wait a few minutes while I get changed?'

'Of course.'

Mary followed her into the lobby.

'Where are you going to take him around here? You know what the fellers are like. All rough and ready and when they spot the uniform . . . well, you know what they call fellers in the Air Force.'

'I know, Mam. "Brylcreem Boys". He'll be teased. But it's *me* who's taking him out, not *them*. And I'm sure he's used to it.'

Nell avoided the Golden Fleece, it reminded her too much of Da; heeding Mary's warning, they went to the Throstle's Nest next door to St Anthony's Church which was a bit more select.

She found a corner in the snug while he got the drinks.

'It's a bit basic in here,' she apologised, glancing around and thinking of the Stork Hotel.

'It's fine. Here, they managed to rustle up a port and lemon.'

She smiled. 'How much did you give him?'

'Oh, just a few extra coppers,' he laughed. She was great to be with, he thought, and she was a good-looking girl. These days you learned to enjoy the moment, and that's what he intended to do now.

'I've been wanting to ask you why you asked me what Dad's name was?'

Nell looked at him. 'It's a bit . . . strange, really. You said his name is David Burton?'

'Yes.'

'Was he adopted, do you know?'

'Yes, he was. My grandparents are long dead, but they adopted him when he was a baby.'

'Was their name Burton?'

'No, but for some reason they gave him his father's name. They didn't want to change it. I asked him once about it and he said they wanted him to know that they'd chosen him. They couldn't have children.'

Nell winced. His last words brought back painful memories.

'What does he do? Where does he live?'

'He's a Chief Engineer with Cunard in peacetime, but he's

away at sea with a convoy at the moment. We live in Crosby.'

Nell sipped her drink. What would his reaction be to finding out that he had a grandfather who was still alive?

'You're very quiet, is there something the matter, Nell?'

She bit her lip. 'I don't know how to tell you this . . .'

He looked at her, concerned at her words. 'Tell me what? That you don't want to see me again?'

'Oh, it's nothing like that, Johnnie. I do want to see you again. It's . . . it's, well, I think you do have a grandfather who's alive.'

He looked puzzled.

'An old lady used to live with us and when she died we found amongst her belongings a birth certificate for a David Burton and an address for a Captain James Burton. I went to see him and the only likely explanation is . . . that he was your dad's real father and that Annie, the old lady, was your dad's mother. They . . . they weren't married.'

He didn't speak. He couldn't take it in.

'You don't have to tell anyone. I wouldn't want to upset you or your parents. You see, they had a huge row when Annie found out she was expecting and she just . . . disappeared. He tried to find her but he couldn't. We only knew her when she was already an old lady.'

'What was her name?'

'Annie Garvey.' Nell paused, watching confusion and incredulity rush across his face. 'What will you do?'

'I just don't know, Nell. It *is* a great surprise. I'll have to think about it. Father's not due back for another week, that's if his ship has survived.'

'Are you sorry I told you?' she asked tentatively.

'No. At least, I don't think so.' He shook his head, as if he was trying to dislodge what she'd told him from his brain. 'Drink up and I'll get another, then I'll have to be getting back.'

She was sorry she'd spoken as for the rest of the time he hardly said a word and she felt miserable.

When they reached Nell's house he stopped and looked down at her.

'Nell, I hope I can go on seeing you. May I?'

Her spirits lifted and she nodded. 'That'd be wonderful, Johnnie,' she said shyly.

He took her in his arms and as he kissed her gently she felt herself melt with happiness. This must be how being in love, felt, she knew, and it was so very different to what she'd felt for Alfred. She suddenly remembered what Annie had said. That there was someone out there for her, and it wasn't Alfred McManus. Had Annie had some strange gift? Had she somehow, without knowing it, been in touch with the fate of her grandson? After all, people had said she could tell fortunes.

'I'll get off when I can, Nell,' he said, 'but I don't know when or for how long. At least tonight there's been no raid.'

'Thank God. I'd like to see you again, Johnnie, I really would, despite everything.'

'Then take care of yourself, Nell.'

'I will, and you take care of *your*self. I hate to think of you being up there in one of those things.'

He laughed. 'You'll get over it. When this is all over I'll take you up in one!'

'You can try!' she laughed.

Inside, Mary was waiting for her. 'So, did you tell him?'

'Yes.'

'And?'

'Well, his father was adopted but kept his real name, David Burton. So it seems Annie was Johnnie's grandmother and James Burton is his grandfather. He doesn't know whether he'll tell his father yet, he's at sea with a convoy.'

'Are you going to see him again, Nell?' Mary asked seriously.

'Yes, Mam.'

'Be careful. I don't want you to get hurt again and Alfred is still your husband. And I notice that you don't wear your wedding ring very often these days.'

'Mam, I just forget, that's all.'

Mary looked sternly at her. 'Nell, you can't get serious about him.'

'Oh, Mam, please don't let's argue about it.'

But Mary persisted. 'Apart from you not being free, he comes from a different background. Could you ever fit into his world?'

'I don't know, Mam. It's . . . it's best not to think like that.'

Mary looked dubiously at her. 'I suppose you're right. I'll be thankful when tomorrow is over and so will Daisy,' Mary agreed grimly.

The morning of the twenty-fourth was cold and a thin mist hung over the streets, partly disguising the wrecked homes and shops.

'It's going to be a bad enough day without the weather

being so flaming miserable,' Mary said as she drew back the blackout curtains in the kitchen.

'I know. I'll be glad when it's all over too,' Nell added.

'At least you can go back to work. I'll have to put in an appearance at the tea at my place afterward, Mam's worked hard to put on a decent show,' Daisy said irritably.

'Who will be there?' Nell asked.

'Just a few cousins and the neighbours.'

'That's a relief.'

'Mam, this black dye hasn't worked very well,' Daisy complained, holding up a blouse and skirt. 'It's all patchy.'

'It's the best I could do under the circumstances. I knew we should have taken them all to Johnson's the cleaners to be professionally dyed black.'

'I wasn't going to waste money, Mam, and, besides the expense, they're really busy.'

Mary nodded her agreement. There were so many families grieving for loved ones after the last few days.

'Did you give Mrs Harper the funeral money?' Daisy asked.

'I did. She said she wouldn't get much with it, but I told her it was all we could afford and that they were our coupons.'

'Some people are so grasping. We've all made sacrifices even though I really don't see why we had to cough up.'

'Because, Daisy, when all's said and done you're his widow and you could show a little more regret and respect.'

'Mam, he never loved me, you know that, and in the end I hated him. I won't be a hypocrite!'

'You'll show some respect for his family if nothing else. Do you want us to be talked about?'

Daisy was exasperated. 'Oh, Mam, I don't care what people in *that* street think of me!'

'Well, *I* care what they think of *me*, Daisy!'

'Oh, for heaven's sake, stop arguing, the pair of you!' Nell intervened. 'Wear your good coat over those things, Daisy, then no one will notice.'

'I can't wear my coat all day, Nell.'

Nell lost patience. 'Oh, wear what you like but it'd better be something warm!'

It took them far longer than usual to walk to the church in Eldon Street because of the mountains of rubble and closed-off streets.

'They never had much in life, now, God help them, they have nothing. Not even a roof over their heads,' Mary said, sadly shaking her head.

The parish priest greeted them at the door of the church.

'Daisy, I am so sorry for your loss. It's a tragedy to be sure, but there are so many cases like theirs.'

'Thank you, Father,' Daisy answered politely but with her head down, so neither he nor the members of the congregation could see the truth in her eyes. Once she'd got this day over she could start to live again. Really live.

It was such a shock, Mary thought, seeing so many coffins at the altar steps. Usually there was just one. That in itself made you realise the magnitude of the tragedy. A whole family! A whole family dead in a few seconds! She bent her head and prayed it would happen to no more families.

Daisy could only feel a slight sense of pity for all of them. She hadn't liked her mother-in-law one bit and the rest of

Sam's family she had ignored, yet now she was supposed to be bowed down with grief. She wasn't interested in the service, she was wrapped in her dreams for the future.

It was just as dismal in the cemetery, Nell thought as she threw the customary handful of soil into the grave. So many people dead, across the whole city, so many small tragedies. But then that was war. At least, her experience of war.

As they turned away, a young woman detached herself from the crowd and came towards them. Nell took in the thin, home-dyed coat and the headscarf tied tightly under the chin. She was carrying a little girl, a bit younger than Joseph.

'Daisy! Daisy O'Grady!' she called and Daisy turned, a look of surprise in her eyes.

'Yes, I'm Daisy O'Grady,' she said, looking curiously at the girl.

'I came today to tell you you're a hard, selfish bitch! You never loved him! But I did!'

Mary, who had been talking to a group of neighbours, came over. 'Daisy, what's going on? People are staring.'

'I don't know, Mam. She's calling me names and I don't even know her.'

'Who are you?' Mary demanded. The girl was vaguely familiar.

'I'm Frances Walshe and this is Sarah, Sam's baby. I loved him and he loved me, but he couldn't get away from *her*! It's me he should have married, not her!'

Mary could see that the girl was genuinely upset but Daisy's face was flushed with anger.

'How dare you come here and insult me! I was his wife and

Joseph is his son and he isn't a bastard like *her*! Clear off! You're not welcome here.'

'She's a bastard because he was *made* to marry you. He hated you, he told me!'

Daisy took a step forward. She was seething. Hadn't he heaped enough humiliation on her head when she'd found out about Joseph? Now she was being humiliated again. 'It was the worst day of my life when I married him, the lying, cheating, useless no-mark! I suppose it was you that he spent his money on while we went short!'

'Yes, he knew how to treat a girl! And it was *his* money, he worked hard for it.'

'And I suppose it was you he'd been with when he got knocked over by that bus. I didn't see you running to take care of him. No one even knew you existed, that's how much he thought of you. He kept you well hidden.'

'He didn't! He didn't! I used to go and see him when you were at work!'

Mary, although shocked, caught Daisy's arm to stop her from slapping the girl.

'Go home, this is no place for a slanging match between you and our Daisy and it seems to me that we're all better off without him. Come on, we're all going home.'

They all turned away, leaving the girl staring helplessly after them.

'Oh, Mam! I've never been so . . . so . . . furious in my life!' Daisy exploded once they were out of the cemetery. 'It was just typical of him! How bloody dare he have that fast piece visiting him while I slaved away to keep a roof over our heads! How dare he! Isn't that just the living end?' Daisy raged.

'You've every right to be annoyed about that.'

'Annoyed! Annoyed! Mam, I'm furious! He . . . he was taking her out on the town while I . . . Oh, I'm glad he's dead! He got what he deserved!'

'Daisy, that's a wicked thing to say!' Mary rebuked her strongly.

'I don't care, Mam! And it's us who are providing the flaming funeral food. Well, I'll soon put an end to that! I'm going round there and telling them it's off, that we're taking all the food home and I don't care what people think of me!'

Mary was about to protest but Nell caught her arm and shook her head.

'Leave her, Mam, she's upset and she's every right to be, he even managed to humiliate her after he was dead!'

Mary nodded sorrowfully. 'I can't go and take away all the food. I just don't feel up to it. Oh, Nell, will all the misery ever cease?'

Nell put her arm around her mother. 'You look worn out. Go home, I'll go with her.'

Mary nodded; she *was* worn out. She really wondered if she could take very much more.

'It's not going to be easy, Daisy,' Nell said as they reached the top of Eldon Street.

'I know, but I honestly don't care what anyone thinks of me! I meant what I said, Nell.'

'Well, at least you're free now,' Nell replied, thinking of Johnnie Burton and Alfred.

'I am and I'm flaming well going to enjoy myself!'

'If the chance comes, will you get married again?' Nell was

trying to divert some of Daisy's anger.

'Not flaming well likely!'

'But you had no choice last time. What if you meet someone who *really* loves you, Daisy?'

Daisy looked irritable. 'Oh, I don't know, Nell. I'm just too shocked and angry at *her* turning up like that!'

'I know, we're all shocked. And I'm worried about Mam, she's not looking well these days.'

'Do any of us? We get no sleep, our nerves are stretched to breaking point, we have to go and do a day's work and Mam has to cope with all the housework and shopping on her own.'

'I've been thinking about the shopping and the queues. Florrie's got the right idea, they all take it in turns. Maybe we could think of some way to share the burden.' She paused outside the Eldon Street house. 'Well, here we are and we're not going to be very welcome.'

'I couldn't care less. I'm not having this lot – none of whom we even know very well – eating food that we've bought using our precious coupons.'

Nell sighed. She just wished the morning was over but at least she could escape to finish her shift.

'How did it go?' Vera asked when Nell took her place at the worktable.

'Terrible.'

'It would be, all those coffins,' Ethel sympathised.

'And – it was awful – Daisy was humiliated.'

'How?' Vera demanded.

Nell sighed and gave them the gist of the morning's events,

while slowly stirring the noxious mixture they all worked with.

'Well, at least I've got some great news,' Nancy interrupted.

'Oh, go on, tell her! Madam here has been like a cat on hot bricks all morning.'

'Oh, honestly, Ethel, you're a real killjoy!'

Nell smiled at the younger girl. 'So, tell all, Nancy?'

'I'm getting engaged.'

'To Harry Larkin?'

'She must be mad,' Ethel muttered. 'She 'ardly knows him and he's a Protestant!'

Nell got up and hugged the girl. 'Nancy, is it what you want? What you *really* want?'

'Of course it is, Nell, but me ma and da . . .'

'What's the matter with them?'

'There was holy murder,' Vera interrupted.

'Oh, no! Why, Nancy?'

'Well, yer know how they carried on when I asked to bring him home and then when I got back last night and told them . . .'

'What happened?' Nell could see the burning disappointment in the girl's eyes.

'Oh, Nell, you'd have thought I was telling them I was going on the streets! Me da called Harry every name under the sun. Said he was no good, a real hard case he called him and me mam said he was trying to ruin me! Ruin me! I love him and he loves me! They won't even meet him, so how can they judge him? All they care about is that he's a Protestant. I told yer, me mam's turning into a religious maniac! She said he's driven by the Devil, trying to drag young girls down to hell. Can yer imagine it! But I don't care, I'm nearly twenty-one and they can't do nothing about it!'

'So, you're going ahead?'

'I am! Too flaming right I am!'

'If you're absolutely sure, Nancy.'

'I *am*, Nell! We're going for the ring as soon as possible and it's going to be a good one. He's been saving his money for ages, waiting to meet the right girl, and I'm it!'

Nell smiled at her. 'You are. I wish you both every happiness and I know Daisy will say the same thing.'

'Thanks, Nell. I . . . I'm going to need all the support I can get unless me mam and da alter their tune and I don't think they will.'

'You never know, Nance, once they see the ring and everything . . .' Vera added, trying to brighten the mood. She thought Nancy's parents were taking the wrong attitude entirely, but she couldn't see what could be done to change their minds.

Chapter Twenty-One

A S NELL SAT ON the tram, making its agonisingly slow
way home, she reflected on the awkward conversation
she had had with Mary before the funeral that morning. Mary
hadn't been able to leave the subject alone.

'Nell, if you're going to see him again it's only fair that you
tell him you're married,' Mary had said seriously.

The light in Nell's eyes had died as she nodded. 'I know
but . . . but I'm afraid I might lose him.'

Mary had shaken her head. 'Sooner or later you will lose
him, luv. You *can't* marry him.'

Nell knew her mam was right but it didn't help. She was so
sure that he was the 'someone out there' that Annie had
spoken of. Now she knew just how Daisy had felt being tied
to Sam for all those years with no hope of any happiness for
the future, but she would never wish Alfred any harm the way
her sister had wished that Sam were dead. It was just not in
her nature. She and Daisy *were* different.

'Oh, Mam,' she'd wailed, 'I wish things were . . . easier.'

'So do I, but they're not. And besides Alfred, there's the question of . . . babies.'

Nell hadn't thought that far ahead, but now she was forced to consider it. As much as she loved Johnnie, she could never give him children. They would never be a family. And she was sure that that was something he would regard as very important.

To her delight and surprise, he was waiting for her when she got off the tram. Her heart missed a beat: he was so handsome. Quite a few of the girls and women turned to look admiringly and curiously to see who this Brylcreem Boy was meeting.

'I had to come and see you, Nell. How did the funeral go?'

She pulled the collar of her coat up around her neck. 'Not too bad but a girl turned up and upset Daisy.'

He looked concerned. 'No! How?'

'She had her child with her and she said it was Sam's and that she used to visit Sam when Daisy was at work. You can imagine how Daisy felt.'

'Very upset, I would imagine.'

'She was absolutely furious and I don't blame her. She was so angry she went up to Bessie Becket's, that neighbour of the O'Gradys in Eldon Street and announced there would be no tea, she was taking all the food home to Mam.'

Johnnie smiled ruefully at the thought of the scene. 'I can't say I blame her. It must have been terribly humiliating.' He paused. 'I've got to be back by ten, would you like to go to an early film? I'm afraid I won't be able to get off over Christmas at all, we're on standby. I'm not supposed to tell you but there is a convoy due in on Boxing Day.'

'Will they get home safely?'

He looked serious. 'I hope to God they will, Dad's with it.'

Nell nodded and they walked on in silence until they got to the corner of Portland Street. 'Will you tell him about Annie and Captain Burton?'

'I think so. I'm still not absolutely sure. I'll wait and see how he is.'

Nell was choosing her words carefully. 'Johnnie, if you like I could take you to meet your grandfather. I said I'd try to go and see him today.'

He looked thoughtful and she waited but when he didn't reply she squeezed his arm.

'Perhaps it's too late in the day to go all that way?'

'No, Nell, it's not that. Anyway, I've no other time. If I . . . we go it will have to be tonight.'

She lapsed into silence again as they walked along the pitch-dark street. It was strange how you got used to the blackout. She really should be helping her mam prepare for tomorrow. Still she'd help when she got back if it wasn't too late.

As they reached number twenty-six Nell turned to him. 'Will you come in? I'm sure Mam can rustle up something for your tea.'

'Just a cup of tea would be great. I can't impose on her, things are so hard to get now. And, Nell, I . . . would like to meet my grandfather. It might be best if I see him before I say anything to Dad.'

She nodded. 'I'll take you after I've got changed and had a bit of something to eat.'

'There's no keeping you away is there?' Mary said laughingly when they got inside, but the quick glance she cast at Nell held no amusement.

'I . . . we're going to Aintree, Mam, after I get changed, if that's all right. Leave some of the chores for me. I'll do them later.'

Mary nodded slowly. It was only natural, she supposed, that the lad wanted to see the old man. She just prayed that an opportunity would arise for Nell to tell him about Alfred. 'I'll make you a buttie, luv, you must be starving.'

'Do that, Mam, he's saying he only wants a cup of tea,' Nell called as she ran upstairs.

'You can borrow my hat and shoes if you like,' Daisy offered when Nell told her of her plans for the evening.

'Thanks, Daisy, I'll take care of them.'

Daisy smiled. 'You always do, I'll give you that.' Now Daisy had moved back home for good the girls were constantly borrowing each other's things. Daisy paused. 'He's very nice, Nell. Are you going to tell him about Alfred?'

Nell sighed and sat on the bed. 'Oh, Daisy, Mam's been going on at me, but I'm afraid I'll . . . lose him.'

Daisy turned away from the mirror. 'Do you love him, Nell?'

'Yes, I do.' She looked down at her hands. 'Now I know how you felt.'

'Trapped was how I felt. Like I'd never escape from the endless misery. Take my advice, Nell, don't take any notice of

271

Mam. Don't tell him. She doesn't understand. She put up with Da for all those years and she thinks we should do the same. Oh, I know she sympathises, but look at the number of times she made me go back to *him* when I was at my wits' end. There were times when if it hadn't been for Joseph, I'd have killed myself.' Daisy sat gently down on the bed next to her sister and put her hand tentatively over hers. 'I know we've never really been very close, but do listen to what I have to say, Nell. Snatch what happiness you can. God knows we might all be dead tomorrow or next week or next month. Don't tell him.'

'Oh, Daisy, I don't know! All the lies, all the cheating.'

'All what lies? You don't have to say anything! He doesn't even suspect. I notice you don't wear your wedding ring very often. Mam has noticed too but I told her we can't wear them at work and often you just simply forget to put it back on, and that we've more important things on our minds, like trying to stay alive!'

Nell smiled wryly. 'You're very persuasive, Daisy.'

'Don't be a fool, Nell. You'll spoil everything. Just enjoy yourself. There's a war on, remember?' Daisy smiled too. 'Well, since you've met him you've stopped being such a pain as you used to be.'

Nell grimaced. 'Was I really a pain?'

'Oh, God, you were!' Daisy laughed. 'Here, go out and enjoy yourself.' She handed Nell the second-hand leather handbag she prized so much.

'I'm glad things are . . . better between us, Daisy. I know it used to upset Mam terribly when we argued.'

'It's what sisters do, Nell. It's only natural. And when you got married to Alfred I was so jealous of everything you had.'

'*I* had nothing, Daisy. Nothing belonged to *me*, it was all *his*.' She shook her head. 'It was the biggest mistake of my life.'

'Well, don't go and make another one. Keep your mouth shut and if Mam asks, tell her you told him and he doesn't mind.'

'There's something else, Daisy.'

'What?'

'You know I can't have children.'

'Oh, Nell! Live for today. Tomorrow might never come! Now, we'd both better get down there or we'll be in trouble.'

Nell hugged her quickly.

'Get off, you'll ruin my hairdo!' Daisy cried, but she was smiling. Life was looking good. She was free! As free as a bird and even the neighbours wouldn't blame her when they heard about the carry-on with Frances Walshe.

'You always look so stylish, both of you,' Johnnie said as, five minutes later, he walked with Nell to the tram stop.

Nell laughed. 'Oh, it's amazing what you can do when you have to and Daisy is very good with hair and make-up.'

'When this lot is all over, perhaps she could find work in a hairdresser's.'

'She'd like that. She hates munitions, she says it ruins your hair and fingernails. She doesn't mind the money though.'

'She seems to be taking her loss very well.'

'She is, but they . . . they didn't get on. He wasn't a cripple when she married him – he was a bit of a "jack the lad", really.

She couldn't abide his family and I can't say I blame her for that, God rest all their souls.'

'It must have been terrible for her to be tied to him like that. Having to spend your life with someone you don't love.'

Nell nodded, but she didn't like the direction in which the conversation was heading. 'It was, but let's not talk about that.' She felt guilty. In a way she *was* lying to him by not telling him that she was in the same position as her sister had been. As he squeezed her hand she told herself that Daisy's advice was sensible. Live for today – they could all be dead tomorrow, like the O'Gradys.

'It's very pleasant around here,' he said as they got off half an hour later at the Black Bull. They crossed over the main road and walked down the darkened, quiet, tree-lined streets.

'Yes, it is. Very quiet and a bit select. Captain Burton's very nice and he'll be so delighted to meet you. Are you feeling all right?'

'Yes. A bit apprehensive, I suppose.'

'He has a terrible housekeeper so don't expect any tea.'

'You didn't tell me that.'

'I didn't want to frighten you off! She's awful.'

'It'd take more than a housekeeper to scare me away.' She squeezed his hand. 'It'll be fine, I know it will.'

She knocked and they waited on the step in silence.

'Oh, it's you again!' the sour-faced woman greeted her. 'I suppose you'd better come in. Wipe your feet, I spent all morning polishing this floor. I know your name but who shall I tell him *he* is?'

Nell glanced up at Johnnie.

'Tell him . . . tell him it's his grandson,' Johnnie instructed.

'His *what?* He never had any children so how can you be his grandson?'

'With respect, it's no business of yours just what relation I am to him.'

Two bright red spots appeared on the housekeeper's cheeks making her look like a painted doll, Nell thought as the woman opened the lounge door and disappeared, closing it firmly behind her.

The next instant the door was thrown open and James Burton stood in the doorway, the shocked face of his housekeeper appearing over his shoulder.

'I brought him to meet you,' Nell said quietly.

Johnnie held out his hand to the old man who looked as though he was near to tears.

'Are you really David's son?' His voice cracked with emotion.

'I am, sir.'

The old man's face was working, and he seemed lost for words.

'Shall we all go in?' Nell suggested.

'Of course! Of course!' Captain Burton stood back, and ushered them in. 'Come in, boy, you don't know how glad I am to see you! I think this calls for a drink. Mrs Armstrong,' he called to the disappearing back of his housekeeper, 'will you bring some glasses and the good bottle of whiskey I've been saving for a special occasion!'

Nell smiled at him as she unbuttoned her coat and sat down. 'I left it up to him. It was his decision to come now. He's not free after tonight. Duty, you understand.'

James Burton was beaming. 'My boy, I'm so glad you did. Has Nell told you . . . everything?'

'She has and I have never been so . . . surprised in all my life.'

'You know, you look like each other,' Nell commented. 'He's an older version of you, Johnnie. I never noticed it before.'

James Burton smiled at her, then turned to Johnnie. 'And your father, does he look like me?'

'He does indeed.'

The captain became serious and when he spoke there was great sadness in his voice. 'I would have married your grandmother if I could have found her. I tried desperately and for so long, she . . . she was the only woman I ever really loved. The last time I saw her we had a furious row. I said she *must* tell her parents. After the shock they would be very helpful to us. They might even help with my career. She turned on me and said that that was all I thought about – cared about – and that she needed no one's help. She'd be fine on her own. She was always hot-headed and stubborn and I could do nothing! I never saw her again. I searched for her everywhere, but to no avail.'

'It's all water under the bridge now, sir,' said Johnnie, unconsciously echoing Nell's words to her mother.

James Burton smiled. 'You're very polite. Could you possibly call me "Grandfather"? It would mean so much to me. I have no other family.'

Johnnie smiled. 'Its all water under the bridge now, Grandfather.'

Johnnie looked around the room as Mrs Armstrong came

276

in with glasses, a crystal jug of water and three crystal tumblers on a tray, her tightly compressed lips and flushed cheeks showing she was still angry.

The captain handed the drinks around but no one spoke until the door had closed behind her.

'Well, here's to happy families,' Nell suggested, wrinkling her nose at the smell of the whiskey. She'd never tasted spirits before and she didn't think she was going to like them.

'I'll drink to that, Nell. It may be very late, but better late than never, especially in times like these.'

Johnnie gestured with his hand to encompass the bric-à-brac and nautical prints. 'I can see where Father gets his love of the sea from.'

'I spent all my working life on the oceans of the world, eventually getting my own ship. What does your father do?'

'Before the war he was a Chief Engineer with Cunard, and now he's on convoy duty. In fact his convoy is due in on Boxing Day. That's why when Nell suggested coming I agreed. As she said, I can't get away over Christmas.'

A troubled look came over James Burton's face and he slowly rotated the glass in his hands. 'They are having it bad on the convoys.'

Johnnie nodded. 'Half the ships are lost before reaching port.'

'I know. I sailed as an escort in the last war. A convoy is only as fast as its slowest ship. I wish to God they all had the speed of the *Queen Mary* and *Queen Elizabeth*. Those two can outrun anything. With a top speed of thirty-two knots they're faster than most trains. Nothing can touch them.'

'I wish they all had that speed too. I get worried sick about Dad.'

James Burton smiled. 'And no doubt he is worried sick about you. You know this country owes a huge debt of gratitude to you boys for fighting off the Luftwaffe.'

'But at what cost? I've lost so many friends, good friends. Lads my age, lads younger too.'

'I thought this was supposed to be a happy occasion?' Nell interrupted brightly, pushing her own worries to the back of her mind.

'It is. Take no notice of us, Nell, men are all the same when they get together. Tell me about your father and your mother, Johnnie, there's so much I don't know.'

Nell sat quietly and listened to them talking. As time passed, she felt as though they'd forgotten that she was there at all. But it didn't matter, she was content just to watch and listen for she was learning so much about Johnnie, about his family, his background, his education. As she listened she wondered if she could ever fit into a world which was so far removed from her own.

At last Johnnie got to his feet.

'I'm sorry, I'll have to get back.' He turned to Nell. 'I feel I've neglected you shamefully.'

'Oh, I don't mind at all,' she smiled. 'I'm so glad I could help.'

'Nell, but for you I would never have known about Johnnie, never have found my family. I can't thank you enough.' James's gaze was as sincere as his obviously heartfelt words.

'She's a great girl, isn't she?' Johnnie enthused.

'One of the best.'

'Oh, stop it, for heaven's sake, or I'll be so embarrassed!' Nell laughed.

'Mother and Dad are meeting me in Southport on the twenty-eighth. It's the first day I'll have some time off. Will you come too, Grandfather?'

James nodded. 'When will you tell your father?'

'As soon as he gets home.'

'Will you telephone me first? I . . . I . . . wouldn't want to come if he isn't very happy with the . . . situation. You do realise that he was born illegitimate and that's something that might upset him. If it does, I'll understand.'

'He was adopted. Doesn't that make it all legal?'

James nodded. 'I can destroy his birth certificate if he wishes.'

'Let's wait and see. Goodnight and happy Christmas!'

James hugged his grandson. 'It will be a *very* happy Christmas, Johnnie.'

Nell wiped away a tear. She was so glad they'd found each other.

'You will come too?' Johnnie pressed as they walked back to the bus stop.

'Do you really want me to? Wouldn't it be better if just you and your parents had a quiet meal with your grandfather? I'm an outsider and they might find it hard. I mean it's going to be hard for everyone.'

'Not for me or for Grandfather. Oh, isn't he a marvellous old chap? I just wish I'd known him long before this.'

Nell smiled. 'He is and he's had such an interesting life. But I meant it would be hard for your father and mother.'

'I'll have already told them. Mother has booked the table but I'm sure two more won't be much trouble. Nell, if it hadn't been for you we'd never have known about him. You must come.'

'But your parents will be surprised to say the least, and won't need another shock. I . . . I'm sure they'll need time to . . . accept me. Especially with my background.'

'I don't care about your "background" as you call it! I'm mad about you! Don't you realise that I love you?'

She pressed her face against his shoulder so he wouldn't see the tears that stung her eyes. It didn't matter what Daisy said, she wasn't free. She was a married woman. Just how would he and his parents react to that news? And Johnnie's new-found grandfather knew she was married. She'd told him on her first visit, though thankfully he seemed to have forgotten, or at least kept quiet about it, for tonight at least.

Blinded with tears, she hugged him back. 'I love you too, Johnnie. I love you so much that it hurts and I want to be with you always, but . . .'

'No buts, Nell! I'll be so miserable and disappointed if you don't come. Please? Please? It will be a wonderful day and I want to share it with you.'

At last she nodded her agreement. 'All right, I'll come, but don't be upset if they can't take it all in. If they don't . . . take to me.'

'Oh, Nell, of course they'll "take to you"! How could they not? You're the best thing that's happened to this family in years!'

Chapter Twenty-Two

<hr>

THEY WERE ALL LATE into work the day after Boxing Day. Nancy, bursting with pride, showed off the engagement ring.

'Oh, Nance, it's gorgeous!' Vera cried, stunned by the size of the diamond in its square-cut setting. It was a far bigger stone than any of them had ever seen.

'I bet that set him back a bob or two,' Ethel commented.

'It did. Fifteen guineas!'

'He paid *fifteen guineas* for a ring!' Daisy was openly envious.

'I told yer, he's been saving up for years and he said I was worth every penny of it.'

'I'm sure you are, Nancy, and he must love you very much.' Nell smiled as she kissed the excited girl on the cheek.

'And what did your mam and da say to that?' Ethel, asked.

Nancy's eyes lost their sparkle. 'Me da wanted to know

where he got the money from and me mam said she was sure it wasn't by honest means.'

'Oh, how can they think like that? The lad's done nothing wrong, in fact he's done everything right,' Daisy said heatedly. Her mam would have been delighted if she'd got engaged and had an expensive ring instead of having to get married so hastily.

'They just won't believe he's a good, decent lad. I said to Mam, "What's the matter with yer? Yer won't even meet him. Just give him a chance?" But she wouldn't hear of it.'

'Oh, I'm so sorry, Nancy.' Nell paused and looked thoughtful. 'Would it help if I went and had a word with them?'

'Nell, don't get involved in family affairs,' Ethel warned.

'It might help.'

'And it might make matters worse if they think she's been running to us with tales.'

Nancy nodded. 'Ethel's right, Nell. They'd go mad and I don't think it would make any difference, but thanks. Yer're a great pal, yer all are.'

'So, when's the wedding then?' Daisy asked to lift the gloom.

Nancy brightened. 'In February. I know it's not the best time of year, but Harry's going to be posted a long way away; he doesn't know exactly where yet.'

'And are yer going to live at home, before and after, like?' Vera asked.

'I'll have to stick it out at home until the wedding, but afterwards Harry said he'd find me somewhere decent. Somewhere in a nice part of Liverpool, even if it's only a couple of rooms.'

'Well, if there's anything we can do to help, Nancy, you only have to ask. You know that.'

'I know, Nell. Yer're all better than me own family and I mean that.'

'God, would yer look at the time! We'll be killed! Better get going and get some work done or we'll be short in our wages – as if Christmas hasn't left us short enough!' Vera cried, pushing both Nancy and Daisy towards the factory gates.

It had been an austere Christmas for everyone. Gifts were mainly the things they'd made themselves, for Daisy had taught her new-found skills to Nell and there'd been scarves and hats and mitts they'd knitted with the wool from old jumpers that had been carefully unpicked and then washed and rewound.

One of the women in Daisy's group at work had also taught Daisy – during their lunch breaks – how to sew and smock. When she wasn't knitting, she was straining her eyes in the dim light of the kitchen and consequently Joseph had had a new romper suit, embellished across the front with delicate smocking.

'Oh, Daisy, it's lovely! Doesn't he look great!' Nell exclaimed.

Daisy smiled. People could say she hadn't been much of a wife and some even hinted that she wasn't much of a mother, seeing as she left Joseph quite a lot, but she loved her baby son and knew he was safe and happy with Mary.

'Mam, where did you get this from?' Nell cried when Mary managed to produce a small chicken from the oven, together with carrots and roast potatoes.

'Don't ask, Nell. I swore I'd never buy anything on the black market but it's been such a terrible year with one thing and another that I thought to hell with it! Let's have a decent meal for Christmas.'

'The table looks great, Nell. It must have taken you hours to make that lot,' Daisy commented smiling.

'It did. I seem to have spent every lunch break since the end of November making them.'

She had made crackers out of cardboard tubes covered with crêpe paper, and had twisted lengths of what had been left over into chains that she had criss-crossed over the tablecloth.

'They don't go bang when you pull them and there are no gifts, but I wrote out the mottoes and made the hats from newspaper.'

'Is there any Christmas pudding, Mam?' Teddy asked, as Mary gently prodded the chicken to make sure it was properly cooked.

'You can't have everything! There's no fruit to be had. Florrie made one with all kinds of weird things Peggy Draper at the shop said you could use but old Mrs Ford said she'd sooner do without than eat what she called "sawdust flavoured with gravy browning". Honestly, I don't know how Florrie manages to feed that lot, even with all their coupons. One small chicken, three pounds of carrots and three pounds of potatoes wouldn't go far amongst them all. Now sit down while I carve. I hope this isn't an old bird otherwise it'll be as tough as old boots. If it is I'll give that feller a tongue lashing for what he charged me.'

'Oh, Mam, it's chicken! It's a real treat! We never had this when we were kids!' Nell laughed, dishing out the meagre portions of vegetables.

'What will you wear?' Daisy had asked on Christmas evening after Nell had confided that she was going to meet Johnnie's parents in three days' time.

'I don't know. I don't have anything good. Of decent quality I mean – they're bound to be better dressed.'

'Not necessarily. I bet his Mam's old fashioned and dowdy and wearing something she's had for years.' Daisy was trying a new way with a turban that Vera had recommended.

'But it will be good quality.'

Daisy pulled a face. 'Cheap and cheerful, that's what all the women's magazines advise us to go for these days.'

'I'll have to wear my black skirt, like always.'

'You can borrow my best white blouse and those nice earrings I bought off Florrie's daughter when she needed a couple of bob.'

'That's a good idea. I'll give my good shoes a polish but my coat and hat aren't up to much.'

'Well, there's nothing we can do about that, unless you borrow Hilda Ford's artificial silk scarf that's doing the rounds of the street. That would look nice around your neck, under your coat. Then maybe people wouldn't notice your other clothes too much.'

'I'll have to mend the only decent pair of stockings I've got, there's a ladder in one of them.'

'If you promise to guard them with your life I'll lend you my new ones.'

'Daisy, you didn't pay ten shillings for a pair of stockings, did you?'

'I did and I got the last pair. God knows when we'll ever get the chance of any more.'

Nell shook her head. 'You're mad. Stark, staring mad!'

'Well, do you want them or not?'

'I'll take extra special care.'

Daisy abandoned her efforts with the turban and sat on the bed. 'Are you nervous?'

'I'm terrified!'

'Oh, don't worry. They'll have plenty to occupy their minds besides you. It's not every day you meet your long-lost father.'

Nell bit her lip. 'That's what worries me, Daisy. How will they get on?'

'Why should you worry about that? All you did was tell Johnnie about Captain Burton and Annie. It was his choice to go and see his grandfather; his decision to tell his parents.'

'Oh, I hope you're right, Daisy.'

It was a sentiment endorsed by Mary.

'Nell, don't be upset if nothing comes of it, if they don't want to meet him.' She shook her head disapprovingly. 'Sometimes it doesn't do to meddle in these things. Don't forget that Annie and Captain Burton were never married.'

'He said something like that, but Johnnie said because he was adopted it made it all sort of "legal".'

'Why does he want you to meet his parents?' Mary quizzed.

'Oh, Mam, probably because I'm the one who got them all together. Nothing else.'

Mary shook her head. She was certain Nell hadn't told him

about Alfred but she'd let the matter lie. Maybe some good could come out of this meeting. Perhaps Johnnie's parents could persuade him that Nell wasn't the type of girl suitable for the wife of an RAF pilot. There'd be heartbreak, she suspected, but it might be for the best in the long-term.

Nell's nerves were very jittery as she came down on the appointed day. She had had to take the day off work, pleading illness and Daisy wasn't there to boost her confidence.

'How do I look, Mam?' she asked.

Mary turned around from the sink and smiled. 'Very nice, luv. That scarf brightens everything up. You look neat and tidy and stylish. I have to say that Daisy's made a good job of cutting your hair. I wasn't too sure at the time but it *does* suit you.'

'I'm very nervous, Mam. The last time I was taken out for a meal was with . . . him.'

'Then just remember that, Nell,' Mary advised ominously, as she turned back to her washing up.

It seemed to have taken for ever to get to Southport, she thought wearily. She'd taken the overhead railway to Seaforth Sands and then changed to the train that had brought her to the elegant seaside resort. The train had been packed and she'd had to stand for half of the journey, but that wasn't unusual these days. She sighed with some relief as she caught sight of Johnnie waiting on the platform for her.

He took her arm. 'I was getting a bit worried, Nell.'

'Oh, the train was so slow and I had to stand for ages! Am I very late?'

'Not too bad. I don't think there's a train in the country that runs to time these days.'

Nell blinked in the frosty sunlight as they walked into Chapel Street. 'Did your father get home safely?'

'He did, thank God, but they lost five ships, almost half the convoy. He seemed very upset and I know how he feels. It's terrible just having to watch and not be able to help. He won't talk about it much.'

'Does your mother find that hard?'

'I don't think she really *wants* him to. She worries herself sick when he's away and if she knew any details she'd be even worse.'

'I can understand that, Johnnie. I'd feel the same and I know Mam would too. She used to worry about Da, although she always denied it, and that was in peacetime. It's strange though, she said she wasn't worrying about him *too* much the last time and that made it even more of a shock when he was killed.'

'That was a bad business, Nell. No one expected them to strike so soon.'

'Oh, let's not think about it.'

'What did he say when you told him about Captain Burton?'

'Nothing for quite some time. I don't think Mother can take it in even now.'

'But he . . . they *are* happy about it?'

'I think so, but they're still apprehensive.'

'Oh, I do hope everything will be all right.'

'I'm sure after they've had a chance to unwind it will be.'

'Where are we going?'

'To the Queens. It's a small hotel on the promenade, but it's very nice and somehow they manage to put a decent meal on the table. Mother is so envious, she says she spends half her life in queues.'

'So does Mam. Where are they meeting him?'

'I thought it would be best if we all met at the hotel. There's less chance of a row somewhere public. But I don't think it will come to that,' he added quickly, seeing the consternation on Nell's face.

She said nothing. Her stomach was beginning to churn. James Burton wasn't the only one who wanted to be accepted.

It was a very nice hotel, she thought as she looked around at the comfortable sofas and chairs in the reception area. It wasn't like the Stork at all. The furnishings and decor there were darker, more ornate, fussy even. She handed her hat and coat to Johnnie and patted her hair nervously, catching sight of herself in a long mirror with a gold frame. Oh, she hoped she wouldn't disgrace herself. Frantically she tried to remember just how she had behaved when Alfred had taken her out for meals in what now seemed a dim and distant past.

'Well, let's see how things are going. I hope the ice has been broken by now,' Johnnie urged, taking her arm and tucking it through his.

At first she didn't see them, for it seemed as though a sea of faces turned towards her. Her throat felt as if it were closing over and her heart was hammering against her ribs.

'There they are, and they look happy!' Johnnie said quietly, ushering her towards a table in the window.

Nell's gaze went quickly over the group. James Burton and his long-lost son David were both smiling at her, and she noticed the resemblance immediately. The small, fair-haired woman was smiling too and Nell's spirits rose.

'Well, I must say everyone seems to be quite content. Mother, Father, this is Nell. We've her to thank for this reunion.'

Both James and David Burton stood up and offered her their hands in greeting.

'It's good to meet you, Nell,' David Burton said warmly. 'We do indeed have a lot to thank you for, don't we, Barbara?'

Nell looked into the kind grey eyes and knew instinctively that this woman was well disposed towards her. She wore a beautifully cut blue wool dress and the pearls at her throat and in her ears were real, as were the diamonds that sparkled on the hand outstretched in formal greeting.

'We certainly do,' she replied. 'It must be a wonderful feeling to be able to make so many people happy.'

'Nell, you look very nice and I'm so glad you could come,' James Burton fussed over her.

'I think we're all glad she could come,' Johnnie agreed, holding the chair out for her.

She smiled shyly. 'I wasn't sure how things would go.'

'Well, I can't say I wasn't surprised when Johnnie told us,' David said.

'It was quite a shock,' his mother added in a quiet voice that held no trace of a Liverpool accent. 'We're still trying to take it all in. I believe you met Johnnie at a dance, Nell?'

'I did. It was the night of the first heavy Christmas raid. I was out with the girls I work with and I was terrified. We all were. That was the night I found out about your husband. I thought it must just be a coincidence, but it wasn't. I was so glad that Johnnie had looked after me and wanted to see me again.'

'You work in munitions?' Barbara Burton said, pouring Nell a glass of water whilst assessing her astutely. She was an attractive girl, and though her clothes were not of a particularly good material, everyone was after all having to 'make do and mend', the girl had added little touches of style to her outfit: the scarf, the cameo and the new stockings. They were particularly hard come by. She must ask her later, in the privacy of the ladies' powder room, where she had obtained them.

Nell smiled at her with relief.

'I work in Kirkby and I'm quite proud of the fact that we're making the shells for the lads at the front.'

'And so you should be, Nell. It's vital work,' David Burton agreed.

'It must be hard and dangerous work. Did you never consider anything else, Nell?' his wife asked. 'Nursing perhaps?'

'That can be dangerous too. To be honest I don't think I'd have made a very good nurse and there are plenty of nurses already trained.'

'Do you know, dear, I've heard that they are going to call up married women soon.'

'I heard that too,' Nell agreed.

'Of course I do my bit with the WVS and I've volunteered to be a fire-watcher. It's hard to think what else I could do. I'm not trained for anything other than running a house.'

'Oh, come on, Mother, you can drive.'

'Yes, I suppose I could drive . . . something. Did you suffer much damage, Nell, in the raids?'

'Not too bad. We've still got a roof over our heads but

houses further down our street were badly damaged.'

'It was dreadful! Dreadful! I could see the flames from the attic window.'

'Barbara, why weren't you in the shelter?' her husband asked, horrified, while the captain shook his head.

She smiled. 'Oh, such a fuss! And it's so cold and damp in that shelter.'

'God forbid that it should happen again but if it does you must promise me you'll get into your motor car and drive down to my house,' James Burton insisted. 'You're not that far from the docks and it's the docks they're after.'

She turned and patted her husband's father on the hand. 'I promise I'll do that, James.'

'Shall we order now?' David Burton asked, pleased that things were developing well between his wife and Nell. She seemed a nice enough girl. Rough and ready, of course, and with an accent you could cut with a knife, but she came from people he considered to be the salt of the earth. People who had stoically endured so much already.

As the meal progressed Nell became more and more relaxed, yet she became ever more aware that the gap between herself and Johnnie and his family was a very wide one. The three men were all talking about the war and she was left to make conversation with Barbara Burton. The woman was obviously trying to put her at her ease but as time went on Nell began to feel unhappy and guilty. Would this woman be so pleasant if she knew her son's girl was in fact a married woman?

It was with some relief that it was deemed time to leave. Johnnie had to get back to his base and his parents and James Burton were going to Crosby.

'Nell, you were very quiet. Are you all right?' Johnnie asked as they left the hotel.

'I'm fine, really I am. It was just . . . nice to sit and listen. Everyone was so happy and your mother was very nice to me.'

'It's been a great day for us all, Nell.'

She smiled at him. 'Good.'

'When can I see you again?'

'I don't know. When can you get time off?'

'Hopefully I'll get a few hours at the end of the week, but I can't promise. I'll come when I can.'

'That'll be fine.'

He touched her shoulder briefly. 'I'll go and say goodbye to my parents now. The car's around the corner. Mother has somehow managed to get some petrol; I'm not asking where from.'

'Probably from the same place as our Christmas dinner,' she laughed, as he ran off through the hotel door, waving cheerily as he went.

'It's been a great day, Nell. A truly *great* day,' James Burton said to her, his face suffused with happiness.

'I'm so glad. We never really think how lucky we are to have a family. Daisy and I have fought and argued in the past and Teddy was a real tearaway when he was younger . . .'

'I always wished I had a family but as you know Marjorie and I were never blessed. I intend to make up for lost time though.' He paused and looked more serious. 'Johnnie seems to be very fond of you and I know it's none of my business, but are you fond of him, Nell?'

Nell nodded, remembering that he knew she was married.

'Don't get upset, Nell,' James Burton said quietly, correctly guessing what she was thinking. 'I won't tell anyone. I don't want to hurt you.'

'It was a huge mistake. He's years older than me and I married him for a secure future, that's all. I never really loved him and he certainly never loved me.'

'Grasp happiness while you can, Nell. I know I'm not the greatest example, but times are different. The world has changed.'

'Has it? Some people will never admit that. My mam for one.'

'Take no notice of her, Nell.'

'My sister told me much the same thing, about living for today, but Mam . . . Mam thinks I've told Johnnie and he doesn't mind.'

'Then don't disillusion her, Nell.' He pulled the collar of his coat up around his ears. 'Well, I have to be going. You will come and see me?'

She smiled. 'Of course I will.'

She looked thoughtful as he walked away to join his son and daughter-in-law. Whom should she take notice of? Did it matter? They were questions that she pondered all the way home.

'Where's Mam?' she asked, walking into the kitchen.

'Gone in to see Florrie. Our Teddy is at the Fords' too. Well, how did it go?'

'Great. His father and mother are very nice. I thought I might have trouble with her but she was so pleasant. She even asked me if I could get her some stockings.'

'So why the long face?'

'Oh, Daisy, all the way home I've been asking myself: is it worth it? I can't marry him, so why get so involved with his family?'

'Well, you don't have to go and live in their pockets.'

'I said I'd visit James and she said I should visit her too.'

'Tell them you haven't time. It's true. By the time we get home from work we're worn out. Too tired to go trailing out to Crosby and Aintree and on Sundays we help Mam as much as we can. Well, you do.'

'Oh, Daisy, I just don't know what to do!'

'Does he want to see you again?'

'Yes.'

'Then don't be a fool, Nell.'

'Oh, I suppose you're right, Daisy,' Nell said, smiling at her sister.

Chapter Twenty-Three

———◆———

To her bitter disappointment and dismay Nancy's parents hadn't changed their rigidly forbidding attitude towards their daughter's choice of husband.

'I don't understand them at all,' Nell sighed as she and Daisy were finishing sewing some silk ruffles on the cuffs and skirt of the wedding dress Daisy had made for Nancy. From somewhere Johnnie had managed to get some parachute silk and Daisy had scoured the shops and markets for the bits of lace and ribbon to trim it. There had been enough to re-cover a wide-brimmed hat that had belonged to Ethel's mother, which she had unearthed from an old trunk in the attic. Out of the pieces that had been left Daisy had managed to make a camisole and french knickers for the bride.

'Thank God that's all finished, I've nearly ruined my eyesight!' Daisy exclaimed, holding up the fashionable white silk dress for Nell's approval.

'You're both very good to that girl, I hope she appreciates

it,' Mary remarked, gathering up the sewing materials.

'Oh, Mam, she does. She's over the moon,' Daisy replied.

'I know she really wanted a church wedding, but with her mam and da not speaking to her and Harry being a Protestant and having no relatives at all, she's happy enough with the Register Office and we're all doing everything we can to make it a great day. I know this isn't the traditional long white dress but it's the next best thing – and there is a war on.'

'I've never been more sick of a saying than I am of that one.' Mary sighed. 'What's he like, this Harry Larkin, apart from being the wrong religion?'

'We've only met him a couple of times but he seems to be a really nice lad and he idolises Nancy. True, he had a terrible upbringing and his early life in the Navy didn't help, but basically I think he just wants to be loved,' Nell replied.

'Well, Nancy certainly loves him,' Daisy added.

'After all the upset they've been through, married life should hold no qualms. I suppose we really should wish them good luck.'

'Yes, Mam, we should,' Nell said quietly. Sometimes she was a little jealous of young Nancy, even though she wished the girl every happiness in life. Nancy at least was free to marry the man she loved so much.

'You're sure you're happy with the idea of her staying here tomorrow night?' Daisy asked.

Mary nodded. At first she had been dubious. If the girl's own parents were so set against the marriage, she felt she shouldn't appear to be siding with Nancy. But the girl was very genuine and seemed really upset by her parents' implacable attitude, although she tried to dismiss it.

'She's really grateful. She said she just couldn't have stood it, having to get herself dressed and leave that house on her own on her wedding day.'

'What time is she coming?'

'About eight. She'll have her things packed and Vera said she'll help her here with her cases, which should save an argument. Nancy doesn't want to leave with a torrent of abuse being hurled at her and Vera said she'd try and keep things calm. I really *can't* understand them. In the middle of a war, when no one knows if they'll survive from one day to the next, you'd think they would just grin and bear it.'

'Oh, there's no accounting for some people's attitudes! I'll try and get a bit of meat and give the girl a decent meal at least,' Mary offered.

Vera and Nancy arrived just before eight o'clock the following evening. Vera was carrying a large case tied up with string and Nancy herself was clutching numerous brown paper parcels and bags.

'I didn't know she had this much stuff otherwise I'd have got in touch with Pickfords!' Vera remarked drily as Mary ushered them in.

'Everything is mine. I've taken nothing I didn't buy meself,' Nancy declared firmly.

'Take your coat off and come and have a cup of tea, luv. I've made a really nice supper for you,' Mary said, smiling.

'How did it go?' Nell whispered to Vera as Nancy stacked up her belongings in a corner of the kitchen.

'Faces like bloody thunder! Right gobs on the pair of them! The rest of the kids never uttered a sound. It's not natural, that. But at least there was no shouting or yelling. I got her out as quick as I could.'

'Did no one say *anything?*' Daisy asked, sotto voce.

'Not a bloody dicky bird. If yer ask me she's better off out of there – and look what she's going to. What wouldn't I give for a couple of nice rooms in that house in Walton Village.'

Nell smiled. 'She'll be all right now. We'll keep her fully occupied.'

'Will you stay for something to eat, Vera? I think I can make it stretch a bit further as our Teddy's at Florrie's,' Mary asked.

'Ta, Mrs C. but I promised me mam I'd get back smartish, like. Her nerves are in a shocking state, she thinks there's going to be an air-raid every flaming night!'

'Please God there won't be, but I know how she feels. It's our Daisy's turn to go fire-watching tonight and Nell's tomorrow night. Any word from your husband, Vera?'

'I had a letter, if yer can call it that, last week. He's fine. Says he quite enjoys this "Army Game" as he calls it! Enjoys! Fellers, I ask yer! Well, I'll see yer all in the morning then. Tarrah!'

'Thanks, Vera, for everything.'

'Right, then, sit you down and get this while it's hot,' Mary instructed. She smiled as Nancy at last seemed to relax.

They were all up early next morning and Nell insisted that Nancy have the first use of the sink in the scullery.

'I've put a big jug of hot water in there, a clean towel and a nice bit of soap I cadged from Florrie's daughter Maureen who married a decent feller, just like you're doing. Then while you're getting washed, I'll clear up the bedroom so you can get dressed,' Nell announced.

'Oh, Nell, yer're dead good to me!'

'It's your wedding day, Nancy! The happiest day in your life and it's *going* to be happy!'

'I know it's not exactly as you wanted it, but it's a damned sight happier than my wedding day was,' Daisy added with feeling. 'Now get started. I want to do your hair and fix your hat on firmly.'

'Mam, will you ask our Teddy to see if there's any sign of those flowers? I know they're not up to much but they cost an arm and a leg,' Nell asked of her mother.

'I told you you should have gone to Lizzie Cassidy,' Mary replied while Daisy cast her eyes to the ceiling and went upstairs.

Half an hour later Nell made some toast and took it up to Nancy with a cup of freshly made tea.

'Put the towel over your knees in case of crumbs, and – *oh!* Nancy!'

'How does she look?' Daisy asked, smiling at Nell.

'She looks gorgeous!'

'Nance, don't you dare touch your hat or your hair, they're both perfect. It's taken me enough time to make sure they are,' Daisy warned her before leaving to see to her own appearance.

'Oh, Nell, I'm so nervous!'

'Why? You look beautiful, he'll be delighted with you.'

'Really?'

'Yes, really! Look at yourself in the mirror.'

'I have and I . . . it doesn't look like . . . me!'

Nell took her hands. 'Today you're not expected to look your usual self. All brides are beautiful.'

'Were you?'

'I suppose I was. Well, everyone said so, including my poor da and that was a big compliment from him. My mam, God love her, had a coat with a real fur collar and a hat and gloves. She looked so smart and I talked Da into taking her out on the town for the first time in her life.'

'I wouldn't have cared if me mam had turned up in a shawl . . .' Nancy said with a tremor in her voice.

'Don't think like that, Nancy, luv. It's her loss, not yours, and you've a good life waiting for you. It's not everyone who gets to go to Rhyl for a few days' honeymoon. Your Harry treats you like a queen.'

Nancy smiled. 'He does, doesn't he? Oh, Nell, I love him so much.'

'He knows that. Come on now, smile.'

Nancy reached out and kissed Nell on the cheek. 'I wish I had you for a mam, I really do.'

'Oh, God help us, Nancy! Are you trying to make me feel a hundred? Now sit there and sip this tea while I put on my jacket and hat.'

A watery sun filtered through the grey clouds as they left the house. Vera, her mother, Ethel, and her two sisters were going straight to Brougham Terrace, as were a few other girls from work. Nell and Daisy had encouraged everyone to go so Nancy wouldn't miss her family too much.

'I'm glad you made me put your coat over my outfit,' Nancy said, shivering a little as they walked to the tram stop.

'Well, you'd have frozen otherwise and you can slip it off when we get there.'

'I hope Harry's on time. He was going out last night with a few of his mates, I hope they didn't get him paralytic!'

'Being in the Navy for as long as he has been, I'm sure he can hold his drink. Stop worrying,' Daisy said firmly

'You won't tell the entire tramload of passengers where we're going?'

'I don't think we'll have to,' Daisy laughed.

She was right. On seeing the white silk dress under the coat and the smartly trimmed white hat and the small posy of flowers Nancy carried, the conductor grinned widely and announced, 'Here comes the bride! Give 'er a cheer, lads!'

For a few seconds the tram reverberated with cheers, whistles and shouted messages and then the irrepressible conductor burst into song.

'"It won't be a stylish marriage, I can't afford a carriage, but you'll look sweet . . ."'

'Never mind the "bicycle made for two" bit!' Daisy interrupted good-naturedly.

'Don't tell me her name's Daisy?' he countered.

'No, it's not! It's Nancy, now shut up and give us the tickets.'

''Ave this one on me, girls! No prizes fer guessin' ter where? West Derby Road?'

'Right first time,' Nell laughed.

'Did yer 'ear that, Fred? Get yer skates on, we don't want ter give the poor feller a fright by lettin' 'im think 'e's been jilted!' he yelled down the tram to the driver.

'A right flaming comedian!' Daisy muttered.

Nell laughed. 'Oh, leave him alone. Look, she's blushing. She's made up with the fuss.'

On the steps of the register office, Daisy tweaked Nancy's hat and Nell slid the coat from around her shoulders.

'Smile! You look gorgeous!'

Nancy still looked a little apprehensive as they entered the small room crowded with her friends but as she caught sight of Harry's blond hair she relaxed. When he turned and she saw the expression on his face she smiled radiantly. It didn't matter that her family weren't there. She had Harry and all her friends.

Nell took her small bouquet and gave her a gentle push forward.

Daisy touched Nell's arm. 'She's really happy. It was worth all the effort,' she whispered. Then they both concentrated on the civil ceremony as Nancy became Mrs Henry Larkin.

By the end of April Nell knew she couldn't go on not revealing the truth to Johnnie. Her mother hadn't spoken of the matter again but Nell often caught Mary looking at her questioningly and with great sadness.

'Daisy, I've been thinking a lot over the last weeks,' she confided as they got ready for bed.

Daisy was carefully hanging up the dress she had spent all evening 'livening up' with rows of white rick-rack braid. They livened a great many things up these days.

'About what, as if I didn't know.'

'Johnnie and everyone else.'

'You've only been to visit James twice and you've managed to steer clear of his mam altogether.'

'Until now. He's insisting that on Thursday night I go out to Crosby with him. His father will be home and James is going too. Oh, Daisy, I can't keep on like this.'

'You love him, don't you?'

'Yes, more than anything in the world. And I'd do anything, *anything* to be able to marry him.'

Daisy looked thoughtful and Nell stopped brushing her hair.

'Well?'

'You could always get a divorce.'

Nell was scandalised. 'A *what!*'

'You heard. That woman in Group One got one.'

'Yes, and everyone's still talking about it. Oh, Daisy, I couldn't! It would kill Mam.'

'Nell, it would be a nine-day wonder. Oh, of course everyone *would* talk and you'd have the street up and Father Mannion would go mad but isn't that a small price to pay to get rid of Alfred? We could send Mam on some sort of holiday for a bit until the worst was over. I know she keeps in touch with those people in Wales who took our Teddy in when he was evacuated. She could stay with them.'

'But what about Joseph?'

'She could take him with her. The country air would do him good.'

'You can only get a divorce if your husband has committed adultery.'

'Or if he's deserted you and he's done that all right. Slung you out on your ear and we've plenty of witnesses to that! Think about it, Nell. You're still young, you shouldn't have to be saddled with that flaming old horror!'

Nell shook her head despairingly. 'I don't think I could go through with it. It would cost the earth and even if I did get a divorce, would Johnnie still want me? What would his mam and dad think of me then? They would have to bear the gossip too, and then . . .'

'Then what?' Daisy asked. Divorce had just been a long shot. A suggestion.

'Have you forgotten that I can't have children?'

Daisy sighed. 'I had forgotten.'

'I couldn't make Johnnie go through all that and then tell him he'll never have a family. I just *couldn't* do it, Daisy.'

'Well, it was just a thought. I *do* feel sorry for you, Nell, I know what it's like.'

'Thanks, Daisy.' She smiled gratefully at her sister. 'I still think that it might be good for Mam and Joseph to have a bit of a holiday, though. At least I could have a couple of weeks not having to bear the reproachful looks she gives me. It's almost as bad as her accusing me outright. Our Teddy's big enough now to see to himself.'

'Big enough and daft enough! The way Mam wet-nurses him, he's useless. God help the girl that gets him, she'll spend her life waiting on him hand and foot. Now we'd better get some sleep.'

But Nell lay awake for hours. It was so tempting to think that a divorce could solve her problem, but it wouldn't and she would be an outcast, shunned by family, friends and the Church.

On Wednesday night Nell broached the subject of a holiday for Mary.

'Are you mad, Nell?' Mary cried.

'It would do you good to get away from here for a while. Away from the queues, the dirt, the rationing.'

'Things are still rationed in Wales.'

'Yes, but staying on a farm you'll have fresh milk, butter, eggs, cheese and vegetables and anything else they've got. Teddy said they were great people and I know you've kept in touch.'

'It's our Teddy I'm thinking of – and what about Joseph? Who'll look after him when you're at work, Daisy?'

'Take him with you, Mam. It will be good for him too. Our Teddy can see to himself, it won't hurt him, and besides we're here of a night.'

'When you're not out gallivanting. I don't think I could leave you all.'

'Oh, Mam, you deserve a break. It won't cost much. It's the first of May tomorrow. The weather is getting better and it's light until much later too.'

'Oh, I'll think about it. I'm not promising anything.' Mary closed the subject with a curt shake of her head.

'Do you think she'll go?' Nell asked Daisy as they were washing the dishes in the scullery after Mary had gone in to see Florrie.

'I hope so. I'd like to invite Freddie Mercer back here.'

'Oh, so this is serious?'

'I don't know, Nell. I really like him. He's fun to be with, he's got a good reserved job and he likes to spend his money.'

'Well, can't you invite him even if Mam is still here?'

Daisy looked doubtful. 'I suppose I could.'

'I mean, you won't get much privacy. Our Teddy'll be here. I would go out but you know him.'

'I could give him money to go to the cinema.'

'That's not a bad idea.'

'Oh, let's wait and see. What are you going to wear for the big night out?'

'Oh, stop that, Daisy, it's just a bit of an outing.'

'Like heck it is! It's a big family get-together, you want to look decent, don't you?'

'Of course I do.'

'Then start thinking. You can borrow something of mine if you like, I'm not going out tomorrow. I'm going to wash my hair and try rinsing it with beer. Vera said it works wonders on my colour hair. Then I'm on fire-watching duty.'

Nell laughed. 'Don't tell the fellers around here what you want the beer for, you'll be killed. The waste of a good pint, they'll say.'

'I couldn't care less. Anyway, it's one pint less for someone to waste their money on!'

Nell was glad she had borrowed Daisy's short swing-back jacket as she stood on the station at Seaforth after changing trains the following evening. It had been fine and dry all day but it had turned chilly once the sun had set. She smiled as she remembered her mam's warning: 'Never cast a clout till May is out.' It was the first of the month today but the chill damp breeze coming off the river reminded her that it wasn't summer yet.

She had really enjoyed herself tonight. She knew she looked well in her pink floral-printed dress, which she'd cheered up with a new white collar and some white braid around the hem. Daisy's jacket was navy blue and matched the small hat she wore. Johnnie had complimented her when he'd met her at the station and his mother had said how nice and fresh she looked.

The meal had been a miracle of improvisation and many hours spent in the queue at the butcher's and greengrocer's, and Johnnie's father had contributed a tin of peaches – a real luxury. There had even been evaporated milk to go with them. Barbara Burton had laughed and apologised for it not being 'real' cream and Nell had joked that if her mam went to stay on a farm there might even be real cream next time Johnnie's father was home.

She began to walk slowly up and down the platform while she waited. Oh, they had made her so welcome, part of the family, and she wished with all her heart that she *could* belongs to that family. She had promised to visit both James and Barbara more frequently, and she would nag the daylights out of Daisy in the hope that she could procure a pair of the promised stockings for Barbara even at the exorbitant prices they asked.

She began to feel miserable. Would this blasted train ever arrive? It must be nearing eleven o'clock and she'd promised Mam she would be back at a decent hour.

Her heart sank further as the wailing, keening sound of the siren shattered the stillness of the night. God knows what time she'd get home now! She hadn't a clue where the nearest public shelter was. She ran back to the ticket office and banged on the glass.

'I thought there was no one on the platform,' the station master said as he appeared, shrugging on his jacket.

'Look, I just want to get home. Is there a train?'

'It's halfway between here and Oriel Road. It shouldn't take long getting here but the driver might decide to abandon it and get everyone to the nearest shelter, depending on how many passengers there are.'

'But I've only got a few stops to go.'

'Sorry, luv, but I'll wait here with you for a few minutes. If it gets bad then we'll *have* to go to the shelter.'

Nell looked up at the night sky. The tracers from the anti-aircraft fire looked like fireworks, she thought. Almost immediately there was a huge explosion and they saw a building erupt into flames across the river in Wallasey.

'Looks like the poor sods over the water are getting it tonight. You're in luck, girl, here comes the train.'

Nell was so thankful when the man pushed her inside and waved the driver on.

The rest of the journey didn't take long but to Nell it seemed interminable as she cowered in a corner of the carriage listening to the whistling and then the roars of exploding bombs. When at last the train pulled into the Pier Head, she got off and ran along the platform and down the steps. Even if she had to run all the way home she would, she hated the public shelters. When she reached Byrom Street she stopped and leaned against a wall, panting. Looking up, she gasped in horror. It looked as if the sky was on fire as hundreds of incendiaries and high-explosive bombs rained down. She couldn't stay here. She *had* to go on. As she ran she prayed to God to let her reach home in safety. At least they would be all together, it would be less worrying than if she were stuck in a public shelter.

By the time she reached Portland Street her breathing was

so laboured that it hurt and her heart was pounding against her ribs. Fear alone had driven her on. She had ignored the shouted instructions and warnings from policemen and firemen and ARP wardens. She *had* to get home. She flung open the front door and made a dive for the stairs.

'Thank God! Get in here, I've been worried sick!' Mary cried.

'Oh, Mam, I was stuck on Seaforth station when the siren went. I've run all the way home from the Pier Head. It's terrible out there. They're dropping thousands of incendiaries!'

'I know, Daisy's on fire-watching duty! Now you're here I'm going out to find her and bring her back with me!'

'You can't! You're *not* going out there! You don't know how terrible it is! I'll go!'

Nell didn't wait for her mother to contradict her but, exhausted and frightened though she was, ran out into the street. She stepped hastily backwards on to the pavement as a fire engine turned the corner, its bell clanging frantically, the firemen still pulling on their jackets. The whole street was illuminated by the dozens of fires that were already beginning to take hold of the dilapidated houses. She watched in horrified fascination as the very last house on the left side of the street began to crumble and the hungry flames leaped upwards from the collapsing roof beams. Everything was in chaos. The firemen were running out the hoses, shouting and yelling instructions to each other and all the men who had come to help. Huge clouds of dense black smoke hung over everything and the roaring and crackling of burning timber and house contents added to the noise and confusion.

She looked around. Just where would Daisy be? So many

houses were already burning. She couldn't look in them all. She began to run, screaming her sister's name at the top of her voice, until she ran into someone.

''Ere, Nell, what are yer doing out 'ere?'

Nell grabbed Eddie Molloy's arm. 'Oh, Mr Molloy, have you seen Daisy?' she pleaded with her neighbour. 'She was fire-watching!'

'She's down at number forty, trying to keep the fire from taking hold of the roof!'

Her heart thumping with fear, she ran towards number forty whose roof was already well alight.

'Daisy! Daisy!' She screamed above the noise of the flames. She *had* to find Daisy. She'd promised her mother she would. She *had* to get her out of this inferno. What was her sister thinking of, going into this?

With the sleeve of her jacket pressed across her nose and mouth, frantically she began to climb the stairs. The smoke was getting thicker. It stung her eyes, burned her throat and made her cough, but she didn't stop. She *couldn't* stop.

'Daisy, for the love of God, where are you?' she yelled but the only reply was the roaring and crackling of the flames.

She gripped the banister rail with her free hand and tried again and again to reach the top of the stairs but the heat and flames beat her back. Her eyes were streaming, her throat felt raw as over and over she screamed for her sister.

'Get out of here, now, luv, the roof's about to fall in!'

She looked up into the face of the fireman. 'My sister! My sister's up there! You've got to save her! You've just got to!' she pleaded.

Strong arms lifted her off her feet and she was half carried, half dragged downstairs and into the street.

'There's nothing we can do, luv. No one could survive up there.'

With tears pouring down her face Nell looked upwards. The whole of the roof was engulfed in flames reaching upwards into the night sky, which was no longer a dark velvety indigo. It was now yellow and orange and red criss-crossed by searchlights picking out the dark shapes of the enemy planes, making them look like a swarm of angry bees. The night air was rent with a cacophany of explosions, anti-aircraft fire, the drone of engines, the furious clanging of ambulance and fire-engine bells and the yells of the fire-fighters, police and wardens.

The noise and the images suddenly began to fade and she was being carried once again.

'Nell! Nell! What's going on? Are you hurt, luv?' The voice became stronger and from the mist a familiar face appeared.

'Mr Ford! It's Daisy!' she gasped, struggling to get up.

'It's all right, Nell! She's fine, I took her home,' Richie reassured her.

Nell grabbed his arm. 'How? She was up there!'

'She got out when she saw it was out of control. We didn't see her in the smoke and dust. Come on, luv, I'll get you home. God blast them to hell and back!' he cried, raising his fist to the skies where the planes still circled, their targets made easily visible now by the raging fires.

Mary uttered a scream of pure relief when Nell was pushed under the stairs by Richie Ford.

'Nell! I thought I'd lost you both!'

'Oh, Mam, it was terrible! Daisy, you gave me a terrible fright! I went after you, but the landing was on fire. I couldn't get up the stairs.'

'But I was already out! If I'd known you were trying to get up to the landing, if . . . anything had happened to you—'

'Just thank God and His Holy Mother that you're both safe!' Mary interrupted and with tears streaming down her cheeks she gathered both her daughters to her. After the events of this night, there was no way she was leaving Liverpool and her family. There would be no holiday for her.

Chapter Twenty-Four

———◆———

'I NEVER WANT TO GO through a night like that again!' Mary said with feeling as at one o'clock the all-clear sounded.

'Neither do I. I've never been so terrified in all my life!' Nell added.

Daisy was very subdued, she had come very near to death and Nell could have been killed too. It was two very quiet, shocked, but thankful sisters who made their way to work just hours later, both aware that their brush with mortality had drawn them closer together.

'The pair of you look like death warmed up, what's up with yer?' Vera asked. She herself looked no better: no one had had much sleep and nearly everyone looked dazed.

'We had a very close shave last night.'

'How come?' Nancy was curious.

'I got caught in the raid and when I got home Daisy was out fire-watching and some fool told me she was still in a blazing house. I thought she . . . she was dead.'

'But I'd already got out. Oh, wait until I see that Norman Lester, I'll give him a piece of my mind. Frightening Nell like that.'

'You'll have to get in the queue behind Mam and me!' Nell said grimly.

'We were on our way to the shelter when me mam remembered she hadn't got her false teeth in. She told me da to go and get them! I ask yer! Her bloody teeth!' Vera was indignant.

'What did he say?' Ethel asked, incredulously.

'He said, "What's up with yer, woman? It's bloody bombs they're dropping, not pork pies."'

Ethel gave a mirthless laugh. 'There's always a comedian, isn't there?'

'Well, yer've got to be a flaming comedian to live in this city!' Vera replied laconically.

'I hope to God they don't come again tonight, me mam's nerves are shot to bits! Are you two going out?' Ethel asked.

'No, I think we've had enough excitement to last us a month,' Nell answered for herself and Daisy.

'How about you, Nancy?' Daisy asked.

'We didn't get much but I got really scared. Yer could see the flames and hear the explosions. When the all-clear went I . . . I went to look for me mam and da.'

'Yer never did?' Vera was surprised. Since the wedding Nancy had neither seen nor heard from her parents.

'What else could I do, Vera?'

'And so? Were they all right?'

Nancy nodded, looking a little pale.

'What did they say?' Ethel demanded.

'They told me . . . they said to get back where I came from. They didn't want . . . nothing from me.'

'Well, may God forgive them, the pair of bloody old bigots!' Vera exploded.

'Nance, don't you go bothering your head about them, luv, they're just not worth it. You've Harry and that woman you live with is dead nice, and there's us, so to hell with them!' Ethel comforted her.

Nancy managed a smile and Nell and Vera exchanged worried looks. How could anyone treat their child like that? Nell wondered sadly.

Mary was dozing in the chair and both girls were knitting when to their horror at twenty past ten the dog started to whine and tremble.

'Oh, God, not again! I'm worn out!' Mary cried, jumping up and grabbing the biscuit tin and the blankets.

Daisy ran upstairs and snatched her child from his cot and as they crowded under the stairs the siren started to wail.

'How long do you think it'll go on for tonight?' Daisy asked, trying to get in a comfortable position with the still-sleeping Joseph.

'God knows and I suggest we all start asking Him,' Mary said, drawing her rosary beads from her apron pocket. She was trying not to think of Teddy who, white with fear and foreboding, had grabbed his gas mask and his jacket and gone cycling down the street at top speed, heading for Victoria Street.

As the hours passed and the house shook from the explosions their fears deepened. God was definitely not listening tonight, Nell thought as they sat huddled together for comfort and strength, never knowing if the next bomb might be the one that would end all their lives.

'Are yer all right under there?' a voice yelled above the din.

'Oh, Richie, is that you?' Mary called and Florrie's husband's face appeared.

'It is.'

'What time is it?' Mary asked.

''Alf past midnight an' there's no sign of them goin' back 'ome!'

'Is it bad, Richie? Is Florrie all right?'

'She was the last time I saw 'er an', aye, it's bad, Mary. Bad as the Christmas raids. The Corn Exchange, the Dock Board offices, the White Star Building, Church House, St Michael's have been destroyed and that's just a few of the buildings. An' Bootle's takin' a 'ammerin' ternight too! Well, I'd best get back.'

'Take care, Richie!' Mary called after him.

'If Bootle is in a bad way, I hope Johnnie's mam is all right. Crosby's not that far from Bootle.'

'If she's any sense she'll have taken herself off to Aintree to Captain Burton's house,' Daisy said grimly.

Mary was silent, thinking about Teddy, out there cycling backwards and forwards in a city that was being systematically and relentlessly destroyed.

It was not until after three a.m. that the all-clear sounded and people could begin to emerge from the shelters and houses to see what was left of their city after a second night's bombardment. What they found was devastation. And when the next morning the girls got to work, after the now familiar long and arduous journey, they found everyone in a sombre mood. Some girls and women were absent and everyone knew that that meant a death in the family.

'I thought we'd had it last night,' Vera informed them. 'The house two doors down got a direct hit and all our windows and doors blew in, the chimney crashed into the street and you can see daylight through the roof, but at least we all came through it.'

'Well, if the Christmas raids are anything to go by, I reckon we've got one more night of it, then they'll go somewhere else,' Ethel put in.

Vera glared at her. 'We can do without your "reckoning". I don't think I can stand another night of it! I can hardly keep me eyes open, I'm that tired. We've had no sleep now for two nights, the worry wears yer out and then it takes hours to get to work. I'm worn to a frazzle.'

'Aren't we all, but at least we've still got a roof over our heads,' Nell finished. After last night she was just glad still to be alive.

It seemed so unfair that the journey home took so long, Nell thought wearily as they finally reached Portland Street, when they had to work so hard all day.

'I always thought Bert Barrett was a bit of a comedian,' Daisy remarked drily as they turned the corner.

'Why?' Nell asked.

'Look!' Daisy pointed to the half-wrecked shop on the corner of Limekiln Lane.

Nell managed a weak smile. Mr Barrett had put a notice

on the door which read: 'Removed for Alterations and Redecoration.'

'It's all we can do, Daisy. Keep our spirits up. Look on the bright side.'

But there wasn't much brightness when, the minute they stepped through the door, they walked straight into an argument between Mary and Teddy. Daisy flung her bag on the sofa in annoyance.

'Oh, what's the matter now, Mam? We're all worn out and want a few hours' peace and quiet, and what do we get? A flaming row!'

'He's insisting on going out tonight! I've pleaded with him not to go.'

'Mam, I *told* you I was going to the pictures with Tommy tonight. I told you days ago,' Teddy said firmly.

'That was before all this bombing started! And what if they start again tonight?'

'If they do we'll go and sign in. I haven't been out to the pictures for ages!'

'Oh, honestly, Teddy, no one's been anywhere for ages! Is the flaming picture house still standing?' Daisy demanded.

'It was when I passed it this morning. Ah, Mam, don't be a killjoy! I bet Mrs Ford isn't carrying on like this!'

'If Florrie's got any sense she will be!' Mary gave in. 'Oh, go! Go on, see if I care!'

'Now can we get some tea and a bit of peace?' Nell asked irritably as at long last she kicked the shoes off her aching feet.

Teddy and Tommy Ford had gone to the pictures, Tommy muttering that he'd had to face similar outrage from his mam, his gran and his Aunty Betty to that endured by Teddy. 'It'll be great ter get out of that flamin' house! Me Aunty Betty's kids are shockin', they'd drive yer mad!' Tommy had said darkly.

Daisy, who had borrowed a paper pattern from Ethel and had managed to get some pretty yellow-and-white polka-dot-printed cotton, was going to make a dress for the summer. 'If I've any left, would you like to make a collar and belt, Nell?' she asked.

'Thanks, Daisy. Will I give you a hand to pin the pattern on?'

'Don't be putting it on the floor, it'll get dirty. I've mopped out but these days it seems to get even muckier,' Mary warned. Daisy's previously hidden skills still amazed her.

'It's all the dust, Mam, it gets everywhere and there's soot mingled with it from all the demolished chimneys.'

They worked in silence while Mary dozed. She wondered how the girls found the energy to even think about clothes.

The dress had all been cut out and Daisy had started to tack the bodice together when the dog – who was under the table – started to whine. 'Oh, not again! Dear God, not again!' Mary groaned.

'Quick, Daisy, get it all together and put it in this paper bag or it'll be ruined!' Nell said, starting to gather up the dress parts.

'Can't they give us a single night's peace?' Daisy snapped. 'Oh, here we go!'

The sound of the siren rose to a crescendo wail and then died away.

'You know we could get some more tacking done if we went to the shelter,' Daisy suggested.

'Well, I'm not going to any flaming shelter,' Mary stated. 'They're not safe.'

'Mam, you're getting as bad as old Mrs Ford!' Nell replied, but neither of them could budge her.

It seemed to all of them that it was a re-run of the previous night. Hour after hour they sat shaking and shivering. It was like the end of the world, Nell thought to herself. How much more could the already battered city take?

At five o'clock on what would have been a sunny May morning, but for the thick pall of smoke that hung over the city, the 'raiders past' sounded.

Daisy was still shaking. 'Oh, Mam, I didn't think it would ever end!'

Mary passed a hand over her aching forehead. 'I hope our Teddy's all right. He didn't come back for his bike. I've been storming heaven with my prayers all night.'

'He'll have gone straight to sign in,' Daisy said tiredly as they went out into the street.

'Oh, my God!' Nell cried and they all fell silent.

Hundreds of fires were still raging and charred and smoking bricks, timbers and shards of broken glass seemed to cover the entire street. There were big gaps where yesterday houses had stood. The corner shop was in ruins and already people were out and beginning to dig with their bare hands to try to salvage something from their ruined homes.

'Oh, we were lucky! So very, very lucky!' Nell breathed.

'Mam, look, here's Florrie!'

Florrie Ford stumbled towards them, her face and hair

covered in dust and soot and with tears pouring down her cheeks.

'Oh, luv, what's wrong?' Mary cried, reaching out for her neighbour's hands.

'It's Richie! Oh, God, Mary . . . he . . . he's dead!'

'No! Oh, Florrie, no!' Mary cried.

'What happened, Mrs Ford?' Nell asked.

'A wall collapsed on 'im. He was tryin' ter get old Ma Jenkins out, 'alf 'er roof 'ad cum in! Oh, Mary, what'll I do?'

Mary put her arms around her. 'Come on inside, luv. I'll make us all a cup of tea and I'm sure I've got some sleeping tablets left somewhere. Nell, go and put the kettle on.'

Old Mrs Ford had joined them and they were sitting in shocked silence when a very grimy and haggard Teddy arrived home, his right arm in a sling and a bandage around one leg of his torn trousers.

'Oh, Teddy, thank God!' Mary cried, throwing her arms around him.

'Teddy, is Tommy all right?' Nell hissed.

He nodded and Nell closed her eyes in relief. Florrie couldn't stand more bad news.

'His da's been killed,' Mary whispered to her son.

'Oh, Mam, it's . . . it's worse than it's ever been!' Suddenly the shaken lad was crying. 'There were five hundred planes! *Five hundred* and for six and a half hours! Nearly everything's gone! I . . . I was terrified!'

'Here, sit down, lad.' Mary pushed him down on the sofa beside old Mrs Ford and Nell handed him a mug of tea.

'Lewis's has gone and Kelly's and Blacklers. The William Brown Library, the Museum, the Art Gallery. All the warehouses in Pall Mall and Cheapside. The General Post Office, and India buildings – but Paradise Street, Lord Street and all the streets round there are the worst. There's hardly anything left standing! It's . . . it's terrible!'

He'd barely finished speaking when a huge explosion made the house shake and Florrie screamed in terror.

'It's all right, Mrs Ford, it's the *Malakand*!' Teddy said wearily.

'What the hell is the *Malakand*?' Mary demanded, shaken by the explosion herself.

'It's the ammunition ship in number two Huskisson Dock. She's alight. No one could put out the fires so they abandoned her. A scuffer told us she'd blow up and take the dock with her. She was loaded with a thousand tons of shells and bombs going out to the Middle East. He reckoned it would take hours . . . maybe days for her to blow herself out.'

'What happened to you?' Mary asked.

'I'd borrowed a bike and I came off it in Canning Place. I ran into a pile of bricks. I went to the Royal Infirmary but it was like a battlefield. A nurse bandaged my leg and wrist. It doesn't half hurt, Mam. She said she thought it wasn't broken, just badly sprained, but I can't ride a bike.'

'And a good thing too if you ask me,' Mary said thankfully. Then, 'Come on, Florrie, luv, I'll take you home and see if there's anything I can do.' Gently Mary raised Florrie to her feet. 'Teddy, you get to bed but have a wash first.'

'Well,' Nell said, getting to her feet too, 'we'd better go and see what we can do to help.'

'I think there'll be plenty, girl,' old Mrs Ford agreed. 'It's shockin', that's what it is. I never thought I'd lose a son. It's all wrong, somehow. Parents are supposed to die before their children.'

They all worked so hard, helping to brush up what seemed like acres of broken glass, helping to retrieve the pathetic remains of people's homes, when Teddy, sent by Mary, arrived to fetch them.

'Tell her I'll be down when I've finished picking the glass and stones out of this blanket for Mrs Jenkins,' Nell shouted.

'Nell, she said to come now because a scuffer has arrived!'

'Oh, God!' Nell dropped the brush and hastily followed her brother. She prayed nothing had happened to James or Barbara Burton.

An enormous policeman was standing in the kitchen, his uniform so covered in dust that it was no longer navy blue but grey. His eyes were bloodshot from lack of sleep.

'Mrs McManus?'

'Yes?' Nell queried.

'It's bad news, I'm afraid. There's no easy way of saying this, luv. Alfred McManus was killed in last night's raid. The burning roof of the Co-op collapsed on top of him. Three other wardens died too.'

Nell sat down on the sofa. She'd never even given him a thought. So he was dead! She felt dazed but somehow not shocked. All she felt was pity for him, the way she would feel pity for a neighbour or acquaintance. He had been her husband and all she could feel was regret. There was no sense of loss, no grief.

'Would you like a cup of tea, sir?' Mary asked.

'Thanks, missus, but I've no time. I've got to get back, there's so much to do.'

Mary showed him out.

'Well, he died better than he lived,' Daisy remarked quietly. 'Doing something for others rather than for himself.'

'I'm so sorry, Nell,' Mary said comfortingly.

Nell looked up at her. 'There's no need to be, Mam. I . . . I'm not upset. Oh, I feel sorry for him in a way, but that's all.'

Daisy sat beside her and took her hand. 'You're free now, Nell.'

'I am, aren't I?' Nell replied with wonder. She hadn't had time to take in the implications of that.

'You stay here, there's no need for you to go back out there. People will understand,' Mary interrupted.

Nell stood up. 'It's fine, Mam, I'll go. It will keep me occupied and we all have to help out.'

Daisy and Nell both returned to the rubble-strewn street but after half an hour Teddy appeared again.

'Now what?' Daisy demanded apprehensively. Not more bad news.

'That feller from Aintree has arrived.'

Nell was confused. 'Captain Burton?'

'Yes. He came in a car with a woman. A posh woman.'

'Mrs Burton! Oh, I hope nothing has happened to Johnnie!' Nell cried.

'Go on, run!' Daisy urged, but Nell needed no further encouragement.

James Burton and his daughter-in-law were sitting on the sofa. Barbara had been out for hours, driving a canteen lorry, and when she'd finally got home she'd driven through the remaining hours of the raid to James's house. Both looked pale and shocked.

'Nell, as soon as the all-clear went, Barbara and I came straight here. It's taken hours, people are coming from miles around just to gape at the devastation and by God it's bad! Never in my life have I seen anything like it!' the captain said grimly.

'I know. Teddy was out in it and Mr Ford, one of the neighbours, was killed and . . . and I've just heard that Alfred . . . is dead.'

'Oh, Nell, I'm sorry,' James Burton said sincerely.

She shook her head, embarrassed. 'Don't be.'

Barbara Burton looked questioningly from Nell to James.

Nell turned to her. 'Alfred was my husband. I'm sorry I didn't tell you about him—'

'He abandoned her,' Mary interrupted. 'He wasn't a nice person at all. He threw her out.'

'Nell, you never told me that!' James cried.

'I know.'

'Well, you can't stay here. What if they come again tonight?'

Mary was incredulous. 'There isn't much left standing now, surely they can't come back again!'

'They might. I want all of you to come out and stay with me in Aintree. It's much safer. And it'll be easier for you girls to get to work.'

'All of us?' Mary queried.

'Yes, there's plenty of room.'

'Is Johnnie all right?' Nell pleaded. It was the question she had been longing to ask.

'As far as we know, although he was up there last night. I believe eighteen enemy planes were shot down.' Barbara's tone became brisk. 'Now I want no excuses, pack up whatever you need and we'll start out.'

The experience of riding in a motor car somehow dimmed the horror of the sights they saw, and the devastation lessened the further into the suburbs they went.

As James solicitously ushered them into the house, he apologised that Mrs Armstrong had given up working for him to devote herself to her WVS duties. Nell couldn't help but feel relieved. Once installed, Mary confided in a whisper to her that James Burton must be a saint for turning his beautiful home over to the likes of them until the raids quietened down.

'But, Mam, he doesn't see it that way. He's so grateful that you took Annie in and gave her a home, the first decent one she'd had for years, that now he's repaying the favour. He genuinely believes we'll be safer here.'

Mary nodded thoughtfully, looking down at the beautiful dining-room table they were sitting round. She'd hated to leave Florrie in her hour of need but old Mrs Ford had urged her to think of the safety of her own family first.

After settling them in and making them a pot of tea, Barbara had gone back to work with the other ladies of the WVS, regardless of James's protests. She promised to come back if there was another raid.

Mary peered at her daughter who seemed lost in thought.

'Are you sure you feel all right, Nell? I know everything's upside down but you'll have to think about burying . . . him.'

'I know, Mam. I'm not looking forward to it but it's my duty.'

'Let's hope that no one comes out of the woodwork at his funeral the way they did at Sam's!' Daisy commented drily, for she had never forgotten her humiliation with Frances Walshe.

'I don't think so, Daisy. He was too careful with his money and his reputation.' Nell paused, worried. 'I hope Mrs Burton doesn't think me awful for not saying anything about Alfred.'

'She looked shocked, but then you would be, wouldn't you? She'll come to terms with it. She seems a sensible woman and she's a brave woman too. She was telling me all about driving that lorry with the bombs falling around her.'

Nell bit her lip anxiously. 'Oh, I just hope Johnnie's safe and well.'

'I wouldn't worry too much, Nell, he's survived so far, which is more than you can say for half of Liverpool,' Daisy reassured her.

The Captain poked his head around the dining-room door.

'Might I suggest that you all go and try and get some sleep?'

Mary got to her feet. 'I think I will. I can't remember when I last had a decent rest.'

'We'll follow you up, Mam,' Nell said. 'Is there any more tea in that pot, Daisy?'

'Yes.' Daisy walked cautiously into the kitchen. 'Oh, Nell, look at all the modern conveniences. An electric kettle, a gas cooker, a toaster, decent pans. It's very kind of him to take us in.'

'He's a good man. It's such a shame about him and Annie. They could have been so happy. She needn't have spent her life pushing that barrow in all weathers.'

Daisy looked meaningfully at her sister. 'Now you're free, Nell, you should start thinking about *your* future and *your* happiness.'

'Oh, it's far too soon and besides . . .'

'Besides what?'

'Daisy, there's the fact that I can't give him a family. And don't you dare suggest that I don't tell him that. I couldn't, I just couldn't do that to him!'

Daisy shrugged. 'Well, it's your decision. It's your life.'

'Daisy, I know you mean well—'

'I just want to see you happy!' She got to her feet. 'Come on, let's go up. Oh, the luxury of a decent bed and bedclothes. If they come again tonight at least we know we're all safe but God help the city . . .'

They all slept heavily, making up the sleep they had lost, but just before midnight they were wakened by the sound of the siren and automatically they got up and dressed and went downstairs. They found the captain in the kitchen, fully dressed also.

'It's nothing to worry about, go back to bed. We haven't needed the shelter yet and you're all exhausted. If I think it's necessary I'll come and wake you.'

Nell looked worriedly at him. 'How much more can we take? The city is in ruins now!'

'They're trying to put the Port out of operation. Close the

ports and the country will starve to death. You all know the amount of food, war materials and men who pass through the Port of Liverpool. It's vital to them that they put us out of action.'

'Well, they won't succeed. We're a tough lot. They've never come across Scousers before,' Mary said firmly.

'A fine sentiment and I'm sure you're right,' James Burton nodded. 'Now go and get some rest.'

After another night of bombardment followed by another day's hard work, Nell and Daisy arrived back at the house in Cedar Road to find Johnnie waiting for them.

Nell flung herself into his arms. 'Oh, Johnnie! Johnnie! I'm so glad to see you!'

'And it's a big relief to me to know you're all safe and well.'

'How *did* you know?'

'Mother told me. I managed to escape for a few hours and went home. I was cross with her for not coming back here but she said she had very little petrol left and she had work to do there.'

Nell was suddenly serious. 'Johnnie, let's go into the sitting room, there's something I have to tell you.'

He looked surprised and Daisy raised her eyebrows. Obviously his mother hadn't told him about Alfred McManus.

As soon as the sitting-room door closed behind them, Nell wrapped her arms around him. 'Oh, Johnnie, it's been a living hell. I've been so scared.'

'You've every right to be. So far we've had nearly eight hundred planes dropping God knows how many tons of explosives and we're preparing for another night of it.'

'Oh, no!'

'You'll be safe out here. Safer than Mother. If they go for Bootle again there's always the chance of stray bombs falling in Crosby.'

She buried her face on his shoulder.

'What's the matter, Nell?'

'I should have told you this long ago, but . . . but I was frightened to.'

'Tell me what?'

'I . . . I was married.'

He held her away from him. 'Married!'

She nodded. 'It was a terrible mistake. I only lived with him for just over a year. He was much older; he . . . he abandoned me.'

'Oh, Nell!'

She hurried on before her courage deserted her. 'He was killed on Saturday night. He was an ARP warden.'

He drew her to him and stroked her hair. 'Poor, poor Nell! You kept all that from me!'

'I didn't want to lose you, Johnnie! I was terrified I would. Mam kept on at me to tell you but Daisy said live for today. She *knew* . . . she understood what it was like to look at the future and *know* there would never be any happiness. Do you remember when you said how awful it would be to be tied for life to someone you don't love?'

'I do. Oh, Nell, why didn't you say something then?'

'I wanted to, but somehow I just couldn't. I *couldn't*. My life, without you in it, wouldn't have been worth living.'

He kissed her gently on the cheek. 'And neither would mine. From the minute I saw you in the Grafton I knew you were the girl for me. You are the one I love and want by my side for ever. Oh, my dear, I love you so much!'

Her eyes were brimming with tears. The barrier of Alfred no longer stood between them but how was she going to tell him about . . . the rest of it?

'Nell,' he went on, 'I know this isn't the right time, in the middle of a war when neither of us knows what tomorrow may bring, never mind next month or next year . . . but will you marry me?'

She felt the band of pain that seemed to encircle her heart grow tighter. Oh, this was far, far worse than having to tell him she was married. Now, when happiness was so near, when she was free of the vows she had made to Alfred, it was being snatched away. Even though she loved him to distraction she could never promise to marry him without telling him that there would be no children. The force of her emotions made her tremble. 'Oh, Johnnie, I wish . . . I wish I could say yes. I love you so much, but . . .' She couldn't meet his gaze. She closed her eyes and the tears fell slowly down her cheeks.

'Why are you crying? If you need more time, I'll understand. It's not really fair of me to ask you so soon after the loss of your husband.'

'It's not that! I never really loved Alfred. I mean it! All I felt when he died was pity. It's not . . . about waiting for a while because I'm upset. I'm not. That part of my life was over more than a year ago.'

He kissed away her tears.

'Then what is it?'

She swallowed hard. She would give anything, *anything* not to have to tell him. Not to see the look in his eyes, the

pain in his voice, the despair when he drew away and tried
to find the words to retract his proposal. But he would *have* to
know.

'I . . . I can't have children. I had to have an operation.
That's why he . . . he threw me out.' There, she'd said it. She
stiffened in his arms.

He didn't speak, nor did he release her.

'Johnnie? Please, say something? Anything?' she begged.
She could see her world falling apart in front of her eyes and
there was nothing she could do about it.

He remained silent and the sobs racked her body. He was
trying to find a way to let her down, to let her go.

'Johnnie, let me go! Please? Leave and go back to your
base. You don't have to say anything. I understand, I really
do!' Oh, please God, she prayed, let it be over soon, let him
go quickly and with no words. She dare not think of the future
and all the pain it would bring, all she could think about was
here and now. She pulled away from him. Let it be over soon,
please, please? Still he didn't speak, and she prayed she
wouldn't break down completely. That would only make it
even more difficult.

He touched her cheek but she couldn't look at him.

'Nell, I can't say now how I feel about . . . children. I've
seen enough of death . . . so many lives snuffed out and . . .
mine could well be the next. Every time we have to scramble
I wonder will I ever come back? Will my plane ever land on
this runway again? When I'm up there there's no time to
think like that. There's no time even to think. Nell, night
after night I've been up there, watching, just watching the
bombs rain down, knowing the death, the mutilation and

the damage they're doing and being helpless, so bloody helpless. Unable to stop them. The other night there were five hundred of them and barely twenty of us! I raged against them, Nell. I raged against God for letting it happen, but it's not His fault. It's the fault of evil men, I know that, but it doesn't help the anger and frustration I feel. What I'm trying to say is that we *have* to live for today. Tomorrow may never come. Oh, Nell, will either of us be alive by the end of this terrible week? Now can you understand why I can't – *won't* think about children? I love you and I'm not going to let your love slip through my fingers! Marry me tomorrow – at the weekend – as soon as possible?'

She felt her knees go weak and she sagged against him. 'I will! Yes, I'll marry you and as soon as possible and we . . . we'll think about the future when this terrible war is over.' They were words she had never expected to hear.

She smiled through her tears. 'Johnnie, we'll get by. We'll be so happy, I know we will. If we can just survive.'

He held her closer. 'I've got *everything* to live for now. We *will* make it! We *will* get through it.' He kissed her forehead. 'As your mother says, "on a wing and a prayer".'

Epilogue

———✦———

April 1947

'NELL, WILL YOU FOR heaven's sake sit still! How I am supposed to fix this hat on properly with you twisting your head from side to side every few minutes?' Daisy was laughing despite trying to sound annoyed.

'How am I supposed to keep my eye on everything?' Nell answered, smiling back at Daisy's reflection in the dressing-table mirror. They no longer shared a bedroom. In fact they no longer shared a house, but they were closer now than they had ever been.

'You don't have to be supervising. You know Mam and Barbara have got everything under control. They're quite capable of seeing to a dozen and a half people, including that mischievous imp, my son.'

Nell looked out of the window to the sky beyond.

'Do you think it will rain? If it does, we can say goodbye to having the party outside in the garden. It's very good of Grandfather to turn his precious garden over to that lot.'

'Oh, Nell Burton! You are the limit! Would the captain have offered if he didn't want "that lot", as you call our family and friends, traipsing over his lawn?'

Nell nodded. 'You're right. You know, Daisy, I still find it hard to call him "Grandfather".'

'I thought he preferred "Grandfather" to anything more formal? At least, that's what Johnnie told me.'

'He does, it's just that for all the time I knew him, even before Johnnie did, I never thought of him being my grandfather.'

'Well, ours died when we were babies.'

'And, talking of babies, doesn't Maria look wonderful? That christening dress you made her is gorgeous! And she won't be cold, not with the beautiful coat Barbara bought her.'

'Hardly! Cashmere with a velvet trim: I get a headache just thinking how much she paid for it.'

'I know, but when I said it was a scandalous price she said she had never expected to be a grandmother and she's thrilled to bits so what does it matter what it cost.'

'I suppose, when you look at it like that, she's right. Nancy would have been thrilled, too, with all the fuss.'

Both girls fell silent and tears welled up in Nell's eyes. Poor Nancy had had so much to live for. The years of her marriage had been such happy ones until Harry had been killed. What had made it seem even more tragically wasteful was the fact that he had survived the sinking of two of the ships he'd served in, but, just a month after the end of the war, the corvette he was returning home in had hit a stray mine. There had been few survivors and young Harry Larkin was not amongst them.

Daisy shook her head sadly. They had all been very fond of Nancy.

'She was never the same . . . after, was she, Daisy?'

'No, God luv her, she wasn't.'

'Not even having Maria seemed to help.'

'I think it made it worse. Harry had wanted a child so much.'

Nell nodded. There had been times in the past when she had cried herself to sleep, thinking of the operation that had saved her life but robbed her of the chance of being a mother. Johnnie had always been so comforting. He stressed it didn't matter that much to him. He was just grateful that he had survived those terrible years when so many of his friends had not. Despite all the horrors of war they had all survived. She wanted to believe him but deep in her heart she knew it *did* matter, despite the fact that he still loved her and had married her.

'Bloody diphtheria! Will they ever find a cure?' Daisy raged, thinking of the epidemic of the disease that had taken Nancy's life and that of so many others.

Nell sighed deeply. 'I pray to God they do. It . . . it's a terrible way to die. Your throat closing over, fighting for breath, choking . . .'

'Oh, don't let's think about that now, Nell! She's gone. She's with Harry and that's all poor Nancy ever wanted.'

Nell wiped away a tear. 'And she left me the most precious gift of all. Her baby.'

'She knew how you'd love and care for her. And that you and Johnnie could give Maria the kind of life she never could have without Harry. Thank God she left that will.'

'She once said she wished I could have been her mam.'

'Well, you would have been a bit different to the one she had. Can you imagine the kind of life that pair of miserable, hard-hearted bigots who have the nerve to call themselves Nancy's mother and father would have made for Maria? No love, no affection . . . nothing.'

'Oh, I know, Daisy. There are times when I just can't bear to think about it. I thank God every day that Nancy wanted me . . . us to take her baby.'

'Well, you'll be able to thank Him "formally", so to speak, today. That's if you will ever be ready, which at this rate I doubt!'

'You two are not still dolling yourselves up, are you?' Mary had appeared in the doorway. 'We're going to be late and I don't think the Reverend Gentleman will be very pleased, especially as that child will be getting hungry and will probably start acting up – and seeing as she's nearly eighteen months old, she can cause mayhem . . .' She was clearly harassed.

'It's not my fault, Mam, tell Madam here to sit still! *You* look very nice, though. A bit flustered but nice.'

'Is it any wonder I'm flustered? That young girl of our Teddy's can talk the hind leg off a donkey. All I said was, "The trouble Mrs Burton and I have had getting decent food and drink for this do", and off she goes, nineteen to the dozen, about how her mam and her sisters can find absolutely anything! My head's aching already.'

'I think you're going to have to get used to it, Mam. He

thinks she's wonderful!' Nell laughed.

Mary groaned. 'Imagine, there's four more like her. I don't think I could get through a wedding like that!'

'You could and, Mam, you do look great.'

Mary smiled at her daughters. In those dark days after the May Blitz she had feared for all their futures. Now everything looked so rosy for both of them. She smoothed down the skirt of the rose-pink velvet suit Daisy had made her and her hand strayed to her hat. She looked as smart as Barbara whose outfit had been purchased at Henderson's. 'I would never have believed that a daughter of mine could be so clever with a needle.'

'Or a hairbrush, scissors and curling tongs,' Nell added.

'I just wish I was being paid more than fifteen shillings a week. How do they expect me to live on that, and with Joseph to keep?'

'Well, you wanted to learn to be a qualified hairdresser and that's all an apprentice gets paid. It'll be worth it in the end, Daisy, you'll see.'

'Sometimes I wonder, Nell. I really do.'

'Well, I'm proud of you.' Mary dropped her voice and looked at the closed door. 'No one would ever know that this suit was made from a pair of old curtains.'

'Oh, Mam! I told you not to say that to *anyone*! And they weren't old, they'd hardly even faded!' Daisy hissed. 'God, wouldn't she have you mortified!' she queried of Nell.

'Hush, Johnnie and his father are coming,' Nell instructed.

There was a tap on the door and the two men entered, Johnnie carrying Maria.

'I've come to see what is keeping my beautiful wife from

my equally beautiful daughter who is getting a bit restless . . .'

'And *my* beautiful wife is getting a bit anxious too,' David Burton added, smiling.

'Are we all ready? Nell's all finished and if she'll keep her hands off that hat she'll be fine,' Daisy laughed.

'Right then, Mary, will you take my arm, and, Daisy, will you take the other one?' David extended both his arms. He admired both Mary and Daisy. Life hadn't been easy for either of them but they were the type of quiet, resolute and courageous women – as was Barbara, his own wife – who overcame everything.

'You have such lovely manners, David. Now, if that had been my Jack he'd have been out the door and we'd be left to fend for ourselves!'

'Oh, Mam!' Daisy cried, raising her eyes to the ceiling.

'But it's true, Daisy,' Mary said with a tinge of sadness in her voice. For all his faults, she missed him and probably always would.

As they left Johnnie turned to Nell and put his free arm around her shoulders.

'Oh, doesn't she look beautiful!' Daisy exclaimed, holding out her arms to take the chubby, rosy-cheeked little girl.

The two men looked on dotingly as Nell tickled her daughter under the chin. She was such a pretty child with her light brown curly hair, blue eyes and the dimple on her chin. The dress Daisy had made really *was* beautiful, Nell thought.

'Come and give your mam a kiss and your grandma and Aunty Daisy. Then we'll all have to go to church.'

The little girl kissed them all, laughing as she did so.

'Come here to Daddy. I'll carry you. We don't want to ruin your pretty dress, do we?'

Maria toddled across to Johnnie and, becoming suddenly shy, clung to his leg and buried her face. Johnnie laughed as he picked her up. 'You're not going to be a "shy baby" are you? Give us all a big smile?'

Maria looked up and beamed at them all.

He bent and kissed her cheek. 'This is a very special day, Nell. We're a family now: you, me and Maria. Out of all the tragedy of the past has come a happiness I never dreamed could exist.'

'Oh, Johnnie. My prayers have been answered. I used to pray so hard that some day, somehow I . . . we would have a child of our own and thanks to Nancy we have.'

'God bless her, she left us something so very, very precious.'

She touched his cheek and then the child's. 'She did, Johnnie, and Maria is our little angel.'

'And Mary's little saying has come true.'

Nell looked a little puzzled. 'Which saying? She seems to have so many these days.'

'"On a wing and a prayer".' He touched the badge on his uniform. 'Well, we have the wings and now the prayer has been answered, so let's go and have our daughter christened. We have so much to look forward to now, Nell. We've come through the darkness, there's only sunshine ahead.'

Heart and Home

by

Cathie Kinrade is all too used to hardship.

Growing up on the Isle of Man in the 1930s, she sees her da
set sail daily on dangerous seas while her mam struggles to put
food on the table. Cathie has little hope for her own future,
until a chance encounter changes her fortunes for ever.

Fiercely determined, Cathie leaves for Liverpool, a bustling
modern city full of possibility. With a lively job as a shop girl
in a grand department store, and a firm friend in kind-hearted
Julia, Cathie has found her niche. But the discovery of an
explosive secret could put everything at risk. And when
love comes calling, Cathie's new friends fear that she may
be set to trust the wrong man with her heart . . .

Available now from

headline

From Liverpool With Love

by

Lyn Andrews

In 1920s Liverpool, Jane, her little brother Alfie and their mother Ellen have faced the horrors of the workhouse together.

But when Ellen dies, two very different paths open up for the siblings.

Jane is sent to work in the Empire Laundry and builds a new life for herself with the neighbours who take her in. She finds solace there and the promise of a happy future when she falls for Joe, their eldest son.

But Alfie absconds from the workhouse and embarks on a life of crime. When their paths cross once more, Alfie turns on his sister. His plans will jeopardise every happiness she hoped for . . .

Available now from

headline

Liverpool Angels

by

Lyn Andrews

*Born at the turn of the twentieth century, Mae Strickland
is only a few days old when her mother suddenly dies.*

Her aunt Maggie brings Mae up together with her own
children, Eddie and Alice, and the girls become like sisters.
In spite of Mae's unhappy start, life feels full of promise.

Then, as the First World War looms, everything changes.
While the local men – including young Eddie – leave to fight,
Mae and Alice train as field nurses. As they travel to the
front line in the wake of family tragedy, nothing can
prepare them for the hardship that lies ahead.

Yet there is solace to be found amid the wreckage of
the war, and for both, romance is on the horizon. But it
will take great courage for Mae and Alice to follow their
hearts. Can love win out in the end?

Available now from

headline

Sunlight On The Mersey

by

Lyn Andrews

Three years have passed since the end of the Great War.

Yet life in Liverpool remains uncertain for shopkeeper's
wife Kate Mundy and her family.

Following recent heartbreak, seventeen-year-old Rose is
sent to work in rural Wales, where she is enchanted by the
'big house' and by David, its tragic young owner. Sister Iris
can't escape so easily, especially when an accident has
devastating consequences for the family. Meanwhile ex-soldier
Charlie is keen to secure a brighter future for himself . . .
even if it means putting ambition above his own happiness.

There is romance in store for each of the family. But can
love blossom amidst the challenges that lie ahead?

Available now from

headline

Lyn Andrews

'An outstanding storyteller' *Woman's Weekly*

The House On Lonely Street
Love And A Promise
A Wing And A Prayer
When Daylight Comes
Across A Summer Sea
A Mother's Love
Friends Forever
Every Mother's Son
Far From Home
Days Of Hope
A Daughter's Journey
A Secret In The Family
To Love And To Cherish
Beyond A Misty Shore
Sunlight On The Mersey
Liverpool Angels
From Liverpool With Love
Heart And Home

Now you can buy any of these bestselling books from your bookshop or direct from Lyn's publisher.

FREE P&P AND UK DELIVERY
(Overseas and Ireland £3.50 per book)

To order simply call this number: **01235 400 414**
Or visit our website: **www.headline.co.uk**

Prices and availability subject to change without notice.